CAVALLERIA RUSTICANA
AND OTHER STORIES

GIOVANNI VERGA was born in Catania, Sicily, in 1840, into a prosperous bourgeois family. He wrote many novels and short stories, and also a number of plays, mostly based on his own stories. While still a teenager he drafted the first of three historical romances, *Amore e Patria (Love and Country)*, which remained largely unpublished. This was followed in 1859 by *I Carbonari della montagna (The Carbonari in the Mountains)*, written while he was reading law at Catania University and published in 1861/2 using money intended for his studies. The third of these early novels was *Sulle lagune (In the Lagoons)*, published in 1863. After serving in the Catania National Guard from 1860 to 1864, Verga made several visits to Florence, then the cultural and political capital, where he settled in 1869. Meanwhile in 1866 he had published *Una peccatrice (A Sinner)*, a tale of disastrous young love, and this was followed in 1871 by the technically different but thematically similar *Storia di una capinera (Story of a Blackcap)*, which proved immensely popular and was widely read until well into this century. Verga moved on to Milan in late 1872, Florence having been replaced the previous year by Rome as the Italian political capital. In Milan he published three further novels, *Eva* (1873), *Tigre Reale (Royal Tigress*, 1873) and *Eros* (1875), in a similar Romantic style to his previous works. Influenced by the *verismo* theories of his friend and fellow-Sicilian, Luigi Capuana, around 1874 Verga adopted a new approach to the writing of fiction, developing a style characterized by dialogue, both naturalistic and dramatic, and with a focus on character. Using this approach, he was to produce the most original and significant writing of his career. This period began with the story *Nedda*, published in 1874, and the novella *Primavera (Springtime)*, in 1875. The year 1880 saw the publication of a collection of short stories dealing largely with Sicilian rural life, entitled *Vita dei campi (Life in the Fields)*. This included the famous tale *Cavalleria rusticana*, later adapted by Verga for the theatre, this adaptation then being used as the basis for the libretto of Mascagni's opera. Two more collections of Verga's tales of Sicilian village life were published, *Novelle rusticane* in 1883 and *Vagabondaggio* in 1887. Back in 1881, Verga had published *I Malavoglia (The House by the Medlar Tree)*, intending it to be the first in a series of five novels to be collectively known as *I vinti* (*The Defeated Ones*). This was followed by the second (and actually the last) of the series, *Mastro-don Gesualdo* (issued originally in instalments, 1888, but heavily revised and published 1889), the last major achievement of his literary career. He produced little in the last thirty years of his life. In late 1894 he returned for the last time to Catania, where he settled in the house he was born in. He died after suffering a cerebral thrombosis in early 1922.

G. H. McWILLIAM, a former Fellow of Trinity College Dublin, is Professor Emeritus of Italian at the University of Leicester. His publications include studies of Dante, Boccaccio, Verga, Pirandello, Ugo Betti, Italian literature in Ireland, Shakespeare's Italy, and the pronunciation of Italian in the sixteenth century. He has translated plays by Italo Svevo, Pirandello and Betti, and poems by Salvatore Quasimodo. His Penguin Classics translation of Boccaccio's *Decameron* (1972) was reissued in 1995 with a new book-length introduction, along with detailed notes, maps and indexes. He holds the Italian Government's silver medal for services to Italian culture.

GIOVANNI VERGA

Cavalleria rusticana
and Other Stories

Translated and with an introduction by
G. H. McWILLIAM

PENGUIN BOOKS

PENGUIN BOOKS

Published by the Penguin Group
Penguin Books Ltd, 27 Wrights Lane, London w8 5tz, England
Penguin Putnam Inc., 375 Hudson Street, New York, New York 10014, USA
Penguin Books Australia Ltd, Ringwood, Victoria, Australia
Penguin Books Canada Ltd, 10 Alcorn Avenue, Toronto, Ontario, Canada m4v 3b2
Penguin Books (NZ) Ltd, Private Bag 102902, NSMC, Auckland, New Zealand

Penguin Books Ltd, Registered Offices: Harmondsworth, Middlesex, England

This translation published 1999

026

Copyright © G. H. McWilliam, 1999
All rights reserved

The moral right of the translator has been asserted

Maps by Nigel Andrews

Set in 10/12.5 pt Monotype Bembo
Typeset by Rowland Phototypesetting Ltd, Bury St Edmunds, Suffolk
Printed and bound in Great Britain by Clays Ltd, Elcograf S.p.A.

www.greenpenguin.co.uk

MIX
Paper from
responsible sources
FSC
www.fsc.org   FSC® C018179

Penguin Books is committed to a sustainable
future for our business, our readers and our planet.
This book is made from Forest Stewardship
Council™ certified paper.

To my children Paul, Laura, Edwin,
Jonathan, Joanna and Rachel

Contents

Other Stories

Acknowledgements

The translator wishes to thank both his good friend Paolo Ruggero Jenna and his sister-in-law Marie-Louise Rossini for their prompt and knowledgeable replies to a handful of queries about Sicilian terminology on the one hand and Milanese locations on the other. He acknowledges the expert advice on Verga's Sicily generously placed at his disposal by his long-standing friend and fellow Italianist, Andrew Wilkin. His grateful thanks are extended also to his text editor, Jennifer Munka, for her helpful suggested amendments to the original typescript.

Introduction

Although the earliest English translations of Giovanni Verga's narrative writings had already appeared in the last decade of the nineteenth century, it was not until after his death that his reputation as one of the foremost novelists and short-story writers of the modern era was given fresh impetus in the English-speaking world. The writer who championed Verga's cause was D. H. Lawrence, whose own translation of Verga's novel, *Mastro-don Gesualdo*, was first published in New York in 1923, and in London two years later. Shortly afterwards, Lawrence also translated two volumes of Verga's short stories, which were published in 1925 and 1928. In an introductory note to the first of these, Lawrence described Verga as a man 'of medium height, strong and straight, with thick white hair, and proud dark eyes, and a big reddish moustache: a striking man to look at'.[1] The description was presumably based on the portraits and photographs of Verga that Lawrence had come across during his stay in Taormina in the early 1920s, for the two writers never met. When Lawrence came to Taormina, Verga was living in Catania, a few miles further down the eastern Sicilian coast, and in the autumn of 1921, when his writings first attracted Lawrence's attention, he was an octogenarian with only a few months left to live. Shortly after Verga's death in January 1922, Lawrence wrote to a correspondent in New York that 'Poor old Verga went and died exactly as I was going to see him in Catania. But he was 82 years old.'[2]

Lawrence's letters of the period reveal his delight and fascination in having discovered a writer of outstanding narrative power and versatility. Never before had he encountered a prose style that was so original and dynamic, a language so rich and colourful. His own brief experience of living in Sicily made him keenly aware of the uncanny accuracy with which Verga had depicted the manners and temperament of that proud island race, attached as if inevitably to its traditional, primitive way of life. Writing to Catherine Carswell in October 1921, Lawrence apologizes for his failure to acknowledge receipt of the plays of Lady Gregory, but claims that he has no time for such trifles ('too much of the insipid old stew'), adding that the only author he has been reading of late is Giovanni Verga:

He exercises quite a fascination on me, and makes me feel quite sick at the end. But perhaps that is only if one knows Sicily. Do you know if he is translated into English? . . . It would be fun to do him – his *langüage* is so fascinating.[3]

Though well aware of the problems involved in reproducing the characteristically Sicilian flavour of Verga's literary style, Lawrence began to toy seriously with the idea of translating him into English. It was the very difficulty of the task that most appealed to Lawrence, who with characteristic immodesty wrote to Edward Garnett from Taormina informing him that Verga 'would be most awfully difficult to translate. That is what tempts me: though it is rather a waste of time, and probably I shall never do it. Though if I dont (*sic*), I doubt if anyone else will – adequately, at least.'[4] It should perhaps be noted in passing that Lawrence's versions of Verga can hardly be regarded as adequate. They were written in considerable haste, and his knowledge of Italian fell some way short of perfection. Hence we find phrases like 'a picnic in the country' being translated as 'the ringing of the bells' (a rudimentary error resulting from confusion of the words *campagna* and *campana*), whilst a fiancée is translated as a wife, and a mother becomes a midwife.

In that same letter to Edward Garnett, Lawrence describes Verga as '*extraordinarily* good – peasant – quite modern – Homeric', adding that 'it would need somebody who could absolutely handle English in the dialect, to translate him.' Here, attention is drawn to three of Verga's outstanding qualities as a narrative writer: his familiarity with popular, colloquial speech; the modernity of his prose style which placed him at the forefront of literary innovation in the latter part of the nineteenth century; and, finally, the epic structure of his two major novels, *I Malavoglia* and *Mastro-don Gesualdo*.

Shortly after Verga's death, Lawrence wrote to his London agent, Curtis Brown, informing him that he was halfway through his translation of *Mastro-don Gesualdo* and promising to send on as much of the manuscript as he had finished before leaving Italy for Ceylon. 'Afraid I shan't have it done,' he wrote. 'Such a good novel. Verga is the man who wrote *Cavalleria rusticana*.'[5]

Even today, despite Lawrence's efforts to ensure that he was more widely read in the English-speaking world, Verga remains 'the man who wrote *Cavalleria rusticana*'. That description is not entirely accurate, as the libretto for Mascagni's celebrated one-act opera was written, not by Verga, but by Giovanni Targioni-Tozzetti and Guido Menasci, who based their text closely on Verga's one-act play (1884), in turn a dramatized version of his own original short story.[6] The first performance of the opera on 17 May 1890 at the Teatro Costanzi in Rome was a phenomenal success, and shortly afterwards it became a permanent fixture alongside Leoncavallo's *I Pagliacci* (1892) in the operatic repertoire. Mascagni had written to Verga on 10 March 1890, only a few weeks before the work was due to be performed, to ask his permission to stage the opera, to which Verga, unable to foresee the extraordinary favour it was to enjoy with operatic audiences throughout the world, consented on 27 March. Before its first performance, Giacomo Puccini had shown the opera libretto to the Milanese music publisher, Giulio Ricordi, who had been unimpressed, saying he could not believe in it ('*non ci credo*').[7] The libretto was eventually published by Eduardo Sonzogno, and for almost the rest of his life, Verga was engaged in fierce litigation with Mascagni and Sonzogno for breach of copyright, pursuing his claim right through the Italian legal system and finally to the *Corte di Cassazione*, the highest Italian court of appeal. But although he received substantial compensation at an earlier hearing in 1893, he never secured a settlement that he would consider adequate.

★

Giovanni Verga was born at 8 Via Sant'Anna, Catania, on 2 September 1840. His mother, Donna Caterina di Mauro, was the daughter of prosperous bourgeois parents in the city. His father, Giovanni Battista Verga Catalano, came from a patrician family that owned an estate at Vizzini, in the hills some thirty-five miles south-west of Catania. Verga's childhood and youth coincided with a period of major historical change, one aspect of which – the transfer of power from the Bourbon to the Savoy monarchy – is amusingly illustrated in the final paragraph of the story 'Getting to know the King'. The invasion and annexation of Sicily in 1860 by Garibaldi and his thousand-strong army was followed in 1861 by its incorporation into the new Kingdom of Italy under Victor Emmanuel II of Savoy. When Garibaldi's forces arrived in Catania in the summer of 1860, Verga, now twenty years old, enrolled in the Catania National Guard, which over the next few years was engaged in suppressing both counter-revolutionary movements and popular uprisings against the bourgeoisie. The mob violence and summary executions witnessed by Verga at this period are graphically recalled some years later in one of his short stories, 'Freedom'. His distaste for military discipline, and for his own involvement in a campaign of repression against the underprivileged, were the probable reasons for Verga buying himself out of the National Guard four years after his enrolment.

During his schooldays, Verga had been encouraged to make a close study of the contemporary historical novel, and while still a teenager he wrote the first of three historical novels of his own, tailored to the prevailing Risorgimento taste for history, adventure and heroism in literature. The first of these, *Amore e patria* (1856–7), remained unpublished until very recently except for one or two excerpts. In 1859, while reading for a degree in law at Catania University, he began to write a novel with equally strong patriotic overtones. *I Carbonari della montagna* (*The Carbonari in the Mountains*), was published in four instalments in 1861–2 with funds intended for the completion of Verga's law studies, now abandoned with his father's consent. It is the tale of a rebellion in Calabria against the French during the final years of Napoleonic rule under Murat. *Sulle lagune* (*In the Lagoons*, 1863), the third of these novels, is set in Venice, where Austria was still the ruling power, but the main emphasis is now switched from political struggle to the chronicle of a love affair between a young Venetian woman and a Hungarian officer in the Austrian army.

I Carbonari della montagna had been favourably received by influential mainland critics, while *Sulle lagune* was actually published on the mainland, as an appendix to the Florentine political and literary journal, *Nuova Europa*. A visit to Florence in May 1865 convinced Verga that his future as a writer was dependent on his breaking away from the somewhat restricted and provincial journalistic milieu of his native Catania, and establishing his credentials with the mainstream literary establishment of the north. Florence had become the political and cultural capital of the new Kingdom of Italy, and it was to Florence that Verga returned several times before taking up residence there in 1869. He had meanwhile published the novel *Una peccatrice* (1866, A Sinner), recounting the story of a young law student's disastrous infatuation with a wealthy young woman of the aristocracy. The novel is set mainly in Catania and Naples, but the modish, cosmopolitan, salon society against which the story unfolds, together with Verga's portrayal of its ambitious young hero, lends to the narrative a distinctly autobiographical flavour.

There followed a novel possessing a similar theme – youthful love and its attendant pitfalls – but wholly different in both form and context. *Storia di una capinera* (*Story of a Blackcap*, 1871) is an epistolary novel consisting of a series of letters written to her confidante by a young woman who has fallen deeply in love while staying in the countryside during a cholera outbreak. Her passionately romantic idyll is shattered when her family compel her to return to the convent where she has been brought up, and to take the veil. The over-exclamatory style of the first edition was toned down in later versions, and the novel attracted a wide readership until well into the twentieth century, being generally thought of as Verga's most important work. Its popularity may be judged by the fact that, by 1907, it had been reprinted twenty-two times, whilst the novel later to be acknowledged as Verga's masterpiece, *I Malavoglia* (1881), had gone through only five reprints.

In 1871, Rome became the new capital of the Kingdom of Italy after being seized from the Papacy in the previous year. The transfer of government from Florence to Rome led also to a decline in the importance of Florence as the foremost Italian literary and artistic centre. Around this same time, Verga's loss of two influential literary friends, one moving to Naples and the other into a mental institution, made his own move from Florence inevitable. Milan had now replaced Florence as the focal point of Italian cultural activity, and it was there that Verga settled towards the end of 1872.

The theme common to both *Una peccatrice* and *Storia di una capinera* was described by one of Verga's commentators as 'the myth of love, as it presents itself to youthful minds, on coming into contact with reality.'[8] After his move to Milan, Verga published three further novels, *Eva* (1873), *Tigre reale* (*Royal Tigress*, 1873) and *Eros* (1875), that once again examined the conflict between human love and the inexorable, destructive forces of life itself. The theme is one that he develops with much greater conviction in his realistic narratives, for instance in 'Nedda', 'Jeli the Shepherd' and 'Black Bread'.

Verga's early, Romantic novels are on the whole undistinguished, being sentimental and melodramatic, even perhaps to excess. *Eva*, for instance, is the story of a love affair between a painter and a ballerina. The painter is a passionate, impetuous southerner, who regards his love for this woman as symbolizing the eternal forces of nature, and sees the woman herself as a kind of demon-goddess who presides over a universe in which evil has triumphed over good. The ballerina, however, is a sensible, earthbound girl, who shatters her lover's complex fantasies. The story ends with the death of the hero, stripped of his grand illusions, and worn away by consumption in a small provincial town. In tone and content, *Eva* and the other romantic narratives of Verga's early literary career resemble many other novels and plays of the period that seem to be aimed at emulating the fabulous success of that notorious best-seller of the mid-nineteenth century, *The Lady of the Camellias* (1848) by Dumas *fils*. His stage adaptation of it, *Camille* (1852), was no less admired and imitated, and supplied Giuseppe Verdi with the plot of *La traviata* (1853).

Those early novels, reflecting the ideas and moral attitudes of the Bohemian milieu of Florence and Milan, abound in stock characters, bogus psychological notions and artificial situations. But it was already clear from what Verga had written in his prefatory comments to *Eva* that he was dissatisfied with the late Romantic style that typifies these works. In that preface, he developed the plausible argument that all societies have the art they deserve, and claimed that his own work was merely reflecting the corrupt society that he observed all around him. Less convincingly, he went on to argue that the kind of novel he was writing had a moralistic function, in that it revealed the shortcomings of the society from which it had emerged. One cannot help feeling that Verga was being a little disingenuous in making such an assertion. Fully three-quarters of the population of the brave new Italy were illiterate, the reading public consisted of a minority of the remaining quarter, and the success or failure of a fictional narrative was dictated by this inevitably restricted consumer demand.

Be that as it may, a change in the attitude of both the writers and the consumers of narrative fiction was soon to become apparent. The mood of disillusionment that followed the attainment of the great Romantic political ideal of Italian unification was accompanied in the mid-1870s by the birth in Italy of the literary movement known as *verismo*. The chief theorist of the new movement was Verga's close friend and fellow Sicilian, Luigi Capuana, who had been persuaded by Verga to join him in Milan. Capuana's aesthetic theories were strongly influenced by his extensive reading of major French novelists, in particular Balzac and Zola. *Verismo*, as propounded by Capuana and others, including Verga himself, was in essence the Italian counterpart of French naturalism. Its practitioners concerned themselves with the presentation of the day-to-day affairs of ordinary people. In Verga's case, he came to see the writer's role as that of studying life and reproducing it faithfully in its most minute particulars. The opening paragraphs of 'Gramigna's Mistress' summarize his intentions, though whether the theory he expounds there could ever accord with his practice is highly debatable.[9] In a famous phrase from those prefatory remarks, he declares that the work of art should seem 'to have created itself, to have grown spontaneously and come to fruition as though it were a part of nature, without preserving any point of contact with its author'. The hand of the author was to remain completely invisible. No longer should the writer engage in the wordy descriptive passages and lengthy moral considerations that characterized the works of earlier, Romantic novelists. The narrative and its implications were to be conveyed through dialogue, which now assumed central importance in the work's overall structure. Even the intervening prose between passages of dialogue had to possess such dialogue characteristics as a *non sequitur* or an imprecation, so that the total impression would be one of a story told exclusively by and through the characters.[10] By this means, Verga introduced an exciting new prose style, a *prosa dialogata*, which is intensely dramatic and naturalistic and which constitutes one of Verga's most significant contributions to the historical evolution of Italian narrative prose.

The first signs of what Benedetto Croce called Verga's 'liberating thrust' (*spinta liberatrice*) are to be found in 'Nedda', which was published in 1874. This pathetic story of a Sicilian peasant girl's struggle against sickness and poverty is introduced by a passage in which Verga claims that the idea of writing it came to him one evening as he was applying poker and tongs to the log fire in his comfortable Milanese apartment. He associates the darting sparks and fluttering flames of the burning logs with the arousal of his 'other self', and in a significant phrase he writes of the sensation he experienced of casting off a suit of clothes as he settled into his armchair and reflected on memories of people and places in Sicily, the region of his birth and upbringing.

Verga's metaphorical change of clothing signalled the beginning of the most original and productive phase in his writing career. From that point onwards, a new concern with the lives and aspirations of his Sicilian compatriots became a regular feature of his narratives. In 'Nedda', as in many of his later stories, he reveals with amazing clarity and understanding the conditions under which the Sicilian peasants attempted to grind out a living for themselves and their families. The evocative opening scene, describing an evening in the huge kitchen of a farmhouse on the slopes of Mount Etna during the olive-gathering season, reflects a part of his own childhood experience. As the son of a Sicilian landowner, he would himself have witnessed annual harvesting rituals of this kind, marked by an atmosphere of tension between the seasonal labourers and their employer. True to his veristic principles, he expresses no opinion on the social justice of the situation he depicts, being content merely to view it through the eyes of his characters, whose own opinions are conveyed through the dialogue. The women's complaint over being forbidden to eat the olives that lie rotting on the ground in the rain is countered by Nedda's 'logical' argument in favour of the owner of the land. The readers are left to decide for themselves whether Nedda's argument is plausible. And the same applies when the proprietor's son, in whom we may detect a brief glimpse of Verga's younger self, orders the steward to supplement Nedda's earnings to make up for what she has lost, and is persuaded that this would arouse the hostility of neighbouring landowners.

Nedda is the victim of a series of catastrophes that culminate at the end of the story with the death of her baby from malnutrition. Her total innocence and resignation in the face of her appalling personal tragedy are the distinguishing characteristics of a narrative that explores in greater depth and with much greater conviction a theme common to several of Verga's earlier works and most of his later ones: the inevitability of defeat in the pursuit of happiness. Hence the overall title that he was later to give to his projected series of novels in which he set out to investigate the human condition at five different levels of society, *I Vinti* (*The Defeated Ones*). As one of his commentators has written, 'there is something about the world in which we live, he seems to be saying, that ineluctably thwarts our dreams, irrespective of our merits or defects'. It is not so much a pessimistic view of life as a tragic one because 'it is permeated by a sense of man's impotence'.[11]

The objective narrative technique that Verga employs in 'Nedda' enables him to achieve a remarkably clear presentation of the compassion-demanding poverty and loneliness of the story's main characters. His depiction of the minor characters, such as Nedda's fellow workers at the olive farm, is equally assured. The contrast between Nedda and the protagonists of Verga's earlier novels is not simply a question of their different social environment. Like Nedda, the painter in *Eva* was a 'defeated one', but he was the victim of his own capricious fantasies. In 'Nedda', and with few exceptions in the stories that follow, the characters are presented as the victims of life itself. Although traces of his earlier manner are still evident in his description of Nedda early in the story, Verga no longer dwells on the personal idiosyncrasies of his main character. His attention has switched to the creation of that atmosphere of tragic inevitability which he sees as enveloping men and women as a whole. It may be objected that in 'Nedda' Verga is dealing with people afflicted by extremes of poverty, and that prolonged poverty inevitably breeds a sensation of hopelessness and tragedy. But as may be observed in several of his other realist narratives, for instance in 'Property', the lives of rich and poor alike are underlain by this same sense of tragic inevitability.

In the year following the publication of 'Nedda', Verga employed a comparable veristic narrative technique, this time in a novella set in Milan. 'Springtime', published in 1875, like his earlier Florentine and Milanese narratives, is a love story with an unhappy ending, but it differs from them in two important respects. Although the tale's literary antecedents can be traced back some thirty years to Henri Murger's *Scènes de la vie de Bohème*, both of the main characters are presented in terms that are psychologically convincing, and immense care is taken to ensure that the background against which the story unfolds is a colourful and accurate representation of post-Risorgimento Milan. One of Verga's contemporaries records that the writer spent his evenings with his artistic and literary friends at the Biffi, a fashionable Milanese café, sometimes going on from there to La Scala, where from the stalls he could be seen, all smiles and elegance, passing from one box to another to chat with the Milanese bigwigs and their ladies. The Milanese world depicted by Verga in 'Springtime', with its Galleria, its famous opera house, its garrets, its cafés, its ambitious young artists and its seamstresses, was to be given definitive form some twenty years later in Giacomo Puccini's *La Bohème*.

After publishing 'Nedda' and 'Springtime', Verga wrote a number of short stories based, like 'Nedda', on Sicilian peasant life in the region around Catania and the slopes of Mount Etna. These tales, published in 1880 under the title *Vita dei campi* (*Life in the Fields*), included 'Picturesque Lives',[12] a powerful and evocative account of the precarious existence of the people living in Aci Trezza, a fishing village north of Catania. As in 'Nedda', so in 'Picturesque Lives' Verga describes the hardships and aspirations of his peasant characters with an unusual degree of sympathy and understanding, but in this case their lives are brought more sharply into focus by the polemical contrast with the futile and self-absorbed existence of the Milanese society woman to whom the novella is ostensibly addressed. The lady concerned has been identified as the Countess Paolina Greppi, one of a number of women whose company Verga cultivated in the course of his strictly bachelor existence. The countess held court in her Milanese salon on Thursdays, and Verga is reported as always being the last to leave.

The contempt that Verga displays in 'Picturesque Lives' towards the trivial and meaningless way of life of the woman to whom the story is addressed may perhaps be taken as a further sign of his rejection – for the time being at least – of his own earlier concern with the portrayal of characters and incidents drawn from the northern Italian *haut monde*, and his resolve to switch his attention to a realistic account of the day-to-day lives of his fellow Sicilians.

With the exception of 'How, When and Why', a tale set against the Milanese high society background of his earlier narratives, that made its curious and unexplained appearance in the second edition of 1882, all of the stories in *Vita dei campi* are concerned with aspects of Sicilian peasant life. When the most famous of these, 'Cavalleria rusticana', was adapted by Verga for the theatre a few years later, he made several major changes to the story, including the expansion of the character of Santa, who now became Santuzza, to provide a starring role for Eleonora Duse. The play was first performed in Turin in 1884, and it was this version on which the libretto of Mascagni's opera was based. In its original form, the tale is notable for its structural compactness and the precision and clarity of its narrative detail. Considering its brevity, the tale is remarkable for the way in which all five of the main characters emerge with clearly defined, distinctive personalities of their own. Verga skilfully creates an atmosphere of tragic inevitability before plunging the narrative into the final, starkly uncompromising encounter between Turiddu and Alfio, a vividly chronicled scene that in the stage version, as in the opera libretto, is replaced by a simple announcement of its fatal outcome: '*Hanno ammazzato Compare Turiddu!*'[13]

Adultery and the satisfaction of honour are themes that reappear in other stories from *Vita dei campi*, for instance in 'Jeli the Shepherd', where the ending is both sudden and intensely dramatic. The tale is notable for its lyrical evocation of the wild and desolate Sicilian landscape against which the events of the narrative unfold. As in 'Nedda', the outlines of the main character are sketched in with enormous sympathy and understanding. The accounts of his childhood friendship with the young aristocrat, Don Alfonso, and with the girl, Mara, who eventually becomes his wife, are characterized on Jeli's part by a deep sense of trust and innocence, and become all the more moving when viewed in retrospect against the tale's final catastrophe. The central episode of the novella, describing the cruel fate of the colt lying wounded and helpless in the ravine, foreshadows the ultimate fate of Jeli himself.

In 'Rosso Malpelo', another of the stories from *Vita dei campi*, Verga creates an unforgettable main character, and brilliantly evokes the atmosphere and working conditions in a sand mine on the slopes of Mount Etna. The personality of Malpelo is a curious compound of intense filial love, cruelty, kindness and superstition. Verga analyses with great subtlety the intimate friendship that develops between Malpelo and the boy who, because of his unfortunate physical handicap, is known by no other name than The Frog. Malpelo unconsciously prophesies his own fate in telling The Frog about the legend current in the village about a miner lost in the maze of underground caverns. Once again, as in 'Cavalleria', 'Jeli', and another immensely powerful narrative from the same collection, 'The She-Wolf', there is a gradually heightening presentiment of the final catastrophe.

Outstanding examples in themselves of the novella form, one or two of the stories in *Vita dei campi* are the original sketches for *I Malavoglia* (*The House by the Medlar Tree*, 1881), the first of the series of five novels, *I Vinti* (*The Defeated Ones*), to which Verga had initially intended to give the collective title *La Marea* (*The Tide*). *I Malavoglia* is prefaced by a brief introductory note in which Verga explains that the work is intended as the first in a series of five novels that will explore people's fruitless struggle for immortality ('the only true happiness') at different levels of the social order. In *I Malavoglia*, the characters are the poor and simple-living inhabitants of a Sicilian maritime community. The setting of the novel, the picturesque fishing village of Aci Trezza, with its characteristic features such as the beacon rock (*il fariglione*) and 'the tiny group of cottages lying huddled up asleep on the shore' had first appeared in 'Picturesque Lives'. So, too, had the prototypes of several of the novel's major figures – the grandfather Padron 'Ntoni, his son Bastianazzo who perishes at sea, his grandson Luca who dies for king and country at the naval battle of Lissa (1866), and his granddaughter Lia who drifts into prostitution in Catania. There are parallels also between the young 'Ntoni, another of the characters in the novel, and Turiddu from 'Cavalleria rusticana', a tale which Verga had originally intended as part of the novel itself. Both are headstrong young men whose lives take on a different and ultimately fateful direction after being torn away from their Sicilian village community to serve as conscripts in the new Italian militia on the mainland.

Verga wrote two other collections of tales based on Sicilian village life: *Novelle rusticane* (1883) and *Vagabondaggio* (1887). Whilst the second could be classified as more of the same, the first contains some of Verga's finest and most original short stories.[14] The collection stands out for the variety of its themes and for characters that are sharply and memorably observed. 'Black Bread' is especially interesting as a study of the strains placed upon human relationships in a primitive rural society where the ceaseless struggle for daily bread subverts traditional concepts of love and honour. In 'Malaria', the reader is presented with an almost tangible sensation of the disease and its consequences in a rural community whose way of life is adversely affected, also, by the advent of the railway era. The effects of natural phenomena on people's livelihoods, such as drought or a volcanic eruption, are graphically described in other stories with the same painstaking eye for detail. The church and the law are prominent elements in several of the tales ('The Reverend', 'Don Licciu Papa', 'Bigwigs'), more often than not as adversaries of the poor, being depicted in a vein that is fiercely satirical. A lighter note is sounded in 'Getting to know the King', where the sense of humour that Verga displays intermittently in most of his stories is broadened, as in 'War of the Saints' from the earlier collection, into pure comedy. 'Property', with its brilliant portrayal of the tale's self-made, ruthless and single-minded protagonist, is of special interest as the initial sketch for *Mastro-don Gesualdo*, the second (and, as it turned out, the last that Verga completed) of the projected series *I Vinti*.

Mastro-don Gesualdo first appeared in instalments in 1888, and was heavily revised before being published in its definitive form in 1889.

Like Mazzarò, the main character of 'Property', Gesualdo Motta is a self-made man, a person of humble origins, who at an early age swears to make himself rich and eventually, by dint of his native wit and tireless energy, amasses a staggeringly large fortune. He moves up the social ladder by marrying into an aristocratic but penniless family, then finds that he is despised not only by the society into which he has moved but also by the one he has abandoned. When he dies, he has been even more thoroughly defeated by life, despite his riches, than the poverty-stricken fisher-folk of *I Malavoglia*. In Verga's estimation, all people are ultimately *vinti*, irrespective of their material wealth or poverty, or the position they occupy in society. The main theme of *Mastro-don Gesualdo*, as of the earlier novella, is the myth of property. Verga accepts the validity of the scriptural warning against the laying up of treasures upon earth, but as his other novels and short stories make abundantly clear, he believes the laying up of treasures in heaven to be no less improvident.

Verga's stories do not, for the most part, have happy endings, but it would be a mistake to think of him as a sombre pessimist. He harboured no illusions about human society, but, at the same time, he was acutely aware of the comic side to our daily lives; even in the midst of catastrophe his characters never lose their capacity to smile at their misfortunes. It is this which endears them to his readers, stirring our compassion and demanding our participation in their joys and sorrows. Verga's great merit lies in his ability to arouse compassion whilst avoiding completely all traces of sentimentality, and this is because he presents life as it is, free from the distortions of idealistic perspectives. His narratives are an unfailing source of interest, not only to those who care about good literature, but also to the historian, for whom his novels and short stories provide an invaluable record of social conditions at a critical stage of modern Italian history. In his style and language he was far ahead of his time, and it is only in comparatively recent times that his true nature as the greatest Italian short-story writer since Boccaccio has been acknowledged in his own country. Outside Italy, he remains grossly underrated, largely because of the extreme difficulty of translation to which D. H. Lawrence referred.[15]

Mastro-don Gesualdo was the crowning achievement of a literary career that had offered vivid and memorable accounts of the society of the Italian mainland cities and the Sicilian countryside in the latter part of the nineteenth century. In addition to the works already referred to, Verga wrote other novels[16] and collections of short stories.[17] He also wrote a number of plays, based for the most part, like *Cavalleria rusticana*, on his own earlier narratives. The last thirty years of his life were relatively unproductive. In December 1894, he returned for the last time from Milan to Catania, where he settled in the house of his birth in the Via Sant'Anna. He died after suffering a cerebral thrombosis on returning from one of his regular visits to his club, the Circolo Unione, on 27 January 1922.

G. H. McWilliam

Professor McWilliam can be contacted by e-mail at ghm4@le.ac.uk

NOTES

1. Introduction to *Little Novels of Sicily* reprinted as 'Note on Giovanni Verga' in *Phoenix II: Uncollected, Unpublished and Other Prose Works*, London: Heinemann, 1968, p. 277.
2. *The Letters of D. H. Lawrence*, vol. IV (June 1921–March 1924), edited by Warren Roberts, James T. Boulton and Elizabeth Mansfield, Cambridge (1987), p. 186.
3. Ibid., pp. 105–106.
4. Ibid., p. 115.
5. Ibid., p. 188.
6. Many reference books, including *The Oxford Companion to Music*, mistakenly claim that the opera was based on the short story, but every schoolboy knows it was based on the adaptation of the story that Verga prepared for the theatre. Confirmation of this is easily obtained by a comparison of the play with the opera libretto. In his introductory note to *Little Novels of Sicily*, D. H. Lawrence wrote (p. 33) that 'Verga made a dramatized version of "Cavalleria rusticana" ', and . . . this dramatized version is the libretto of the ever-popular little opera of the same name.'
7. 'Edoardo Sonzogno . . . instituted a prize competition for one-act operas – the *Concorso Sonzogno*. At first no outstanding work was discovered in these *concorsi* – until in 1889 "Cavalleria rusticana" was brought to light in this way.

It is interesting to mention that, before Mascagni entered the work for this competition, Puccini had shown the score to Giulio Ricordi, who rejected it because "I don't believe in this opera" ... (Mosco Carner, *Puccini: a critical biography*, second ed., London (1974), p. 36).

8. '*il mito dell'amore, così come si presenta alla fantasia giovanile, nei suoi urti con la realtà*' (L. Russo, *Gli scrittori d'Italia*, Florence (1951), vol. II, p. 753).

9. In his introductory note to *Little Novels of Sicily*, Lawrence writes (p. 27) that 'the moment Verga starts talking theories, our interest wilts immediately. The theories were none of his own: just borrowed from the literary smarties of Paris. And poor Verga looks a sorry sight in Paris ready-mades.'

10. An example of this technique is the reaction of Turiddu, in 'Cavalleria rusticana', on hearing that Lola has become engaged during his absence to Alfio, the carter: 'When Turiddu first got to know about it, Christ in Heaven! he wanted to tear the guts out of that chap from Licodia, he really did!'

11. *See* D. Woolf, *The Art of Verga*, p. 111.

12. The title given by Verga to this novella was 'Fantasticheria', for which the nearest English equivalent, 'Daydreaming', inadequately conveys the ironic contrast between appearance and reality that provides the story with its *raison d'être*. Lawrence's version of the story is entitled 'Caprice'.

13. 'They've killed Turiddu!'

14. In the introductory note to his own translation of *Little Novels of Sicily*, D. H. Lawrence remarks that 'most of the sketches are said to be drawn from actual life, from the village where Verga lived and from which his family originally came. The landscape will be more or less familiar to anyone who has gone in the train down the east coast of Sicily to Syracuse, past Etna and the Plain of Catania and the *Biviere*, the Lake of Lentini, on to the hills again. And anyone who has once known this land can never be quite free from the nostalgia for it, nor can he fail to fall under the spell of Verga's wonderful creation of it, at some point or other.'

15. *See* p. xii.

16. *Il marito di Elena* (1882) and *Dal tuo al mio* (1905).

17. *Per le vie* (1883), *I ricordi del capitano d'Arce* (1891), *Don Candeloro e C.*[i] (1894).

Bibliography

CRITICAL STUDIES

A. Alexander, *Giovanni Verga: A Great Writer and his World* (London, 1972)

T. Bergin, *Giovanni Verga* (New Haven, 1931. Reprint Westport, Conn., 1983)

L. Capuana, *Verga e D'Annunzio*, a cura di M. Pomilio (Bologna, 1972)

G. M. Carsaniga, 'Realism in Italy' in F. W. J. Hemmings (ed.), *The Age of Realism* (Harmondsworth, 1974), pp. 323–55

G. Cattaneo, *Giovanni Verga* (Turin, 1963)

G. Cecchetti, *Giovanni Verga* (Boston, 1978)

G. Cecchetti, *Il Verga maggiore* (Florence, 1968)

B. Croce, *Giovanni Verga* (Bari, 1964)

F. De Roberto, *Casa Verga e altri saggi verghiani* (Florence, 1964)

G. L. Lucente, *The Narrative of Realism and Myth: Verga, Lawrence, Faulkner, Pavese* (Baltimore, 1961)

A. Momigliano, *Dante, Manzoni, Verga* (Messina, 1944)

S. Pacifici, 'The tragic world of Verga's primitives' in *From Verismo to Experimentalism: Essays on the Modern Italian Novel* (Bloomington, 1969), pp. 3–34

L. Pirandello, 'Giovanni Verga' in *Saggi, Poesie, Scritti Varii* (Milan, 1960), pp. 389–428

G. Raya, *Vita di Giovanni Verga* (Rome, 1990)

L. Russo, *Giovanni Verga* (Bari, 1966)

G. Viti, *Verga verista* (Florence, 1974)

D. M. White (ed.), *Pane Nero and Other Stories* (Manchester, 1962)

D. Woolf, *The Art of Verga: A Study in Objectivity* (Sydney, 1977)

TRANSLATIONS

Little Novels of Sicily (Novelle rusticane), translated by D. H. Lawrence, with an Introduction and Glossary by Andrew Wilkin (Harmondsworth, 1973)

Cavalleria rusticana and other stories (from *Vita dei campi*), translated by D. H. Lawrence (London, 1928. Reprinted Westport, Conn., 1975)

The She-Wolf and Other Stories, translated with an Introduction by Giovanni Cecchetti (second ed., revised and enlarged, Berkeley, Los Angeles and London, 1973)

The House by the Medlar Tree (I Malavoglia), translated by Raymond Rosenthal, with new Introduction by Giovanni Cecchetti (second ed., Berkeley, Los Angeles and London, 1983)

Mastro-don Gesualdo, translated by D. H. Lawrence (Harmondsworth, 1970)

Note on Sicilian Terms

SICILIAN TITLES

Comare   Term widely used in Sicily and Calabria as a courtesy title before a female Christian name among friends and neighbours. The male equivalent is *Compare*.

Don   From Latin *dominus*, a courtesy title given in Sicily to men who enjoy an elevated social standing based on their supposed affluence. The female equivalent is *Donna*.

Gnà   Title deriving, not from *signora*, but from *donna* (*doña*), and used before women's Christian names in Sicilian and Calabrian peasant communities.

Massaro   Title applied to a Sicilian peasant farmer or smallholder.

Zio   *Zio* ('Uncle') is a title applied in Sicilian peasant communities to men of a certain age who command some degree of respect or authority. The female equivalent is *Zia*.

MONETARY UNITS

Carlino   Coin worth 25 *centesimi*.

Centesimo   One hundredth of a *lira*.

Lira   Basic Italian unit of currency, worth 100 *centesimi* or 20 *soldi*. In Verga's day roughly equivalent to one-tenth of the pound sterling or one-fifth of the American dollar.

Onza   Coin worth 12.75 *lire*.

Soldo   Coin worth five *centesimi*

Tarì   Old Sicilian coin worth 8.5 *soldi*.

Nedda

SICILIAN SKETCH

The family fireside was for me a figure of speech, useful as a frame for the mildest and calmest of emotions, on a par with moonbeams kissing blonde tresses; but I used to smile whenever I heard people telling me that the fire in the hearth is a sort of friend. There were times when in truth it seemed to me to be too demanding a friend, annoying and despotic, that would have liked to take you gradually by the hands, or by the feet, and drag you into its smoky cavern and kiss you after the manner of Judas. I was unaware of the pastime of poking the logs, or the joy of feeling yourself engulfed in the warmth of the flames; I had no understanding of the teasing language of the log that crackles and grumbles as it burns; my eye never grew accustomed to the bizarre designs of the sparks rushing like fireflies over the blackened firebrands, to the fantastic shapes that the wood assumes as it blazes away, to the thousand and one chiaroscuro effects of the blue and red tongues of flame that timidly lick and gracefully caress before bursting petulantly and arrogantly into life. But once I was initiated into the mysteries of the tongs and the bellows, I fell hopelessly in love with the hearth's potential for blissful idleness. I fling my body on to the armchair beside the fire as though I were casting off a suit of clothes, allowing the flames to make the blood flow more warmly through my veins and cause my heart to quicken its beat, and entrusting the sparks, darting and fluttering like enamoured moths, with the task of keeping me awake and making my thoughts wander off in the same capricious fashion. There is something charming and indefinable in the spectacle of your thoughts taking leave of you and flying off at random into the distance, whence they shower your heart with unsuspected tokens of bittersweet melancholy. Your cigar half-spent, your eyes half-closed, your fingers holding loosely on to the tongs, you see your other self careering dizzily off into the far distance; you sense the currents of strange worlds passing through your sinews; you smile as you experience a thousand and one sensations that would turn your hair grey and line your forehead with wrinkles, without moving a finger or taking a solitary step.

It was during one of these nomad excursions of the soul that the flame flickered a little too closely perhaps, and brought back the vision of another gigantic flame I had once seen burning in the enormous fireplace at Piano, on the slopes of Etna. It was raining, the wind was howling angrily, and the twenty or thirty women employed to gather the olives on the farm were drying out their clothes, sodden by the rain, in front of the fire. The contented ones, those who had money in their pockets, or those who were in love, were singing, whilst the others sat talking about the olive harvest, which had been poor, about the weddings in the parish, or about the rain that was stealing the bread from their mouths. The steward's elderly wife was busy at her spinning-wheel so as not to waste the light from the lantern that hung from the fire's canopy, and the big, wolf-coloured dog lay with its muzzle stretched out across its paws towards the fire, pricking up its ears at every new wailing of the wind. Then, while the minestra was cooking, the shepherd began to play a mountain song that made your legs itch to be moving, and the girls started dancing on the uneven tiled floor of the vast, smoke-blackened kitchen, while the dog growled for fear of their stepping on his tail. The ragged skirts fluttered merrily, and the beans too danced away in the pot, mumbling amid the froth boiled up by the heat of the flames. Once they were tired from dancing, it was time for the singing to begin, and several of the girls called out 'Nedda! Nedda Varannisa![1] Where's Varannisa hidden herself?'

'I'm over here,' a voice replied from the darkest corner of the room, where a girl was squatting on a bundle of firewood.

'What are you doing there?'

'Nothing.'

'Why weren't you dancing?'

'I'm too tired.'

'Sing us one of those lovely songs of yours.'

'No, I don't want to sing.'

'What's the matter?'

'Nothing.'

'She's got her mother dying,' said one of her companions, as though she were saying she'd got toothache.

Crouching there with her chin over her knees, the girl raised her big, black eyes, shining but tearless and seemingly impassive, towards the young woman who had spoken, then lowered them again to stare down towards her bare feet, without uttering a word.

Most of the girls turned away, all chattering at once, like magpies making merry over rich pickings, but two or three of them turned towards her and said, 'Why have you left your mother on her own, then?'

'To find myself a job.'

'Where do you come from?'

'From Viagrande, but I'm staying at Ravanusa.'

The steward's goddaughter, who was due to marry the third son of Massaro Jacopo at Easter, who wore a fine gold cross round her neck, and who thought she was very clever, said as she turned her back on her, 'That's not far! If the news is bad, they can send it by pigeon.'

Nedda shot her retreating figure a glance similar to the one that the dog curled up by the fire had been shooting at the clogs threatening its tail.

'No!' she exclaimed, as though replying to herself. 'Zio Giovanni would come and tell me!'

'Zio Giovanni? Who's he?'

'Zio Giovanni of Ravanusa. Everyone calls him that.'

'You should have got Zio Giovanni to lend you something instead of leaving your mother alone,' said another girl.

'Zio Giovanni isn't rich, and we already owe him ten *lire*! What about the doctor's bill? And the medicines? And the bread we have to eat every day? Oh, it's easy for you to talk,' Nedda added, shaking her head and allowing for the first time a more sorrowful tone to creep into her coarse, almost savage voice, 'but as you stand in the doorway and watch the sun go down, knowing there's no bread in the

3

cupboard, no oil in the lamp and no job to go to next day, it leaves a bitter taste in your mouth when you have a poor old woman lying ill in bed!'

She fell silent, but continued to shake her head without looking at anyone, her eyes dry and expressionless except for a hint of benumbed sorrow such as eyes more accustomed to tears would be incapable of betraying.

'Your soup plates, girls!' shouted the steward's wife, raising the lid from the pot with an air of triumph.

They all crowded round the fire, where the steward's wife was ladling out the beans with the parsimony of long experience. Nedda, her soup bowl under her arm, was last to come forward, and when she finally found a place, the flames lit up her whole person.

She was dark-skinned and poorly dressed, with that air of coarseness and timidity brought on by poverty and loneliness. She might have been beautiful, if toil and hardship had not profoundly altered not only whatever delicate womanly features she had possessed but also the very shape of her body. Her hair was black, thick, unkempt, and tied up with string, her teeth were white as ivory, and there was something attractive about her coarse features that became more evident whenever she smiled. She had big black eyes, moistened with tints of blue, that would have aroused the envy of a queen for that wretched girl curled up on the lowest rung of the human ladder, had they not been overlain by the shadow of timidity that comes with poverty, or rendered so lacklustre through her unchanging air of sorrowful resignation. Her limbs, whether because they had suffered so much beneath enormous burdens, or because they had been forcibly wrenched into shape through painful exertions, had lost their natural form, but without becoming sturdy. She worked as a builder's labourer whenever she was not clearing rocks from ground being broken up for ploughing, or carrying other people's heavy goods into town, or attending to one of the many demanding tasks that in those parts are considered too demeaning for any man to perform. As for the jobs women normally undertake in farming areas, harvesting the grapes and the corn and gathering the olives, they were like holidays to her, a time for merrymaking, a genuine pastime rather than hard work, though on the other hand they brought in less than half the amount she could earn – thirteen *soldi*! – as a builder's labourer for a good day's work in the summer.

The rags that covered her person by way of clothing served only to distort what otherwise might have been seen as delicate womanly beauty. It would have taken a vivid imagination to think that those hands, condemned to a daily round of unrelenting toil in burning heat and freezing cold and scratching a living through dense brambles and jagged fissures in the rock, or that those feet, accustomed to tramping bare in the snow and over rocks seared by the sun, torn by the thorns and hardened by the rocks, could ever have been beautiful. It was impossible to guess the age of this derelict human creature; poverty had crushed her from infancy with all the trials that harden and deform the soul, the mind and the body. It had been just the same for her mother and her grandmother, and it would be just the same for her daughter. The only trace that remained in her of her brothers was a sufficient amount of intelligence to understand their orders and carry out the hardest and most menial of tasks on their behalf.

Nedda held out her soup bowl, and the steward's wife poured into it the miserable helping of bean soup left in the pot.

'Why do you always come last? Don't you realize that the last ones only get the leftovers?' said the steward's wife in an effort to make amends.

The girl lowered her eyes towards the steaming black soup in her bowl as though to acknowledge the reproof, then walked away very slowly so that none of it would be spilt.

'I'd gladly let you have some of mine,' said one of Nedda's more charitable companions, 'but if it goes on raining tomorrow I shall have to eat the rest of my bread as well as losing my day's wages.'

'No fear of that for me,' said Nedda, with a sad little smile.

'Why not?'

'Because I have no bread of my own. What little I had I left with my mother, along with the few coppers I had in my pocket.'

'Are you living on soup and nothing else?'

'Yes, I'm used to it,' Nedda replied simply.

'A curse on this foul weather that robs us of our wages!' swore another of the girls.

'Come on, then, take some of mine.'

'I don't feel hungry any more,' Varannisa retorted briskly, thanking her for the offer.

'You there, who curse the rain of the good Lord, don't you ever eat bread like the rest of us?' said the steward's wife to the girl who had sworn at the foul weather. 'Don't you know that autumn rain means a good harvest?'

Her words were greeted with a general murmur of approval.

'Yes, but it also means that your husband will be docking three half-days from our week's wages!'

This brought another murmur of approval.

'What work have you done in those three half-days that needs to be paid for?' replied the old woman triumphantly.

'That's true! That's true!' the other girls responded, with the instinct that ordinary people have for justice, even if it causes someone to suffer.

The steward's wife recited the rosary, and the monotonous mumbling of the Ave Marias ensued, accompanied by one or two yawns. After the litany came prayers for the living and the dead, at which point the eyes of poor Nedda filled with tears, and she forgot to say her Amen.

'What are things coming to when you don't say your Amen?' said the steward's wife in a severe tone of voice.

'I was thinking about my poor mother so far away,' Nedda replied, putting on a serious air.

The steward's wife bade them goodnight, took up the lantern, and went away. A picturesque array of pallets was made up in different parts of the kitchen or around the fire, the dying flames of which cast their flickering light over the various groups and the postures of the sleepers. It was a good farm, whose owner, unlike many others, spared no effort to provide a sufficiency of beans for the minestra, wood for the fire, and straw for the pallets. The women slept in the kitchen, and the men in the barn. But when you have a miserly owner or a small farm, men and women bed down wherever they can find a space, in the stable or anywhere else, on straw or a few rags, children alongside their parents, and if the father is well off and has a blanket of his own, he spreads it over his family. Anyone feeling cold will huddle up against his neighbour, or settle down with his feet in the warm ashes, or cover himself with straw as best he can. After toiling away for a whole day, and before beginning all over again on the next, sleep comes easily, like a benevolent despot, and the owner turns a blind eye to everything except for denying work to the girl who is about to become a mother, and unable to complete her ten hours of back-breaking labour.

Before dawn the early risers had gone out to see what the weather was doing, and the kitchen door banged and swung continually back and forth, allowing rain and an icy wind to sweep in over the slugabeds who were still asleep. At first light the steward had come and flung the door wide open so that even the laziest would wake up, for it is not right to cheat your master out of a single minute of the ten-hour day that he pays you so handsomely for, sometimes as much as three *carlini* as well as the minestra!

'It's raining!' The dread words were on everyone's lips, repeated here and there in tones of sullen resentment. Nedda leant against the door-post, gazing sadly out on the enormous, leaden clouds that suffused her figure with the grey tints of the dawn. The day was cold and misty. Leaves curled up and separated from the trees, slithering along the branches, then fluttering for a while in the air as they fell to the muddy earth, and rivulets spread into puddles where the pigs rolled about in ecstasy. The cows pressed their muzzles against the gate of the shed, fixing their sorrowful eyes on the falling rain. From their nests below the tiles of the gutter, sparrows chirruped an endless mournful lament.

'There's another day wasted!' muttered one of the girls, as she sank her teeth into a loaf of black bread.

'Look, the clouds are separating from the sea over there,' said Nedda, raising her arm in that direction. 'Perhaps the weather will change before midday.'

'Even if it does, that swindler of a steward will only pay us a third of a day!'

'That's better than nothing.'

'Yes, but who's going to pay us back for the bread we're having to eat?'

'What about the losses the owner has to bear on account of the olives going bad, and the ones he's losing in the mud out there?'

'That's true!' said another of the girls.

'But just you go and pick up a single one of those olives that in half an hour's time will be no good to anyone, to go with your dry bread, and see what the steward has to say about it.'

'He'll be quite right, because the olives don't belong to us.'

'Nor do they belong to the ground that's making a meal of them!'

'The ground belongs to the owner, doesn't it?' Nedda replied, her eyes aglow with pride in the force of her logic.

'That's very true,' said another girl, who could think of no better way to reply.

'If you ask me, I'd rather let it rain all day than spend half a day crawling through the mud in this weather for three or four miserable *soldi*.'

'Three or four *soldi* mean nothing to you, I suppose!' Nedda retorted sadly.

On the Saturday evening, when it was time to settle the week's accounts, and the steward's table was littered with papers and little heaps of *soldi*, the men with the loudest voices were the first to be paid, then the most quarrelsome of the women. The last of all, and those who were paid the least, were the timid and the weak among the women. When the steward had made up her account, Nedda discovered that after her wages had been docked for the two and a half days of forced inactivity, she was left with only forty *soldi*.

The poor girl dared not open her mouth, but simply stood there, her eyes filling with tears.

'You can shed as many tears as you like, you crybaby!' yelled the steward, who was always shouting to show how dutifully he was safeguarding the owner's money. 'I pay you the same as the others, even though you're weaker and smaller than they are! The wage you get from me for a day's work is higher than any other landowner pays in the whole of Pedara, Nicolosi and Trecastagni put together! Three *carlini*, as well as the minestra!'

'I'm not complaining,' said Nedda, timidly pocketing the few *soldi* the steward had counted out for her coin by coin to make it look bigger. 'It's the bad weather that's to blame, for taking away from me nearly half of what I could have earned.'

'Complain to the Lord God then!' bawled the steward.

'Not the Lord God! If anyone's to blame, it's myself for being so poor!'

'Pay the poor girl for the whole week,' the steward was told by the master's son, who was there to supervise the olive-gathering. 'You only lose a few *soldi*.'

'I can only give her what's right and proper!'

'I'm telling you to pay her for the whole week!'

'All the landowners for miles around will be up in arms against both of us if we go changing the rules.'

'You're right,' replied the son of the employer, who was a rich landowner with a fair number of neighbours.

Nedda gathered up her rags and tatters and bade farewell to her companions.

'You're not going back to Ravanusa at this hour, are you?' some of them asked her.

'My mother's ill in bed!'

'Aren't you afraid?'

'Yes, I'm afraid about having so little money in my pocket. But my mother's ill, and now that I don't have to work tomorrow, I wouldn't be able to sleep if I stayed here overnight.'

'Shall I come along and keep you company?' the young shepherd asked, in a jesting tone of voice.

'The only company I need is God and the Virgin,' she replied simply, bowing her head as she set off across the fields.

The sun had set some little time before, and the mountain-top was casting its shadow ever more deeply across the valley. Nedda quickened her step, and when darkness fell completely she began to sing like a bird to keep up her courage. After every dozen steps she turned round in alarm, and whenever a stone was dislodged from the wall alongside her by the rain, or the water lying on the leaves of the trees was driven like hailstones into her face by a sudden gust of wind, she stopped dead and trembled all over like a lamb that has strayed from the flock. An owl pursued her from tree to tree hooting a mournful lament, and every so often, glad of its company, she whistled back at it as the bird never grew tired of following her. As she was passing a shrine by the gate of a farm, she stopped for a moment to recite a hurried Ave Maria, on the alert in case the guard-dog that was baying furiously leapt on her over the boundary wall, before hurrying on and looking over her shoulder two or three times at the tiny lamp burning in homage to the Virgin that lit the way for the farmer whenever he came back late in the evening. Its light strengthened her courage, and prompted her to pray for her poor mother. From time to time a sharp pain would pierce her heart as she recalled how ill her mother was, whereupon she would begin to run, singing at the top of her voice to drown her sorrows. Or she would try and remember the carefree days of the wine harvest, or those wondrous moonlit summer evenings when they all flocked back from La Piana[2] to the joyful sound of the bagpipes, but in her mind's eye all she could see was the wretched pallet on which her sick mother was lying. She tripped on a jagged chip of lava and gashed her foot, the darkness was so complete that at almost every turning of the path she stumbled against the wall or the hedge, and she began to lose her nerve and think she had lost her way. But suddenly she heard the church clock at Punta booming out nine strokes, so close at hand that they seemed to be falling on her head, and she smiled as if a friend had called to her by name in the midst of a crowd of strangers.

She turned happily down the village street, singing her enchanting song at the top of her voice, and holding on tightly to the forty *soldi* in her overall pocket.

As she passed by the chemist's shop she looked inside and saw the chemist and the notary, wrapped up in their cloaks, playing at cards. A little further on she came across the poor village idiot of Punta, who was going up and down the street with his hands in his pockets singing the same old song he had been singing night and day, in the cold midwinter and hot midsummer, for twenty years. On reaching the first trees of the avenue leading in a straight line to Ravanusa she met a pair of oxen, lowing peacefully as they ambled slowly towards her.

'Hey! Nedda!' shouted a familiar voice.

'Is that you, Janu?'

'Yes, it's me, with the master's oxen.'

'Where are you coming from?' Nedda asked, without stopping.

'From La Piana. I called at your house. Your mother's expecting you.'

'How is she?'

'Still the same.'

'God bless you!' the girl exclaimed, as if she had been expecting the worst, and she began to run on again.

'Goodbye, Nedda!' Janu called after her.

'Goodbye,' Nedda responded from the distance.

And she thought the stars were shining like so many suns, that all the trees, every one of which she recognized, were spreading their branches over her head to protect her, and that the stones of the road were caressing her aching feet.

Next day, it being a Sunday, there came the visit of the doctor, who set aside for his destitute patients the day he could not devote to his farms. It was truly a joyless visit, because the doctor was not accustomed to standing on ceremony with his customers, and in Nedda's poor cottage there was neither waiting-room nor any friend of the family to whom he could speak frankly about the invalid's true condition.

There followed another sorrowful event when the parish priest arrived in his rochet,[3] accompanied by the sexton with the extreme unction, and two or three parishioners mumbling various prayers. The sexton's bell jingled out keenly across the fields, and the cart-drivers halted their mules along the road when they heard it and raised their caps. When Nedda heard it coming up the stony path leading from the road to the house, she pulled the tattered blanket up to the invalid's chin so that no one would notice the absence of any sheets, and spread her best white pinafore over the rickety table, which she had levelled up with the aid of one or two tiles. While the priest was carrying out his office, she went and knelt outside the front door, muttering her prayers mechanically, staring with a faraway look at the boulder beside the doorway where her old mother used to sit and warm herself up in the April sun, bending an inattentive ear to the customary sounds of the neighbourhood and the bustling of all the people going about their business without a care in the world. The priest went away, and the sexton paused in the doorway, vainly waiting for them to offer him the usual alms for the poor.

Late that evening Zio Giovanni saw Nedda hurrying down the road towards Punta.

'Hey there! Where are you going at this hour?'

'I'm going for the medicine the doctor ordered.'

Zio Giovanni was a thrifty man, who liked to grumble.

'More medicines!' he muttered. 'Wasn't it enough for them to order the medicine of the holy oil? They're all in league with the chemist to drain the blood from the poor! Take my advice, Nedda, save your money and go back and stay with your poor mother.'

'You never know, it could do her some good!' the girl replied, lowering her eyes sorrowfully and quickening her step.

Zio Giovanni moaned, then called after her, 'Hey, Varannisa!'

'What is it?'

'I'll go to the chemist's. Don't worry, I'll be back sooner than you would have been. And you won't have to leave your poor mother alone.'

The girl's eyes filled with tears. 'God bless you!' she said, as she tried to hand him the money.

'You can pay me back later,' growled Zio Giovanni, and he sprinted off as though he were a twenty-year-old.

The girl returned to her mother, saying, 'Zio Giovanni's gone for us,' in an unusually tender sort of voice.

The dying woman, hearing Nedda replacing the handful of coins on the table, gave her a questioning look.

'He told me we could pay him back later,' said her daughter.

'God bless him for his charity!' murmured the sick woman. 'So you'll still have something to spend.'

'Oh, Mother!'

'How much do we owe Zio Giovanni?'

'Ten *lire*. But don't worry, Mother! I shall carry on working!'

The old woman gazed at her at length through half-closed eyes, then embraced her without a word.

Next day the undertakers called, along with the sexton and several of the women living nearby. When Nedda had arranged the body of her mother on the bier in her best clothes, she placed in her hands a carnation she had grown in a cracked pot, along with the finest tress of her own hair. She gave the gravediggers the few *soldi* she had left so that they would do their job in a proper fashion and be sure not to jolt the dead woman too much on the rocky path leading to the cemetery. Then she tidied up the bed and the house, put away the last bottle of medicine on a high shelf, and went and sat in the doorway gazing up at the sky.

A robin, the bird of cold November mornings, began to sing in the bushes and the brambles that hung above the wall opposite, and from time to time, as it hopped among the thorns and the brushwood, it fixed its mischievous eyes upon her as though it had something to tell her. Nedda thought to herself that her mother, the day before, had heard it singing. In the garden next door magpies were still pecking away at the olives strewn about the ground. She had driven them off by throwing stones at them, so that the dying woman would not have to listen to their funereal croaking. But now she watched them impassively, without making a move, and as the lupine-seller or the vintner or the carters made their way down the neighbouring street, shouting so as to be heard above the noise of their cartwheels and the bell-collars of their mules, she said to herself, 'That'll be so-and-so, that'll be whatsisname.' When the Angelus rang, and the first stars appeared in the evening sky, it struck her that she no longer needed to go to Punta to buy any more medicines, and as the noises gradually subsided in the street, and darkness descended on the garden, she thought to herself she no longer needed to light the lamp.

Zio Giovanni found her standing in the doorway.

She had got to her feet on hearing footsteps approaching along the path, because she was not expecting anyone to call.

'What are you doing there?' Zio Giovanni asked. She shrugged her shoulders, without bothering to answer.

The old man sat down beside her on the doorstep, and asked no further questions.

'Zio Giovanni,' said the girl, after a long pause, 'now that I have no one else to care for, and I don't have to look for work nearby, I'll go to Roccella where the olives are still being harvested, and when I return I'll pay you back the money you lent us.'

'I didn't come here asking for the money!' Zio Giovanni gruffly replied.

She said no more, and they both sat there in silence listening to the hooting of an owl. Nedda thought perhaps it was the one that had kept her company coming back from Piano, and her heart swelled with emotion.

'Do you have work to go to?' Zio Giovanni asked her finally.

'No, but I'll always find a charitable soul to offer me something to do.'

'I heard that over at Aci Catena they pay good women workers about a *lira* a day to pack oranges, no minestra of course, and I thought of you at once. You did that sort of job last March, so you must know what it's all about. Do you want to go and see?'

'Of course!'

'In that case, you must turn up at dawn at Merlo's orchard, on the corner of the lane that leads to Sant'Anna.'

'I can even go tonight. My poor mother made sure she wouldn't leave me doing nothing for long!'

'Do you know the way?'

'Yes. But if I get lost I'll inquire.'

'Ask the innkeeper on the main road to Valverde, just beyond the chestnut copse to the left of the road. Find Massaro Vinirannu, and tell him I sent you.'

'I shall go,' said the girl, delighted at her good fortune.

'It occurred to me you wouldn't have enough bread to last the week,' said Zio Giovanni, pulling out a huge black loaf from his deep coat pocket, and placing it on the table.

Nedda turned red with embarrassment, as though she were the one doing someone a favour. Then, after a moment, she said, 'If the priest were to say Mass for my mother tomorrow, I would give him two days' pay when the bean harvest comes.'

'I've already had him say Mass for her,' Zio Giovanni replied.

'Oh! My poor dead mother will be praying for you in return!' the girl murmured, huge tears filling her eyes.

When Zio Giovanni finally left, and she heard his footsteps trailing away into the distance, she closed the door and lit a candle. She now felt all alone in the world, and afraid to sleep in the little bed where she had always lain down beside her mother.

The girls in the village spoke ill of her for going to work the very next day after her mother's funeral, and for not wearing mourning. The parish priest gave her a sound telling off when he caught sight of her the following Sunday in her doorway sewing up her overall, which she had dyed black, the only sign of mourning the poor girl was able to display, and he took all this as his text for preaching in church against the evil habit of failing to observe feast days and the sabbath.

So as to requite her dreadful sin, the poor girl went and worked in the parish priest's field for two days to persuade him to say Mass for her dead mother on Sundays and the first Monday of the month. The girls in their Sunday best drew away from her in the church pew or giggled behind her back, and when the young men shouted coarse witticisms at her as she came out of the church, she wrapped her tattered mantilla tightly round her head and hurried off, fixing her eyes on the ground and allowing no bitter thought to disturb the serenity of her prayer. Sometimes she would tell herself she deserved their contempt because she was so poor, at others, holding out her two strong arms, she would say to herself, 'Blessed be the Lord that gave them to me!' and she would go on her way with a smile.

One evening, soon after she had turned out the light, she heard a familiar voice in the lane singing out loud, with the melancholic oriental cadence of the Sicilian folksongs, '*Picca cci voli ca la vaju' a viju. A la mi' amanti di l'arma mia.*'[4]

'It's Janu!' she whispered, like a startled bird, her heart pounding in her breast, and she buried her head in the bedclothes.

When she opened her window next morning, she saw Janu basking in the warm April sun as he leant against the orchard wall in his brand new velveteen suit, doing his best to force into its pockets his big, swart hands, calloused from his labours. A fine new bright-red silk scarf peeped out invitingly from the inside pocket of his jacket.

'Ah, Janu!' she said, feigning total surprise.

'Hello there!' called the young man, with a broad grin all over his face.

'What are you doing here?'

'I've come back from La Piana.'

The girl smiled back at him, and looked towards the larks still hopping across the grass in the early morning sunlight.

'You've come back with the larks.'

'The larks are like me. They know where to find better things to eat.'

'What do you mean by that?'

'They've given me the sack.'

'Why?'

'Because I caught a fever down there, and could only work three days a week.'

'Poor Janu!'

'Damn La Piana!' cursed Janu, stretching out his arm towards the valley.

'Did you know that my mother . . . ?' Nedda began.

'Yes, Zio Giovanni told me.'

She said no more, and turned to gaze down on the garden beyond the wall. Steam rose from stones moistened by the morning dew, whose drops glistened on every blade of grass. Almond trees in full bloom whispered in the gentlest of breezes, their pink and white blossom drifting on to the cottage roof and filling the air with its fragrance. A petulant sparrow chirped angrily away from the edge of a gutter, issuing its own brand of menace to Janu, whose suspect looks made it seem likely he would raid its nest, of which a few telltale blades of straw protruded from the tiles. The church bell was summoning the people to Mass.

'Doesn't it make you feel good to hear the parish bell!' Janu exclaimed.

'I recognized your voice last night,' said Nedda, blushing as she forked up the soil round the flowers in her window-box with a piece of broken pottery.

He turned the other way and spent some time lighting up his pipe, as any man must.

'Goodbye, I'm off to Mass now!' said Nedda abruptly, withdrawing from the window after waiting in vain for him to speak.

'Here, take this,' he said, displaying his fine silk scarf, 'I brought it back for you from the city.'

'It's lovely! But it's far too good for me!'

'Why's that? It doesn't cost you anything!' the young man replied, with the logic of the countryman.

She turned scarlet, as though the huge expense had made her realize the warmth of the young man's feelings towards her. Smiling, she cast him a glance both savage and affectionate, and withdrew rapidly into the house. When she heard the sound of his boots retreating over the stones of the path, she peeped out and kept him in view as he went on his way.

At Holy Mass, all the village girls admired Nedda's fine new silk scarf, imprinted with roses that were so true to life you could almost smell them, on which the sun poured its brightest rays as it shone through the church windows. And as she was passing Janu, who was standing alongside the first cypress in the churchyard with his back to the wall smoking that pipe of his that was all so intricately carved, she blushed and felt her heart pounding in her breast, and quickly walked on. The young man followed her, whistling as he went along, and watching her as she hurried on without looking round, in her fine new heavily pleated velveteen dress, her elegant little shoes, and her flaming red silk scarf. 'Poor soul,' he thought to himself. 'Now that her mother has gone to Heaven and she no longer needs to provide for her, she's managed to put together an outfit from her earnings.' Amid all the misery the poor have to suffer, there's also the solace that comes with the losses that pierce the heart with the greatest sorrow!

Nedda heard the young man's heavy footsteps behind her, unable to tell whether she felt deeply happy or deeply afraid, and on the pale grey dust of the sun-drenched road ahead of her, her eyes were glued to a second shadow that every so often separated itself from her own. Suddenly, when she came in sight of her cottage, for no apparent reason she began to run like a frightened deer. Janu caught up with her, and, leaning against the door, she landed a punch on his back with a cry of 'Take that!'

He returned the blow with a rather exuberant show of gallantry.

'How much did you pay for your silk scarf?' Nedda asked, filled with delight as she took it from her head to hold it out in the sunlight and admire it.

'Five *lire*,' Janu replied, with a slight puffing out of his chest.

She looked away from him with a smile, folded up the scarf along its original lines as best she could, and began to sing a song that returned to her lips for the first time in ages.

The cracked pot on the window-sill was teeming with carnations still in bud.

'What a shame,' said Nedda, 'that none of them has come out yet,' as she picked the one with the biggest bud and gave it to him.

'What use is that to me if it isn't in flower?' he said, uncomprehending, casting it aside.

She turned away from him for a moment, then asked, 'Where are you going to work now?'

He shrugged his shoulders. 'What about you? Where are you going tomorrow?'

'To Bongiardo.'

'I'll find a job, as long as I don't have to catch any more fevers.'

'You have to stop staying out at night to sing in people's doorways!' she said, blushing all over and moving from side to side against the doorpost in a coquettish sort of way.

'I won't, if you don't want me to.'

She gave him a push and ran inside the house.

'Hey there! Janu!' the voice of Zio Giovanni came bellowing from the road.

'I'm coming!' Janu shouted, then to Nedda, 'I'll come with you to Bongiardo, if they want me.'

'Listen to me, young man,' Zio Giovanni said to Janu when he joined him on the road, 'Nedda is on her own now, and you're a good fellow, but it isn't right for the two of you to be together. You understand?'

'I understand, Zio Giovanni. But God willing, we shall be all right together after the harvest, when I've put aside the bit of money we need.'

Even though no one could see her, Nedda blushed as she overheard what they were saying from behind the wall.

Before dawn next morning, as she opened the door to leave, she found Janu standing there with his bundle and stick.

'Where are you going?' she asked.

'I'm coming to Bongiardo with you to look for a job.'

The sound of their voices so early in the morning awoke the fledgling sparrows, which began to chirrup in the nest. Janu hooked Nedda's bundle on to his stick alongside his own, and they set off at a brisk pace while the first glimmers of day tinged the sky on the horizon, and the air turned chill in the morning breeze.

At Bongiardo anyone looking for work was bound to find it. The price of wine had risen, and a wealthy landowner was having a broad tract of smallholdings cleared for the planting of vines. The smallholdings were yielding 1,200 *lire* a year from lupines and olives, but in five years' time, once they were turned into vineyards, they would bring in twelve to thirteen thousand *lire* a year after an outlay of only ten to twelve thousand, half of which would be covered from cutting down the olives. It was clearly a deal too good to be missed, and the landowner was more than willing to pay a decent wage to the peasants clearing the terrain, thirty *soldi* to the men and twenty to the women, but no minestra. It was hard work, certainly, and even the ragged clothes they worked in were getting torn to bits, but Nedda was not accustomed to earning twenty *soldi* every day of her life.

The supervisor noticed that Janu, as they filled up their wicker baskets with rocks, kept leaving the lighter one for Nedda, and when he threatened to send him packing, the poor devil had to rest content with a cut of ten *soldi* in his day's wage.

The trouble was that the smallholdings, being relatively uncultivated, lacked any sort of farmhouse. At night the men and the women had to sleep higgledy-piggledy in a hut without a door, and the nights were decidedly cold. Janu pretended he was always feeling hot, and gave Nedda his corduroy cloak to keep herself well covered. And on Sunday all the labourers went their separate ways.

Janu and Nedda had taken shortcuts, and as they walked through the chestnut copse they laughed and chatted and sang together, jingling the big money in their pockets. The sun was as hot as it is in June, the distant meadows were beginning to turn brown, the shadows cast by the trees had a festive air about them, and the grass beneath their feet was still green and flecked with dew.

Towards midday they sat in the shade to eat their black bread and their white onions. Janu also had some of that special Mascali wine, and he never stopped handing it over to Nedda, so that the poor girl, who was not used to drinking so much, was getting a thick head and a furry tongue to go with it. From time to time their eyes met and they burst out laughing for no apparent reason.

'If we were husband and wife we could eat bread and drink wine together every day,' Janu said, with his mouth full, and Nedda lowered her eyes because of the way he was looking at her. The deep silence of noon enveloped them all around, the tiniest leaves of the trees were motionless, shadows were rare; the air was filled with a stillness, a warmth, a sensuous murmuring of insects that made the eyelids droop. The loftiest tops of the chestnuts suddenly started to sigh in a fresh breeze coming off the sea.

'It's going to be a good year for the poor as well as the rich,' said Janu, 'and at harvest time, God willing, I shall put aside a bit of money . . . and then, if you love me . . . !' He handed her the flask.

'No, I won't drink any more,' she said, blushing all over her face.

'Why do you turn so red?' he said, laughing.

'I won't tell you.'

'Is it because of the wine?'

'No!'

She struck him on the shoulder and started laughing.

In the distance they heard the braying of a donkey that had caught a whiff of fresh grass.

'Do you know why the donkeys are braying?' Janu asked.

'You tell me, since you know the reason.'

'Of course I know. They're braying because they're in love,' he said, staring at her with a meaningful smile on his lips. She lowered her eyes as though they were dazzled by flames of fire, and she felt as if all the wine she had drunk had gone to her head, and all the warmth of that golden sky was rushing through her veins.

'Let's go now!' she exclaimed, tormentedly shaking her head, still heavy with the wine.

'What's the matter?'

'I don't know, but let's go, quickly!'

'Do you love me?'

She nodded her head.

'Will you marry me?'

She looked him calmly in the eyes and gripped his rough hand tightly between her own dark hands, at the same time raising herself unsteadily on to her knees in order to get away. Distraught, he held on to her by her dress, murmuring unintelligible words, as though no longer in control of his actions.

When they heard the crowing of a cock from the nearby farm, Nedda suddenly sprang to her feet and looked anxiously all around.

'Let's go! Come on, let's go!' She was all flushed, and the words came out from her lips in a rapid stream.

As she was about to turn the corner before reaching her cottage she paused for a moment and trembled, as though afraid she would find her old mother waiting on the doorstep, deserted now for six whole months.

Then it was Easter, the joyous festival of the countryside, with its enormous bonfires, its merry processions through fields turning green and beneath trees laden with blossom, with the village church decked out in all its glory, the cottage doorways festooned with flowers, and the girls parading abroad in their bright new summer dresses. Nedda was seen in tears as she came away from the confessional, and failed to appear among the girls lined up at the choir to receive communion. From that day forth no respectable girl addressed so much as a single word to her, and when she went to Mass she found no room in her usual pew, and had to stay on her knees for the whole service. Whenever they saw her crying they conjured up all the nasty sins they could think of, and turned their backs on her in horror. And anyone offering her a job of work took advantage to lower her day's wage.

Meanwhile she waited for her fiancé to return from La Piana, where he had gone reaping to scrape together the money they needed to set up some sort of home together, and pay the parish priest.

One evening, as she was spinning, she heard an ox-cart coming to a halt at the end of the lane, and saw Janu coming towards her, looking pale and strange.

'What's the matter?' she said.

'I've been ill. The fever took hold of me again, down there in that accursed Piana. I lost a full week's work, and spent what little money I'd earned on food.' She led him quickly into the house, unfolded the straw pallet, and tried to give him the small amount she had tucked away there in the foot of a stocking.

'No,' he said. 'Tomorrow I shall go to Mascalucia for the pruning of the olives, and that'll keep me going. When the pruning is over we'll get married.'

He had a troubled air about him as he made this promise, and stood leaning against the doorpost, with his scarf wound over his head, looking at her with eyes that were close to tears.

'But you're not well!' said Nedda.

'I know, but I'm hoping to get better now that I'm here, and in any case the fever only comes on every three days.'

She looked at him without saying a word, and felt as if her heart was breaking to see how pale and thin he looked.

'Will you be able to keep your balance up there on the high branches?'

'With God's help!' Janu replied. 'Goodbye now, I can't keep the carter waiting after giving me a lift here from La Piana. I'll soon be back!'

It was some little time before he could drag himself away from her, and when he finally did, she went along with him to the main road. She stood and watched him disappearing into the distance without shedding a tear, even though she felt she would never see him leaving her again. Her heart missed another beat, like a sponge being squeezed just one more time, and he waved and called out her name as he passed from view round the bend in the road.

Three days later she heard a great commotion outside in the road. She looked over the wall and saw a group of peasants and neighbours crowding round Janu, who was stretched out on the rungs of a ladder, white as a sheet, his head bound round with a scarf that was sodden with blood. As she trod the *via dolorosa* along the road leading back to his house, he held her by the hand and told her how the fever had weakened him so much that he had fallen from the top of a tree and ended up in the sorry state she could see him in.

'You knew in your heart what would happen!' he murmured, with a sad smile on his lips. She was wide-eyed as she listened, holding him by the hand, her face as pallid as his own. On the following day he died.

As she felt the sad legacy of her dead companion moving about inside her body, Nedda hurried off to the church to pray for his soul to the Holy Virgin. But in the churchyard she came face to face with the priest, who knew of her shame, and, hiding her face in her mantilla, she turned back again in utter despair.

From then on, whenever she went looking for a job, they simply laughed in her face, not so much to pillory the girl for her sins as because she could no longer work as diligently as before. After being rejected and laughed at so many times that she no longer dared show her face, she stayed inside the house, like a bird that has retired wounded to its nest. The few *soldi* she had put away in the foot of the stocking were spent one after the other, to be followed by her fine new dress, and the fine silk scarf. Zio Giovanni gave her what little help he could, drawing on that sense of tolerance and reviving charity without which the moralizing of a parish priest is barren and unjust, and so prevented her from dying of hunger. She eventually gave birth to a rickety and stunted baby girl, and when they told her it was not a boy she wept in the way she had wept on the evening when she had closed the front door of the cottage behind her in the wake of the coffin, and realized she no longer had a mother. But she refused to let the baby go to the Sisters of Charity.

'You poor little child,' she said. 'If you have to suffer, let's at least delay it as long as possible!' The neighbours called her a shameless hussy because she had not acted the hypocrite and abandoned her child. But the baby went short of milk because the mother couldn't get enough to eat. It was wasting rapidly away, and in vain did Nedda try to squeeze into its hungry little lips the very blood from her breast. One winter's evening, at sunset, while the snow fell thickly on the cottage roof and the ill-fitting door rattled in the wind, the poor infant, its whole body purple with the cold, its tiny fingers clenched tightly into the palms of its hands, fixed its lifeless eyes on the fervent eyes of its mother, let out a sob, and breathed its last.

Nedda shook it, hugged it madly and savagely to her breast, tried to give it warmth with her breath and her kisses, and when she realized it was really dead, she laid it on the bed where her mother had slept, and knelt beside it, her eyes quite dry and popping out from their sockets.

'Ah! Blessed are you that are dead!' she exclaimed. 'Ah! Blessed Holy Virgin, who has taken away my child so as not to let it suffer as I have suffered!'

From Vita dei campi

Cavalleria rusticana

When Turiddu Macca, the son of Gnà Nunzia, came back from the army, he strutted round the piazza every Sunday in his sharpshooter's uniform and his red forage-cap, as though he were the fortune-teller setting up stall with his cage of canaries. The girls couldn't take their eyes off him as they went along to Mass with their faces half hidden in their mantillas, and the little boys buzzed round him like flies. He had even brought back a pipe carved with a lifelike image of the king on horseback, and he would strike matches on the seat of his pants, raising his leg as if to take a kick at something. But all the same, Massaro Angelo's daughter Lola failed to show up either at Mass or on her veranda, as she had got engaged to a fellow from Licodia, who was a cart-driver with four Sortino[1] mules in his stable. When Turiddu first got to know about it, Christ in Heaven! he wanted to tear the guts out of that chap from Licodia, he really did! But the only thing he did was to give vent to his feelings by going and singing all the abusive songs he could think of under the fair young woman's window.

'Doesn't Gnà Nunzia's Turiddu have anything better to do,' the villagers were saying, 'than to spend his nights singing away like a thrush without a mate?'

He eventually bumped into Lola on her way back from the shrine of Our Lady of Peril, and when she saw him she didn't turn a hair, as though he was none of her business.

'Nice to see you!' he said.

'Ah, Turiddu, I did hear you'd come back on the first of the month.'

'I heard one or two other things as well!' he replied. 'Is it true you're going to marry Alfio, the cart-driver?'

27

'If that's the will of God!' Lola replied, drawing her neckerchief up over her chin by its two corners.

'You play around with the will of God in whatever way it suits you! It was the will of God that made me come all that way back to be faced with a fine bit of news like this, Lola!'

The poor wretch tried again to put a brave face on it all, but his voice trailed off, and he doddered along behind her with the tassel of his cap swinging from side to side across his shoulders. To be honest, the girl was feeling sorry to see him pulling such a long face, but she had no wish to encourage him with a lot of fine words.

In the end she turned round and said, 'Look here, Turiddu, leave me alone so I can go and catch up with the other girls. What would people say in the village if they were to see me with you?'

'Fair enough,' replied Turiddu, 'now that you're marrying Alfio, with four mules in his stable, we mustn't start people's tongues wagging. My poor old mother, on the other hand, was forced to sell our own bay mule and that patch of vineyard along the main road while I was away in the army. Times have changed, and you no longer remember standing at the window to chat with me down in the courtyard, or when you gave me that handkerchief, just before I went away. God knows how many tears I've shed into it since I wandered off so far from home that our village had never been heard of. Goodbye then, Lola, let's forget we were ever friends with one another.'

Lola went ahead and married the cart-driver, and on Sundays she would stand on her veranda with her hands across her belly to show off all the big gold rings her husband had given her. Turiddu continued to pass up and down the street, pipe in his mouth and hands in his pockets, with an air of indifference, eyeing all the girls. But deep inside he was distraught to think that Lola's husband had all that gold, and that she pretended not to notice him as he passed by.

'I'm going to teach that bitch a thing or two,' he muttered.

Opposite Alfio's lived Massaro Cola, the vine dresser, who was said to be as rich as a pig, and had a daughter in the house. Turiddu said and did all the things required to worm his way into Massaro Cola's good books, and began to hang around the house and fill the girl's ears with sweet nothings.

By way of reply, Santa would say, 'Why don't you go and say these fine things to that Lola girl?'

'Lola's a great lady! Lola's married now to a big wheel!'

'Big wheels are too good for me.'

'You are worth a hundred Lolas, and I know someone who wouldn't even look at her or anybody else, if you were around. Lola isn't worth as much as your little finger, that she isn't.'

'When the fox couldn't get at the grapes . . .'

'He said: what a lovely girl you are, my currant bun!'

'Hey, Turiddu! Keep those hands to yourself!'

'Are you afraid I'm going to eat you?'

'I'm not afraid of you or anyone else.'

'Ah! Your mother came from Licodia, and don't we know it! You've got fiery blood in your veins! Oh, I could eat you up simply looking at you!'

'Keep on looking, then, and we shan't leave any crumbs lying around. But, for the time being, just pick up that bundle for me, would you?'

'For you I would pick up the whole house, honestly I would!'

So as to save herself from blushing, she hurled a log at him that happened to be within her reach, missing him by a hair's breadth.

'Let's get on. Fine words butter no parsnips.'

'If I were a rich man, I'd be looking for a wife like you, Santa.'

'I won't be marrying any big wheel, the same as Lola, but I do have a dowry of my own when the good Lord sends me the right man.'

'We all know you're rich, we know that.'

'Get moving then, if you know it, because my father's due any minute, and I don't want him to find me out here in the courtyard.'

Her father began to turn up his nose at the affair, but the girl pretended not to notice, because the tassel on the sharpshooter's cap had begun to tickle her fancy, and kept on dancing up and down in front of her eyes. When the father showed Turiddu the door, the daughter opened the window for him, and stayed there chatting away to him every evening, so that the whole neighbourhood talked of nothing else.

'I'm crazy about you,' said Turiddu. 'I can't sleep and I can't eat.'

29

'Rubbish!'

'If only I were the son of King Victor Emmanuel, I'd be able to marry you!'

'Rubbish!'

'By all that's holy, I could gobble you up like a loaf of bread!'

'Rubbish!'

'I really could, honestly!'

'Oh, for goodness' sake!'

Lola was all ears every evening, concealed behind her pot of basil, now turning pale, now blushing, and one day she called out to Turiddu.

'Hey there, Turiddu, don't you ever say hello to your old friends any more?'

'Ah!' sighed the young fellow. 'It would be a happy man who could say hello to you!'

'If you want to say hello to me, you know where I live!' Lola replied.

Turiddu called to say hello to her so often that Santa took notice, and slammed her window in his face. The neighbours gave each other a nod and a wink whenever the sharpshooter passed down the street. Lola's husband was away with his mules, doing the rounds of the country fairs.

'On Sunday I'm going to confession. I had a terrible dream last night!' said Lola.

'Don't worry about it! Don't worry!' Turiddu pleaded.

'No, now that Easter's coming, my husband will be wanting to know why I haven't been to confession.'

'Ah!' murmured Cola's daughter Santa as she waited her turn, kneeling in front of the confessional where Lola was laundering her sins. 'I swear I won't let you get away with it by crawling to Rome!'

Alfio returned home with his mules, laden with shekels, and with a fine new Easter dress for his wife.

'You do well to bring her presents,' his neighbour Santa told him, 'because while you're away your wife dresses up your home with a pair of horns!'

Alfio was one of those cart-drivers who take offence easily, and when he heard his wife being talked about in that fashion his colour changed as though he'd been knifed.

'By Almighty God!' he exclaimed. 'If you haven't been seeing clearly, you'll have no eyes left to cry with by the time I've finished with you, and that goes for all your family as well!'

'I don't do much crying!' Santa replied. 'I didn't even cry when I saw Gnà Nunzia's son Turiddu going in to your wife's house every night.'

'Right,' Alfio replied, 'and thank you very much.'

Now that the cat was back, Turiddu no longer hung about the street every day, but filled in his time at the tavern, with his friends. On the evening of Easter Saturday, they were sitting round one of the tables with a dish of pork sausages. As soon as Alfio came in, Turiddu knew, simply from the way he stared at him, that he had come to settle the unfinished business of theirs, and put his fork down on his plate.

'Can I do anything for you, Alfio?' he said.

'I don't need any favours from you, Turiddu. I haven't seen anything of you for a while, and I just wanted a word on that matter you know about.'

Turiddu began by holding out a glass of wine to him, but Alfio brushed it aside with a sweep of his arm.

Then Turiddu got up and said, 'If you want me, Alfio, here I am.'

The cart-driver flung his arms round Turiddu's neck.

'If you'd like to come down to the cactus grove at Canziria tomorrow morning, we can talk the thing over, my friend.'

'Wait for me at dawn on the main road, and we'll go there together.'

With these words they exchanged the kiss of the challenge. Turiddu took the tip of the cart-driver's ear between his teeth and bit it, by way of a solemn promise to keep the appointment.

His friends left the sausages where they were without uttering a word, and took Turiddu home. Poor Gnà Nunzia had been waiting up for him till a late hour for nights on end.

'Mamma,' Turiddu said, 'do you remember when I went off to the army, and you thought I would never come back? Give me a big kiss like you did then, because tomorrow morning I'm going on a long journey.'

Before dawn he dug out the flick-knife that he'd hidden under a pile of straw before going off as a conscript, then he set off for the cactus grove at Canziria.

'Oh! Jesus, Mary and Joseph! Where are you off to in such a hurry?' wailed the terrified Lola, as her husband was about to leave.

'I'm not going very far,' Alfio replied, 'and it would be better for you if I never came back.'

Lola, in her nightdress, knelt down to pray at the foot of the bed, pressing to her lips the rosary that Brother Bernardino had brought back for her from the Holy Land, and she recited as many Ave Marias as there were beads on it.

'Listen, Alfio,' Turiddu began, after walking a fair stretch of the road alongside his companion, who remained completely silent, his cap pulled down above his eyes, 'as God is my witness I know I did wrong and I'd be glad to let you kill me. But before coming to meet you I caught sight of my old mother, who had got up to see me leaving with the excuse of cleaning out the chicken run, looking as though her heart was breaking, and as God is my witness I'm going to kill you to stop my mother shedding any tears.'

'That's all right,' Alfio replied, stripping off his jacket, 'let's give it all we've got.'

They both knew how to use a knife. Turiddu took the first blow, stopping it with his arm just in time. He gave back as good as he'd got, striking Alfio in the groin.

'Ah, Turiddu! So you really do want to kill me!'

'Yes, I already told you. After seeing my old mother with the chickens, my eyes can see nothing else.'

'Open them wide, those eyes of yours!' roared Alfio, 'and I'll give you something to do them a bit of good.'

Keeping up his guard, hunched up in pain, clutching his wound with his left hand, and crawling over the ground with the use of his elbow, he suddenly grabbed a handful of dust and hurled it into the eyes of his opponent.

'Ah!' yelled Turiddu, blinded by the dust. 'I'm a dead man.'

He tried to escape, leaping backward in desperation, but Alfio struck him another blow in the stomach and a third in the throat.

'That's three! For dressing up my home. Now your mother can stop bothering about the chickens!'

Turiddu pawed the air for a while amid the cactuses, then dropped to the ground like a stone. The blood foamed up with a gurgling sound into his throat, and he couldn't even get out the words, 'Ah, mamma mia!'

The She-Wolf

She was dark-haired, tall and lean, with firm, well-rounded breasts, though she was no longer young, and she had a pale complexion, like someone forever in the grip of malaria. The pallor was relieved by a pair of huge eyes and fresh red lips that looked as though they would eat you.

In the village they called her the She-Wolf because, no matter what she had, she was never satisfied. The women crossed themselves whenever they saw her coming, lone as a stray bitch, with the restless and wary appearance of a starving wolf. She would gobble up their sons and their husbands in the twinkling of an eye with those red lips of hers, and draw them to the tail of her skirt and transfix them with those devilish eyes, as though they were standing before the altar at St Agrippina's. Luckily the She-Wolf herself never set foot inside the church, either at Easter or at Christmas or to hear Mass or to go to confession. Father Angiolino of St Mary of Jesus, a true servant of God, had lost his soul on her account.

Maricchia, poor girl, a good and worthy soul, shed tears in secret because she was the She-Wolf's daughter and nobody would ever want to marry her, even though she too had a fine trousseau tucked away in a chest and a patch of decent land in the sun, like any other girl in the village.

Then it happened that the She-Wolf fell in love with a handsome young fellow back from the army, when the two of them were hay-making on the notary's farm. She'd fallen for him lock, stock and barrel, her flesh burning beneath her thick cotton bodice, and, staring into his eyes, she was overcome with the kind of thirst you would experience down in the valley on a hot midsummer day. But he just kept scything calmly away, head down over the hay, saying, 'What's the matter, Pina?' In the vast expanse of the fields, where all you could hear was the chirping of the crickets as they leapt, with the sun beating straight down, the She-Wolf tied up sheaf after sheaf, bundle after bundle, showing no sign of fatigue, never looking up for an instant, never putting her lips to the flask, just as long as she could be there behind Nanni, while he scythed away, asking her every so often, 'What is it you want, Pina?'

One evening she told him, while the men, exhausted from their long day's labours, were nodding off to sleep in the barn, and the dogs were filling the dark air of the countryside with their howling, 'It's you I want! You that are beautiful as the sun, and sweet as the honey! I want you!'

'It's that unmarried daughter of yours that *I* want,' Nanni replied, laughing.

The She-Wolf thrust her hands into her hair, tearing at the sides of her head without uttering a word, then strode off and stayed away from the barn. But when the olive-crushing season came round in October, she set her eyes on Nanni again because he was working next door to where she lived, and the creaking of the press kept her awake the whole night long.

'Pick up that sack of olives,' she said to her daughter, 'and come with me.'

Nanni was pushing the olives under the mill wheel with his shovel, and shouting 'Gee up there!' to the mule to keep it moving.

'Do you want my daughter Maricchia?' Pina asked.

'What are you going to give her?' Nanni replied.

'She's got the things her father left, and she can have my house into the bargain. All you need to leave me is a corner of the kitchen to spread out my palliasse.'

'In that case we can talk it over at Christmas,' said Nanni.

Nanni was covered in grease and sweat from the oil and the fermenting olives, and Maricchia wanted nothing whatever to do with him, but when they got home her mother grabbed her by the hair and said to her through clenched teeth:

'If you don't take him, I'll kill you!'

★

You would have thought the She-Wolf was ill, and people were saying that when the Devil grows old he goes into hiding. She never wandered about the village any more, she didn't stand on the doorstep flashing those crazy eyes of hers. Her son-in-law, whenever she fixed those eyes on him, began to laugh, and pulled out his scapular[1] to bless himself with. Maricchia stayed at home, breastfeeding the children, while her mother went off to the fields to work alongside the men; just like a man, in fact, digging, hoeing, rounding up the cattle, and pruning the vines in all weathers, in January with an icy wind from the east, or August with a sirocco from the south, when at the end of the day the mules would be drooping their heads and the men would be sitting asleep, propped against the wall with their mouths hanging open. 'In hours that run from dusk till dawn goes no good woman ever born,' and Pina was the only living soul you could see out and about, picking her way over the torrid stones of the country lanes, across the parched stubble of the boundless fields that stretched into the heat haze of the far distance towards Etna, shrouded in mist, where the sky bore down on the horizon.

'Wake up!' said the She-Wolf to Nanni, who was lying asleep in the ditch under the dust-laden hedgerow, resting his head between his arms. 'Wake up, I've brought you some wine to wet your throat.'

Nanni opened his eyes wide, stupefied, still half-asleep, to find her standing over him, white-faced, thrusting her breasts towards him and fixing him with her coal-black eyes, and he stretched out his hands, groping the air.

'No! No good woman's abroad from dusk till dawn!' bewailed Nanni, pressing his face down again into the dry grass of the ditch as hard as he could, with his fingernails tearing at his hair. 'Go away! Go away! Keep away from the barn!'

She did go away, did the She-Wolf, tying up her splendid tresses as she went, staring ahead of her towards the hot fields of stubble with her coal-black eyes.

But she kept going back to the barn, and Nanni said nothing. In fact, whenever she was late arriving, in hours that run from dusk till dawn, he would go and wait for her at the top of the ashen-white, deserted lane, with beads of sweat standing out on his forehead. And afterwards he would thrust his hands through his hair and repeat every time, 'Go away! Go away! Don't come back to the barn!'

Maricchia wept day and night, and stared at her mother with tear-filled eyes aflame with jealousy, looking like a wolf-cub herself, every time she saw her returning pale and silent from the fields.

'You wicked slut!' she cried. 'You wicked slut of a mother!'

'Shut up!'

'You thief! Thief!'

'Shut up!'

'I'll tell the police sergeant, that's what I'll do!'

'Go ahead and tell him!'

She did go ahead, with her children clinging round her neck, totally unafraid, and without shedding a tear. She was like a mad woman, because now she too loved the husband they had forced upon her, all greasy and covered in sweat from the fermenting of the olives.

The sergeant had Nanni called in, and threatened him with prison and the gallows. Nanni stood there sobbing and tearing his hair. He denied nothing, and didn't even try to make excuses.

'I was tempted!' he cried. 'I was tempted by the Devil!'

He threw himself at the sergeant's feet, pleading with him to send him to prison.

'For pity's sake, sergeant, take me out of this hell on earth! Have me killed, send me to prison, never let me set eyes on her again, ever!'

But when the sergeant spoke to the She-Wolf, she replied, 'No! I kept a corner of the kitchen to sleep in, when I gave him my house as a dowry. The house is mine. I don't intend to leave it.'

Shortly after that, Nanni was kicked in the chest by a mule, and was at death's door. But the parish priest refused to bring him the bread of Christ until the She-Wolf left the house. The She-Wolf went away, and her son-in-law could then prepare to take his leave of the world as a good Christian. He confessed and made communion with such an obvious show of repentance and contrition that all the neighbours and onlookers were in tears at the bed of the dying man. And it would have been better for him if he had died then and there, before the Devil returned to tempt him and to take him over body and soul as soon as he recovered.

'Leave me alone!' he said to the She-Wolf. 'For God's sake, leave me in peace! I stared death in the face! That poor Maricchia is in despair! The whole village knows all about it now! It's better for both of us if I don't see you . . .'

He would have liked to tear out his eyes so as not to see the eyes of the She-Wolf, who made him surrender body and soul when she fixed them upon him. He no longer knew what to do to release himself from her spell. He paid for Masses for the souls in Purgatory, and asked the parish priest and the sergeant to help him. At Easter he went to confession, and did penance in public by crawling on his belly for six feet over the cobblestones in front of the church. After all that, when the She-Wolf returned to torment him, he said to her:

'Listen! Just you stay away from the barn, because if you come looking for me again, I swear to God I'll kill you!'

'Go ahead and kill me,' replied the She-Wolf. 'It doesn't worry me. I can't live without you.'

When he saw her coming in the distance, through the sown fields, he stopped digging at the vine with his mattock, and went and wrenched the axe from the elm. The She-Wolf saw him coming, pale with frenzy, the axe glittering in the sun, but she never stopped for a moment or lowered her gaze as she carried on walking towards him, with her hands full of bunches of red poppies, devouring him with her coal-black eyes.

'Ah!' Nanni stammered. 'May your soul roast in Hell!'

Picturesque Lives

Once, when the train was passing by Aci Trezza, you looked out of the carriage-window and exclaimed, 'I'd like to spend a month down there!'

We went back there and spent, not a month, but forty-eight hours. The villagers who stared in disbelief at your enormous trunks must have thought you would be staying for a couple of years. On the morning of the third day, tired of seeing nothing but green fields and blue sea, and of counting the carts as they trundled up and down the street, you were at the station, fiddling impatiently with the chain of your scent-bottle, and craning your neck to catch sight of a train that couldn't arrive too soon. In those forty-eight hours we did all it was possible to do in Aci Trezza. We walked down the dusty street and we scrambled over the rocks. Under the pretext of learning to row you got blisters beneath your gloves that had to be kissed better. We spent a marvellously romantic night at sea, casting nets so as to do something to convince the boatmen it was worth their while to be catching rheumatism. Dawn came upon us at the top of the beacon rock. I can still see that dawn – pale and unassuming, with broad, mauve-coloured shafts of light playing across a dark green sea, caressing the tiny group of cottages that lay huddled up asleep on the shore, while above the rock, silhouetted against the dark and cloudless sky, your tiny figure stood out clearly in the expert lines designed for it by your dressmaker, and the fine, elegant profile of your own making. You were wearing a grey dress that seemed to have been specially made to blend with the colours of the dawn. A truly pretty picture! And you certainly knew it, to judge from the way you modelled yourself in your shawl and

39

smiled with those enormous, tired, wide-open eyes at that strange spectacle, and at the strangeness, too, of being there yourself to witness it. What was going on at that moment in your little head, as you faced the rising sun? Were you asking it to tell you where in the world you would be, a month into the future? All you said, in that ingenuous way of yours, was, 'I don't understand how people can spend the whole of their lives in a place like this.'

But you see, the answer is easier than it looks. For a start, all you need is not to have an income of a hundred thousand *lire*, and to take comfort in suffering a few of the many hardships that go with those giant rocks, set in the deep blue sea, that caused you to clap your hands in wonder. Those poor devils, who were nodding off in the boat as they waited for us, need no more than that to find, in among their ramshackle, picturesque cottages, that seemed to you from a distance to be trembling as if they too were seasick, everything you search for high and low in Paris, Nice and Naples.

It's a curious business, but perhaps it's better that way for you, and for all the others like you. That cluster of cottages is inhabited by fishermen, who call themselves 'men of the sea' as opposed to your 'men about town', people whose skins are harder than the bread that they eat, when they eat any bread at all, for the sea is not always as calm as it was when it was planting kisses on your gloves. On its black days, when it roars and it thunders, you have to rest content with standing and gazing out at it from the shore, or lying in your bed, which is the best place to be on an empty stomach. On days like that, a crowd gathers outside the tavern, but you don't hear many coins rattling on the tin counter, and the kids, who throng the village as if poverty was a good way to multiply their numbers, go shrieking and tearing around as though possessed by the devil.

Every so often typhus, or cholera, or a bad harvest, or a storm at sea come along and make a good clean sweep through that swarm of people. You would imagine they could wish for nothing better than to be swept away and disappear altogether, but they always come swarming back again to the very same place. I can't tell you how or why they do it.

Did you ever, after an autumn shower, find yourself scattering an army of ants as you carelessly traced the name of your latest boyfriend in the sand along the boulevard? Some of those poor little creatures would have remained stuck on the ferrule of your umbrella, writhing in agony, but all the others, after five minutes of rushing about in panic, would have returned to cling on desperately to their dark little ant-heap. You wouldn't go back there, certainly, and neither would I. But in order to understand that kind of stubbornness, which in some respects is heroic, we have to reduce ourselves to the same level, restrict our whole horizon to what lies between a couple of mounds of earth, and place their tiny hearts under a microscope to discover what makes them beat. Would you, too, like to take a look through this lens here, you who contemplate life through the other end of a telescope? You'll think it a curious spectacle, and it might amuse you perhaps.

We were very close friends (do you remember?), and you asked me to dedicate a few pages to you. Why? *à quoi bon*, as you would put it. What value does anything I write possess for anyone who knows you? And to those who don't, what are you anyway? But never mind all that, I remembered your little whim, on the day I set eyes once again on that beggar woman you gave alms to with the pretext of buying the oranges she'd laid out in a row on the bench outside the front door. The bench is no longer there, they've cut down the medlar tree in the yard, and the house has a new window. It was only the woman that hadn't changed. She was a little further on, holding out her hand to the cart-drivers, crouching there on the pile of stones blocking the entrance to the old outpost of the national guard. As I was doing the rounds, puffing away at a cigar, it struck me that she too, poor as she is, had seen you passing by, fair of skin and proud of bearing.

Don't be angry if I've remembered you in such a way, and in such a context. Apart from the happy memories you left me, I have a hundred others, indistinct, confused, all different, gathered here, there and everywhere – some of them mere daydreams, perhaps – and in my confused state of mind, as I walked along that street that has witnessed so many happy and painful events, the frail-looking woman crouching there in her mantilla made me somehow feel very sad, and made me think of you, glutted with everything, even with the adulation heaped at your feet by the fashion magazines, that often splash your name in the headlines of their elegant feature articles – glutted to such a degree as to think up the notion of seeing your name in the pages of a book.

Perhaps, when I have written the book, you won't give it a second thought. But meanwhile, the memories I send you now, so far away from you in every sense, inebriated as you are with feasting and flowers, will bring a refreshing breeze to play upon the feverish round of your endless revelry. On the day you go back there, if you ever do go back, and we sit together again, kicking up stones with our feet and visions in our thoughts, perhaps we shall talk about those other breezes that life elsewhere has to offer. Imagine, if you like, that my mind is fixed on that unknown little corner of the world because you once stepped into it, or in order to avert my gaze from the dazzling glare of precious stones and fevered expectation that accompanies your every movement, or because I have sought you out in vain in all the places smiled upon by fashion. So you see, you always take the lead in my thoughts, as you do in the theatre!

Do you also recall that old man at the tiller of our boat? You owe it to him to remember, because he saved you a dozen times from soaking your fine blue stockings. He died down there, poor devil, in the town hospital, in a huge white ward, between white sheets, chewing white bread, assisted by the white hands of the Sisters of Charity, whose only weakness was their failure to comprehend the string of woes that the wretched fellow mumbled forth in his semi-barbaric dialect.

But if there was one thing he would have wanted above all else, it was to die in that shaded little corner beside his own hearth, where he had slept for so many years 'below his own roof', which is why, when they carried him away, he was in tears, whining as only the old are able to.

He had spent his whole life between those four walls, looking out on that lovely but treacherous sea with which he had had to wrestle every day of his life to extract what he needed to survive without coming to a watery end. And yet for that brief moment in time when he was silently relishing his place in the sun, huddled on the thwart of the boat with his arms round his knees, he wouldn't have turned his head to admire you, and you would have looked in vain into those spellbound eyes for the proud reflection of your beauty, as when so many of the high and mighty bow their heads as they make way for you in the fashionable salons, and you see your reflection in the envious eyes of your best women friends.

Life is rich, as you see, in its inexhaustible variety, and you can enjoy that part of its richness that has come your way, just as you please.

Take that young woman, for instance, who peeped out from behind the pots of basilica when the rustling of your dress set off a clamour in the street. When she espied your famous face in the window opposite, she beamed as though she too were dressed in silk. Who knows what simple joys filled her thoughts as she stood at that window behind the fragrant basilica, her eyes fixed intently on the house opposite, bedecked with branches of vine. And the laughter in her eyes would not have turned later into bitter tears in the big city, far away from the four walls that had witnessed her birth and watched her grow up, if her grandfather hadn't died in the hospital, and her father hadn't drowned, and her family hadn't been scattered by a puff of wind that had blown right through it – a puff of ruinous wind, which had carried one of her brothers off to prison on the island of Pantelleria, or 'into trouble', as they say in those parts.

A kinder fate lay in store for those who died, one in the naval battle of Lissa. He was the eldest son, the one you thought resembled a David sculpted in bronze, as he stood there clutching his harpoon, with the light from the flame of the lanterns playing about his features. Big and tall as he was, he too glowed with pleasure whenever you darted your brazen eyes in his direction. But he died a good sailor, standing firm at the rigging of the yardarm, raising his cap in the air and saluting the flag for the last time with the primitive shout of the islander bred and born. The other man, the one who was too timid to touch your foot on the island to free it from the rabbit trap where you got it caught in that heedless way of yours, was lost on a dark winter's night, alone at sea amid the raging foam, when between his boat and the shore, where his loved ones awaited his return, rushing here and there as though possessed, there lay sixty miles of storm and darkness. You would never have guessed the amount of sheer dauntless courage that man was capable of, who allowed himself to be overawed by the handiwork of your shoemaker.

The ones who are dead are better off. They are not eating 'the king's bread', like the poor devil locked up on Pantelleria, or the kind of bread his sister is eating, nor do they go around like the woman with the oranges, living on the charity of God, which doesn't flow too freely in Aci Trezza. At least the dead need nothing any more! That's what the son of the woman who keeps the tavern said, the last time he went to the hospital to inquire about the old man and smuggle in some of those stuffed snails that are so good to suck for anyone who has no teeth, and he found the bed empty, with the blankets neatly folded up on it. He crept out into the hospital yard and planted himself at a door with a lot of waste paper piled up against it, and through the keyhole he spied a large empty room, hollow-sounding and icy even in summer, and the end of a long marble table, with a thick, starched sheet draped over it. And thinking to himself that the ones inside no longer needed anything, and the snails were of no use to them any more, he began to suck them one after the other to pass away the time. It will comfort you to think, as you hug your blue fox muff to your bosom, that you gave a hundred *lire* to the poor old fellow.

Those village kids who followed you like stray dogs and raided the oranges are still there. They are still buzzing round the beggar woman, pawing at her clothes as though she's hiding a crust of bread, picking up cabbage stalks, orange peel and cigar stubs, all the things thrown away in the street but obviously still having some value because the poor live on them. They live so well on them, in fact, that those starving, blown-out ragamuffins will grow up in the mud and the dust of the street, and turn out big and strong like their fathers and grandfathers. Then they in turn will populate Aci Trezza with more ragamuffins, who will cling on to life as long as they can by the skin of their teeth, like that old grandfather, wanting nothing else but simply praying to God they will close their eyes in the place where they opened them, attended by the village doctor who goes round every day on his donkey, like Jesus, to succour the departing ones.

'The ambition of the oyster!' you may say. Exactly, and the only reason we find it absurd is that we were not born oysters ourselves.

But in any case, the tenacious clinging of those poor souls to the rock on to which fortune decreed they should fall, as it scattered princes here and duchesses there, their brave resignation to a life full of hardships, their religion of the family, reflected in their work, their homes, and the walls that surround them, seem to me, for the time being at any rate, deeply serious and worthy of respect. It seems to me that the anxieties of our wandering thoughts would find sweet solace in the tranquil calm of those simple, uncomplicated feelings that are handed down, serene and unchanging, from one generation to the next. It seems to me that I could watch you passing by, to the sound of your horses' trotting hooves and the merry jingling of their brasses, and greet you without a care in the world.

Perhaps because I have tried too hard to penetrate the whirlwind that surrounds and pursues you, I have now learnt to understand the inevitable need for that solid, mutual affection among the weak, for the instinct of the underprivileged to cling to one another to survive the storms of their existence, and I have tried to unravel the humble, undiscovered drama that has dispersed to the four winds its plebeian actors whom we once got to know together. The drama of which I speak, which perhaps one day I shall unfold to you in its entirety, would seem to me to depend essentially on this: that whenever one of the underprivileged, being either weaker, or less cautious, or more selfish than the others, decided to break with his family out of a desire for the unknown, or an urge for a better life, or curiosity to know the world, then the world, like the voracious fish that it is, swallowed him up along with his nearest and dearest. From this point of view you will see that the drama is not without interest. The main concern of oysters must be to protect themselves from the snares of the lobster, or the knife of the diver that prises them from the rock.

Jeli the Shepherd

Jeli, who tended the horses, was thirteen when he first made friends with the young gentleman, Don Alfonso. He was so small that he didn't reach up to the belly of Bianca, the old pack-horse that carried the herd's cowbell. You might come across him anywhere, in the hills or on the plain, grazing his beasts, standing erect and motionless on some stretch of high ground, or squatting on top of a boulder. His friend Don Alfonso, when he was down there at Tebidi on holiday, would go and see him every single day, and they would share the young lord's goodies and the herd-boy's barley bread, or the fruit scrumped from a nearby orchard. At first, Jeli addressed the young lord as Your Excellency, as people do in Sicily, but once they'd had a good scrap with one another, their friendship was cemented for good. Jeli taught his friend how to climb right up to the magpies' nests, at the tops of the highest walnut trees in Licodia, he taught him how to hit a sparrow on the wing with a stone, and how to get up with a flying leap on to the bare backs of fillies not yet broken in, grabbing by its mane the first one that came within range, without being discouraged by the angry snorts of the untamed colts as they leapt around desperately this way and that. Ah! Those wonderful rides across mown fields, the manes of their mounts flowing in the wind! Those fine April days when the wind swept in waves across the lush green grass and the mares whinnied in the meadows! Those wonderful summer noontides when the countryside, bleached and overhung with leaden skies, lay silent except for the crackling sound of crickets on the farmland, as though the stubble had been set on fire! Those clear winter skies framed in the bare branches of almond trees quivering in the north wind, and the crisp clip-clop of horses' hooves along the lane, and the larks trilling away as they hovered high up in the hot, blue sky! Those summer evenings with dusk creeping up like a mist, the fresh smell of hay when you sank your elbows into it, and the plaintive hum of insects in the twilight, and those two notes from Jeli's whistle – eeh ooh! eeh ooh! – that brought back memories of distant things, of the feast of San Giovanni, of Christmas nights, of waking up on the day of the picnic, of all those great events of the past that seemed so distant now as to fill you with sadness and to look up, your eyes moist with tears, and feel that all the stars as they lit up one by one in the sky were raining down upon you and breaking your heart!

As for Jeli, he didn't suffer from those feelings of sadness. He would simply crouch there on the hillock, puffing out his cheeks, all intent on blowing those two notes from his whistle. Then he would round up the animals by shouting and aiming stones at them, and drive them into the stables, on the other side of the Hill of the Cross.

He would pant his way up the hill on the far side of the valley, and sometimes he would call out to his friend Alfonso, 'Call the dog! Hey there, call the dog!' or 'Aim a good big stone at the chestnut that's playing me up and dawdling by the bushes down there in the valley' or 'Tomorrow morning bring me one of Gnà Lia's big needles.'

He could do all sorts of things with a needle, and in his canvas bag he had a bundle of rags to patch his breeches and the sleeves of his jacket whenever the need arose. He could also make plaited cord from the manes of the horses, and he could use pumice from the valley to launder the scarf that he wore round his neck when he was feeling cold. In short, as long as he had his shoulder-bag with him, he had no need of anyone to keep him company, whether in the woods of Resecone, or miles from anywhere in the open country round Caltagirone. Gnà Lia used to say, 'You see Jeli the herd-boy? He's spent his whole life alone out there in the fields as though his mares had given him birth, which is why he can cross himself with either hand!'

True though it is that Jeli had no need of anyone, all the same everyone at the farm would gladly do him a favour, because he was an obliging sort of lad, and there was always the possibility of getting something out of him. Gnà Lia would bake bread for him out of neighbourly love, and he would return the compliment with one or two fine wicker egg-baskets, cane spools for winding her wool, and other little things of that sort.

Gnà Lia put it this way: 'We scratch one another's backs, like his horses.'

Everybody in Tebidi had known him since he was a tiny child, lost among the tails of the horses as they grazed on the high plateau, and they had watched him grow up, so to speak, though nobody ever actually saw it happen as he wandered from one place to another with his animals. 'He fell from the sky to be caught by the earth!' as the proverb goes, and he was truly one of those people without either home or close family. His mother worked as a housemaid in Vizzini, and only saw him once a year when he took his ponies to the fair of San Giovanni. On the day she died, they came to collect him on a Saturday afternoon, and on the Monday he was back with his herd, so that the peasant who'd stepped into his place to look after the horses missed not a single day's work. But the poor boy came back so upset that he sometimes allowed the foals to stray into the sown fields. 'Hey, Jeli!' Massaro Agrippino would yell at him from the barn. 'Are you looking for a sound flogging, you son of a bitch?'

Jeli would start running after the foals that had strayed, and gradually force them back up the hill. But in his mind's eye all he could see was his mother, with a white scarf wrapped round her head, no longer uttering a sound.

His father worked as a cowherd on the far side of Licodia, where malaria was so rife it could be harvested, as the peasants in those parts used to say, but in the malaria regions the pasture lands are good, and cows don't catch any fevers. So Jeli was in the fields all year round, either at Donferrante, or in the enclosures at Commenda, or in the Jacitano valley, and he could always be seen, wandering about like a dog without a master here, there and everywhere, by hunters or by people taking shortcuts through the fields. He had no complaints, because he was used to being with the horses as they ambled along in front of him and paused every so often to munch the clover, and to the flocks of birds that circled around him the whole day long, as the sun inched its way across the sky till the shadows lengthened, then disappeared. He had all the time in the world to watch the clouds as they piled up gradually one on top of the other, and to pick out the distant hills and the valleys. He could sense a thunderstorm in the air from the way the wind was blowing, and a snowstorm from the colour of the clouds. Everything had its own shape and its own meaning, and there was always something to look and listen out for at every hour of the day. That was how it was at the setting of the sun, when the herd-boy would begin to play on his whistle, and the black mare would come lazily up chewing the clover, and stand there watching him with her huge, contemplative eyes.

Where he did feel rather sorry for himself was in the deserted plains of Passanitello, where not a bush or a hedgerow can be seen, and in the hot summer months not a bird is flying. The horses would gather round in a circle, hanging their heads so as to shade each other from the sun, and throughout the long days of the threshing season that intense silent light bore down in a steady, oppressive stream for sixteen hours at a time.

But since the fodder was plentiful, and the horses were in no hurry to move on, the boy turned his attention to other things. He made reed cages to catch crickets, he carved pipes, he fashioned wicker baskets from a handful of rushes. And he could knock up a shelter for himself when the north wind whirled long lines of crows down the valley, or when the cicadas clapped their wings under the sun that was scorching the stubble. He roasted acorns from the oak woods in the embers of sumac twigs, imagining as he ate them they were roast chestnuts, or toasted over the fire thick slices of bread that had started to grow a beard of mould, because at Passanitello in the winter, the roads were so bad that sometimes you could spend a whole fortnight without catching sight of a single living soul passing by.

Don Alfonso, whose parents kept him wrapped in cotton wool, envied his friend Jeli with his canvas bag containing all his things: his bread, his onions, his flask of wine, his winter scarf, his bundle of rags with the reel of thread and the big needles, and the metal box where he kept his bait and his flintstone. Another thing he envied was his splendid mare with ears of different colour, that animal with wicked eyes and a tuft of hair standing up on her brow that blew out her nostrils like a bad-tempered mastiff when anyone tried to mount her. But she allowed Jeli to mount her and tickle those ears of hers, of which she was so proud, and sniffed at him to hear what he had to say to her.

'Keep away from the mare,' Jeli warned him. 'She's not a bad creature, but she doesn't know you.'

Once, when Scordu, the trader from Buccheri, took away the Calabrian mare he had bought at San Giovanni and asked Jeli to keep with his herd till the grape harvest, its chestnut foal, being left an orphan, couldn't be consoled, and ran off up into the mountain crags, whinnying endless sad laments and puffing its nostrils into the wind. Jeli ran after it, calling out loudly to it, and the foal stopped to listen, stretching out its neck and twitching its ears, swishing its tail against its flanks. 'It's because they've taken away its mother, and it doesn't know where to put itself,' said the herd-boy. 'We'll have to keep an eye on it, otherwise it could let itself go over the precipice. I felt the same when my mother died, and I couldn't see a thing in front of my eyes.'

Later, when the foal began to sniff once more at the clover, and reluctantly chew off a mouthful or two: 'You see!' he said. 'It's gradually beginning to forget. But it'll only be sold off. Horses are made to be sold off, as surely as lambs are born to go to the slaughter-house, and clouds bring rain. Only the birds have nothing else to do but sing and fly about the whole day long.'

Ideas never came to him in an orderly row one after the other, because he'd seldom had anyone to talk to, and so he wasn't very quick to dislodge them and dig them out from the depths of his mind. Instead he was accustomed to let them come into being and blossom gradually, like the buds on the branches in the warmth of the sun. 'But even the birds,' he added, 'have to find things to eat, and when the snow covers the earth they die.'

Then he thought a little more about it. 'You are like the birds, but when winter comes you can stay by the fire and do nothing.'

However, Don Alfonso replied that he also went to school, to learn things. Whereupon Jeli opened his eyes wide, and he was all ears if the young gentleman began to read to him, and he looked at him and the book suspiciously, listening with that slight blinking of the eyelids that marks intense concentration in the animals closest to man. He liked to listen to verses that caressed his ears with the harmonies of a song that was beyond his understanding, and sometimes he knitted his brows, stuck out his chin, and felt that something was busily working away inside him. Then he would keep on nodding his head with a knowing smile, scratching his head as he did so. Again, when the young gentleman started to write so as to show him how many things he could do, Jeli would simply stare at him for days on end, then suddenly screw up his eyes with a look of distrust. He was quite unable to come to terms with the fact that one could put down on paper the words that he or Don Alfonso had spoken, and even the things he hadn't let fall from his lips, so that in the end he drew back, incredulous, with that same knowing smile.

He treated with suspicion every new idea that knocked on his head to be admitted, and seemed to sniff away at it with all the distrust of his wild mare. Yet nothing in the world ever seemed to amaze him. If anyone had told him that in town the horses went round pulling carriages, he would have remained impassive, with that mask of oriental indifference that marks the dignity of the Sicilian peasant. He seemed to entrench himself instinctively in his ignorance, as though poverty forced him into it. Whenever he was short of an answer, he always replied, 'I don't know anything. I'm poor,' with that stubborn smile of his that had a hint of mischief about it.

He had asked his friend Don Alfonso to write the name Mara for him on a scrap of paper he had picked up somewhere, just as he collected everything he saw lying about, and had stuffed into his bundle of rags. One day, after saying nothing for a while and looking absent-mindedly this way and that, he said to him in a really serious tone of voice, 'I've got a girl-friend.'

Although he could read well enough, Alfonso opened his eyes wide. 'It's true,' said Jeli. 'Mara, the daughter of Massaro Agrippino who used to live here. She's living in Marineo now, in that big tenement block in the valley that you look down on from the high plateau.'

'Are you going to marry her then?'

'Yes, when I'm grown up and earning six *onze* a year in wages. Mara knows nothing about it yet.'

'Why haven't you told her?'

Jeli shook his head and stopped to think. Then he unwrapped his bundle and spread out the piece of paper he'd got his friend to write on.

'It really does say Mara, I know it does, because Don Gesualdo, the gamekeeper, read it, and so did Brother Cola, when he came down here looking for beans.'

'Anyone who knows how to write,' he went on, 'is like a person who stores his words in a steel safe, and who could carry them around in his pocket, and even send them wherever he wants.'

'So what are you going to do now with that piece of paper, when you can't read what's written on it?' asked Don Alfonso.

Jeli shrugged his shoulders, and continued to roll the sheet of paper carefully up in his bundle of rags.

He had first met Mara when she was a little girl, and they had begun to pitch in to one another down in the valley, as they were both picking blackberries along the hedgerows. The girl, who knew she was on her own land, grabbed Jeli by the neck and called him a thief. They stood there, pummelling away at one another's backs like the cooper hammering the metal rings of a cask, but once they grew tired they gradually calmed down, still holding on to each other.

'Who are you, anyway?' asked Mara.

And since Jeli, being the wilder of the two, wouldn't tell her who he was, 'I'm Mara,' she said, 'the daughter of Massaro Agrippino, who's in charge of all these fields around here.'

Jeli then let go of her without saying a word, and the girl began to gather up the blackberries that had fallen on the ground, every so often stealing inquisitive glances at her adversary.

'On the other side of the bridge, in the hedge alongside the orchard, there are lots of big blackberries,' added the little girl. 'The chickens feed on them.'

Jeli sloped off quiet as a mouse, and Mara, after keeping him in sight until he reached the oak wood, turned her back on him and ran off, heading for home.

But from that day onwards they began to make friends with one another. Mara would go and sit on the parapet of the bridge, spinning tow, and watching as Jeli drove his herd very slowly towards the lower slopes of Bandit Hill. At first he stayed away from her, hanging round and eyeing her warily from a distance, then he gradually came closer with the watchful air of a dog grown accustomed to being stoned. When they finally came side by side, they would remain for hours at a stretch without opening their mouths, Jeli staring in fascination at the intricate knitting that Mara's mother had given her to get on with, whilst she watched him carving neat zig-zag patterns on walking-sticks fashioned out of almond wood. Then they would go their separate ways without uttering a word to one another, and the little girl, once in sight of home, would start to run, lifting her petticoat high to reveal her rosy little legs.

Later, when the Indian figs were in season, they settled down together in the dense thicket, peeling figs the whole day long. They wandered about together under the ancient walnut trees, and Jeli beat the branches so vigorously that the walnuts came raining down like hailstones. Shrieking with joy, the girl tried her utmost to gather up as many as she could, then ran off holding on tightly to the corners of her apron, and staggering from side to side like an old woman.

During the winter it was so cold that Mara never dared poke her head out of doors. Towards evening, you could sometimes see smoke rising from the sumac fires lit by Jeli on the high plateau or in the hills near Macca, to prevent himself from freezing to death like the great tits he would come across next morning behind a rock, or in the shelter of a mound of earth. Even the horses liked to dangle their tails a little around the fire, huddling close together to keep warm.

In March the larks returned to the high plateau, the sparrows to the cottage roofs, the leaves and the nests to the hedgerows, and Mara ventured out again to go walking with Jeli over the tender grass, through the flowering scrub, beneath the trees, still bare, that were just starting to be dotted in green. Jeli poked around in the brambles like a bloodhound, to go uncovering the broods of blackbirds, that peered out at him in bewilderment with their tiny peppercorn eyes. Often they would pick up baby rabbits, driven out of their burrows half naked but already with long twitching ears, and tuck them into their shirt fronts. And they would run about the fields behind the horses, and drive them step by step across the stubble in the wake of the reapers, pausing every so often whenever one of the herd stopped to take up a mouthful of grass. By the time evening came they were at the bridge, where they went their separate ways without so much as saying goodbye to one another.

In that way they spent the whole summer. Meanwhile the sun began to set behind the Hill of the Cross, and the redbreasts flew after it towards the mountain as the light began to fade, pursuing it across the cactus scrub. The crickets and the cicadas fell silent, and at that hour of the day an air of great sadness seemed to spread itself over the whole of the countryside.

It was then that Jeli's father, the cowherd, who had caught malaria at Ragoleti, arrived at Jeli's hut, almost falling off the donkey that was carrying him. Jeli very quickly lit a fire, and ran over to the farm to find a few eggs for him. 'Don't bother with all that,' said his father. 'Just spread a bit of straw close to the fire. The fever's coming over me again.'

The shuddering effect of the fever was so strong that the father, Menu, buried as he was under his own big cloak, the donkey's saddle-bag, and Jeli's knapsack, was trembling all over like leaves in November, and in the light of the fire his face was a deathly white all over. The peasants came across from the farm to ask him how he was feeling, but all the poor wretch could do by way of reply was to yelp like a puppy taking suck from its mother. 'It's the kind of malaria that kills you quicker than a shot from a gun,' said his friends, warming their hands at the fire.

They even called the doctor, but it was money entirely wasted, because all he said was that the illness was so well known and straight-forward that even a child could treat it, and that if the fever was not of the lethal variety, a course of sulphur would clear it up in no time. They filled old Menu up to his eyebrows with sulphur, but for all the good it did him they might have thrown him down a well.

'Take a good dose of *ecalibbiso*.[1] It doesn't cost anything,' Massaro Agrippino suggested, 'and if it does no more good than the sulphur, at least you won't be crippling yourself with the expense.' So he took a dose of eucalyptus, but the fever kept coming back, even stronger than before.

Jeli did all he could to look after his ailing parent. Every morning, before leaving with his ponies, he left him his medicine in a bowl, sticks close at hand for the fire, eggs in the warm ashes, and he came back early in the evening with more wood to keep the fire going overnight, and a flask of wine, and one or two bits of mutton he had run as far as Licodia to buy for him. The poor lad saw to everything conscientiously, like a good housewife, and his father, following his every movement with his tired eyes as Jeli went about his various tasks in the hut, smiled to himself from time to time with the thought that the boy would know how to look after himself when he was left all alone in the world.

On the days when the fever let up for a few hours, Menu staggered to his feet, tightened the scarf round his head, propped himself in the doorway while the sun was still shining, and waited for Jeli to come back. Once Jeli had dropped his bundle of firewood at the door and laid the wine-flask and the eggs on the table, his father would say, 'Go and boil up the *ecalibbiso* for tonight,' or 'Remember, when I'm not here any more, your mother's gold is with your aunt Agata,' to which Jeli would nod his head to show he had taken it in.

'It's no use,' Massaro Agrippino kept repeating every time he called again to see how the old man was coping with his fever. 'Your whole system's racked with it.'

Menu listened without batting an eyelid, his face whiter than the scarf round his head.

In the end he could no longer get up, and Jeli started crying when he found his strength was insufficient to help him turn over from one side to the other. Gradually Menu lost the power of speech altogether. The last words he spoke to his son were these:

'When I'm dead, go to the man who owns the cows at Ragoleti, and get him to hand over the three *onze* and twelve sacks of grain owing to me from May up to the present.'

'No,' Jeli replied, 'it's only two and a quarter, because you left the cows over a month ago, and you mustn't steal from the hand that feeds you.'

'That's true!' Menu declared, as he closed his eyes for the last time. Now I really am alone in the world like a lost foal, ready to be eaten up by the wolves! Jeli thought to himself after they had taken his father away to the cemetery at Licodia.

Mara, too, had come to have a look at the dead man's house, spurred on by the restless curiosity aroused in people by frightening events.

'You see what's happened to me?' said Jeli. The girl drew back from him in alarm, worried in case he got her to enter the house where the corpse had been lying.

Jeli went and collected his father's money, then set off with his herd for Passanitello, where the grass was already tall on the fallow land, and the grazing was good, so that the ponies had no reason to move on. Meanwhile Jeli had grown up, and he often thought to himself, as he played on his whistle, that Mara must have grown up as well. And when he returned after a long absence to Tebidi, driving his horses slowly along the slippery lanes around Cosimo's Spring, he kept looking out for the bridge over the river, and the tenement block in the Jacitano valley, and the roofs of the big houses where the doves were always flying back and forth. But just at that time the landowner had given Massaro Agrippino notice to quit, and Mara's whole family was moving. Jeli came across the girl, now a pretty young woman, at the farmyard gate, keeping an eye on her belongings as they were being loaded on to the removal cart. Their empty room now seemed more drab and blackened with smoke than he remembered. The table, and the bed, and the chest of drawers, and the images of the Virgin and St John, and even the nails for hanging up pumpkins for seed, had left their mark on the walls against which they had rested for so many years. 'We're leaving,' Mara told him, as she saw him looking all about him. 'We're going to Marineo, where the big tenement block is, down in the valley.'

Jeli gave a hand to Massaro Agrippino and his wife Lia in loading the cart, and when there was nothing left to take away, he went and sat with Mara on the edge of the trough. 'Even the houses,' he said, when he saw that the last of the baskets had been loaded on to the cart, 'even the houses look different once everything has been taken out.'

'At Marineo,' Mara replied, 'my mother says we'll have a nicer room, bigger than the store where the cheeses are kept.'

'Now that you won't be here any longer, I don't want to come back. It'll feel like winter again, seeing that door locked and bolted.'

'At Marineo we'll get to know a lot of new people, like Pudda the redhead and the gamekeeper's daughter. We'll be happy there, and at harvest time over eighty reapers will come with bagpipes, and we'll go dancing on the threshing-floor.'

Massaro Agrippino and his wife had set off with the cart, and Mara was running happily along behind them, carrying the basket with the pigeons in it. Jeli decided to go with her as far as the bridge, and when Mara was about to disappear down the valley he called out to her: 'Mara! Hey, Mara!'

'What do you want?' said Mara.

He no longer knew what he wanted.

'You, Jeli, what are you going to do here, all by yourself?' the girl continued.

'I'll be staying with the ponies.'

Mara went skipping off, and he remained rooted to the spot for as long as he could hear the sound of the cart trundling over the stones. The last rays of the sun were touching the high rocks on the Hill of the Cross, the grey foliage of the olives was fading in the dusk, and the whole of the countryside was immersed in silence except for the sound of the grey mare's cowbell.

Once Mara had gone to Marineo and found new friends, and the grape harvest came round, she forgot about him. But Jeli thought about her the whole time, because he had nothing else to occupy his mind during the long days he spent with only the tails of his animals to look at. Moreover, he no longer had any reason to descend to the valley on the far side of the bridge, and he never set foot inside the farm any more. That was the reason he took so long to find out that Mara was engaged to be married, because so much water had passed under the bridge since their last meeting. He only saw the girl again at the feast of San Giovanni, when he took his ponies to be sold at the fair. The gala turned into a real nightmare for him, and cost him his living, God help him, when one of his master's ponies was involved in an accident.

On the day of the fair the farm-bailiff was waiting from dawn for the ponies to arrive, striding up and down in his well-polished boots behind the cruppers of the horses and the mules lined up on each side of the road. The fair was nearly over, and there was still no sign of Jeli coming round the bend of the road. On the parched slopes of Calvary and Windmill Hill, one or two flocks of sheep with lacklustre eyes lingered in compact groups nuzzling the earth, and a few pairs of oxen of the sort that a farmer sells to pay his rent stood motionless under the baking rays of the sun. Further down the valley, the church-bell of San Giovanni began to ring for High Mass, as fireworks crackled away in the background. Suddenly the fair seemed to come alive, and a shout went up from the people milling round the tented stalls along the side of the road, that echoed down the valley to the church itself: 'Viva San Giovanni!'

'Holy Mother of Christ!' screamed the bailiff. 'That idiot of a Jeli is going to cost me the fair.'

Startled by the noise, the sheep raised their heads and began to bleat in unison, and even the oxen took a languid step or two, looking round with their great, attentive eyes.

The reason the bailiff was so angry was because that was the day ('on the advent of San Giovanni neath the elm' as the contract was worded) when the rent for the main enclosures was due, and to make up the sum that was owed he was counting on selling the ponies. But there he was, surrounded by as many ponies, horses and mules as the good Lord ever created, all of them combed and gleaming, and tricked out in their bows and their tassels and their bells, shaking them merrily away to relieve the tedium, and turning their heads towards every passer-by, as though waiting for some charitable soul to make up his mind to buy them.

'He must have fallen asleep, that blockhead!' the bailiff kept roaring. 'And now he's left me with a bellyful of ponies!'

In fact, Jeli had been walking all through the night so that the ponies would arrive fresh at the fair and take up a good position when they got there, and had reached Piana del Corvo when the stars known in those parts as the Three Kings were still twinkling on the horizon above Mont'Altore.[2] Carts and people on horseback kept overtaking him along the road on their way to the fair, and the young fellow was keeping a careful watch in case the ponies took fright at the unusual comings and goings and ran off in all directions, making sure they kept in line along the edge of the road behind the grey, that ambled calmly

ahead with the cowbell strung round her neck. Every so often, when
the road ran over the crest of a hill, you could hear the church-bell of
San Giovanni in the far distance, breaking the nocturnal silence of the
countryside with its festive sound, and all the way along the road,
wherever there were people on foot or on horseback going to Vizzini,
you could hear shouts of 'Viva San Giovanni!' And you could see
rockets lighting up the sky on the far side of the Canziria hills, like
shooting stars in August.

'It's like Christmas night!' Jeli was saying to the boy helping him
drive the herd. 'They're celebrating and letting off fireworks on all the
farms, and the whole of the countryside's dotted with bonfires.'

The boy made no reply, as it was all he could do to push one leg in
front of the other to prevent himself from nodding off to sleep. But Jeli's
whole body tingled with excitement at the sound of the church-bell, and
he couldn't stop talking, as though every one of those rockets flashing
up silently through the dark beyond the mountain was blossoming forth
from his soul.

'Mara will be there, too, at the gala of San Giovanni,' he said. 'She
goes every year.'

Unperturbed at the lack of any reply from Alfio, he went on, 'D'you
know what? Mara's really grown up now, taller than her mother who
brought her into the world. When I saw her again I could hardly believe
she was the same girl I went gathering the Indian figs with, and beating
down the walnuts.'

And he started singing all the songs he knew, at the top of his voice.

'Hey there, Alfio, have you fallen asleep?' he shouted at him when
he'd finished. 'Make sure the grey stays behind you the whole time.
Watch what you're doing!'

'No, I'm not asleep,' Alfio replied, in a sullen tone of voice.

'Do you see *Puddara*³ winking at us up there, over towards Granvilla,
as though they were firing off rockets as far away as Santa Domenica?
It'll soon be dawn, but we'll arrive at the fair in time to find a good
place. Hey, Blackie, my pretty one, you'll have a nice new halter and
little red tassels for the fair! And you too, Star, my beauty!'

He went on talking like this to each of the ponies in turn, so that
they would be comforted by hearing his voice in the dark. But it made

him sad to think that Star and Blackie were going to the fair to be sold.

'Once they're sold, they'll go off with their new owner, and be seen no more in the herd, just like Mara, when she went to Marineo. Her father's doing well down there at Marineo. When I called to see them they filled me up with all the fruits of the earth, bread, wine, cheese, everything you can think of, because he's almost the head farmer now, and has the keys to everything, and I could have eaten the whole farm if I'd wanted to. It's such a long time since we saw one another that Mara had a job to recognize me, and she cried out, "Oh, look! It's Jeli, from Tebidi!" It was like someone coming back from faraway places, when the sight of a hilltop is enough for him to recognize the village where he grew up. Lia, her mother, didn't want me to call Mara by her Christian name, because people are so ignorant and they start gossiping. But Mara laughed, and turned so red in the face that she looked as if she'd just been putting bread in the oven. The way she spread out the tablecloth and laid the table, she seemed a different girl altogether. "Do you still remember Tebidi?" I asked her as soon as her mother went out of the room to pour fresh wine from the cask. "Of course I remember," she said. "I remember the church-bell at Tebidi, and the campanile shaped like a salt-cellar, and the music from the veranda, and the two cats carved in stone that seemed to be purring away on the garden gate." I could picture all these things in my mind as she was talking about them. Mara looked me up and down goggle-eyed, and she said, "My goodness, how you've grown!" Then she started laughing again, and gave me a slap on the side of the head.'

That was how Jeli the horsekeeper lost his job, because just at that moment a carriage, which no one had heard coming as it made its way slowly up the hill, came over the brow and rushed suddenly past with a great commotion of horse-whip and bells, as if it had the devil inside it. The ponies, terrified out of their wits, scattered in a flash as though an earthquake was happening, and it took a great deal of shouting and calling and *whoa*s! from Jeli and the lad before they managed to round them up around the grey, which was also rearing up a little as she trotted on with the cowbell round her neck. As soon as Jeli had taken stock of his animals, he saw that Star was missing, and started tearing his hair out because at that point the road ran alongside a ravine, and it was in the ravine that Star lay badly smashed up, a pony worth all of twelve *onze*, a king's ransom! Weeping and shouting, Jeli went round calling out 'Ho there! Ho there!' to the colt, but still no sign of him, until finally Star responded from the foot of the ravine with a pathetic whinny, as if the poor beast was actually able to talk.

'Oh, my God!' cried Jeli and the lad. 'My God, how terrible!'

On hearing them wailing so loudly in the dark, people on their way to the fair stopped to ask them what they had lost, but once they were told what the trouble was, they just carried on along the road.

Star was lying motionless where he had fallen, his legs in the air, and as Jeli gently prodded him all over, crying and talking to him as though he could understand his every word, the poor beast twisted his head round with an effort and turned it towards him, gasping for breath in his agony.

'He must have broken something!' Jeli wailed, in despair at being unable to see anything in the dark, and the colt, dropping its head again like a stone, lay there lifeless. Alfio, who had stayed behind on the road to look after the herd, was the first to calm down, and took some bread out of his bag. The sky had now begun to turn a pale blue, and the tall, black outlines of the surrounding hills seemed to steal into view one after the other. From the bend in the road you could begin to pick out the village, with Calvary and Windmill Hill silhouetted against the dawn, still in dark shadow, flecked with the white dots of the sheep. And as the oxen grazing on the ridges moved this way and that against the blue of the sky, it seemed that the profiles of the mountains themselves were coming to life and swarming with activity. From the foot of the ravine the church-bell could no longer be heard, fewer people passed by along the road, and those who did were hurrying to get to the fair. Poor Jeli couldn't think what saint to commend himself to in that wilderness. As for Alfio, he was unable to lend a hand by himself, so he simply went on chewing his hunk of bread.

Eventually they caught sight of the bailiff in the distance galloping up on horseback and yelling and swearing so loudly to see the animals standing still on the road that Alfio took to his heels up the hillside. But Jeli stayed where he was by the side of Star. The bailiff left his mule on the road and descended into the ravine, where he tried to encourage the animal to stand up, pulling it by its tail. 'Leave him alone,' said Jeli, turning so white in the face that you would have thought it was he who had broken his bones. 'Leave him alone! Don't you see the poor beast can't move?'

In fact, with every movement and every effort he was forced to make, Star let out a piercing cry that sounded almost human. The bailiff took it out on Jeli with a barrage of kicks and blows to the body, cursing and swearing till he was blue in the face.

Meanwhile Alfio, slightly reassured, had returned to the road to keep an eye on the animals, and tried to defend himself by calling out, 'It wasn't my fault. I was walking on ahead with the grey.'

'There's nothing we can do about it,' said the bailiff, by now convinced that it was all a waste of time. 'The only thing it's good for now is its hide, while it's still fresh.'

Jeli began to tremble like a leaf when he saw the bailiff go and collect his shotgun from the pack-saddle of his mule.

'Get out of the way, you useless idiot!' roared the bailiff. 'I don't know what stops me from laying you out as well alongside that colt, which was worth a lot more than you are. The devil take the robber of a priest who baptized you!'

Star, unable to move, turned his head and stared at them with his great, wide-open eyes, as though he had understood every word, and his coat bristled in waves along his ribs as though he was shuddering all over. The bailiff destroyed Star on the spot for his hide, and the dull thud of the shot at point-blank range into his living flesh gave Jeli the feeling it was all happening to him.

'If you want my advice,' the bailiff put it to him, 'make sure you don't go near the master for the wages he owes you, or you'll get more than you bargained for!'

The bailiff rode off with Alfio and the rest of the ponies, which didn't even look round to see what had happened to Star whenever they paused to take up a mouthful of grass from the verge. Star was left all alone in the ravine, waiting for them to come and peel his hide, with his eyes wide-open as ever and his four legs in the air, at peace with the world because at last he was out of his suffering. Now that Jeli had seen the bailiff take deliberate aim at the pony and pull the trigger as the beast turned its head pathetically towards him, he stopped crying and sat on a boulder staring intently away at it until the men came to strip the carcase.

After what had happened to Star, he was free to wander at will, enjoy himself at the fair, or hang around for the rest of the day in the village square, watching the playboys at the gaming house for as long as he liked. But because he was without any means or a place to live, he also had to find out if anyone had a job to offer him.

That's the way things happen in the world. While Jeli, with his bag slung over his shoulder and his stick in his hand, went looking for a new employer, the band played merrily away in the square in their plumed hats, amid a crowd of white-capped people swarming about like flies, and the playboys sat enjoying themselves in the gaming house. Everyone was dressed up, like the animals at the fair, and in one corner of the square there was a woman in a short skirt and flesh-coloured stockings that made her legs look bare, beating away on a large chest in front of a painted sheet depicting Christians being put to the torture, with blood running in rivers. One of the crowd of people gaping open-mouthed was Massaro Cola, who had known Jeli when he was at Passanitello, and who told him he would find him a new employer, because Isidoro Macca wanted someone to look after his pigs. 'But don't tell him anything about Star,' Massaro Cola warned him. 'That's the sort of accident that can happen to anyone. But it's best not to talk about it.'

So they went off in search of Isidoro Macca, who was dancing at the wine-cellar, and while Cola went in to make inquiries Jeli waited outside in the street, surrounded by the crowd looking in at the doorway. The dingy room was filled with an enormous crowd of people leaping about and enjoying themselves, all red-faced and out of breath, making such a clatter with their boots on the tiled floor that you couldn't even hear the steady beat of the double-bass. As soon as one tune was finished, for which they'd paid five pence, the dancers shot up their fingers to demand another, whereupon the double-bass player made a cross on the wall with a piece of coal to keep the record straight, then started up all over again. 'These people spend money like water,' Jeli kept saying to himself. 'Their pockets must be full of it. They're not penniless like me, or out of a job, the way they're sweating buckets and jumping about all over the place as though they're being paid to do it!' When Massaro Cola came out and told him that Macca needed nobody, he turned round and walked sadly away.

Mara was living down towards Sant'Antonio, where the houses sprawl over the bridge, facing the Canziria valley, with its rich green carpet of cactus and its watermills stirring up the stream at intervals lower down. But now that he was not even wanted to look after the pigs, Jeli hadn't the courage to go near the place, and as he wandered through the crowd, with people mercilessly pushing and shoving him this way and that, he felt more lonely than he ever did on the uplands of Passanitello, and wanted to burst into tears. In the end Massaro Agrippino, who was striding around all over the place swinging his arms and having a good time at the gala, came up behind Jeli in the square, shouting 'Hey, Jeli! Hey there!' and took him back home with him. Mara, dressed up to the nines, with huge ear-rings flapping against her cheeks, was standing in the doorway with her hands spread out across her belly to show off all her rings, waiting for it to grow dark so that she could go and see the fireworks.

'Oh!' said Mara. 'Are you here as well for the feast of San Giovanni?'

Jeli really didn't have the courage to enter because he was so poorly dressed, but Massaro Agrippino gave him a shove from behind, telling him he was an old friend of the family, and that they knew he had come to the fair with his master's ponies. His wife Lia poured him a generous glass of wine, and they insisted on taking him with them to see the illuminations, along with their friends and neighbours.

On arriving in the square, Jeli was struck dumb with amazement. The whole place was a sea of fire, like burning stubble fields, because of the huge number of rockets being set off by his devotees in the presence of the saint, who was standing there at the entrance to the church, a figure draped in black beneath his silver canopy. The devotees were running in and out of the flames like a pack of devils, and there was even a woman, half undressed and dishevelled, her eyes popping out of her head, and a priest, hatless, with his cassock round his ears, who seemed to be possessed by the zeal of his devotion.

'That fellow over there is the son of Massaro Neri, the farm-bailiff on the Salonia estate. He spends a small fortune on fireworks!' said Mara's mother, Lia, pointing towards a young man who was going round holding a firework in each hand like a pair of candles. All the women gazed admiringly at him, with shouts of 'Viva San Giovanni!'

'His father's a rich man,' Massaro Agrippino added. 'He owns more than twenty head of cattle.'

Mara also knew that he had carried the main standard in the procession, and that he held it up straight as an arrow because he was so strong and handsome.

Massaro Neri's son seemed to hear what they were saying, and lit a pair of Roman candles for Mara, dancing round her in a circle. And when the fireworks had died down he came over and joined them, and took them to the dance, and to the cosmorama, where you could see the old world and the new. He paid for everyone, of course, including Jeli, who brought up the rear of the party like a dog without a master, only to see Massaro Neri's son dancing with Mara, who skipped around him and curtsied like a lovesick dove, prettily holding a corner of her pinafore at arm's length. As for Massaro Neri's son, he leapt this way and that like a pony, causing Gnà Lia to weep with ecstasy, while Massaro Agrippino nodded his head in approval and expressed his satisfaction at the way things were turning out.

Eventually they grew tired, joined the people walking up and down the street, and were drawn bodily along by the crowd as though caught up in a strong current, past the illuminated screens showing a beheading of San Giovanni that would have even brought tears to the eyes of the Saracens themselves, with the saint gambolling about like a goat under the executioner's axe. Nearby, the band was playing under a great wooden canopy dotted with lanterns, and the square was packed with more Christian souls than any fair had ever witnessed.

Mara was walking along on the arm of Massaro Neri's son like a young woman of the quality, whispering in his ear and laughing so much you could tell she was enjoying every minute of it. Jeli by this time was utterly exhausted, and he fell asleep sitting on the pavement, until he was suddenly woken up by the first bangers of the firework display. Mara was still at the side of Massaro Neri's son, leaning up against him with her arms entwined round his shoulders, and in the light of the coloured fireworks, in turn she appeared white then red all over. When the last salvo of rockets burst in the sky, Massaro Neri's son turned towards her, his face lit up in green, and gave her a kiss.

Jeli said nothing, but at that moment the whole gala, which until then he had been enjoying, turned into poison for him, and he began to reflect once more on his misfortunes, which had completely disappeared from his mind. He remembered that he had no job, no prospects, nowhere to go, nothing to eat and no roof over his head; in other words it would be better to go and fling himself into the ravine like Star, who by that time was being eaten up by the dogs.

Meanwhile the people around him were in high spirits. Mara was singing as she skipped along the stony path with her companions on their way back home.

'Good night! Good night!' her friends called out as they left the group one by one along the road.

When it came to Mara's turn to bid them good night, her voice had such a contented ring about it that she seemed to be singing, and Massaro Neri's son had got so worked up about her that he didn't want to leave her, as Massaro Agrippino and Gnà Lia stood there arguing before opening the front door.

Nobody was taking any notice of Jeli, until Massaro Agrippino remembered he was there, and asked him, 'And where will you go now?'

'I don't know,' said Jeli.

'Come and see me tomorrow, and I'll help you to look for somewhere to stay. Just for tonight, go back to the square where we listened to the band playing, and find yourself a place on one of the benches. You must be used to sleeping out in the open.'

Used to it he certainly was, but what distressed him most was that Mara never said a word to him, and left him standing on the doorstep like a beggar. So next day, as soon as he was able to find her alone for a moment in the house, he said to her, 'What's got into you, Mara? Don't you remember your friends any more?'

'Don't be silly, Jeli!' said Mara. 'I haven't forgotten you. It's just that I was tired out after the fireworks!'

'Do you mean to say you're not in love with Massaro Neri's son?' he asked, twirling his stick between the palms of his hands.

'What nonsense you do talk!' Mara replied in a brusque tone of voice. 'My mother's in the next room, listening to everything.'

Massaro Agrippino found him a place as a shepherd on the Salonia estate, where Massaro Neri was the head farmer, but since Jeli had little experience in the job he had to content himself with a very low wage.

So now he tended his sheep, and learnt how to make different kinds of cheese, from ricotta to Sicilian hard cheese, and all the other products that a flock can provide. But when evening came, and the other shepherds and the peasants started chatting among themselves in the farmyard while the women were shelling beans for the minestra, if they happened to mention Massaro Neri's son who was going to marry Mara, Jeli shut up like a clam, not even daring to open his mouth.

Once, when the watchman made fun of him by telling him that Mara had dropped him like a hot potato after everybody had been saying they were going to be husband and wife, Jeli, who was busy warming up the milk in the pot, replied as he slowly separated the curds from the whey, 'The older she gets, the more beautiful she becomes. Mara looks like a real lady nowadays.'

Being so patient and hard-working, he soon learnt to do his job better than people who had done nothing else for the whole of their lives, and since he was accustomed to being with animals, he tended his sheep with all the loving care of a father, so that on the Salonia farm there were fewer deaths from the sickness, and the flock came on so well that whenever Massaro Neri visited the farm he was delighted with it. As a result, when new year came along he decided to persuade the landowner to increase Jeli's wages, so that he was now getting almost as much as he had earned when tending the horses. It was money well spent, because Jeli was prepared to wander for miles and miles to find the best grazing lands for his flock, and if they were lambing or feeling out of sorts he would get them to eat from the donkey's hay-bags, and he would carry the lambs with their heads popping out of a sack round his shoulders in such a way that they bleated into his face and sucked the tips of his ears. During the famous snowstorm on St Lucy's night, the snow fell so thickly over Salonia that by daybreak it was lying four palms deep over the lower valley, and nothing else could be seen for miles in the whole of the countryside. Neri would have been ruined on that occasion, as so many other farmers were, if Jeli hadn't got up three or four times in the night to drive his flock into the fold so that the poor sheep could shake the snow off their backs and save themselves from being buried like so many in the neighbouring flocks. 'They would have been buried up to their ears,' Massaro Agrippino said when he called later on to take a look at a small field of beans that he had on the estate, and he also said that all that talk about Massaro Neri's son marrying his daughter Mara was a lot of nonsense, and that Mara had different ideas in her head.

'But everyone said they were going to marry at Christmas,' said Jeli.

'It's completely untrue, no one had any intention of marrying. It's all gossip put about by envious busybodies meddling with other people's affairs,' Massaro Agrippino replied.

But after Massaro Agrippino had left, the watchman, who was better informed because he had heard people talking about it in the square during a visit he had paid to the village on the previous Sunday, explained how matters really stood. The marriage was off because Massaro Neri's son had got to know that Massaro Agrippino's daughter, Mara, had formed a close relationship with Don Alfonso, the young gentleman, who had known Mara ever since she was a child, and Massaro Neri had declared that his son wanted to be respected like his father, and that he was having no horns in his house except the ones his oxen were carrying.

Jeli was present as he was saying all this, sitting in a circle with the others over the midday meal, and just at that moment he was slicing the bread. He said nothing, but lost his appetite for the rest of the day.

As he was leading his sheep to pasture, he began to think again about Mara, when she was a little girl, and how they used to keep one another company the whole day long in the Jacitano valley and on the Hill of the Cross, and how she would sit watching him with her head held high as he climbed to the tops of the trees to bring down birds' nests. And he thought about Don Alfonso, too, who would come and see him from the big house nearby, and of how they would lie face downwards on the grass poking at crickets' nests with a small twig. All these things he turned over in his mind for hour after hour, sitting on the bank of the torrent with his arms clasped round his knees. And then there were the tall walnut trees at Tebidi, and the thick scrub of the valleys, and the hill-slopes clad in the green of the sumacs, and the grey olives piling up like mist, one on top of the other, and the red roofs of the tenement block, and the bell-tower 'shaped like a salt-cellar' in the middle of the orange grove. But here the countryside stretched out barren and deserted before him covered in patches of parched grass, silently fading away into the sultry haze of the distant horizon.

In spring, as soon as the bean-pods began to droop their heads, Mara turned up at the Salonia farm to pick the beans with her father and mother, and the boy and the donkey, and they all bedded down at the farm for the two or three days the harvest lasted. So Jeli was able to see the girl morning and evening, and they would often sit with one another on the low wall of the sheepfold, talking to each other while Jeli counted the sheep.

'It's like being at Tebidi,' said Mara, 'when we were small, and we sat on the little bridge down the lane.'

Jeli could remember it all just as clearly, but being such a pensive sort, never having much to say, he offered no reply.

When the harvest was over, on the eve of their departure Mara came to say goodbye to the young man, just as he was making the ricotta, intent on skimming off the curds with his ladle.

'I just came to say goodbye,' she said. 'We're going back to Vizzini tomorrow.'

'How did the bean-picking go?'

'Badly! They were all eaten up by the mildew this year.'

'That's because we haven't had much rain,' Jeli said. 'You wouldn't believe it, but we even had to kill the lambs because there wasn't enough for them to eat. There's been no more than three inches of grass on the whole of the Salonia estate.'

'I don't suppose that worries you. You always get your wages, whether it's a good or a bad year.'

'That's true,' he said, 'but it makes me feel sad to hand those poor beasts over to the butcher.'

'Do you remember coming to the feast of San Giovanni, that time when you'd lost your job?'

'Yes, I remember.'

'It was my father who found you a job here, with Massaro Neri.'

'Yes, but how is it that you and Massaro Neri's son didn't get married?'

'Because it wasn't God's will,' she replied. She paused a little, then continued, 'My father's been unlucky. Ever since we moved to Marineo everything has turned out badly. It's not just the beans, it's the main crop, even the vines on that little patch of land we have up there. And then my brother was called up into the army, and we even had a mule that died on us that was worth forty *onze*.'

'I know,' said Jeli. 'The bay mule!'

'Now that we've lost everything, who do you think is going to marry me?'

As she spoke, Mara was idly snapping bits off a blackthorn twig, staring at the ground, her chin tucked tightly in, and she accidentally poked Jeli on the arm with her elbow. Jeli, his eyes fixed on the churn, offered no reply, so she continued, 'Do you remember how the people at Tebidi said we would be husband and wife?'

'Yes,' said Jeli, hanging the ladle on the rim of the churn. 'But I'm only a poor shepherd, not good enough to marry a farmer's daughter like yourself.'

Mara remained silent for a few moments, then she said, 'If you love me, I'll be happy to take you.'

'Do you really mean it?'

'Yes, of course I do.'

'But what will your father say?'

'My father says you've learnt your job now, and you're not the sort of man to spend all your wages, but you make them stretch twice as far, and because you don't eat for the sake of eating you'll have sheep of your own one day, and become a rich man.'

'If that's what he says,' Jeli concluded, 'I'll be just as happy to take you.'

'There!' said Mara, now that it was dark, and the sheep were beginning to quieten down. 'If you want a kiss now I'll give you one, because we're going to be husband and wife.'

Jeli was at a loss for words, but accepted the kiss like a lamb, then added, 'I've always loved you, even when you wanted to leave me for Massaro Neri's son and . . .' But he hadn't the courage to name the other.

'You see? Fate intended us for one another!' Mara concluded.

Massaro Agrippino duly gave his consent, and his wife Lia rapidly made up a new overcoat and a pair of velvet breeches for her son-in-law. Mara was fresh and lovely as a rose, looking like an Easter lamb in her white bridal gown, and her neck glowed white beneath her amber necklace. As Jeli walked stiffly down the street at her side in his new jacket and velvet breeches, not daring to blow his nose into his red silk handkerchief in case anyone was looking, the villagers and everyone else who knew about the business of Don Alfonso were making fun of him behind his back. When Mara had said 'I will,' and the priest had joined them in holy matrimony with a great big sign of the cross, Jeli led her proudly back home with the feeling that they had given him pots of gold and all the lands he had ever set eyes upon.

'Now that we're man and wife,' he said to her when he brought her home and sat down facing her, making himself look as tiny as he could, 'believe me, now that we're man and wife, I can't understand why such a beautiful woman as you should have chosen to marry me, when you could have had any number of men who are better than I am!'

The poor wretch could think of nothing else to say to her, but was simply bursting out of his new clothes with contentment as he watched Mara going about the house as its mistress, arranging everything with her own hands. When Monday came, it was all he could do to drag himself away from her in the doorway to return to the Salonia farm, and he lingered at length as he fixed the bags on the donkey's pack-saddle, along with his cloak and his waterproof clothing.

'You should come too to Salonia!' he said to his wife as she stood watching him at the front door. 'You ought to come with me.'

But the woman began to laugh, and replied that she wasn't cut out to be a shepherdess, and there was nothing for her to do at Salonia.

Mara was not in fact cut out to be a shepherdess, and she was not accustomed to going about in the north winds of January, when your hands freeze up on your shepherd's crook and you feel as if your fingernails are dropping off. Nor was she accustomed to being caught in the violent downpours that soak you to the skin, or to choking in the clouds of dust along the roads, when the sheep are moving on under the baking sun, or to lying on a hard pallet, or having nothing but mouldy bread to eat. Not for her the long, silent, lonely days, when you see nothing in the whole of the burnt-up countryside except occasionally in the distance some peasant or other, blackened by the sun, silently driving his donkey forward along the white and never-ending road. At least Jeli knew that Mara was tucked up warm under the bedcovers, or spinning in front of the fire with a few of her neighbours, or enjoying the sun on the veranda, as he made his way back from the pasture, tired and thirsty, or wet through from the rain, or when the wind blew the snow into his hut, dousing the sumac fire.

Every month, Mara went and collected his wages from his master, and she never went short of eggs for the brooding, or oil for the lantern, or wine for the flask. Jeli came home to see her twice a month, and she would wait for him on the veranda, holding her spindle. Then, when he had tied up the mule in the stable and removed its saddle-pack and put down fodder for it in the manger, he would stow away most of the firewood in the lean-to shed in the yard and bring the rest into the kitchen. Mara would hang up his cloak on the nail and help him off with his damp leggings in front of the fire, then pour him out some wine while the minestra simmered merrily away. Then she would quietly go about laying the table like a dutiful housewife, chatting away to him on this, that and the other as she did so, telling him about the hen that was brooding, the cloth on the loom, the calf they were rearing, and every little thing that had happened, so that Jeli had the feeling he was living like a prince.

But on St Barbara's night he came back home at an unusual hour, when all the street lamps were already out and the town clock was ringing midnight. It was the sort of night when wolves go on the prowl, and one of them had got into his house while he was away earning his living in the wind and the rain. His reason for coming back was that he urgently needed the vet to come and tend to his master's mule, which had fallen sick. He knocked and hammered away at the door, calling out to Mara at the top of his voice, while the water poured down on him from the broken gutter, soaking him from head to foot. Finally Mara came and opened up, and began to swear at him, looking daggers at him as though she were the one who had been roaming through the fields in that awful weather.

'What's the matter?' he asked. 'What's got into you?'

'You put the fear of God into me, that's what, knocking on the door at this time of the night! Is this the hour for any honest man to be coming home? I'll be catching my death of cold!'

'Go and lie down, leave it to me to light the fire.'

'No, I'll have to go and fetch the wood.'

'I'll go.'

'No, you stay here!'

When Mara returned with the wood in her arms, Jeli said to her, 'Why did you open the back door? Wasn't there any wood left in the kitchen?'

'No, I had to go and fetch it from the shed.'

She stood there stiffly, turning her face the other way, and allowed him to kiss her.

'His wife leaves him on the doorstep getting drenched,' the neighbours said, 'when she has a songbird in the house!'

Although he was a cuckold, Jeli knew nothing about it, and the others didn't bother to tell him because he never worried about anything, and he only had himself to blame for taking on the woman after Massaro Neri's son had ditched her on hearing about the Don Alfonso affair. But Jeli carried on, happy as a sandboy and blissfully unaware of his dishonour, because as the saying goes, 'Though the horns may be spindly, they fatten up the home!'

In the end the boy who helped him tend his flock told him everything to his face when they were having an argument over certain bits of cheese that were missing. 'Now that Don Alfonso has taken your wife,' he said, 'you treat him like a brother-in-law, and you walk around with your nose in the air like a crowned prince, with those horns on your head.'

The farm-bailiff and the watchman were expecting to see blood flow any minute when they heard these words, but Jeli remained silent as though none of it concerned him, with an ox-like expression on his face that seemed to fit his horns to perfection.

With the approach of Easter, the bailiff sent all the farmhands to make confession, in the hope that the fear of God's wrath would stop them from robbing him. Jeli went along too.

As he left the church he sought out the boy who'd turned nasty on him and flung his arms round his neck, saying, 'The father confessor told me to forgive you, but I'm not angry with you for saying what you did, and as long as you stop filching my cheese I don't care about what you said to me in the heat of the moment.'

It was from that day forth that they gave him the nickname Goldhorns, and the nickname remained with him and all his family, even after he had washed away his horns in blood.

Mara too had gone to confession, and as she made her way home, casting her eyes downward with her mantilla wrapped tightly round her head, she looked like St Mary Magdalen. Jeli was waiting for her silently on the veranda, and when he caught sight of her returning in that fashion, as though her whole body was filled with the grace of the Lord, he turned pale all over, feeling as if he was seeing her for the first time, or that his Mara had been changed into another woman. He never even dared to raise his eyes towards her, as she went about unfolding the tablecloth and setting out the plates, calmly and daintily as ever.

After thinking for a long time about it, he asked her in a very cold sort of voice, 'Is it true that you're in love with Don Alfonso?'

'What are you trying to do? Turn me into a sinner on this of all days?' she exclaimed.

'I never did believe it, because when we were small boys Don Alfonso and I always went about together, and when he was staying nearby in the country he never let a day pass without coming over to see me. Besides, he's a wealthy man with pots of money, and if he wanted a woman's company he could marry and still have all the things he wanted, and plenty to eat.'

Mara was working herself up into a rage, and began to shower him with so much abuse that the poor wretch didn't dare to raise his nose from his bowl of soup. But in the end, to prevent the food they were eating from turning into poison, Mara changed the subject and asked him whether he had found the time to dig round the patch of flax they had sown in the bean field.

'Yes,' Jeli replied, 'and we're going to have a good crop.'

'In that case,' said Mara, 'I'll make a couple of new shirts to keep you warm this winter.'

The fact is that Jeli didn't know the meaning of the word cuckold, and it never entered his head to act the jealous husband. It was difficult for him to grasp anything that was unusual, and this business seemed to him so extraordinary as to throw his mind into total confusion, especially when he could see his Mara there in front of his eyes, so beautiful and pale-complexioned and neatly dressed. Besides, it was she who had told him she wanted to marry him, and ever since he was a child he had loved her so much and thought about her for so long over so many years that when he heard she was going to marry someone else he could neither eat nor drink for the rest of the day. And it was just the same when he thought about Don Alfonso, and all the days they had spent together, and how he had brought him sweets and white bread every time he came. He could picture him now in his pretty new clothes, with his curly hair, and his face as smooth and pale as a girl's. That was the way he still remembered him, because being a poor shepherd who spent the whole year out in the wilds, he had never come across him again. But the first time he had the misfortune to see Don Alfonso again, after all those years, Jeli felt as if a fire was raging inside his body. Now that he had grown up, Don Alfonso no longer seemed the same person, with his fine bushy beard as curly as his hair, his velvet jacket, and a gold watch-chain dangling across his waistcoat. He recognized Jeli, though, and slapped him over the shoulders by way of greeting. He had come with the farm's owner and a party of friends on a trip to the country at the sheep-shearing season, and Mara had turned up as well under the pretext that she was pregnant and wanted some fresh ricotta.

It was a fine, hot day in the sun-blanched fields, with the hedges in bloom and the long green rows of vines, the sheep were bleating and gambolling about from the joy of finding themselves short of all that wool, and in the kitchen the women were building a big fire to cook all the good things the owner had brought along for the meal. While they were waiting, the gentlemen sat in the shade of the carob trees, or relaxed by dancing with the farm-girls to the sound of tambourines and bagpipes. As Jeli went on shearing the sheep, without knowing the reason for it he felt a sharp pain, like a thorn or a nail or the tip of his shears, working steadily away inside him, as though he had been poisoned. The owner had given orders for two sucking kids to be slaughtered, along with a yearling bullock, and chickens and a turkey. He was putting on a big party, in other words, sparing no expense to entertain his guests, and while all those beasts were writhing in pain, and the sucking kids were squealing under the knife, Jeli felt his knees start to tremble, and little by little it seemed that the wool he was shearing and the grass where the sheep were gambolling became awash with blood.

'Stay where you are!' he said to Mara, when Don Alfonso called her over to dance with the others. 'Stay where you are, Mara!'

'Why should I?'

'I don't want you to go. Stay where you are!'

'Don't you see they're calling me?'

Nothing more that he said had any clear meaning, as he remained bent over the sheep he was shearing. Mara shrugged her shoulders and went to join in the dance. She was flushed with joy, her dark eyes lit up like two stars, her teeth shone white through her laughter, and all the gold trinkets she was wearing tinkled and glittered on her cheeks and her breast so that she looked like a painting of the Madonna come to life. Jeli stood up straight, with the long shears in his hands, and turned as white in the face as his father the cowherd once had turned when he was shuddering in the hut from his fever beside the fire. Suddenly he saw that Don Alfonso, with his fine curly beard and his velvet jacket and his gold watch-chain, had taken Mara by the hand to dance with her, and at the very moment he saw him touch her, he leapt on him and cut his throat with a single slash of his shears, just like a sucking kid.

Later, when they brought him up, a broken man in handcuffs before the judge, without having offered the slightest resistance to his arrest: 'What!' he said. 'Didn't I have every right to kill him? He took away my Mara!'

Rosso Malpelo

He was called Malpelo[1] because he had red hair, and he had red hair because he was a mischievous rascal who promised to turn out a real knave. So everyone at the red sand mine called him Malpelo, and even his mother, hearing him always referred to in that way, had almost forgotten the name he was christened with.

In any case, she only saw him on Saturday evenings, when he came back home with his paltry weekly wage, and since he was *malpelo* she was always afraid he had kept a bit of it back. Just in case he had, and to be on the safe side, his elder sister greeted him with one or two clouts around the ear.

However, the pitowner had confirmed that his wages amounted to such and such a figure and no more, and to tell the truth even that was too high for Malpelo, a ragamuffin nobody wanted to see anywhere near him, a person to be avoided like a mangy dog, and they greeted him with the toes of their boots whenever he came within range.

He truly was an ugly-looking creature, with a surly, quarrelsome and excitable temperament to match. At noon, when all the other mineworkers were sitting round in a circle eating up their minestra and taking a break, he would squat some distance away with his wicker basket between his knees, nibbling away at his mouldy bread like an animal, and they all joined in to poke fun and throw stones at him until the foreman sent him back to work with a kick in the pants. He thrived on being kicked about, and allowed them to load him up more heavily than the grey mule, without ever daring to complain. He always went around in rags, covered from head to foot in red sand, because his sister was engaged to be married now and had other things to think about.

But all the same everyone in Monserrato and Carvana knew who he was, so much so that they called the mine where he worked Malpelo's Mine, much to the annoyance of the owner. In fact, they only kept him on out of charity and because his father, Misciu, had died in the mine.

The way he died was that, one Saturday, he'd decided to finish off some piece-work he had taken on, which involved removing a pillar, originally erected to hold up the roof of the cave but now no longer needed, and he'd agreed with the owner to extract at a rough estimate thirty-five to forty cartloads of sand. Misciu had been digging away for three whole days, and there was still enough work left to keep him busy till lunch time on Monday. It was a rotten deal, and only a fool like Misciu would have let himself be cheated in that way by the owner. No wonder he was called Misciu Blockhead, and people thought of him as the pack-mule for the whole mine. Instead of laying into his workmates and arguing with them, the poor devil simply ignored them and got on with earning his daily bread. But Malpelo sulked as if their remarks were being aimed at him, and although he was very small he pulled such long faces that they told him to cheer up, saying, 'Come on, now, you're not going to die in your bed, like that father of yours.'

However, Misciu never died in his bed at all, even though he was such an inoffensive creature. Old Mommu, known as The Cripple, had said all along that the pillar was so dangerous that he wouldn't have gone near it for all the money in the world. But then, life in the caves is a dangerous business, and if you listen to all the nonsense people spout, you might as well go and become a lawyer.

That Saturday evening, Misciu was still scraping away at his pillar long after sunset had come and gone, and all his mates had lit up their pipes and left the site, telling him to enjoy himself as he scratched away for the owner's benefit, and to be careful not to die like a rat in a trap.

He was used to their taunts and paid no attention to them, but simply replied with his groans of 'Ah! Ah!' as he dug away with his spade, meanwhile muttering to himself, 'That's for the bread! That's for the wine! That's for Nunziata's new skirt!' And in this way he worked out how he would be spending the proceeds of the piece-work he had let himself in for.

Outside the cave, the sky was teeming with stars, while down there his lantern was pouring out smoke and swinging from side to side. The big red pillar, ripped open by the blows of his spade, twisted and bent itself into an arc as if it had stomach-ache, and groaned on its own account. Malpelo cleared everything from the floor of the cave, making sure the pickaxe, the empty lunch-bag and the flask of wine were in a safe place. His father, poor fellow, was very fond of him, and kept shouting, 'Stay back!' or 'Watch out! Watch out for stones or thick sand falling from above.' Then suddenly his voice was no longer heard, and Malpelo, who had turned away to stow the tools in the wicker bag, heard a dull, thunderous roar as of sand shifting en masse all at once, and the light went out.

The pit-engineer was at the theatre that evening, and would not have exchanged his seat in the stalls for a royal throne when they came to tell him about Malpelo's father, who had died like a rat in a trap. All the women of Monserrato were shrieking and beating their breasts to announce the terrible distress that Santa, Misciu's wife, was suffering because of the accident. She was the only one saying nothing, but simply stood there with her teeth chattering as though she had caught a tertian fever. When they had explained how the accident had happened, three hours before, and told the engineer that Misciu Blockhead must be well and truly in Paradise by now, he set off with ropes and ladders to drill holes in the sand, more for the sake of his conscience than for any other reason. Forty cartloads, indeed! The Cripple said it would take a whole week at least to clear the floor of the cave. A colossal amount of sand had fallen, fine as it ever comes and well scorched by the lava, so you could work it into mortar with your hands, one part sand to two parts lime. There was enough there to keep you filling up carts for weeks. Blockhead had made a really good job of it!

In the crowd of people all talking at once, nobody was taking any notice of a child's voice, yelling like a lunatic, 'Dig! Dig here! Quick!'

'Hello!' someone said in the end. 'That must be Malpelo! Where's he sprung from? If it had been anyone else he would have been dead by now.' And one of them said he was in league with the Devil, and another that he was like a cat with nine lives.

Malpelo ignored them. He wasn't even crying, but carried on

burrowing furiously away at the sand with his fingernails. Nobody had noticed him, and when they approached him, carrying a lantern, they caught sight of a face that was frightening to behold, contorted with distress, glassy-eyed, and foaming at the mouth. His nails had been torn off and were dangling from his fingers, covered in blood, and it took a great effort on their part to extract him from the scene. No longer able to scratch them, he started to bite like a rabid dog, and they had to grab him by the hair and drag him away by main force.

Eventually, however, after a few days he went back to work at the mine on the arm of his mother, who was crying and holding him by the hand. People have to eat, after all, and jobs are not always easy to come by. There was no way to shift him from the cave, and he dug away furiously, as though every basketful of sand was relieving the weight on his father's chest. Every so often he would suddenly stop digging, holding his spade in the air to stare grimly ahead of him, rolling his eyes, as if to listen to what the Devil was whispering in his ears from the other side of that mountain of fallen sand. For several days he behaved more badly and wickedly than ever, so much so that he hardly ate a thing and threw his bread to the dog, as though it wasn't fit for human consumption. The dog came to love him, because dogs never look further than the hand that feeds them, but the grey mule, poor beast, bow-legged and emaciated, was the target for every outburst of Malpelo's frustrated anger. He beat it mercilessly with the handle of his spade, muttering as he did so, 'That'll kill you off more quickly!'

After the death of his father he seemed to be possessed by the Devil, and worked like one of those wild buffaloes that are led by an iron ring through the nose. Knowing he was *malpelo*, he lived up to his name more conscientiously than ever, and if an accident happened, or a workman lost his tools, or a mule broke its leg, or the roof of a tunnel caved in, everyone put the blame on him. He took without a murmur all the blows they rained on him, like mules that bend their backs but go on doing what they have to do in their own good time. He treated the younger boys with sheer brutality, and seemed intent on avenging himself on the weak for all the misfortunes he imagined that others had inflicted on himself and his father, and for the way they had let him die. When he was alone he would mutter to himself, 'They'll do the same to me! They called my father Blockhead because he let them walk all over him!' On one occasion, as he was passing the pitowner, he gave him a withering look and mumbled, 'He's the one who did it, for thirty-five *tarì*!' Then again, behind The Cripple's back, he said to himself, 'And he's another one! He was even laughing that night! I heard him myself!'

By way of a refined piece of cruelty he appeared to take under his wing one of the poorer boys, who had come to work at the mine a little while before, and who had given up his trade after dislocating a thigh bone when he fell from scaffolding. When he was carrying his basket of sand on his back, the poor wretch would hop along as if he was dancing the tarantella, and all the mineworkers laughed at him and called him The Frog. But frog or no frog, when he was working below ground he earned his crust, and Malpelo even gave him some of his own, simply for the pleasure, so they said, of playing the tyrant over him.

In fact, he found a hundred different ways to torment him. He would beat him for no reason at all without mercy, and if The Frog failed to put up a fight, he would turn really nasty and hit him harder, saying, 'Take that, you idiot! You're an idiot! If you don't have the courage to defend yourself against someone like me, who doesn't wish you any harm, it means you'll let anybody come and trample all over you!'

Again, if The Frog was mopping up the blood flowing from his mouth or his nose, he would say, 'The more you feel the pain of being beaten, the better you learn to hand it out to others.' Whenever Malpelo, driving a laden mule up the steep slope below ground, found it digging in its hooves from exhaustion and bending its back under the load, leaden-eyed and panting for breath, he would use the handle of his spade to beat it without mercy, and the blows would ring out loud and clear as he struck it on its shins and its bare ribs. There were times when the beast was bent double under the battering, but being powerless to move one leg in front of the other, it sank to its knees, and there was one mule that had fallen so often that it had two wounds on its forelegs. Malpelo would say to The Frog, 'The mule gets beaten because it can't fight back, and if it could, it would trample us under its feet and steal the food out of our mouths.'

Or else he would say, 'If you happen to give anyone a hiding, make sure you beat him as hard as you can, and then the others will respect you and you'll have a lot fewer of them on your back.'

Apart from that, when he was working with his pick and shovel he went at it like a maniac as though he had it in for the sand, and he hacked and dug away at it through clenched teeth, groaning, 'Ah! Ah!' as his father did. 'The sand can never be trusted,' he muttered to The Frog under his breath, 'it's like all the others, who stamp on your face if you're weaker than they are, and if you're stronger than them, or have the crowd on your side, like The Cripple, it surrenders. My father beat away at it regularly for his whole life, which is why they called him Blockhead, and in the end the sand crept up on him and swallowed him, because it was stronger than he was.'

Every time The Frog had a heavy job to do, and cried over it like a frail old woman, Malpelo slapped him on the back and shouted, 'Be quiet, you sissy!' But if the lad couldn't get it done, he gave him a hand, saying to him in a proud sort of voice, 'Leave it to me. I'm stronger than you are.' Or else he would let him have his half-onion and be content with eating dry bread, shrugging his shoulders and saying, 'I'm used to it.'

He was used to everything, in fact, to being beaten, being kicked, being struck with the handle of a spade or the strap of a pack-saddle, being knocked about and taunted by everybody, and sleeping on stones, with his arms and his back aching from a fourteen-hour shift. He was used to going hungry as well, whenever the pitowner punished him by denying him his bread or his minestra. He used to say the pitowner never denied him his ration of beatings, but the beatings didn't cost him anything. He never complained, however, and cunningly took secret revenge with some devilish trick or other, with the result that they gave him a beating for various things that happened even when he was not to blame, on the grounds that if Malpelo was not responsible, he was quite capable of having done it. He never attempted to prove they were wrong, which would not have helped in any case. Sometimes, when The Frog, frightened to the point of bursting into tears, pleaded with him to tell the truth and prove his innocence, he repeated, 'What's the use? I'm *malpelo*!' and nobody could tell whether he was shaking his head and shrugging his shoulders from a sense of fierce pride or hopeless resignation, or whether it was a case on his part of obtuseness or timidity. What was certain was that his own mother had never known him to embrace her, so she had never done the same to him either.

On Saturday evenings, once he had arrived home with his ugly, freckled face spattered with red sand, and his tattered clothes hanging shabbily from his frame, his sister would grab the broom-handle if he attempted to show himself at the front door in that pickle, afraid that her fiancé would run a mile if he saw what kind of a brother-in-law he was letting himself in for. His mother was always round at one of her neighbours, so he sloped off and huddled up on his straw mattress like a sick animal. Then, on Sundays, when all the other boys of the neighbourhood put on a clean shirt to go to Mass or run about in the playground, the only way he seemed capable of amusing himself was to go wandering along the garden paths throwing stones at lizards and the other wretched creatures that had never done him any harm, or hacking gaps in the cactus hedgerows. At all events he was in no mood to expose himself to the taunts and the stone-throwing of the other boys.

Misciu's widow was in despair at having such a problem child, as they all described him, which in fact is what he had become. He resembled one of those dogs that have been kicked and stoned so often that they end up with their tails between their legs and run away as soon as any living soul comes near them, turning all skinny and mangy like a wild wolf. At least when he was below ground in the sand mine, no matter how ugly and ragged and filthy he was, they could no longer taunt him, and he seemed to be cut out on purpose for that sort of job even down to the colour of his hair and his piercing, cat-like eyes, that blinked in the light of the sun. There are mules in that same condition, that work in the caves for years and years without ever coming out again, and because the pit-shaft is vertical, they are lowered in on ropes and remain down there for the rest of their lives. True enough, they are old mules, bought up for twelve *lire* or so on their way to be strangled at the Plaja,[2] but still good enough for the work they have to do below ground. Malpelo, certainly, was no better off than they were, and although he came out of the pit on Saturday evenings, that was only because he had hands to haul himself up the ropes and because he had to take his week's wages home to his mother.

Without a doubt he would have preferred to earn his living as a builder's labourer like The Frog once had done, singing as he worked high up on scaffolding with the sun shining down on his back from the clear blue sky, or as a cart-driver like Gaspare, who came to collect the sand from the pit, nodding off to sleep over the shafts of his cart with his pipe in his mouth as he drove the whole day long through the quiet country lanes, or better still, he would have liked to be a peasant spending his life in the heart of the green countryside, with the densely wooded carob groves to retire to, the dark blue sea in the background, and the song of the birds overhead. But his father had been a sand-miner, and he too was born to ply the same trade.

As he thought about all that, he told The Frog about the pillar that collapsed and how his father had been buried in the fine, scorched sand that was still being carried away by the driver with the pipe in his mouth who nodded over the shafts of his cart, and he told him that when they had finished digging they would find his father's body, wearing the corduroy trousers that were still as good as new. The Frog felt frightened, but not Malpelo, who was thinking that he had spent his whole life there ever since he was a small boy, and had always been familiar with that black hole plunging into the depths to which his father used to lead him by the hand. He spread out his arms to the right and the left, and described how an intricate maze of tunnels extended far and wide below their feet in all directions under the whole of the black, deserted volcano[3] with its dried-up clumps of gorse bushes. And he told him about all the men who had been buried or lost their way in the dark, who had been wandering about for years down there and were wandering yet, unable to find the vent of the shaft by which they had entered, and unable to hear the desperate cries of their children searching for them in vain.

But once, as they were filling up their sand-baskets, they came across one of Misciu's shoes, and Malpelo was overcome with such a fit of trembling that they had to bring him up on ropes to the fresh air, like a mule about to breathe its last. There was no sign of the other shoe, however, or of the trousers that were as good as new, or the rest of Misciu for that matter, even though the experts affirmed that it was the very spot where the pillar had toppled over on him. One of the workers, who was new to the job, made the curious comment that the sand must be very fickle, since it had tossed Blockhead this way and that, leaving his shoes in one place and his feet in another.

From the moment the shoe was found, Malpelo was so terrified of seeing his father's bare foot coming into view in the sand that he refused to dig any further with his spade, saying he would rather they hit him over the head with it. He went to work in another section of the mine, and refused to come back to the place where the shoe had turned up. Two or three days later, in fact, they discovered Misciu's body, lying flat on its face, trousers and all, looking for all the world as if it had been embalmed. Old Mommu remarked that he must have taken a long time to die, because the pillar had bent over in an arc above him and buried him alive. And you could still see the proof that Blockhead had tried instinctively to escape by scraping away at the sand, because the nails were broken on his lacerated hands. 'Just like his son Malpelo!' The Cripple kept repeating. 'He was digging on this side and his son was digging on that.' They said nothing to the boy, however, for they knew exactly how malign and vindictive he was.

The carter cleared the mine of the corpse in the same way that he cleared it of the sand that had fallen and of dead mules, except that this time he was dealing, not only with the smell of a carcase, but with the carcase of a baptized fellow worker. Misciu's widow shortened the trousers and the shirt and altered them to fit Malpelo, who thus went about in clothes that were almost new for the first time in his life. The shoes were put away for when he had grown up, because you can't make shoes any smaller than they already are and also because his sister's fiancé was not going to wear the shoes of a dead man.

Malpelo ran his hand over the good-as-new corduroy trousers on his legs, thinking to himself they were as soft and smooth as the hands of his father when he used to stroke his hair, rough and hardened as they were. He carefully hung the shoes on the same nail where he kept his pallet, as though they were the Pope's slippers, and on Sundays he would take them down, polish them and try them on. Then he would place them on the floor, one beside the other, and stare at them for hours on end with his elbows on his knees and his chin resting in the palms of his hands, and it was anybody's guess what ideas were running through that calculating little head of his.

He had some strange ideas, did Malpelo. He had also inherited his father's pick and spade, and insisted on using them, even though they were too heavy for a boy of his age. When they asked him if he wanted to sell them and offered him what they would have cost if they were buying them new, he turned them all down. His father's hands had left the handles so smooth and shiny that he would never have been able to create the same effect with a new pick and spade if he worked with them for a hundred years or more.

Around that time the grey mule died from exhaustion and old age, and the carter arrived to take away the corpse and dispose of it miles away in the *sciara*.[4] 'That's what they always do,' muttered Malpelo. 'When tools have served their purpose, they're taken miles away and dumped.'

He went to have a look at the carcase of the grey mule lying in the ravine, and forced The Frog to go along with him, although he didn't want to. Malpelo told him that in this world you had to get used to looking things squarely in the face, whether they were beautiful or ugly, and he stood there gazing with the eager curiosity of a street-urchin at the dogs that had rushed to the scene from all the farms in the neighbourhood to vie with one another for the grey mule's flesh. When the boys came into view, the dogs ran off whining, and they circled round, howling, on the other bank of the ravine. The Frog started throwing stones at them, but Malpelo restrained him, saying, 'Don't you see that the black bitch is not afraid of your stones? She's not afraid because she's hungrier than the others. Do you see how the grey's ribs are sticking out? At least he's not in pain any more.'

The grey mule lay still on its back with its four legs sticking up in the air, letting the dogs gorge themselves as they emptied out its deep eye-sockets, and stripped the flesh off its milky-white bones. The teeth tearing away at its innards could never have made it bend down an inch, as it used to do when they hammered it on its back with their spades to force enough strength into its body to climb the steep incline.

'That's the way things go in this world!' said Malpelo. 'The grey took some blows from spades in his time, and suffered from the sores on his back. And when he bent double under the blows, or couldn't summon up the strength to go on, he seemed to be saying: "That's enough! That's enough!" as they kept on beating him. But now that his eyes are being swallowed up by the dogs, he can laugh at all those blows and the sores he had on his back, lying there with his teeth sticking out from a mouth that's been stripped of its flesh. But it would have been better for him if he'd never been born at all.'

The *sciara* spread out as far as the eye could see, deserted and melancholy, black and wrinkled as it rose and fell in ridges and ravines, with not a cricket that was chirping or a bird that was singing. Not a sound could be heard, not even the sound of the mineworkers' picks as they toiled away below the ground. Malpelo kept repeating that the ground underneath was hollowed out with tunnels running in every direction, both towards the mountain and towards the valley, so much so that one miner had entered them once as a young man and come out with grey hair. And another, whose lamp had gone out, had been shouting for help in vain for years on end.

'He's the only one who can hear all the shouting he's doing!' he said, and the idea of it made him shudder, though his heart was as hard as the *sciara* itself.

'The pitowner regularly sends me to some distant part of the tunnels, where the others are afraid to go. But I'm only Malpelo, and if I never come back, nobody will go looking for me.'

On clear summer nights, the stars shone no less brightly over the *sciara* than they did elsewhere. The surrounding countryside was just as black as the *sciara* itself, but Malpelo, tired from his long day's work, would lie down on his pallet, looking up at the sky, enjoying the stillness and the luminous majesty of it all. He hated the moonlit nights, when the sea is swarming with sparks of light and here and there you can vaguely pick out the shapes of the countryside, because then the *sciara* seems even more barren and desolate.

For people like us who are born to live underground, he thought, it should always be dark everywhere.

An owl would screech above the *sciara*, swooping this way and that, and he thought to himself, Even the owl knows there are dead men under the ground in these parts, and it's crying with despair because it can't go down there and find them.

The Frog was afraid of owls, and of bats too, but Malpelo told him not to be so stupid, because nobody who has to live alone should ever be afraid of anything, and not even the grey mule was afraid of the dogs that were stripping away his flesh, now that he no longer felt any pain from being eaten.

'You used to crawl about like a cat when you worked on the roofs,' he told him, 'but then it was totally different. Now that you have to live underground like a rat, you shouldn't be afraid of either rats or bats, which are only old rats with wings. They love to keep company with the dead.'

The Frog on the other hand was dying to explain to him what the stars were doing up there in the heavens, and he told him that Paradise was up there, where the dead go if they have been good and not annoyed their parents. 'Who told you that?' Malpelo asked, and The Frog replied that his mother had told him.

At this, Malpelo scratched his head, and with a mischievous smile he peered at him sideways like a street-urchin who thinks he knows everything. 'Your mother told you that because you should be wearing a skirt instead of trousers.'

He thought about it for a while, then added, 'My father was good, and never did any harm to anybody, and they called him Blockhead. But he's finished up down below, and they even found his tools and his shoes and these trousers I'm wearing.'

Shortly afterwards, The Frog, whose health had been failing for some time, was taken so poorly that he had to be carried from the pit on the mule's back, straddled across the sand-baskets, shaking with fever like a drowned rat. One of the miners said the boy would never develop a thick enough skin for that job, and to work in a mine without dropping dead you had to be born to it. Hearing him say this, Malpelo came all over proud at having been born to it, and remaining so strong and healthy, despite having to face so many hardships in that unwholesome atmosphere. He lifted The Frog up on to his shoulders and tried to force some life into him in his own fashion, by hitting him and shouting at him. But on one occasion, after striking him on the back, The Frog started bleeding from the mouth. Malpelo was alarmed, and tried his best to find out what he had done, by looking into the boy's mouth and up his nostrils. He swore that he could not have done him any great harm by hitting him as he did, and just to prove it he beat himself severely about the chest and the back with a large stone. A workman who happened to be present gave him an almighty kick in the back that made a noise like a drumbeat, yet Malpelo never budged an inch, and after the workman had gone he added, 'You see? He never hurt me in the least! And he hit me twice as hard as I hit you, honestly he did!'

Meanwhile The Frog was getting no better and continued to spit out blood, and every day he was just as feverish. So Malpelo set aside some money from his weekly earnings to buy him wine and hot soup, and gave him his good-as-new trousers to cover up his legs. But The Frog kept on coughing, and at times he seemed to be choking. When evening came there was no way to stop him shaking from his fever, no matter how much they covered him with sacks or layers of straw, or how close to the fire they settled him down. Malpelo bent over him, silent and motionless, with his hands on his knees, staring at him with those huge eyes of his bulging out of his forehead, as though he was going to paint his portrait, and when he heard him moaning softly away and saw him gasping for breath with a glassy look in his eyes, exactly like the grey mule panting on its last legs as it tried to climb up the tunnel, he murmured, 'It's best for you to drop dead now and be done with it! If you have to suffer like this, it's best for you to drop dead!'

The pitowner said Malpelo was capable of smashing the boy's head in, and they should all keep an eye on him.

Then, one Monday morning, The Frog failed to turn up at the mine, and the pitowner washed his hands of him, because by now his state of health was so poor that he was more of a hindrance than anything else. Malpelo found out where he lived, and on the Saturday he went to see him. The Frog was more dead than alive, poor wretch, and his mother was weeping and wailing as if her son were somebody earning ten *lire* a week.

All this was quite beyond Malpelo, who asked The Frog why his mother was making such a fuss, when for two months he had been earning less than it cost to feed him. But The Frog paid no attention to him, and simply seemed intent on lying there in his bed. So Malpelo came to the conclusion that The Frog's mother was screaming like that because her son had always been weak and sickly, and she had coddled him like one of those youngsters who had never been weaned. He, on the other hand, had always been strong and healthy, and his mother had never wept over him, because she had never been afraid of losing him.

Shortly after that, they heard at the mine that The Frog was dead, and he thought to himself that the owl was now screeching for him as well, and he went back to take a look at the fleshless bones of the grey, in the ravine where he and The Frog had gone together. By now, all that was left of the grey was the skeleton, and The Frog would end up in the same state. His mother would dry up her tears as his own mother had dried up hers after Misciu had died, and she had now remarried and gone to live at Cibali with her married daughter, where they kept the door securely locked. From now on they no longer cared if he was beaten, and he didn't care either, because when he had got to the same state as the grey or The Frog, nothing would hurt him any more.

Around that time a man turned up to work in the mine whom nobody had ever set eyes on before, and who kept himself concealed as much as he could. The other miners whispered among themselves that he had escaped from prison, and that if he was caught they would take him back and throw away the key. Malpelo found out on that occasion that prison was a place where they kept thieves, and scoundrels like himself, and that they kept them locked up and guarded them the whole time.

From that moment on he was filled with an unhealthy longing to find out more about the man who had been in prison and escaped. But after a few weeks the fugitive declared in no uncertain terms that he had had enough of living like a filthy mole and would rather go back to prison for the rest of his life, because prison was like Paradise in comparison, and he preferred to crawl back to prison on his hands and knees. 'In that case,' Malpelo asked, 'why doesn't everyone who works in the mine get himself put in prison?'

'Because they're not *malpelo* like you!' The Cripple replied. 'But don't worry, you'll end up there sooner or later! And that's where you'll end your days.'

Instead of which Malpelo ended his days in the mine like his father, but in a different fashion. One day it was decided to explore a passage that was supposed to connect up with the main shaft, over to the left towards the valley, and if all went well, half at least of the labour cost would be saved in excavating the sand. On the other hand, there was a danger that whoever went in would lose his way and never come back. So none of the men with families would take the risk or put his life in jeopardy for all the money in the world.

But even if his life was worth all the money in the world, Malpelo had no one left to collect it for him, so he was the obvious choice. As he was about to set off, he thought about the miner who had been lost for years and was still wandering about in the dark, calling for help with nobody to hear him. But he said nothing. Anyway, what was the point? He collected his father's tools, the pick and spade, the lantern, the bag with some bread in it, the flask of wine, and off he went. He was never heard of again.

So Malpelo met his end down there as well, and the boys working at the mine lower their voices when they mention his name below ground, because they are afraid he might step out in front of them any minute, with his red hair and his grey, deep-set eyes.

Gramigna's Mistress

To Salvatore Farina[1]

My dear Farina, here is a story for you, or rather, the outline of a story. At least it has the merit of being very short in length, and of being historically authentic – a slice of life, as they say nowadays, that will possibly be of interest to you and to all those who study the hearts of men and women. I shall tell it to you just as I picked it up along the country byways, in roughly the same simple and picturesque terms of popular narrative. You certainly would prefer to be confronted by the plain simple facts rather than having to go searching for them between the lines with the lens of the writer.

The events in people's lives will always arouse curiosity, because they have actually happened, bringing the tears or the excitement or the many other sensations those people have experienced for themselves. The mysterious process through which human passions become entangled and interwoven as they ripen and develop in their hidden course, in their often contradictory meanderings, will long continue to form the powerful and fascinating basis of the psychological phenomena that underlie the plot of a story, which modern critical analysis takes so much trouble to follow with scientific precision. As for the story I narrate to you today, I shall merely tell you how it began and how it ended, which is all you need to know. Perhaps one day it will be all that anyone needs to know.

At the present day we are renewing the artistic process to which we owe so many of our glorious monuments of the past, using a different method, more precise and more intimate. We gladly sacrifice the narrative's climax and its psychological effect, grasped through a kind of divine instinct by the great artists of the past, to the logical and

93

necessary development of the passions and events leading up to the climax, which is thereby perhaps rendered less startling and dramatic, but no less inevitable. We are more modest in our ambitions, but no less humble, believing that the discoveries we make about psychological truths will certainly be no less valuable to the art of the future. Will the study of human passions ever reach such a degree of perfection that it becomes pointless to persevere in the analysis of the inner life of the characters? Will the science of the human heart, around which all contemporary art is based, exhaust so completely the writer's powers of imagination that in future the only novels that are written will be chronicles of various events?

For the time being I believe that the triumph of the novel, which of all works of art is the most complete and most closely related to the human condition, will come about when the affinity and cohesion of all its separate parts are so entire that the process of its creation remains as much a mystery as the unfolding of the human passions, and the harmony of its forms is so perfect, the sincerity of its reality so obvious, its manner and *raison d'être* so assured, that the hand of the artist will remain completely invisible. When that happens it will carry the imprint of the real event, the work of art will seem to have created itself, to have grown spontaneously and come to fruition as though it were a part of nature, without preserving any point of contact with its author. In its living contours, it will preserve no imprint of the mind that brought it to life, no shadow of the imagination that first conceived it, no trace of the lips that murmured its first words in a stroke of the creator's pen. It will stand on its own account, simply because it is what it has to be out of necessity, throbbing with life and unchangeable as a bronze statue whose author has had the godlike courage to allow himself to be eclipsed and to disappear within his immortal work.

Some years ago, down in Sicily along the banks of the Simeto, they were giving chase to a brigand, one Gramigna[2] if I am not mistaken, who was as much accursed as the grass that bears the same name, and whose reputation had struck terror into people's hearts from end to end of the province. Carabinieri, soldiers and cavalrymen had been on his trail for two months without managing to lay their hands on him.

He worked on his own but he was the equal of a band of ten, and the weed was threatening to spread still further. Moreover, harvest time was approaching, the hay was lying close to the ground in the meadows, the ears of corn were drooping on the stalks and saying yes to the reapers who were already waiting with their scythes in their hands. But none of the owners dared to raise his head above the hedgerows of his farm, for fear of finding Gramigna lying between the furrows on the other side with his carbine between his knees, ready to blow the head off anyone who came and poked his nose into his affairs. Complaints were coming in from everywhere, so the prefect called a meeting of all the senior commanders of the police, the carabinieri and the armed forces, and gave them a stern lecture. Next day it was as if an earthquake had happened. There were patrols and squads of men everywhere, look-outs concealed in every ditch and behind every wall all over the province, determined to track him down day and night, on foot, on horseback, and by telegraph. Gramigna steered clear of them, and responded with one or two shots from his gun if they ventured too close on his heels. In the whole of the countryside, in the villages, on the farms, outside the taverns, in the holiday haunts, they talked of nothing else except Gramigna, the relentless manhunt, and his desperate attempts to escape. The horses of the carabinieri were dropping dead from exhaustion, the armed soldiers, overcome with fatigue, were collapsing on to the floors of the stables, the patrols were falling asleep on their feet. Gramigna alone never tired, never slept, was always on the run, climbing over crags, crawling through the cornfields, running on all fours through the cactus, slipping away like a wolf across the dried-up beds of the mountain streams. The legend of his exploits spread for two hundred miles all around, people were talking of his strength and his courage, of the desperate struggle of one man against a thousand, tired, starving, dying of thirst in the boundless plains, that were burnt dry beneath the rays of the midsummer sun.

Peppa, one of the prettiest girls in Licodia, was due to be married around this time to Finu, known as Tallow-Candle, who owned sunlit lands and had a bay mule in his stable. He was a big, strong, handsome young fellow, who carried the standard of Santa Margherita in procession as straight as a pillar, without bending his back.

Peppa's mother was positively weeping with joy over her daughter's good fortune, and spent her time turning the bride's trousseau over and over again in the trunk, so white and pure it could have belonged to a queen, and there were ear-rings that came down to the shoulders, and enough gold rings for every one of her ten fingers. She had as much gold as you could see on Santa Margherita in the fresco, and in fact the wedding was arranged for that very saint's feast day in June, after the haymaking. Every evening, when he returned from the fields, Tallow-Candle tied up his mule at Peppa's front door, and came to tell her how marvellous the crops were going to be if Gramigna didn't set them alight, and how the big wicker basket in front of the bed wouldn't be big enough to contain all the grain from the harvest, and how he couldn't wait to lead her back home as his bride on the cropper of his bay mule.

But one fine day Peppa said to him, 'You can keep your mule. I don't intend to marry you.'

Poor Tallow-Candle was struck dumb with amazement, and Peppa's mother began tearing her hair out when she heard that her daughter was turning down the most eligible man in the whole village.

'The man I love is Gramigna,' her daughter told her. 'I want to marry him and nobody else!'

'Ah!' Her mother rushed shrieking through the house, her grey hair trailing behind her, making her look like a witch. 'Ah! That demon has been here and cast a spell on my daughter!'

'No!' replied Peppa, with a look of steel in her eyes. 'No, he never came here.'

'Where did you see him then?'

'I've never seen him. I heard about him. I just feel him here, burning inside me!'

The news caused a stir in the village, even though they tried to keep it quiet. The women who had been envying Peppa over the rich cornfield, the bay mule, and the handsome young fellow who carried the standard of Santa Margherita without bending his back, went around telling all sorts of fancy stories about how Gramigna came to see her at night in the kitchen, and how they had seen him hiding under the bed. Her poor mother had lit a lamp for the souls in Purgatory, and even the parish priest called at Peppa's house to touch her breast with his stole, so as to exorcize that demon of a Gramigna who had taken possession of her.

However, she continued to maintain that she did not know the man even by sight, but that she dreamt about him at night, and when she got up next morning her lips were parched, as if she too had known the thirst from which he must have been suffering.

Her mother then locked her inside the house so that she would hear no more of Gramigna, and she blocked all the cracks round the front door with pictures of saints. Peppa listened to what people in the street were saying on the other side of the holy images, and turned hot and cold as if all the fires of Hell were being blown into her face by the Devil himself.

Eventually she heard them saying that Gramigna had been run to earth in the cactus scrub at Palagonia. 'He fired away at them for two hours!' they were saying. 'There's one carabiniere dead and at least three soldiers injured. But they peppered him with such a hail of bullets this time that they found a pool of blood at the spot where he'd been shooting from.'

Peppa made the sign of the cross at the bedside of her mother, and escaped through the window.

Gramigna was still lying low in the rabbit warren of the cactus scrub at Palagonia, where they had not yet managed to dig him out. He was wounded, bleeding, pale and weak from two days of going without food, feverish, and levelling his gun at his pursuers.

When he saw her approaching with such a resolute air through the thick scrub, in the dim light of dawn, for a moment he was undecided whether to pull the trigger.

'What do you want?' he asked her. 'What are you doing here?'

'I've come to be with you,' she said, fixing her eyes on him. 'Are you Gramigna?'

'Yes, I am Gramigna. If you've come to collect money, you've made a mistake in your calculations.'

'No, I've come to be with you!' she insisted.

'Clear off!' he said. 'You can't stay here. I don't want any company! I've already told you, if you've come looking for money you've come to the wrong place, because I don't have any. See for yourself! It's two whole days since I last had even a crust of bread to eat.'

'I can't go back home now,' she said. 'The road is swarming with soldiers.'

'What do I care? Clear off!'

He aimed his gun at her, but much to Gramigna's amazement she stood her ground. So he went up to her and started to rain punches on her, saying, 'What is this? Are you mad? Are you a spy or something?'

'No!' she said. 'No, I'm not a spy.'

'Right you are, then, go and fill up this flask with water for me down at the stream. If you want to stay with me, you have to put your life at risk.'

Peppa went without saying a word, and when Gramigna heard the sound of rifle shots he burst out laughing, and said to himself, 'That was meant for me.'

But shortly after that, when he saw her coming back carrying the flask, pale and bleeding, he first of all pounced on her to seize the flask, and after he had drunk so much that he was out of breath, he said, 'You got away with it, then? How did you manage that?'

'The soldiers were on the far bank, and the scrub was thick on this side of the stream.'

'All the same they hit you. There's blood on your clothes.'

'Yes.'

'Where are you wounded?'

'On the shoulder.'

'That's nothing. You can still walk.'

He let her stay with him, and she followed him everywhere, feverish from her wound, ragged and barefoot, and she risked her life to go and fetch him flasks of water and crusts of bread. Whenever she came back empty-handed through the rifle fire, her lover, dying of thirst and hunger, gave her a good thrashing.

Finally, one night when the moon was shining brightly over the cactus grove, Gramigna said to her, 'They're coming!' And he got her to stand at the foot of a wall of rock while he ran off in the opposite direction.

Rifle shots rang out amid the cactus scrub, and here and there brief flashes of flame penetrated the darkness. Suddenly Peppa heard someone coming and turned round to see Gramigna dragging himself back with a broken leg. He steadied himself against the cactus stumps to reload his rifle.

'It's all over!' he said. 'Now they are going to get me.'

What caused her blood to run cold more than anything else was the glassy expression in his eyes, that made him look like a madman.

When he dropped to the ground like a bundle of sticks, the soldiers piled on to him in a flash.

Next day they dragged him on a cart through the village, all bedraggled and covered in blood. Everybody rushed to see him, and they began to laugh when they saw how tiny he was, as pale and ugly-looking as a doll in a peep-show. So this was the man Peppa had deserted Finu Tallow-Candle for! Poor Tallow-Candle stayed out of sight as if he was the one who ought to feel ashamed, while Peppa was led away in handcuffs by the soldiers as a common thief, Peppa who had as much gold as Santa Margherita!

Peppa's poor mother had to sell all the white linen of the trousseau and the gold ear-rings, and all the ten rings for her fingers, so as to pay her daughter's lawyers and bring her back home, penniless, ill, put to shame, as plain-looking as Gramigna, with Gramigna's child clinging to her neck. When they handed her daughter over at the end of the trial, surrounded by carabinieri in the bleak and gloomy barracks, she recited an Ave Maria. The poor old woman, who had lost everything she possessed, felt they were giving her a treasure, and she wept like a fountain from the sheer relief of it all. Peppa, on the other hand, seemed to have no tears left, and she said nothing, nor was she ever seen again in the village, although the two women earned their living with their own hands. People said that Peppa had learnt her trade out there in the woods, and went out at night to steal.

The fact was that she stayed curled up in a corner of the kitchen like a wild animal, and only reappeared after her mother died from her labours, and the house had to be sold.

'You see!' said Tallow-Candle, who was still in love with her. 'I could kill you with these two hands for all the wrong you have done to yourself and to others.'

'It's true!' Peppa replied. 'I know! But it was the will of God.'

When the house and its few remaining bits of furniture had been sold, she left the village by night just as she had entered it, without bothering to turn round and look for the last time at the roof under which she had slept for so long, and went to pursue the will of God in the city with her child, near the prison where Gramigna had been put away. All she could see were the sinister peepholes lining its mute façade, and the sentries drove her away if she lingered to pick out the cell where he might be lying. Eventually they told her he had left some time before, to be taken away in handcuffs and transported across the seas with his wicker bag slung over his shoulders.

She said nothing, simply staying where she was because she had nowhere else to go, with nobody to wait for her to come any longer. She scraped a living for herself working for the soldiers and the prison warders, as though she felt that she herself was a part of that huge, silent edifice, and also for the carabinieri who had seized Gramigna in the heart of the cactus grove after shooting him and breaking his leg. For them she felt a kind of tender admiration that was akin to the deference shown by an animal to brute force. On public holidays, when she saw them standing stiffly to attention in their dress uniform with their plumes and their shining epaulettes, she eyed them longingly, and she was to be seen so often around the barracks, sweeping out their sleeping quarters and polishing their boots, that they called her The Carabinieri's Duster.

But every time she saw them loading their weapons at night and going out in pairs, with their trousers turned up and their revolvers strapped to their waists, or when they mounted their horses in the light of the lamp that gave a sheen to their carbines, and when she heard the sound of the horses' hooves and the rattling of their sabres receding into the darkness, she turned a deathly pale, and trembled all over as she closed the stable-gates after them. And whenever her little boy was playing with the other boys on the esplanade in front of the prison, running in and out among the soldiers' legs, and the other boys shouted 'Son of Gramigna! Son of Gramigna!' at him, she flew into a rage and pelted them with stones until they ran away.

War of the Saints

Suddenly, as San Rocco[1] was proceeding calmly on his way beneath his *baldacchino* surrounded by the throng of his devotees, with the dogs on the lead, a huge number of lighted candles, and the band leading the procession, there was a general stampede and massive uproar, and all hell broke loose. There were priests rushing about with their cassocks flying, heads being thumped with clarinets and trumpets, women screaming, blood flowing in rivers, and blows raining down like over-ripe pears right under the nose of the blessed San Rocco. The chief of police, the mayor, and the carabinieri all rushed to the scene. The injured were carried off to hospital with broken limbs, and the main troublemakers were clapped into jail for the night. The festival had turned into a Punch and Judy show, and the saint returned to the church at more of a gallop than a walking pace.

It all arose from the envy of the people living in the San Pasquale parish, because that year the devotees of San Rocco had spent a small fortune to put on a grand spectacle. The municipal band had turned up from the city, over two thousand firecrackers had been let off, and there was even a new standard, all embroidered in gold, that was reckoned to weigh a quarter of a ton, and in the midst of the crowd it looked like a splash of real gold. All of this had a diabolic effect on people's nerves in the San Pasquale parish, and in the end one of them lost his patience, turned pale with fury, and began to shout, 'Long live San Pasquale!' That was when the fists started flying.

There can be no doubt about it, to go shouting 'Long live San Pasquale!' right under the nose of San Rocco in person is an act of extreme provocation. It's like someone coming and spitting in your own house, or someone who thinks it amusing to pinch the bottom of the girl you have on your arm. At moments like that, you forget about Christ or the Devil, and abandon even the modicum of respect that you have for the other saints who, after all, are no different from your own. If it happens in church, pews are hurled into the air. If you are in a procession, oaths rain down on you like bats. If you are at table, dishes go flying all over the place.

'Holy Mother of God!' shouted Nino, who was battered and bruised all over. 'I'd just like to see anyone else having the nerve to come along here shouting "Long live San Pasquale!"'

'I will!' screamed Turi the leatherworker, whose sister was engaged to Nino, and who was quite beside himself because of a punch he had picked up in the mêlée, leaving him half-blind. 'Long live San Pasquale to the death!'

'Oh, for the love of God! For the love of God!' shrieked Saridda, Turi's sister, flinging herself between brother and fiancé, who until that moment had always gone about together as the best of friends.

Her fiancé Nino cried out derisively, 'Long live my boots! Long live Saint Boot!'

'Take that!' shouted Turi, foaming at the mouth, his eye swollen and black as an aubergine. 'Take that and put it in your boots. And that for San Rocco!'

The pair of them went on exchanging punches that would have felled an ox until their friends managed to kick and hammer them apart. But by that time Saridda was no less worked up, and shrieking 'Long live San Pasquale!' so loudly that she and her fiancé almost started hitting one another, as if they were already husband and wife.

On these occasions parents come to blows with their children, and wives leave their husbands if a woman from the San Pasquale parish has had the misfortune to marry a man from San Rocco, or vice-versa.

'I never want to hear that fellow's name ever again!' Saridda bellowed, her fists clenched on her hips, to the neighbours who were asking her why the marriage had been called off. 'Not even if they hand him over to me dressed in silver and gold! Do you understand?'

'As far as I'm concerned Saridda can rot in Hell!' Nino said for his part while they were wiping all the blood off his face at the tavern. 'Those leatherworkers are nothing but a gang of beggars and layabouts! I must have been drunk when I took it into my head to go over there to look for a girl-friend.'

'If this is what's going to happen,' the mayor had concluded, 'and people can't carry a saint into the square without coming to blows, which is an absolute disgrace, I want no more festivals and no more forty-hour vigils! And if I hear so much as a single curse being uttered, I'll have them all arrested.'

The situation was in any case building up to a crisis, because the bishop of the diocese had granted the privilege to the canons of San Pasquale of wearing the *mozzetta*,[2] and the parishioners of San Rocco, whose priests had no *mozzetta*, had sent a delegation to Rome to kick up a fuss at the feet of the Holy Father, carrying a petition on official paper and all the rest of it. But it was totally in vain, because the new leather industry had made their opponents from the lower quarter as rich as pigs, although they could remember them going around without any shoes on their feet, and as everybody knows, in this world justice is bought and sold like the soul of Judas.

At San Pasquale they were awaiting the arrival of the bishop's delegate, a man of some importance who, according to those who had seen him, wore silver buckles on his shoes weighing half a pound at the very least. He was bringing the *mozzetta* with him to hand over to the canons; the San Pasquale folk had also hired a band to go and meet him three miles out from the village, and rumour had it that there would be fireworks in the square that evening, with 'Long live San Pasquale!' repeated over and over again in block capitals.

The people living in the upper quarter were thus in a state of considerable unrest, and some of the more excited amongst them fashioned cudgels out of pear or cherry branches as big as ten-foot poles, muttering, 'If there's going to be any music, they'll need someone to beat out the rhythm!'

The bishop's delegate was running a serious risk of ending up with broken limbs from his triumphal entry into the village. But the Reverend was a crafty old bird, and left the band waiting for him outside the village whilst he made his way quietly on foot, using shortcuts, to the house of the parish priest, where he called a meeting of the leaders of the two factions.

When these gentlemen found themselves face to face after quarrelling for so long, they stood there staring at each other as if they had a great longing to tear one another's eyes out, and it required all the authority of the Reverend, who was wearing a new silk hood for the occasion, to arrange for the ice-creams and the other refreshments to be served without incident.

'That's the way to behave!' purred the mayor, with his nose in his glass. 'If you want me to attend a peace gathering, you'll always find me ready and willing.'

The delegate said, in fact, that he had come to reconcile the two parties with the olive twig in his mouth, like Noah's dove, and, entreating them all to keep the peace, he went round handing out the smiles and the handshakes, saying, 'Do come and join me in the sacristy for cocoa, gentlemen, on the day of the festival.'

'Cancel the festival altogether,' said the magistrate, 'otherwise it'll lead to more trouble.'

'What leads to trouble is when they go pushing people around, and nobody is free to do what he wants to do with his own money,' exclaimed Bruno the coachbuilder.

'I shall have no part in it. The Government's instructions are quite clear. If you go ahead with the festival I shall call in the carabinieri. I want public order.'

'I shall answer for that!' exclaimed the mayor, tapping his umbrella on the floor and casting his eyes round the assembly.

'That's a good one!' the magistrate responded. 'As if we didn't know it's Bruno, that brother-in-law of yours, who dictates everything you decide on the Council!'

'You're just making a fuss because you couldn't stomach the fine we slapped on you for hanging out the laundry!'

'Gentlemen! Gentlemen!' the delegate implored. 'If we go on like this we can't start anything.'

'We can start a riot, that's what!' shouted Bruno, waving his arms in the air.

Luckily the parish priest had seen to it that the crockery and glasses were swiftly moved out of harm's way, and the sacristan had left at breakneck speed to pay off the members of the band, who had learnt of the delegate's arrival and were hurrying in to the village to give him a rousing welcome, blowing away on their horns and their clarinets.

'We shan't get anywhere like this!' complained the delegate, who was also annoyed because from his own point of view everything was cut and dried, and yet there he was, wasting his time trying to stop Bruno and the magistrate from killing one another. 'What's all this about a fine for hanging out the laundry?'

'The usual bullying tactics. You can no longer hang out a handkerchief to dry at the window without someone slapping a fine on you. Until now people have always treated authority with respect, and the magistrate's wife, knowing her husband held the office that he did, felt it was safe to hang out the week's washing on the terrace as she always had done. All she needed was a little sympathy, but now, under the new by-law, it's become a mortal sin. I can tell you with the greatest respect that you're not even allowed to keep dogs or chickens or other animals, that up to now have kept our streets free of rubbish. When we get the first rains, may God preserve us all from being drowned in the filthy mess. But the fact is that Bruno has got it in for the magistrate on account of a judgment he gave against him.'

In trying to reconcile the various parties, the delegate was stuck all day long in the confessional like an owl. All the women wanted to be confessed by him because he could give plenary absolution for every kind of sin, as though he were the bishop in person.

'Father!' said Saridda, with her nose right up against the grille of the confessional. 'That Nino makes me sin in church every Sunday.'

'And how does he do that, my daughter?'

'The fellow was to have been my husband, before all these arguments started in the village, but now that the marriage is off, he plants himself near the main altar, staring at me and laughing with his friends the whole time during Holy Mass.'

When the Reverend tried to make Nino see the error of his ways, he replied, 'She's the one to blame. She turns her back on me every time she sees me, as if I were some sort of beggar.'

But the fact was that, whenever Saridda passed through the square on Sundays, he pretended to be a great friend of the police sergeant and various other notables, and never even cast a glance in her direction. Saridda was very busy making fairy-lamps out of coloured paper, and she set them out on her window-sill under his very nose, with the pretext of drying them out. On one occasion when they were both attending a christening, they never even acknowledged each other's presence, as though they were total strangers, and, in fact, Saridda made eyes at the fellow holding his baby girl over the font.

'A fine fellow to be ogling!' sneered Nino. 'All he can do is produce a girl! It's a sure sign when a girl is born that the roof of your house is going to collapse.'

But Saridda, pretending to speak to the mother, said, 'Every cloud has a silver lining. Sometimes, when you think you've lost a treasure, you should be giving thanks to God and San Pasquale. We all have to eat a peck of dirt before we die.'

'That's true. You have to take misfortunes as they come, it's no use crying over spilt milk. When the Pope dies, they make another one.'

'Children are fated to be born the way they are, and marriages are the same. That's why it's better to marry a man who really loves you rather than for some other reason, even if he has nothing, neither mules, nor land, nor property.'

A drum-roll was sounding in the square, summoning the populace.

A whisper went through the crowd. 'The mayor says the festival is going ahead.'

'Over my dead body! I'll spend every penny I possess and end up like Job in nothing but my shirt. And I won't pay that fine, even if I have to lay it down in my will!'

'Bloody hell!' Nino exclaimed. 'What sort of a festival do they think they're going to have when we're all going to die of starvation before the year is out?'

Not a drop of rain had fallen since the month of March, and the crops, all yellow and tinder-dry, were dying of thirst. Bruno the coachbuilder ventured the opinion that once San Pasquale came out in procession it would start raining for certain. But what did it matter to him, a coachbuilder, whether it rained or not, or to all those leatherworkers on his side of the argument? All the same, they did carry San Pasquale in procession to all points of the compass, and even took him to the top of the hill to bless the countryside. It was a sultry day in May,[3] overcast with dark clouds, one of those days when the farmers tear their hair out as they survey the parched fields, and the ears of the crops droop low as if they are dying.

'A curse on San Pasquale!' Nino cried, spitting into the air, and running through the cornfield like a madman. 'You've ruined me, San Pasquale! All you've left me is the sickle to cut my throat with!'

The upper quarter was in despair. It was one of those years when the hunger begins in June, and the women stand about in their doorways doing nothing, their hair in disarray and their eyes staring out in bewilderment. When Saridda heard that Nino's mule was up for sale in the square, so that he could pay the rent for the land that had yielded him nothing, she immediately flew into a rage and sent Turi, her brother, running off to help him out with the few *soldi* they had saved up between them.

Hands in his pockets, Nino was standing in a corner of the square with a faraway look in his eyes as they were selling his mule, all got up in ribbons and a new halter.

'I don't want your charity,' he snarled. 'I still have the use of my arms, thank God! A fine saint, that San Pasquale of yours, eh?'

Turi turned his back on him and walked away so as to avoid a fight. But the truth was that people's nerves were on edge, now that San Pasquale had been carried in procession to all points of the compass to no effect. The worst of it was that many of the San Rocco parishioners had been persuaded to join in the procession, beating their breasts like donkeys and wearing crowns of thorns on their heads, for the sake of the crops. And now they were cursing away so violently that the bishop's delegate had to make good his escape on foot and without a band, in the same way he had come.

To get his own back on the coachbuilder, the magistrate telegraphed to say the people were growing restless and that public order was under threat, with the result that one fine day news began to circulate that soldiers had arrived during the night, and if anyone wanted to see them, he only had to go to the stables.

Others, however, were saying they had come because of the cholera, and that down in the city people were dying like flies.

The chemist bolted the door of his shop, and the doctor was the first to make himself scarce, so as not to be set upon and bumped off.

'It won't come to anything,' said the few people left in the village who hadn't been able to escape to various parts of the countryside. 'San Rocco will keep watch over the village, and if anyone shows his face in the streets after dark we'll kill him.'

Even the people from the lower quarter were rushing barefoot into the church of San Rocco. But before long men and women were going down with the cholera as thick and fast as raindrops before a thunderstorm, and people were saying that So-and-so was a greedy pig who had died on purpose to fill his belly with manna, and that So-and-so had returned from the country in the middle of the night. In other words, the cholera had struck with a vengeance despite the vigil and the beard of San Rocco, and notwithstanding the fact that a pious old woman claimed he had come to her in a dream and told her in person, 'Be not afraid of the cholera, I shall deal with it, for I am not like that good-for-nothing of a San Pasquale.'

Nino and Turi had seen nothing of one another since the affair of the mule, but as soon as Nino heard that brother and sister had both been taken ill, he rushed round to their house to find Saridda lying at the end of the room, her features dark and withered, alongside her brother, whose condition was less serious, but who was at his wits' end to know what to do.

'Ah! Villain of a San Rocco!' Nino sobbed. 'I never expected this of you! Saridda, don't you recognize me? It's Nino, don't you remember?'

Saridda looked at him through eyes so sunken in their sockets that you needed a lantern to find them, while Nino's eyes were gushing like fountains.

'Ah! San Rocco!' cried Nino. 'You've played a worse trick on me than San Pasquale ever did!'

However, Saridda recovered, and as she stood in the doorway, pale as wax, with her scarf wrapped round her head, she said to him, 'San Rocco has performed a miracle for my sake, and we must all go and light a candle to him on his feast day.'

Nino, proud as a peacock, nodded his head in agreement. But then he too caught the disease, and lay at death's door. Saridda clawed at her cheeks, saying that she wanted to die with him, and that she would cut off her hair and lay it in his coffin, and no one would ever set eyes on her again for as long as she lived.

'No! No!' Nino replied, his face all drawn and haggard. 'Your hair will grow again, but I shall be the one who doesn't set eyes on you again.'

'A fine miracle San Rocco has performed on *you*!' Turi said, in an effort to cheer him up a little.

As they both convalesced, warming themselves in the sun with their backs to the wall and scowling at one another, they each kept hurling San Rocco and San Pasquale into the other's face in turn.

When the cholera had run its course, Bruno the coachbuilder returned to the village, and as he was passing by he said, 'We'll have a big festival to thank San Pasquale for saving our lives. There won't be any more opposition from troublemakers, now that the magistrate has gone to glory and left the lawsuit in his will.'

'You're right,' Nino jeered. 'We can thank him for all the people who died!'

'And do we have San Rocco to thank for keeping *you* alive?'

'Do stop it,' Saridda yelled at them, 'or it'll take the cholera to come back before we have any peace!'

How, when and why

Signor Polidori and Signora Rinaldi were in love – or thought they were – which sometimes amounts to the same thing; and if there is such a thing as love on this earth, they were truly made for one another. Polidori enjoyed an income of forty thousand *lire* and a dreadful reputation as a thoroughly bad lot, and Signora Rinaldi was a vapid, pretty little woman with a husband who worked his fingers to the bone to ensure that she could live as though he, too, were earning forty thousand. But she never did anything to provoke the tiniest shred of gossip, even though the proud beauty had aroused the interest of all Polidori's friends, parading before her with flowers in their buttonholes. Finally chance, destiny, the will of God or that of the Devil tugged at the hem of her dress, and the proud beauty fell.

When we say she fell, we mean that she had let fall on Polidori that first soft, languid, come-hither look that causes the serpent hidden at the foot of the tree of seduction to tremble at the knees. Falls at breakneck speed are rare, and they sometimes frighten the serpent away. Before descending from one branch to the next, Signora Rinaldi was careful to see where she should place her feet, and pulled a thousand pretty faces, pretending she really wanted to escape towards the top of the tree. She had perched for about a month on the branch of epistolary contact, an unstable and hazardous branch that stirs in every little scented breeze. They had begun with the excuse of borrowing or returning a book, requiring a piece of information, that sort of thing. The fair lady would have liked to perch for quite a while on that branch, chirping prettily away as only women can, rocking to and fro between heaven and earth. But once he had unburdened himself, Polidori quickly turned monosyllabic, laconic and impatient, like a man driven to despair. The poor dear had no option but to shut her eyes, raise her wings, and allow herself to glide a little lower.

'I didn't read your letter, and I don't intend to!' she told him when she met him at the last ball of the season, as they joined a line of other couples. 'As you are not the gentleman I thought you were, leave me alone to remain as I want to be.'

Polidori gave her a very serious look, twitching his moustache, his head bowed. The other dancers, having no reason to stand chattering in the doorway, pushed them in towards the ballroom. The woman blushed, as though she had been surprised in a secret tête-à-tête with him.

Polidori – the serpent – took note of that fleeting change of colour.

'You know I shall always obey you, whatever happens,' he replied smoothly.

The diamond cross glittered on her bosom as it billowed in triumph. All that evening, a horde of admirers in her wake, Signora Rinaldi danced like a madwoman, choosing a new partner each time she took to the floor. Her eyes were aglow with joy, they sparkled like the gems that swarmed across her heaving bosom. Then suddenly, finding herself face to face with her reflection in a large mirror, she turned very serious and refused to dance another step. To everyone who asked, she replied that she was utterly exhausted, and she looked round instinctively for her husband. There was no sign of the fellow! In the ten minutes she lay sprawled on the sofa, unconcerned with crumpling her dress in so ungainly a fashion, strange visions passed before her eyes, mingling with the waltzing couples. Polidori was not among the dancers, and was nowhere to be seen. What sort of man was he? She caught sight of him later at the end of a deserted room, face to face with a bald-headed man with obviously nothing to say, smiling as usual. Even his smile was one of indifference. On her word of honour, she would rather have surprised him in the company of the belle of the ball. Polidori was not to know that. He stood up, solicitous as ever, and offered her his arm.

At that very moment, who should turn up out of the blue but her husband, who had been looking all over for her. She turned smartly on her heels and, adjusting the neckline of her dress with a pretty little jerk of the shoulder, she said to Polidori, so softly that the rustling of the silk almost smothered the sound of her voice, 'Very well, tomorrow at nine, in the Gardens.'

Polidori made a deep bow as, radiant and overjoyed, she passed by him on her husband's arm.

Never in her charming Brianza[1] villa had a spring morning seemed so mysteriously beautiful to Signora Rinaldi, and never had she gazed with more distracted eyes, through the gleaming coupé window, as when her carriage was rapidly crossing Piazza Cavour. The avenues of the Gardens were flooded with the warm, golden light of the sun, shining down from a deep blue sky on to new green grass. She was quite unaware that all of this was being reflected in her big, dark eyes as she looked into the distance, knowing neither what she would find, nor where, whilst leaning her hand and pale forehead against the head-rest. Every so often, whether because she was cold or feeling tired, she was seized by an involuntary shudder of the shoulders.

When the carriage stopped at the gate, she was filled with alarm and drew back in her seat, as though her husband had suddenly appeared at the window. She paused for a moment before stepping out, holding on to the handle of the carriage-door and musing, as in a dream, over how her husband seemed now to appear in a different light. Then, stepping to the ground, she covered her face with her thickly embroidered dark black veil, through which her eyes began to glow with excitement as her features turned pale as death. The carriage moved swiftly off, making no noise, being the sort of carriage that was discreet and well brought up.

The Gardens, too, seemed to have awoken earlier than usual, completely taken by surprise to be starting the day so early. Men in shirt sleeves were busy washing down the Gardens, putting a comb through them, giving them their morning's beauty treatment. The few people she encountered gave one the impression they were there for the first time at that hour of day, and on doctor's orders. They attempted to penetrate the veil of the lady taking her morning stroll, and to identify the scent of the handkerchief concealed in the muff she held tightly to her breast. An old man, dragging himself slowly along in search of the early spring sun, stopped to gaze at her as she overtook him, leaned unsteadily on his stick, and sadly shook his head.

Signora Rinaldi paused at the edge of the lake, glancing cautiously this way and that to see whether anything or anyone was about. As she stood there all alone, listening to the murmuring of the ripples on the surface of the water and the gentle rustling of the chestnut trees, she raised her veil a little, and from her glove she drew out a tiny note, smaller than a playing card. For two or three minutes the rippling of the water and the rustling of the leaves continued of their own accord. As the woman stood there, wholly absorbed in her dreams, a tear came into her eyes.

Suddenly, the sound of rapid footsteps caused her to lift her head, and the blood welled up in her cheeks, as though the ardent expression of the newcomer had grazed her face with a kiss. Just as Polidori was about to raise his hand to his hat, she prevented the gesture with an imperceptible glance in his direction, then walked straight past without looking at him.

She walked with eyes cast downward, listening to the sand crunching beneath her pretty little boots, without looking ahead of her. Every so often she covered her mouth with her handkerchief to breathe in deeply, as though her heart was greedily gulping down all the air around her. Murmuring *sotto voce*, the peaceful flow of the stream escorted her softly along; the shade of the cedars and the silence of the deserted avenue stabbed her gently with a sweet sensation of desire.

When she stopped at the leopard's cage, her heart came near to bursting and she trembled at the knees as Polidori, too, halted at her side, fixed his gaze on the proud beast with the stupefied expression of a peasant cast down on that spot by accident, and whispered, 'Thank you!'

She offered no reply, blushed a deep crimson, and took a firm hold on the bars of the safety fence, against which she was resting her forehead. As she did so, a pleasant sensation coursed along the skin of her gloveless hand. Who would ever have imagined that such a delicious feeling could stem from so simple a greeting in so deserted a place! A woman could lose her head completely over it! She felt she was on fire down to the back of her neck, which Polidori, standing behind her, could see turning red. A tempestuous flood of jumbled words came into her head. She told him that her husband had left the house at dawn, whereas she had lain awake all night, thinking what a wonderful time she had had at the ball.

'But I'm not a bit tired! This cool air's good for you, it's wonderful! Changes your outlook on life, doesn't it?'

'Yes! That's true!' Polidori replied, staring at her eyes, which she dared not raise towards him.

'When I go to Brianza I intend to get up with the sun every day. We live such impossible lives in the city. But I suppose you gentlemen prefer it.'

She spoke rapidly, her voice a shade too shrill and high-pitched, her lips often parting at random into a smile. Without being aware of it, she was grateful to find him so reluctant to interrupt what she was saying, to mingle his voice with hers.

Eventually Polidori said, 'But why didn't you ask me to call on you at home?'

For the first time that morning, she looked him straight in the eye with a shocked and pained expression. In nothing they had done until now, in nothing they had said, had any wrong ever been intended, except perhaps in an exquisitely delicate way that her ultra-sensitive nature had savoured agreeably, just as the leopard lying there at their feet loved to bask in the rays of the sun, blinking its wide, golden eyes in the warmth, and sensually stretching out its limbs, with that same unawareness. Summoned back so brusquely to reality, she clenched her fists and puckered her lips in an expression of deep sorrow. Her eyes became clouded with tears as the magical spell of her reverie was broken, and she fixed her desolate gaze upon him. All the experience Polidori possessed could do nothing to unravel the meaning of what he was seeing.

'Yes!' she exclaimed, changing her tone of voice. 'It would have been more prudent, would it not?'

'How cruel you are!' Polidori murmured.

'No!' she replied, raising her head and blushing a little, but in a firm voice. 'I'm not like all the other ladies, I'm not prudent! When I decide to break my neck, I want to savour the horror of looking down into the abyss! So much the worse for you if you don't understand.'

He then took her hand firmly into his, devouring all of her pulsating beauty with ravenous eyes, and stammered, 'Will you, then? Will you?'

She did not reply, and made an effort to withdraw her hand.

Polidori implored her compliance in tones of deep agitation, of delirium almost. He repeated the same question, the same entreaty, with different inflections of the voice aimed at penetrating the most intimate core of the woman's being. Her whole body glowed from the warmth of his passion, she had the delicious sensation of being utterly devoured and swept off her feet. Pale, anxious, her lips trembling, she tried to release herself, casting her terror-stricken eyes up and down the avenue, twisting this way and that under his powerful grip, making an effort with both of her feverish hands to tear herself free from that other hand, which she could feel burning hotly beneath her glove.

In the end, no longer able to control her feelings, she murmured 'Yes! Yes!' then took to her heels at the sound of approaching footsteps.

As she left the Gardens her head was in such a whirl that she almost stepped under a horse and carriage. She had made a lovers' tryst! That was a tryst! In a low murmur she repeated it to herself over and over again, 'A tryst! A tryst!' The word took over her whole being, she was intoxicated by it, she spoke it on her pale lips without uttering a sound, dreamily savouring a sense of guilt.

She walked unsteadily up to the first carriage she saw, and gave instructions to be taken to Erminia's house, as though seeking help. When her friend saw her approaching with so anxious a look, she rushed to meet her at the door of the drawing-room.

'What is it?'

'It's nothing! Nothing at all!'

'How lovely you look! What's the matter?'

Instead of replying, she threw her arms round her neck and gave her two wild kisses.

Erminia was accustomed to Maria's extravagant displays of friendship. The pair of them cast their eyes over photographs they had seen a hundred times before, then emerged on the balcony to admire the flowers that had been in bloom for the past month.

At that moment, Polidori happened to be passing by the house in the open carriage of his friend Guidetti, a cigar between his lips, and he gave Erminia the sort of greeting he could have given to Maria, if he had caught sight of her as she crouched behind the shrubs, her hands pressed tightly to her heart as if to prevent it from bursting. It was nothing, but it was one of those nothings that pierce a woman's breast like the point of a needle. So when she got home, Signora Rinaldi wrote Polidori a long letter, asking him in a calm and dignified manner to forget about their appointment, to which she had agreed in a moment of aberration, a moment that continued to fill her with shame and remorse. There was so much sincerity in the denial of her feelings towards him that an hour after the event, that moment in which she had surrendered seemed to lie in the remote past; and if, reading between the lines of her letter, some tiny echo could still be heard, it was simply her regret over dreams that vanished so rapidly. She appealed to his sense of honour and his delicacy of feeling to help her forget the error of her ways and restore her self-esteem.

Polidori had been half-expecting her letter. Signora Rinaldi was too inexperienced a woman not to repent several times over before repenting in earnest. He did something that showed how this pretty, untutored little woman had reawakened his deep and genuine feelings with all the freshness of first impressions: he sent back her letter together with this brief reply.

> I love you with all the respect and tenderness that your innocence must inspire. I am returning the letter you addressed to me, because I am unworthy of keeping it, and I would not venture to destroy it. But your boldness in writing such a letter is the clearest proof that all true gentlemen must hold you in their highest esteem.

'My husband!' exclaimed Maria in a strange tone of voice. 'My husband couldn't be happier! The ups and downs of the market are just to his liking, silk's been doing well, orders are flooding in from all over the place. He's making fifty per cent clear profit.'

Erminia stared at her open-mouthed.

'Listen, darling, you're feverish. Let's make some tea.'

Two days later, to recover from the fever that Erminia had told her about, she told her, 'I'm going with my husband to Brianza. The fresh air, the oxygen, the peace and quiet, the song of the nightingales . . . A pity we don't have children to rock off to sleep!'

There, beneath the verdant trees, gazing out on broad horizons, in a strange sort of way she was annoyed, despite herself, by the sensation of calm her surroundings induced in her. As evening approached, she would often climb, muddying her pretty little boots, to nearby beauty spots, where she would fill her head on purpose with sentiments borrowed from novels. Polidori had the good manners to stay out of sight, remaining in Milan without making any dramatic or conventional move, as though determined to be polite even to the point of letting her forget him. Nor could she say for certain whether she still thought about him; rather was she filled with aspirations of an indefinable sort to keep her company in her solitude. They wrapped her tenderly and inseparably in a vulnerable state of inertia, and spoke for her in the sombre silence that encircled her and kept her in its shadow. She gave vent to her feelings by writing long letters to Erminia, singing the praises of the hidden delights of the countryside, the Angelus echoing round the valleys, the sun rising over the mountains. She told her how many eggs the steward's wife had collected, and how much wine they would be bottling that autumn.

'Tell me a little more about your books and your outings on horse-back,' Erminia replied. 'Tell your husband to keep you away from the chicken-run, or keep you company.'

One day, having no word from her Maria for a while and feeling slightly anxious, she set off, and went to pay her a visit.

'Were you worried about me?' she said. 'Did you think I was in total despair, ready to do away with myself?'

'No. I thought you might be getting bored, cooped up here in this absolute wilderness, with only God or the Devil to turn to. Come with me to the Villa d'Este.² You won't object, Rinaldi, will you, if I deprive you of her company?'

'I want only for her to enjoy life and be happy.'

★

Life was certainly enjoyable at the Villa d'Este, what with music, dancing, sailing, trips by steamer, excursions to the country nearby, lots of people, beautiful dresses, and Polidori, who was the life and soul of all the parties.

Signora Rinaldi was unaware that he, too, was there; and if, indeed, Polidori could have foreseen that she was coming to the Villa d'Este, he would have had the good manners to be elsewhere. But by this time he had accepted the role of organizer for the boat races, and was unable to move without attracting people's notice before the races had finished. He explained all this in a few nicely turned phrases to Signora Rinaldi when they first came across one another in the salon, making obscure apologies to her, and skating unconcernedly over what had happened between them. Once Maria had got over her initial shock, not only did she feel reassured but in a strange sort of way his self-contained demeanour stirred violent feelings of contempt within her. He told her he would be leaving as soon as the races were over, because he had promised to join some friends of his in Piedmont for a big hunting party, and he was truly sorry to be leaving behind so many lovely ladies at the Villa d'Este.

'Are you really?' Signora Rinaldi asked, with a smile. 'Which one do you like best?'

'Oh . . . all of them,' Polidori calmly replied. 'Your friend Erminia, for instance.'

What a revelation! The thought had never entered her head, but her friend Erminia must have turned many a gentleman's head in her direction on account of that lively little face and the spirit of devilry she had about her. She was so indifferent to the respect to which she was naturally entitled, being married to a marquis, and one of those marchionesses who wear their tiaras with pride, that there was no man on earth who would not die happily for her sake.

She and her friend Erminia were always together, whether boating on the lake, walking in the hills, sitting in the salon, or resting in the shade of the trees. But now she observed her every move as if she was seeing her for the first time. She studied her, copied her, and sometimes went so far as to envy her over something quite trivial. Without wishing to, she had discovered that her friend Erminia, for all her regal airs, was a bit of a flirt, the sort of flirt who never committed herself, but who nevertheless had all the men eating from the palm of her hand. It was a serious business! They could not go anywhere without running into Polidori, the handsome Polidori, pursued by all those society ladies, who was badly compromising her friend Erminia without appearing to know it. But the worst of it was that she herself seemed equally unaware, and not everyone was convinced by the way she laughingly dismissed the whole thing. But for the fact that the subject was so delicate, Signora Rinaldi would have had a word in her friend's ear to impress upon her how falsely her denials always rang.

So she tried not to give her the slightest hint of the distress that all these manoeuvrings were causing her, being very concerned about Erminia's welfare, naturally, whereas Polidori was of no importance to her. He, after all, was a man, he was his own master, and besides, he was the kind of person who would always find comfort elsewhere. Erminia, on the other hand, had everything to lose from playing this sort of game, with a husband like hers, who loved her and was truly the ideal husband. What magic power did Polidori possess, then, for him to supplant a man like the Marquis Gandolfi in the affections of such a beautiful, intelligent and admired woman as Erminia? Certain things defy logical explanation.

Nothing in the world would have made her want a living soul to notice what was happening, and she would have liked to close her eyes to everyone else, just as Erminia was doing; but quite frankly, one's patience could only stretch so far.

'My dear, I just don't understand,' said Erminia, laughing, coolly and collectedly, as if she had nothing to do with it. 'What's the matter? I sometimes feel as though I've done you some terrible wrong without knowing it!'

Oh dear! How could her poor Erminia remain so blind to what was happening? It was a constant torment to see how she was becoming entangled so mindlessly in such a messy affair, or rather, allowing herself to become entangled, because that Polidori was winding her round his little finger with the cunning of the Devil. The fellow must have done a great deal of wrong in his time, to have become such a master of deception He truly was a bad lot!

'Maria, my dear!' Erminia said one fine day, giving her a big kiss. 'You seem to be filling up your head far too much with that Polidori. You must be careful! He's too dangerous an individual for a child like you!'

'Like me?' she replied, utterly amazed. 'Me . . . ?' She was struck dumb under Erminia's penetrating gaze.

'That's good! Good! I was beginning to worry about you. Good!'

Considering she was only a child, thought Maria, her friend Erminia should be taking more notice of how she was feeling. Some things are so obvious!

For elegant suitors, fixed-hour Casanovas during the stroll in the garden or at evening concerts, or womanizers wearing chamois-leather gloves, Signora Rinaldi felt nothing but contempt. Once, when Polidori allowed himself to make one or two polite remarks in his defence, she burst out laughing straight into his face.

He seemed to turn pale. The fellow was finally turning pale! If other women buzzed round Polidori like bees round a honeypot, they were the ones who should take the blame for spoiling him.

'Don't tell anyone,' she added. 'It would make me feel very sorry.'

'For whom?'

'For you, for me . . . for the others. For everyone.'

This time, refusing to let her sarcasm put him off his stride, he calmly replied, 'I would only be sorry for you alone.'

She was just about to hit him between the eyes with another salvo of that pitiless, mordant wit of hers, but the laughter died on her lips because of the way those two words – you alone – altered his whole appearance.

'You can insult me,' he replied, 'but you have no right to mistrust the feelings you have sown in my heart.'

Maria, overcome, lowered her head.

'Have I not carried out your wishes to the full? Have I ever asked you for an explanation? Did I not foresee in advance what you wanted of me? Have I not managed to pretend I had forgotten what no man on earth would be able to forget . . . coming from you? And if I suffered on that account, did anyone on earth see that I was suffering?'

He spoke in a calm voice, in such a tranquil manner that the placatory words he uttered took on an air of irresistible eloquence.

'So you . . . !' Maria stammered.

'I!' Polidori replied. 'I, who love you still, and would never ever have told you.'

She, who had paused to pluck leaves from the bushes, now took a few steps to distance herself from him, poor child! Polidori took not a single one to follow her.

Signora Rinaldi suddenly took on a dreamlike, melancholy air. She sat for hours on end with her book open at the same page, with her fingers wandering over the keyboard of the piano, or with her needlework draped over her knees, staring out at the water, the mountains, and the stars. The surface of the lake reflected every trace of the indefinite thoughts running through her mind, and she experienced an exquisite delight as she sat there and listened to them echoing within her, completely engrossed and absorbed. And so she stayed away from all the convivial gatherings, preferring to go alone by boat around the lake, when the mountains were casting deep green shadows over its surface, when the oars gleamed like swords of steel in the gathering gloom, and the magenta-coloured rays of the sun were disappearing sorrowfully into the dusk. She drew the curtain across between herself and the boatmen, lay back on the cushions, and revelled in the feeling that she was cradled over the abyss, drawn into it almost, as she trailed a hand in the water and felt her whole body quiver with a mysterious sense of well-being. She loved to stare out into the endless darkness, beyond the stars, and to imagine what some tiny distant light, flickering in the dark on the mountainside, was shining down upon. She would set off in search of grass-lined, shady paths in the silence of the mysterious woods, or to delight in the spectacle of the lake at the time of day when the sun was shining down upon it as though on to a looking-glass, or of the hotel when all its shutters were still closed, and the dew glistened on the grass of the lawn, and thick shadows lay beneath the huge trees, and the crunching sound of the sand beneath her feet whispered into her ears, evoking magical daydreams. She would often go and read or stroll by the lakeside, along remote paths of the Campi Elisi,[3] when the moon sat gently above the lake and caressed her pale hands, or when the hotel windows pierced the gloom of the avenue with broad rectangular shafts of cold light, and the music coming from the salon stirred up arcane visions within the mute and dormant shadows of the giant trees. From beyond those strange shadows, behind those brightly lit windows, the veiled and deadened motion of the party inside took on a blend of outlines, colours, and sounds that gave it a strangely fascinating air, akin to something between an orgy and a dance of winged spirits. There she remained, looking in and resting her forehead against the window-panes, a slight sensation of tingling at the roots of her hair.

Then one evening, she suddenly turned up in the midst of the dancers like some captivating vision, paler and more lovely than ever. There was something no one had ever seen about her eyes and her lips, and, overawed by her looks, everyone stood aside to let her through. Erminia ran up to embrace her, and a swarm of handsome young men crowded round her to extract the promise of a waltz or a square dance. She stopped for a moment to look around, with that same smile on her lips, her eyes shining out like fireflies in the avenue, and when she spotted Polidori she dropped her handkerchief at his feet.

'God save the queen!' Polidori exclaimed, bending his knee.

'You see!' Maria said to Erminia, brimming with high spirits. 'I'm stealing your dancing partner. I'm simply dying to take the floor myself, for a change.'

Polidori was one of those dancers the ladies compete for with sweet smiles and fan-rapping over the palms of their hands, when their smiles have been overdone. He combined bodily strength with elegance, verve with tenderness, and no one could match his way of transporting you to your seventh heaven with a sharp tap of the back of his heel, setting you gently down on his right arm as if on a velvet cushion. It was said that he alone possessed that exquisite skill of Strauss for taking away your breath and your sanity, knowing as he did how to charge his arm, his muscles, his whole body with passion, abandon, and ecstasy.

'I don't want you to dance any more. I don't want you to dance with anyone else,' Maria told him as she came to a stop, breathless, misty-eyed and red in the face. And that, for that evening, was that.

Ah! how triumphant she felt, and how her heart pounded in her breast, as her envied dancing partner led her through the throng of her admirers, and thence, as she wrapped her black stole tightly round her shoulders, out into the avenue where the sounds of revelry grew weaker, and vague, formless visions came longingly again into being! It was as though she was suspended in a delicious dream, when the waltz gave way to a Mendelssohn nocturne, a nocturne that, like the waltz, flowed across her forehead, hair and shoulders like a fresh and fragrant velvet hand. Without prior warning a dark figure interposed itself between herself and the window pouring its light on to the avenue; like a shadow her dream came suddenly to life before her eyes. Startled, she stood up, dazed and bewildered, murmuring something or other that meant 'No! No! No!' and made her escape to the salon, taking refuge in the noise and the light. She half closed her eyes in the dazzling light, and the noise, agreeably deafening to the ears, left her looking stunned, rather stiff and thoughtful, a smile hovering about her lips. Erminia folded her in her arms like an adorable plaything. The ladies agreed that she looked a real picture, surrounded as she was by all those adventure-hunters, elegant to a fault, with her back to the wall, like a fawn huddled against a steep cliff-face. You would have said that the hint of a tear of surrender flickered in her eyes.

Polidori, like a hunter destined by fate to administer the *coup de grâce*, was one of the last to assail her, and seemed to be feeling pity for his victim, for he spoke very gravely to her about the weather, restricted his wooing to a minimum, and, showing much concern, asked her about things of no great importance, such as whether she had taken her trip by boat on the lake, and whether she would be going to the Campi Elisi next morning. Without replying, she looked into his eyes. He questioned her no further.

Erminia had seated herself at the piano, and everyone fixed their attention on her playing. Maria only had eyes for her, even when she turned them vaguely towards daydreams of the unknown, for it was Erminia who was creating those visions and enticing her to pursue them. The whole of the warm splendid ballroom reverberated with melodic sound. It was one of those fatal moments when the heart swells within the breast, overpowering all reason.

Maria trembled from head to toe as she sank deeper into the armchair, forehead resting on hand, while Polidori whispered impassioned words into her ear, that caused the curls of the hair to quiver above the back of her lily-white neck. The poor woman could no longer take in a thing, neither the gleaming ballroom nor the throng charged with emotion, nor Erminia's bright and piercing eyes, and she yielded to what she believed to be her destiny, drained of strength and glassy-eyed, like a dying woman.

'Yes! Yes!' she murmured, with a sigh.

Polidori walked slowly away to allow her time to recover, and went off to smoke a cigarette in the billiard room.

The breeze from the lake kept the flames of the candelabras on her mantelpiece aflutter the whole night long, as she stared into the mirror for hours on end without seeing herself, her eyes staring, afire with the fever of it all.

Signor Polidori had been walking for some time along the path at an hour of the morning that reminded him of a hunt meeting. He remained oblivious to the wonderful scenery except for casting his eyes across it impatiently and at great length. All of a sudden he stopped to listen, and raised his head like a greyhound. Finally the light and timid footfall of his elegant prey could be heard. Maria came into view, and as soon as she saw Polidori, though she knew she would find him there, she was alarmed, and suddenly stopped in her tracks, still as a statue. Her fine, classic profile seemed to cut through her thick black veil. Polidori raised his hat and bowed deeply, daring neither to touch her hand nor say a single word to her.

Anxious and out of breath, she instinctively realized how embarrassing it was for the silence to continue.

'I'm tired!' she mumbled.

She was choking with emotion, and as she spoke she set off again along the path winding up the hillside. He walked along beside her without a word; both were overcome by the strength of their feelings. Finally they came to a kind of funeral monument. Maria came abruptly to a stop, leant back against the rock wall with her face in her hands, and eventually burst into tears, whereupon he took her hands in his and, slavelike, implanted a gentle kiss upon them.

When at last he felt a lessening of the tremor of those poor little hands, he said softly, but in tones of ineffable tenderness, 'Are you afraid of me, then?'

'You don't despise me for coming, do you?' said Maria.

He pressed his hands together in a gesture of ardent passion and exclaimed, 'I? Despise you? Never!'

Maria raised her troubled face, stared at him wide-eyed, and, with the tears still visible on her cheeks, she stammered out a series of jumbled and meaningless phrases. 'It's the first time! I swear to you! Do believe me!'

'Ah!' exclaimed Polidori impetuously. 'Why do you say that to me? To the one who loves you? To the one who loves you so deeply!'

His words pounded away inside her like some living thing. She held them tightly inside her breast with both hands, at the same time closing her eyes. But at once they blazed forth on her cheeks, as if they had sped through the whole of her body in a flash, and set all her veins on fire.

'No! No!' she kept saying. 'It's wicked of me! It's very wicked! I made a mistake! Do believe me, sir! It's not my fault; I made a mistake! I'm a child, really, everyone says so, even my best friends.' Poor woman! She tried to smile, staring wildly this way and that. 'I need to know you don't despise me for coming!'

'Maria!' Polidori cried out.

Startled, she drew back abruptly, alarmed at the sound of her own name.

Polidori bowed his head towards her, and in humble, tender, loving tones he said, 'How lovely you are! And how lovely it is to be alive for moments like these!'

Maria passed her hands over her eyes and through her hair. Confused and bewildered, she stumbled backwards, and like a machine she repeated over and over again, 'If you only knew what an effort it was to get myself here, along the path I walk along every day. I would never have believed it would need so much effort. Honestly! I would never have believed it!' She smiled to bolster her courage, without daring to look in his direction, allowing the rock face behind her to take the weight of her body, pulling her gloves up over her arms, that were still shaking a little, and continuing to talk to herself like a child cheering itself up as it walks along the road in the dark. 'Poor little me! Yes, I know what a featherbrained person I am! I have these mad ideas about living in a world that perhaps is only a dream, a dream of a mind that's diseased, if you like! Sometimes I feel I'm being choked by all the reason of our world, I feel the need of fresh air, of climbing up high to breathe it in, where it's more pure and closer to the blue of the sky. It's not my fault if I can't accept how foolish I am, if I can't resign myself to the world as it is, if I can't understand what concerns other people. Of course it isn't my fault. I've tried my best. I'm a few hundred years behind the time. I should have been born when knights errant were roaming the earth.' Her hesitant smile had a sorrowful sweetness about it, as she yielded unawares to the magic that she herself had helped to create. 'You're so lucky to be able to live your life in your own way!'

'I would simply like to live at your feet.'

'Your whole life?'

'My whole life.'

'You'll tire yourself out if you're not careful,' she gaily replied. 'You must tire yourself out quite often!' Maria spoke these words in as bold and confident a manner as she could manage.

Polidori found her charming in the embarrassment she displayed, but it was lasting too long for his liking.

At the very last moment before coming to meet him, as she was passing through the door, Maria had experienced all the conflicting emotions aroused by the lure of the unknown, the attraction of sin, the thrill of the fear that coursed through her veins with arcane, irresistible tremors. She was gripped by a whole mass of contradictory feelings and ideas, of misgivings and impulses that had driven her to fling herself helter-skelter into the unknown, into a kind of somnambulistic trance, without knowing what exactly she was intending to do. If Polidori had held out his arms to her on first catching sight of her, she would probably have beaten her head against the rock on which at this moment she was gently allowing herself to lean. But now, reassured by seeing that envied and sought-after man at her feet, she derived a delicious sensation from the velvet-smooth moss that was caressing her back, just as the tender and passionate words he whispered were sweetly caressing her ears, and gently pervading the whole of her body with exquisite feelings of languor. He was so good, so kind, so considerate!

He would not even dare to touch the tips of her fingers, being content gently to let her bathe in the ardent breath of his passion, which left him prostrate at her feet as though before an idol. In all of this, there was no hint of transgression, it was just wonderful. Polidori had gradually taken her by the hand which, all unawares, she had held out towards him. He too was deeply and sincerely moved at that moment, and tried to gaze into her eyes with a look of inebriated longing. She felt the flames of his longing but dared not raise her eyes, and the laughter died on her lips. She attempted over and over again to withdraw her hand, but hadn't the strength to do it, as though the sound of his words had lulled her, body and soul, into the sweetest of sweet dreams, transported her into a state of agonizing ecstasy.

In the attitude she had assumed, Polidori was unable to take his eyes off her as she stood there lost to the world, her arms quite still, her head bowed, her breast heaving with emotion, and finally, in an outburst of passion, he stretched out his trembling arms and exclaimed, 'How beautiful you are, Maria, and how I love you!'

She raised herself up abruptly, looking stern and serious, as though she were hearing it said to her for the first time.

'You know how deeply I love you, and for how long!' he repeated.

She offered no reply, but arched her whole body backwards and lowered her head in distrust, knitting her brows and instinctively waving her arms as if trying to protect herself, her lips pale and tightly closed. Then, suddenly, resting her eyes on his anguished features and meeting his gaze, she gave out a strangled cry and retreated to the entrance of the nearby sepulchral monument, white with terror, defending herself with outstretched arms against this passion which terrified her now that she had met it face to face for the first time and knew what it involved.

'Please . . . ! Oh, please . . . !' she murmured.

Beside himself, he implored her once again in an animated entreaty of delirium and love, 'Maria! Maria!'

'No!' she repeated in tones of bewilderment. 'No . . . !'

Polidori stopped in his tracks, and passed a hand over his forehead and his eyes in a gesture of despair. Then, in a voice now hoarse, he said, 'You've never loved me, Maria!'

'No! No! Let me go!' she repeated, when already Polidori had stepped back. 'Please . . . ! Oh, please . . . !'

Despite himself, Polidori shared the powerful emotion of this moment, and he too, like the poor ingenuous woman, was trembling all over.

'You must listen,' she said, utterly convulsed. 'We've done wrong! I swear it was wrong of us! I swear it, I swear it. We've done wrong . . .' She felt as if she were about to faint.

At that moment, they suddenly heard a noise among the trees, and the sound of someone's footsteps stopped no great distance away, as if the person was hesitant to go on.

'Maria!' called a voice so perturbed that neither of them recognized it. 'Maria!'

Polidori, having instantly become his normal self again, took Maria by the arm and pushed her firmly towards the path in the direction from which the voice was coming, and disappeared in a flash in the maze of the burial ground. On reaching the path, Maria found herself face to face with Erminia, likewise pale in the face, who was making a strenuous effort to hide her concern, and wanting to explain something to her, with an air of indifference. Maria looked her between the eyes with a strange expression.

'What is it?' she asked simply, in a hollow voice, after what seemed like an eternity.

'Ah! Maria . . . !' Erminia replied, throwing her arms round her neck.

And that was all. Walking side by side, they made their way back, heads bowed, without uttering a word. But as the hotel came into view, they both felt the need to put on a brave face.

'Lucia told me you'd gone for a walk in the garden,' said Erminia, 'and that gave me the idea of doing the same, with the excuse of coming to look for you.'

'Thank you!' Maria replied, simply.

'But it's beginning to get too late for taking a walk. The sun's already hot.'

Maria had taken such a strong touch of the sun, in fact, that she had been dazzled and stunned by it. It had left her feeling utterly shaken and confused. At times she could be found clasping her hands tightly together, as if to make sure they were really her own, or to find something there, some trace of what had happened, and she would close her eyes in a sort of trance. Whenever people stared at her, and all eyes were cast inquisitively in her direction, or simply those of her friend, her face would turn a bright crimson. She stayed out of sight in her apartment as much as she could, so much so that many people thought she had left. The mere sight of Erminia would cause her to knit her brows, and a sort of cloud would come over her features. Yet she had enough savoir-faire to be able to conceal to some extent whatever it was she was feeling. Erminia, who was not taken in by it all, felt truly sorry for her.

'I'm still your one and only Erminia, you know!' she would say whenever she got the chance, taking Maria's hands lovingly into her own. 'I'm still your Erminia, the same as I always was, and always will be!'

Wrapped in thought, Maria gave her a gentle hint of a smile.

'You're wrong, you know!' said Erminia. 'You're mistaken . . . ! You're mistaken, if you think I don't love you as much as ever!'

She always, in fact, displayed much motherly concern for her Maria, a concern which often irritated the other woman, as though it were a way of keeping her under discreet and affectionate supervision.

One day Erminia took her by surprise as she was starting to read a letter, and simply asked her whether it was from her husband. The question was so ill-timed that Maria almost blushed, as though she were on the point of telling a lie.

'No, my husband doesn't spoil me that much! He's too busy.'

'Oh, yes, of course, he's too busy!' Erminia repeated, without taking in the irony of her reply. 'Terribly busy. The poor man's up to his neck in his affairs.'

'What do you mean? He lives for his business. It's his one and only passion.'

'Do you really think so?' Erminia asked, fixing her with those big, knowing eyes of hers.

'But of course!' Maria replied, a smile hovering at the corners of her lips. Then she added, by way of a corrective, 'I have no reason to be jealous, though. My husband never gambles, never spends his time in cafés, never goes hunting, never goes riding, never reads anything but the prices on the stock exchange. And that's the honest truth!'

'Yes, I know. You are the only woman he loves!'

Maria bowed her head and forced herself to smile. For a while she sat without saying a word, and then, in a regretful tone of voice, 'You're right. I'm not worthy of him!'

'No, that isn't the point. You're a spoilt little woman, with a cracked little brain, that gets certain things wrong and doesn't see some others. Your husband's only fault is not to have made you realize how deeply he loves you.'

'Luckily he relied on you to tell me.'

'Yes, and I love you as well, I really do! Shall we leave here tomorrow?'

'Oh, I don't know about that.'

'Don't you want to?'

'It's not that I don't want to. It's just the sudden way you ask me that takes me by surprise, as though it were a play that was written by a pair of young women who have drafted a romantic novel.'

'I'm sorry, I was just asking whether you would come with me. But if you prefer to stay . . .'

'No, I want to come too. Only we must think of a plausible pretext, so as to prevent our inquisitive fellow-residents from thinking about the novel when they see us packing our cases in such a hurry.'

'We already have the perfect excuse, especially because it happens to be true. I'm going to meet my mother-in-law who arrives tomorrow from Florence, and you naturally are coming with me, so as not to be left here by yourself at the Villa d'Este.'

'Excellent! Since leave we must, the sooner we leave the better. I want to go by the first train.'

They left the hotel, in fact, early next morning. Her heart was pounding as she passed by the shuttered windows, on which the shadow of the tall trees was still asleep, and as she left behind the now-deserted avenue through which she had wandered so often, dreaming her dreams.

In the still of the early morning, the lake had a singular magic about it, and the surrounding landscape came alive down to the tiniest detail as though it were a living part of her own being, leaving a lasting impression in the depths of her heart. As soon as she was settled in the railway carriage, she opened the book she had brought along on purpose, and hid her face and tear-filled eyes behind it. Erminia pretended not to notice, and had the good sense to leave her to luxuriate blissfully in the sorrow of the parting.

They found Erminia's carriage awaiting them at the station, and Erminia insisted on taking her friend with her back to her house.

'Rinaldi is not in Milan,' she said, in response to Maria's look of surprise on finding nobody there to meet her. 'He's gone to Rome.'

'Without writing to tell me!' Maria murmured. 'Without sending me any word!'

'He did write. His letter will be with my husband.'

She suddenly broke off, as she was beginning to grow alarmed at the concern becoming evident on Maria's face.

'Oh, very well,' she said, 'you'll have to be told sooner or later. Rinaldi's hurried off to Rome to put his affairs in order. You know how it is. When you're doing business at a distance it doesn't always go as it should. Your husband was worried. By going to Rome he'll put everything right.'

'What's it about?' whispered Maria, who was now even more concerned because, coming at that moment, the news had taken her by surprise. 'What's happened?'

'Don't be alarmed. Your husband is fine. It's just that one of his debtors has gone into liquidation. It's a question of funds.'

'Ah!' said Maria, with a sigh. Her face betrayed a hint of the irony of it all.

It looked as if her husband was deliberately doing all he could to justify her bitter little smile. He was so worried about his business that nothing else in the world could penetrate his thoughts. Several days went by without any further word from him. Then finally a telegram arrived that filled his business partner with great consternation, and he left at once for Rome.

'Oh!' exclaimed Maria, in the worried tone of voice that had become habitual with her over the previous week. 'It really must be a serious business! But then, to my husband all business is serious. At a time like this, my place must be at his side. He doesn't write to tell me anything, of course, because he doesn't want to upset me. But now that his partner has gone to see him, I must go as well.'

Although Erminia put on an air of nonchalance, Maria was surprised to find that she approved of her decision, which made her feel uneasy. For a moment a black thought crossed her mind, draining her face of its colour, but she soon recovered her composure and gave another of her nervous little laughs.

'If my husband hadn't trained me never to interfere in his business, I really would have reason to be alarmed.'

'Alarmed over what? Making a journey to Rome? At the best time of year, and through such wonderful countryside?'

'You're right. It'll be like going on holiday. Whether Rome or Brianza, they're both the same to me. What about you? Will you be going back to the Villa d'Este?'

'No.'

'Oh . . . !'

'I shall take my mother-in-law back to Florence.'

'What a shame! I mention the Villa d'Este, because there must be a lot of interesting people staying there just at present. Your mother-in-law will be telling you what a wonderful young woman you are.'

That same evening, she left for Rome, but she was filled with an unaccountable state of anxiety, and her agitation increased as she neared the end of a journey that seemed to be going on for ever. When she first caught sight of her husband, she found that such a change had come over him in so brief an interval that she almost died of fright. Rinaldi took her hands affectionately into his own, but seemed to be taken aback by her sudden arrival. He was so flustered that he did nothing but ask her over and over, 'Why did you come? What brought you here?'

'I'd never seen my husband in such a state!' Maria said to Erminia a few months later, the first time she saw her after returning to Milan. 'I'd never imagined that the expression on that man's face could affect me so deeply, or that he could say what he did, or talk to me in the sort of tone that touches you to the very core. I'd never seen him like that!'

Poor Maria! She too was very different now. The faintest of wrinkles had appeared above her eyebrows, delicately lining the clear pure white of her forehead, at times spreading like a shadow across the whole of her face.

'Yes, they were terrible times, and they still affect me like a black cloud, a painful memory to which I've almost become attached because it has rooted itself so deeply within me. It left so indelible an impression that I could never erase it without doing harm to myself. What a moment that was, when I saw my husband with the revolver in his hand, and I found the strength to cling on to him, to prevent him from killing himself! What a moment! He really did want to kill himself; he told me so afterwards. He couldn't bring himself to tell me he could no longer buy horses for me, or a box at La Scala, or jewellery, or anything! There he was, crying as certain men cry who have never cried before, with tears that drive an arrow clean through your heart. I can't begin to tell you how many thoughts flashed through my mind at that moment, when I pressed my heart close to his own, that was beating still, for me alone, and he buried his head against me, burning with affection! It was good of you to climb all those stairs to the fourth floor to pay me a visit. You've done so much for me!'

'You're not doing a great deal for me, my dear Maria, by paying me all these compliments. You must have had a low opinion of me!'

'Of course not! But what can you expect, when you've been through all the things that I have? Besides, the worst thing about falling on hard times is that it makes you distrust people. You can just imagine what an effect it had on me when the rumour got about that I'd been left a widow, and it never occurred to anybody that I was down there in Rome, all alone, with no one to come to my aid, not even a single one of those who claimed to be such good friends! Mind you, I'm not complaining. I hadn't been altogether honest with you. I still love you!'

She hesitated for a moment, then rushed up to Erminia and threw her arms round her neck.

'Forgive me! Forgive me! I was mistaken about you, and about everyone else! I've been wrong so many times!'

Erminia returned her embrace. She too was greatly moved, but uttered no word in reply.

'It was foolish of me!' Maria murmured, after hesitating once again, her face buried in Erminia's bosom. 'I never even think about him any more.'

'And I never thought about him at all,' said Erminia, laughing as broadly as ever, but in tones and appearance of utter sincerity.

Maria suddenly raised her head and looked her straight in the face, her eyes blazing with astonishment.

'Never, you say? Never?'

'Never.'

'But in that case . . . In that case, I never loved him either! No, really! Never!'

From Novelle Rusticane

The Reverend

He was not exactly reverend in appearance. He no longer wore the bushy beard or the scapular of a Capuchin, now that he had a shave every Sunday and went about in his elegant, finely woven cassock, and the cloak with its silk turnings round the armholes. If it should ever have occurred to him, as he puffed away at his clay pipe with his hands in his pockets, surveying all his fields, his vineyards, his cattle and his farmhands, that he had once washed up the pots and pans for the Capuchins, and that they had covered him in a sackcloth out of charity, he would have crossed himself with his left hand.

But if, out of charity, they had not taught him to say Mass and to read and to write, he would not have managed to worm his way into the leading families of the district, or to fill his ledgers with the names of all those tenants who worked for him and prayed God to send him a good harvest, and who cursed like troopers when the time came for him to settle their accounts. 'Judge me by what I am, not by the one who bore me,' says the proverb, and everybody knew who had borne him, because his mother still swept his house for him. The Reverend had no sense of family pride, not he, and whenever he called on the baroness for a game of cards, he would get his own brother to wait for him with a lantern in the ante-room.

For the Reverend, charity began at home, as Heaven decrees it should, and he had taken into his house a niece, good-looking but poor as a church mouse, who would never have found a scrap of a husband. Not only did he maintain her, but he set her up in a splendid room with glass panes in the window and a four-poster bed, and she was not required to work, or soil her hands performing any humble service.

Hence everyone took it to be God's judgement when the poor girl came over scrupulous, as happens to women who have nothing to occupy their minds, and spent her days in church beating her breast over living in mortal sin – but not when her uncle was there, for he was not the sort of priest who likes to show himself off at the altar in all his pomp and glory to his mistress. As far as women were concerned, outside his own house it was enough for him to tweak them paternally on the cheek between forefinger and thumb. And he did the same through the window of the confessional after they had cleared their conscience by unloading their own and other people's sins, for there is always something useful to be learnt, by imparting blessings, for anyone who speculates in country affairs.

The Lord be blessed! He never claimed to be a saintly man, not he! Saintly men died of hunger, like the parish priest who went on celebrating Mass even when they left nothing in the plate, and who dragged himself round the houses of the poor in a threadbare cassock that was a scandal to religion. The Reverend was determined to move forward, and that was what he did, with a fair wind in his sails, after being side-tracked to begin with by that blessed habit that was such a hindrance that in order to leave it behind in the monastery garden he pleaded his case before the royal law-courts. His fellow-brethren had helped him to win the case so as to be rid of him, because ever since he had joined the monastery, benches and soup-bowls went flying round the refectory whenever a new provincial was elected. Father Battistino, a true servant of God who was sturdy as an ox, had almost been decapitated, and Father Giammaria, the sacristan, had lost a whole row of teeth. The Reverend, who had stirred it all up, retired to his cell and stayed there quiet as a mouse, which was how he managed to retain all the teeth a Reverend required, while everyone told Father Giammaria, who had set this scorpion in their midst in the first place, 'Serve you right!'

Father Giammaria, being a decent sort of fellow, rubbed his toothless gums over his lips, and replied, 'What do you expect? He was never made out to be a Capuchin. He's like Pope Sixtus, who started out as a swineherd and became the man he was. Don't you remember the promise he showed as a boy?'

No wonder Father Giammaria had simply remained a sacristan of the Capuchins, without a shirt to his back or a penny to his name, listening to people's confessions out of the love of God, and cooking minestra for the poor and the needy.

When the Reverend was still a boy, and saw his brother, the one with the lantern, breaking his back digging, and his sisters unable to find a husband even if you gave them away, and his mother spinning in the dark to save the oil for the lamp, he had said, 'I'm going to be a priest!' They sold their mule and their tiny bit of land to send him to school, hoping that once they had a priest in the house, it would more than compensate for a mule and a bit of land. But more than that was needed to maintain him at the seminary! So the boy started hanging round the monastery so that they would take him on as a novice, and one day when the provincial was expected and there was work to be done in the kitchen, they invited him in to lend a hand. Father Giammaria, who was a kindly soul, said to him, 'If you like the job you can stay.' And Brother Carmelo, the warden, in order to while away the time as he sat on the low wall of the cloister, idly flapping his sandals one against the other, ran up a bit of a scapular for him with pieces of sackcloth draped over the fig tree to scare away the sparrows. His mother, brother and sisters protested that if he became a friar they were finished, and their investment in his schooling was wasted, as they would never get a penny back. But being a friar to the very core, he shrugged his shoulders, saying, 'Do you mean to say a man can't follow the vocation God has called him to?'

Father Giammaria had taken him on willingly because he was quick as lightning, whether in the kitchen or performing any other menial task, and he would even serve Mass as if he had never done anything else in his life, with his eyes cast downward and his lips sealed like a seraph. Now that he no longer served Mass, he still had those downcast eyes and those sealed lips whenever he was negotiating some shady deal with the local bigwigs, or bidding at auction for common land, or swearing on oath before the chief of police.

As to oaths, in 1854 he was forced to swear a real whopper at the altar, as he was reciting Holy Mass in front of the ciborium, when people were accusing him of spreading the cholera, and threatening to beat him up.

'By this consecrated Host that I hold in my hands,' he said, to the kneeling faithful, 'I am innocent, my children! Moreover, I promise you that within a week the scourge will come to an end. Be patient!'

They were patient, right enough! They had no option, because people said he was hand in glove with the judge and the army commandant, and that King Bomba¹ not only sent him capons at Easter and Christmas to pay him off, but had also sent him an anti-cholera remedy, in case anything went wrong.

An elderly aunt of his, whom he had been forced to take into his house to stop people talking, and who was good for nothing except to steal the food from his mouth, had uncorked a wrong bottle, and caught a real dose of cholera. But her own nephew, so as not to allow anyone to suspect him, refused to give her the antidote. 'Give me the antidote! Give me the antidote!' pleaded the old woman, already black as coal, paying no attention to the doctor and the notary who, also present, were exchanging embarrassed glances with one another. The Reverend, pretending bare-faced that it was none of his business, shrugged his shoulders and muttered, 'Take no notice, she's delirious.'

If he really did have the antidote, the king had sent it to him in the strictest confidence, forbidding him to pass it on to a living soul. The judge had called round in person and pleaded with him on bended knee to give him some for his dying wife, only to be told, 'Ask me to lay down my life for you, dear friend, but in a matter of this sort I'm powerless to help.'

All of this was common knowledge, and because everyone knew that his intrigues and his cleverness had won him the intimate friendship of the king, the judge, and the army commandant, who controlled the police, and whose reports arrived in Naples without passing through the hands of the provincial governor, nobody dared to argue with him. And whenever he set his sights on a farm that was up for sale, or a plot of common land that was up for auction, even the local bigwigs, if they ventured to bid against him, bowed and scraped to him as they did so, and offered him a pinch of snuff. He once spent a whole morning playing cat and mouse with the baron himself. The baron was the soul of amiability as the Reverend, seated opposite him with his cloak gathered up between his knees, kept offering him his silver snuffbox every time he raised the bidding, sighing,

'What else are we to do, my dear baron? If the donkey drops, one has to help it to its feet.' And when the time came for the lot to be knocked down, the baron raised the pinch of stuff to his nose with bile coming out of his ears.

The villagers were quite content about all this, because the big dogs will always fight one another over a juicy bone, and the poor never get a smell of it. But what caused them to mutter was that this servant of the Lord would milk them dry worse than the Antichrist whenever they had any dealings with him, and he had no scruples about seizing his neighbour's goods, because he was holding the confessional reins in his own hands, and if he committed a mortal sin he could give himself absolution.

'It all comes from having a priest in the house!' they sighed. And the ones who were better off starved themselves so as to send their sons to the seminary.

'When you depend on the country for your living, you have to give the whole of your time to it,' the Reverend would say, which was his excuse for never considering anyone except himself. As to the Mass itself, he only celebrated it on Sundays, when there was nothing else to do. He wasn't one of those petty priests who ran after three *tarì* just for saying Mass. He could do without it. And that was why the Lord Bishop, after arriving at his house on a pastoral visit, and finding his breviary covered in dust, wrote 'Deo gratias' on it with his finger. But the Reverend had too many other things on his plate to waste his time reading the breviary, for he was not one of your petty priests who recite Mass for a handful of coppers, and he laughed off the Bishop's reproof. His breviary might have been covered in dust, but his oxen were gleaming, his sheep were thick with wool, and his crops were taller than the top of a man's head. His farmhands could revel in the sight of the crops and build castles in the air; until, that is, their master came along to settle up. The poor fools opened their hearts out to him. 'The crops have grown like magic! The Good Lord's been passing over them in the night! They belong to a servant of God, no mistake about it. We'd be a right set of fools not to work for the farmer with Mass and benediction at his fingertips.'

In May, the time of year when they were looking up at the sky to exorcize every passing cloud, they were happy with the thought that their master was saying Mass for a good summer, which would do more good than all the images of saints, or the sanctified bread left lying around to ward off the evil eye and a poor harvest. The Reverend did not, in fact, want sanctified bread scattered about his fields, because it merely attracted sparrows and other birds to come along and damage the crops. And as for images of saints, he had his pockets full of them, being able to pick up as many as he wanted in the sacristy to hand them out to his peasants.

But at harvest time he rode up on horseback with his brother, who, acting as his watchman, had a shotgun slung over his shoulder. He never moved from the spot, bedding down with all that malaria around to keep a close watch on his affairs, without a care for anyone, not even Christ Himself. Those poor devils, who in the balmy days of summer had forgotten the hardships of the winter, stood open-mouthed to listen to him reciting the litany of what they owed him. 'Your wife borrowed so many kilos of beans when it was snowing.' 'Your son was given so many kilos of firewood.' 'So many kilos of seed-corn advanced at so much a month with interest.' 'Reckon it up for yourself.' Some sort of reckoning! In the year of the famine, Zio Carmenio had slaved away and ruined his health in the Reverend's fields, and when the harvest came he had to hand over his donkey to pay off his debts and went away empty-handed, yelling such a stream of foul-mouthed abuse as to shake Heaven and earth. The Reverend, not being there to listen to confessions, let him get on with it and led the donkey away into the stable.

After becoming a wealthy man he discovered that his family, which had always gone hungry, held certain rights to a benefice that was rich as a canonry, and at the time when mortmain[2] was abolished, he applied for the land to be released, and grabbed the farm in perpetuity. The only thing that annoyed him was the fee one had to pay for the land to be released, and he called the Government robbers for not allowing people to take over gratis a benefice that belonged to them anyway.

He had almost had a fit over this Government earlier on, in 1860, when the revolution took place,[3] and he had been forced to take refuge in a cave like a rat, because all the villagers who had been in dispute with him wanted to polish him off. Then later on came the rigmarole of the taxes, that he was forever having to pay, and the very thought of it turned his wine at table into poison. And now they were laying siege to the Pope, and wanted to strip him of his temporal power. But when the Pope excommunicated everyone who had taken over its mortmains, the Reverend completely lost his temper, and spluttered, 'Who does the Pope think he is? What belongs to me has nothing to do with his temporal power.' And he went on celebrating Holy Mass more boldly than ever.

The villagers went and listened to him, but they could not help thinking about the robberies the celebrant had committed, and they kept being distracted. And their womenfolk, as they were confessing their sins, were unable to stop themselves whispering in his ear, 'Father, I have sinned by speaking ill of you, a servant of God, because this winter we were left with no beans and no corn because of you.'

'Because of me! Am I the one who brings a fine summer or a poor harvest? Do I own these lands for you to sow them to your own profit? Are you without any conscience, any fear of God? Why bother coming to confession? All this is the work of the Devil, tempting you to lose the sacrament of penance. When you spawn all those children, do you never think of how you are going to feed them? Is it my fault that you run short of bread? Did I force you to have all those children? I don't have any, which is why I became a priest in the first place.'

He gave them absolution, however, as he was obliged to. But none the less those simple people could not come to terms with the contradiction between the priest who raised his hand to bless them in God's name, and the master who cooked the books and sent them away from the farm with an empty sack, and a sickle under their arm.

'There's nothing to be done! Nothing!' the poor wretches muttered, resigned to their lot. 'You can't squeeze blood out of a stone, and there's no way of taking the Reverend to court because he knows what the law says!'

He certainly did know! When he was in court before the judge, with his lawyer, he would shut everyone up by saying, 'The law says this,' or 'The law says that.' And what the law said was always on his side. In the good old days he could laugh at his enemies and those who were smitten with envy. They could create as much uproar as they liked, they could appeal to the bishop, they could confront him about his niece, about Massaro Carmenio and his unlawful seizure of his goods, they could stop him saying Mass and hearing confession. That was all very well, but what good would it do them? He had no need of the bishop or anyone else. He was his own man, he was respected as one of the people who controlled the affairs of the village, the baroness made him welcome in her own household, and the more fuss they made about him, the greater the scandal. Instead of interfering with the big guns, even if you were a bishop, you raised your hat to them for the sake of peace and quiet, to be on the safe side. But what was the use of all that after the revolution, now that the heretics had come into power? The villagers were learning to read and write, and to add up better than you could yourself. Political parties were challenging one another in the town hall, and splitting up the cake among themselves without a care in the world. Any Tom, Dick or Harry could get legal aid if he took you to court, and make you pay the costs of the hearing out of your own pocket! A priest counted for nothing any more, either with the judge or the chief of police. A word in their ear was no longer enough to have people locked up for treating you with disrespect, and all you were fit for was to say Mass and hear confession, like a public servant. The judge was always worrying about the press, about public opinion, about what Roman law might have said, and was handing out judgements like Solomon! They had even put a curse and the evil eye on the property he had won with the sweat of his brow, out of pure envy. The very food he ate at table gave him nightmares, while his brother, who led a hard life and whose diet consisted of bread and onions, had the stomach of an ostrich, knowing that in the years to come, when the Reverend was dead, he would inherit everything and find himself a rich man without lifting a finger. His poor old mother was a millstone round his neck, lingering on so as to suffer and make other people suffer, so bedridden by paralysis that it was he who now had to look after her. His own niece, plump, well dressed, with every little thing she wanted, and with nothing to do but go to church, tormented him whenever she took it into her head that she was living in mortal sin, as though he were one of those excommunicates who had dispossessed the Holy Father, and she had got the bishop to prevent him saying Mass.

'There's no such thing as religion any more, no justice, nothing!' the Reverend would grumble as the years went by. 'Nowadays everyone wants to have his say. The people with nothing would like to grab what is yours, saying "Move aside, I want to get in there!" People with nothing better to do come along and pester you in your own home. They would like to turn priests into sacristans, good only for saying Mass and sweeping out the church. They won't obey God's will any more, that's the trouble!'

Getting to know the King

Cosimo, the litter-driver,[1] settled his mules down for the night, lengthened their halters a little, spread a bit of straw under the feet of the bay, which had slid twice on the wet street-cobbles of Grammichele after the heavy rain, then stood at the doorway of the stable, hands in pockets, yawning at all the people who had come to see the King. There were so many comings and goings in the streets of Caltagirone that it looked like the festival of San Giacomo. So he was all ears, and kept a close watch on his animals, that were munching away at the barley very slowly, so as not to eat him out of house and home.

Just at that moment they came to tell him the King wanted a word with him. It was not exactly the King who wanted a word, because the King never talks to anyone, but one of the people who act as spokesmen for the King when he has something to say. What the spokesman told him was that His Majesty wanted his litter at dawn next morning to go to Catania, and had no wish to become obliged to the bishop or the lord-lieutenant, preferring to foot the bill out of his own pocket like anyone else.

Cosimo ought to have been happy, because litter-driving was his trade. He was waiting there for someone to come along and hire his litter, and the King is not the sort of person to haggle over a penny more or a penny less, like so many others. But Cosimo was so worried about having to drive the King in his litter that he would have preferred to return to Grammichele without a fare. The very thought of it turned the festivities into poison, and took all the joy out of the illuminations, the band playing in the square, the triumphal chariot touring the streets with the portraits of the King and Queen, and the church of San

Giacomo, all lit up and spitting out flames, where the Holy Saint himself was on display, and the bells were pealing out in the King's honour.

In fact, the more he saw and heard of the festivities, the more terrified he became about having to drive the King in his own litter. All the fireworks, the crowds, the illuminations and the bell-ringing turned his stomach over to such an extent that he was unable to sleep a wink, and he spent the night checking the hooves of the bay, currycombing the mules, and stuffing them with barley up to their ears to keep up their strength, as though the King weighed twice as much as anybody else. The stable was full of cavalrymen, with spurs all over their boots, which they never took off even when they bedded down to sleep on the benches. There were so many sabres and pistols hanging from the nails on the pillars that poor old Cosimo was convinced they would cut off his head if one of his mules happened to slip on the wet cobbles while he was carrying the King. The rain had been pouring out of the sky for the past few days; people must have been stark raving mad to come all the way to Caltagirone in such terrible weather. As far as he was concerned, God's truth, he would have preferred at that moment to be back in his little cottage where, as he lay in bed, he could hear the mules, tucked up in their stalls, munching away at their barley. He would gladly have given away the two *onze* he was getting from the King to find himself in his own bed, with the door locked, peeping out over the blankets at his wife as she went round with the lantern, putting everything neatly away for the night.

At dawn, half-asleep, he leapt to his feet at the sound of the soldiers' trumpet blaring away like a rooster aware of the time of day, which threw the whole of the stables into uproar. Carters reared their heads from the pack-saddles they had laid down as pillows, dogs started barking, and the hostess peered down sleepily from the hay-loft, scratching her head. It was still pitch dark, but people were strolling up and down the street as if it were Christmas night, and the nougat-vendors, standing behind their Chinese lanterns beside the fires, were clattering their knives on their benches to drum up business. What a wonderful time all those people must have been having, buying nougat and dragging themselves wearily through the streets, half-asleep, waiting for the King! When they saw the litter coming with all the bells and the woolly pom-poms, they stared at it wide-eyed, envying Cosimo like mad because he was going to face the King eyeball to eyeball, while none of them had so far been able to catch so much as the smallest glimpse of him in the forty-eight hours they had been standing in the streets day and night, with the rain coming down in buckets. The church of San Giacomo was still spitting out fire and flames, perched at the top of its endless flight of steps waiting to wish the King *bon voyage*, and ringing all its bells to tell him it was time for him to be pushing off. How much longer could all those lights be kept burning? And what about that poor sexton? Were his arms made of iron, that he could keep on ringing those bells day and night without stopping? The grey light of dawn was at last approaching across the plain, revealing a sea of mist covering the whole valley. Yet all those people were still swarming about like flies, their coats buttoned up to their noses, and as soon as they saw the litter arriving they practically smothered Cosimo and his mules, thinking the King was inside.

But the King was in no great hurry. At that moment he was pulling on his trousers perhaps, or wetting his whistle with a drop of brandy, which Cosimo had not even thought of doing that morning as he was unable to swallow a blessed thing. An hour later the cavalry arrived with sabres drawn, forcing people to stand aside. In their wake came another wave of people, then the brass band, then a bunch of notables with their ladies, who were wearing pretty hats, their noses glowing red from the cold. The street-vendors, too, hurried on to the scene, holding their benches high above their heads and setting up stall wherever they might sell a little more of their nougat. The great square was so tightly packed that there was no room to swing a cat in it, and the mules would not even have been able to swish away the flies if it were not for the cavalry clearing the way ahead. But then, the cavalry was accompanied by a swarm of horseflies, of the kind that drive litter-mules crazy, and every time Cosimo spotted one of them landing on the belly of one of his beasts he sent up a prayer to God and all the souls in Purgatory.

Finally the bells seemed to go mad and rang out twice as loud, rockets went shooting up for the King, a further torrent of people came rushing in, and the King's carriage made its appearance, seeming to float on people's heads in the middle of the crowd. Then trumpets sounded a fanfare, drums rolled, another salvo of rockets went up, and Cosimo's mules, God help him, tried to break free of their harness, kicking out left, right and centre. The soldiers, who had sheathed their sabres, drew them out again, and the crowd shouted 'The Queen, the Queen! That little woman there, beside her husband. It's unbelievable how tiny she is!'

The King on the other hand was a fine figure of a man, tall and well built, with red trousers and a sabre dangling from his paunch. Tagging along behind him came the bishop, the mayor, the lord-lieutenant, and another swarm of bigwigs wearing gloves and white neckerchiefs. They were dressed in black, and looked as if they were suffering from St Vitus's dance because of the chill north wind that was dispersing the mists from the plain of San Giacomo. Before mounting his horse, as his wife was getting into the litter, the King stood there chatting with this person and that as if the whole thing was none of his business. Then finally he went up to Cosimo, clapped him on the shoulder, and addressed him with these very words in his Neapolitan twang, 'Just remember you are carrying your Queen!' Cosimo felt as if his knees were giving way under him, the more so when at that moment the crowd swayed this way and that like a vast cornfield, a cry of despair went up, and a young woman in a nun's habit, looking pale as death, flung herself at the King's feet crying, 'Mercy!' She was begging for mercy for her father, who had got himself involved in an attempt on the King's life[2] and been condemned to have his head cut off. The King had a brief word with someone standing next to him, which was all that was needed to save the girl's father from losing his head. She turned away again, feeling so relieved that she fainted with joy and had to be carried off unconscious.

What it boiled down to was that the King could order the head to be cut off anyone he pleased, including Cosimo if one of his mules put a foot wrong and caused his wife, being so tiny, to fall out of the litter.

Poor old Cosimo could think of nothing else as he walked along beside the bay with his hand on the shaft of the litter, biting hard on his scapular[3] coin and sending up a prayer to God as though about to breathe his last. Meanwhile the whole caravan, with the King, the Queen and the soldiers, had moved off amid the shouting, the bell-ringing and the firing of rockets. These could still be heard down in the plain, and by the time they reached the foot of the valley they could look back and see the hillside bathed in sunlight and crawling with black dots, as if the plain of San Giacomo had been hosting a cattle fair.

What did it matter to Cosimo if it was a fine, sunny day? There was nothing fine or sunny about the way he felt as he walked along, never daring to raise his eyes from the cobbles on which the mules were plonking their hooves. To Cosimo it was as if they were walking on eggs. Nor did he register how the crops were progressing, or take any pleasure in seeing the bunches of olives overhanging the hedgerows, or think of all the good the torrential rain had done that week, for his heart pounded away like a hammer every time he thought of how the stream would be swollen, forcing them to cross it by ford! He didn't dare to sit astride the shafts, as he normally would when he was not carrying the Queen, so as to let his head droop and snatch forty winks in the warm sun, with a clear road ahead that the mules would follow with their eyes closed. The mules were not the most sensible of creatures, and had no idea who they were carrying. They were so happy to be on a dry and level stretch of road that they were merrily swishing their tails and shaking their bells, and almost breaking into a trot. The mere sight of his mules turning so frisky frightened Cosimo out of his wits, making his heart leap into his mouth. Those animals of his were without a care in the world, whether for the Queen or for anything else.

Meanwhile the Queen herself was chatting away to another lady they had shoved into the litter to keep her company, in a lingo you couldn't understand a blessed word of. She was sitting there admiring the countryside through her flax-blue eyes, resting on the litter-door a hand that was so tiny that it seemed to have been made on purpose to do nothing. Had it really been worth filling up the mules with barley so as to carry that pathetic little thing, queen or no queen? But no matter how tiny she was, a single word from her was all that was needed for people to have their throats cut. And now here were these thoughtless mules being tempted to start leaping and dancing all over the road and lose Cosimo his head.

Cosimo, poor fellow, did nothing but recite Ave Marias and Paternosters between clenched teeth and commend himself to the souls of his departed ones, whether or not he had known them personally, all the way to Catania, where a great crowd had hurried into town to see the King, and every tavern had its side of skinned pork hanging outside for the festivities. When he arrived home after delivering the Queen safe and sound, it seemed like some sort of miracle, and he kissed the wall of the manger as he tied up the mules. Then he went off to bed, touching neither food nor drink, and put the Queen's money right out of his mind. And it would have remained in his overcoat-pocket for goodness knows how long, if it were not for his wife who took it and stuffed it into the bottom of the stocking under the mattress.

His friends and neighbours, who were curious to know what sort of people the King and the Queen were, came and asked him all about the journey, under the pretext of finding out whether he had caught malaria. He refused to say anything, as it made him feverish just to talk about it, and twice a day they had to call the doctor, who took away about half the money he had got for carrying the Queen.

But some years later, when they came and seized his mules in the King's name because he was in debt, Cosimo couldn't help thinking these poor beasts were the very mules that had delivered the King's wife safe and sound, when there were no proper roads to drive on. The Queen would have broken her neck if it were not for his litter, and people said that the King and Queen had come on purpose to Sicily to make proper roads to drive on, of which there was still no sign whatever, and it was an absolute disgrace. Litter-drivers could make a decent living in those days, and Cosimo would have been able to pay his debts and would not have had his mules seized, if the King and Queen hadn't come to make proper roads to drive on.

Later on, when his son Orazio, who was so dark-skinned and powerful that they called him Turk, was taken away to be a gunner, and that poor old woman of a wife of his was crying her eyes out, he remembered the girl who had come and thrown herself at the King's feet pleading for mercy, and how the King had sent her away happy with a single word. It never occurred to him that the King was a different one now, and the old one had been toppled from his saddle. He said that if the King had been there, he would have sent them away happy, himself and his wife, because he had been clapped on the shoulder by the King, he knew him, he had faced him eyeball to eyeball and seen his red trousers and the sabre dangling from his paunch. A single word from him was enough for people's heads to be cut off, and whenever he liked he could come and seize your mules if you were in debt and take away your sons to serve as soldiers.

Don Licciu Papa

The women were sitting on their doorsteps at their spinning wheels in the sun, and the poultry scratching about in the dirt, when a great shout went up, and people came running down the street, because Zio Masi, the pig-snatcher, had been spotted in the distance with his noose over his arm. The chickens darted off squawking, as if they knew who was coming.

The town hall paid Zio Masi 50 *centesimi* for chickens and 3 *lire* for every pig he caught breaking the law. He preferred pigs, and when he spotted Comare Santa's piglet, peacefully sticking its snout into the mud outside her front door, he whipped his slipknot round its neck.

'Holy Mother of God!' cried Comare Santa, turning pale as death. 'What are you doing, Zio Masi? For pity's sake, Zio Masi, don't slap a fine on me, or you'll ruin me!'

So as to give himself time to haul the piglet over his shoulders, that rat of a Zio Masi laid on the charm, saying, 'What can I do, my love? I'm only carrying out the mayor's orders. He doesn't want pigs on the streets any more. If I don't take your piglet, I lose my job.'

Comare Santa ran after him like one possessed, tearing her hair out, and screaming, 'Hey! Zio Masi! Don't you know it cost me 14 *tarì* at the San Giovanni fair, and it's all I have in the world! Leave me my baby pig, Zio Masi, in the name of your dead mother's soul! God willing, it'll be worth two *onze* by the end of the year.'

Zio Masi had a heart of stone, and, saying nothing, he simply kept his head down to see where he was placing his feet, so as not to slip in the mud, with the piglet across his shoulders grunting and staring into space. In order to save her piglet, Santa in desperation aimed a solid kick at his backside and sent him tumbling.

When the women saw the pig-snatcher sprawling in the mud, they set about him with their clogs and their distaffs, determined to make him suffer for all the pigs and chickens he had on his conscience. But at that moment they were seen by Don Licciu Papa, swaggering about with his sabre dangling over his belly, who started shouting like a madman, keeping well out of range of the distaffs, 'Make way for the Law! Make way for the Law!'

The Law sentenced Comare Santa to a fine and payment of damages, and she only escaped going to prison by the skin of her teeth through the intervention of the baron, whose kitchen window faced on to the street. He proved to the Law that there was no question of an insurrection, because on that particular day the pig-snatcher was not wearing his official town-hall cap with the braid round it.

'You see!' the women exclaimed in chorus. 'It takes a saint to get into Heaven! None of us knew anything about that cap business!'

But the baron also added a word of warning. 'The mayor was quite right to order pigs and chickens to be cleared from the neighbourhood. It was beginning to look like a pigsty.' From then on, the baron's servant emptied the refuse over the women's heads without a word of complaint. But they grumbled that the chickens confined to the house laid fewer eggs, and the pigs, tethered to the bedposts, seemed like so many souls in purgatory. 'At least they kept the streets clean before this happened!'

'All that manure would be like gold for the Grilli Fields[1]!' Massaro Vito sighed. 'If I still had the bay mule, I'd sweep up the streets with my bare hands.'

Don Licciu Papa played a part in that business, too. It was he who had come with the bailiff to seize the mule, because Massaro Vito would sooner have died than allow the bailiff to take it from the stable by himself, he would have gobbled the fellow up for breakfast. And when Massaro Venerando took him to court for what was owing from the tenancy, with the magistrate sitting there on the bench like Pontius Pilate, Vito was completely tongue-tied. That piece of land was only good for breeding crickets, it was his own fault if he was left empty-handed at harvest time, and Massaro Venerando was right to demand payment instead of all these promises and delays, causing him to bring along a lawyer to speak on his behalf. When the judge finished, and Massaro Venerando strode happily away in his big boots, swaying from side to side like a bloated duck, Vito simply had to ask the clerk of the court whether it was true they were going to sell his mule.

'Silence!' bawled the judge in the middle of blowing his nose before passing on to the next case.

Don Licciu Papa, asleep on a bench, suddenly woke up and shouted, 'Silence!'

'If you'd brought a lawyer along,' Compare Orazio said to Vito to cheer him up a little, 'you'd be allowed to go on talking.'

In the piazza, below the town-hall steps, the auctioneer was selling his mule. 'Fifteen *onze* for Vito Gnirri's mule! Who'll bid me fifteen *onze* for this fine bay mule? Fifteen *onze*!'

Compare Vito sat on the steps, cradling his chin in his hands, unwilling to tell anyone it was an old mule he had been working with for over sixteen years. She was standing there with her new halter, happy as a bride. But once they led her away, it made him furious to think that for a single year's tenancy Massaro Venerando had swindled him out of 15 *onze*, which was more than the land was worth. Now that he had no mule he would not be able to work it, and at the end of the year he would be in debt up to his ears all over again. He began yelling like a madman to Massaro Venerando's face, 'What'll you take from me when I have nothing, you Antichrist!' And he would have knocked him senseless then and there except that Don Licciu Papa, who was close at hand with his sabre and his braided cap, pulled him away, shouting, 'Stop in the name of the Law! Stop in the name of the Law!'

'What law?' Vito yelled, as he returned home with the mule's halter. 'There's one law for the rich and one for the poor.'

Arcangelo the shepherd was another who knew all about that. When he took the Reverend[2] to court over his cottage because the Reverend was trying to force him to sell it, everyone told him, 'You must be mad to be picking a quarrel with the Reverend. You're hammering your head against a brick wall! With all the money he's got, he'll hire the best lawyer for miles around and you'll end up poor, ready for the funny farm.'

After he became rich, the Reverend had enlarged the family house in different places, like a hedgehog growing fat and pushing the others out of the nest. Once he had widened the window overlooking Arcangelo's roof, he said he needed the cottage to build a kitchen on top of it and turn the window into a doorway. 'You see, Arcangelo my friend, I can't do without a kitchen! You must be reasonable.'

Arcangelo was nothing of the sort, and insisted on claiming he was going to die in the house where he was born. True, he was only there once a week on Sundays, but he knew every inch of the cottage walls, and whenever he thought of the village, as he wandered over the pasture lands above Carramone,[3] in his mind's eye he could see that rickety front door and the window without any glass. Very well, thought the Reverend to himself, in that case, if these yokels can't see reason, we'll have to knock some of it into their heads.

From then on, out of the Reverend's window on to Arcangelo's roof there poured a shower of broken pots, stones, and dirty water, turning the corner of the cottage where Arcangelo had his bed into a pigsty. If Arcangelo complained, the Reverend stuck his head out and complained even louder, shouting, 'Is no one allowed to keep a pot of basilica on his window-ledge? Does no one have a right to water his own plants?'

Arcangelo the shepherd was more obstinate than one of his rams, and he went to law over it. The judge came along, with the clerk to the court and Don Licciu Papa, to see whether the Reverend had a right to water his own plants, which were not in the window that day, and all the Reverend had to do was remove them every time the law people were due to turn up, and put them back again as soon as their backs were turned. The judge could not very well keep passing up and down the road to keep an eye on Arcangelo's roof. Every visit he made was costing good money.

They were left with the question of deciding whether the Reverend's window should have a grille or not, so the judge, the clerk to the court, and everyone else went over the place with optical gear, taking so many measurements you would have thought it was a baron's roof rather than the simple, mould-covered, tiny roof of Arcangelo's cottage. The Reverend also dug up certain ancient rights to a window without a grille and tiles jutting out over the roof, and poor Arcangelo just stood there looking up and wondering how his roof could possibly be to blame. He was unable to sleep at night and was no longer his normal, cheerful self. The expense of it all was bleeding him to death, and he had to leave a shepherd-boy in charge of the flock so that he could run after the judge and the justices' clerk. Not only that, but his sheep were dying like flies in the early winter frosts, and people started saying the Lord was punishing him for arguing with the church.

In the end he told the Reverend to go ahead and take it, because after so much litigation and so much expense he could no longer afford a rope to hang himself with from one of the beams. All he wanted was to sling his rucksack over his shoulder, take his daughter to live with him alongside his sheep, and never set eyes on that blasted house for the rest of his life.

Then battle was joined by his other next-door neighbour, the baron, who also had windows and tiles overlooking Arcangelo's roof, and since the Reverend wanted to put in a new kitchen, the baron claimed he needed to enlarge his pantry, so the poor shepherd no longer knew who his own house belonged to. The Reverend discovered a way to settle his dispute with the baron by dividing Arcangelo's house between the two of them, and because of this second easement, Arcangelo got at least a quarter less for it than it was worth.

When they were about to leave the house and go away from the village, Nina, Arcangelo's daughter, was in floods of tears, feeling as though her very heart was permanently nailed to those walls. Her father, poor fellow, tried to comfort her as best he could, telling her they would be living like royalty down there in the Carramone caves, with neither neighbours nor pig-snatchers to worry about. But the women of the village, who knew how matters stood, winked at one another and whispered among themselves, saying, 'There'll be no young man to call on her every evening at the Carramone caves when Arcangelo is minding his sheep. That's why Nina's shedding so many tears.'

When Arcangelo discovered what had been going on, he began swearing and shouting, 'You wicked hussy! Who d'you think is going to marry you now?'

But Nina had no thought of getting married. She simply wanted to stay in the same place as the young man she saw every morning from her window as soon as she got up, giving him a signal to show whether he could call on her that evening. That was how she had fallen from grace, by looking out of the window every morning at the young man, who at first smiled back at her, then blew her kisses along with the smoke from his pipe, while her neighbours were dying of envy. After that their love had grown so strong that the girl was blind to everything else in the world, and she told her father bluntly and clearly, 'You can go where you like, but I'm staying right here.' And the young man had given her a promise that he would look after her.

Arcangelo the shepherd was having none of that, and wanted to call in Don Licciu Papa to take his daughter away by force. 'At least when we get away from here, nobody'll know about what's happened to us,' he said. But the judge told him that Nina had reached the age of consent, and was her own mistress to do whatever she pleased.

'Her own mistress, eh?' Arcangelo muttered. 'Well, I'm my own master!' And as soon as he came face to face with the young man, who blew smoke in his face, he split his head open like a walnut, with a single blow of his club.

Once they had him securely tied up, Don Licciu Papa came running up, shouting, 'Make way for the Law! Make way for the Law!'

At the trial they even gave him a lawyer to put up a defence. 'At least the Law doesn't cost me anything this time,' Arcangelo said. And it worked out well for him. The lawyer managed to prove that two and two make four, that Arcangelo the shepherd had not tried deliberately to kill the young man with his wild pear cudgel, because it was part of his stock in trade, and he used it to give the rams a clout on their horns when they wouldn't listen to reason.

The result was that he was sentenced to only five years, Nina stayed behind with her young man, the baron enlarged his pantry, and the Reverend built a fine new house over Arcangelo's old one, with a balcony and two windows full of greenery.

Malaria

You feel as if you could touch it with your hands, like the rich, steaming earth lying everywhere around the mountains that encircle it, from Agnone to snow-capped Mongibello.[1] It hovers stagnant over the plain, in the same way as the sultry, oppressive July heat. In those parts the sun rises and sets like burning coals, the moon is pale, and the *Puddara*[2] seems to sail across a sea hung over with mist. In the spring there are birds and the plain is flecked with white daisies, but the summer is parched and dry, and in the autumn ducks fly in long black lines across a cloudy sky. The river flows gleaming like a metal strip between broad, abandoned banks, white, irregular, littered with pebbles; and at the foot of the valley lies the Lake of Lentini, swamp-like, smooth and motionless, with the flat plain all around it, and not a boat in sight, or a single tree on its banks. On the pebbly shore a few scattered oxen graze listlessly, their shaggy coats caked in mud to their chests. Whenever one of the herd's cowbells breaks the great silence, yellow wagtails take to the air, and the herdsman, he too yellow from fever and white with dust, opens his swollen eyelids for a moment, raising his head from the shade of the dry reeds.

The fact is that malaria enters your bones with the bread that you eat and whenever you open your mouth to speak, as you make your way on foot along paths that are choking with dust and the heat of the sun, and you feel your legs giving way under you. Or else you collapse in a heap over the pack-saddle of your mule, that hangs its head low as it ambles along. In vain do Lentini, and Francofonte, and Paternò attempt to climb like lost sheep over the first hills to escape from the plain, surrounding themselves with orange groves, with vineyards, with evergreen gardens. The malaria fells the townspeople in the deserted streets, it pins them down in the doorways of houses whose plaster is peeling in the sun, as they shudder from the fever, wrapped up in their overcoats, and with all the blankets from their beds round their shoulders.

Down below, in the plain, along lanes devoured by the sun, the few scattered houses stand melancholy-looking between two heaps of steaming manure, alongside crumbling stable roofs where relief horses wait with lifeless eyes, tethered to empty mangers.

Or cast your eyes down there to the shore of the lake, at the inn with its tattered old bush hanging on the door,[3] its empty reception rooms, and its innkeeper huddled up asleep on the doorstep, his head bound round in a handkerchief, waking up from time to time and surveying the deserted landscape to see if any thirsty traveller should be coming his way. Or see those objects like white wooden boxes, framed by a few slender, grey eucalyptus trees, beside the railway line that splits the plain in two as though by a blow from an axe, where the locomotive flies whistling along like the autumn wind, and fiery sparks coruscate through the night. Or lastly, here and there you will come across an occasional farm, its boundaries marked by rickety posts, with the shored-up roof, shutters dangling loose, and the threshing-yard riven with cracks. In the shade of tall haystacks, chickens sleep with their beaks tucked under their wings, the donkey hangs its head, still with a mouthful of straw, and every so often the dog springs warily up to growl at a stone detaching itself from the pebble-dash, a darting lizard, or a leaf that stirs in the dormant farmland.

The sun no sooner goes down in the evening, than sunburnt men under straw hats appear at the doorway in loose canvas shorts, yawning and stretching their arms. And women too appear, half-dressed, their shoulders black from the sun, suckling babies already so pale and wasted in appearance that you wonder how they are ever going to grow up tall and dark-skinned, and whether they will even survive to play on the grass next winter, when the farm turns green again, and the whole of the land comes joyously back to life in the sunlight, beneath a deep blue sky. Nor can you tell where or how all those others live, who on Sundays flock to Mass in secluded chapels bordered by hedges of prickly pear within a ten-mile radius, drawn by the feeble sound of the church-bells ringing out across that endless open plain.

Yet where there is malaria, the land overflows with God's blessings. In June, the ears of corn droop low beneath their weight, and when the plough comes along in November, the furrows will steam as though they have blood in their veins. But then, both the sowers and the reapers will fall like the ripe ears of corn, because as the Lord said, 'In the sweat of thy face shalt thou eat bread.'[4] And when the sweat of the fever leaves a body stone dead on a straw mattress, and the sulphur or eucalyptus remedies are of no further use, it is laid on the haycart or across the donkey's saddle or sometimes set on a ladder, with a sack over its face. Then it is taken away and set down in the secluded churchyard beneath the prickly pears, whose fruit no one ever eats for that very reason. The women huddle together in tears, and the men stand and watch, smoking their pipes.

That was how they carried off Massaro Croce, the watchman from the farm at Valsavoia, who had been dosing himself for thirty years with sulphur and eucalyptus. He had been feeling better in the spring of that year, but in the autumn, when the wild ducks were passing over again, he wrapped his head in his handkerchief. He was such a bag of bones that he only appeared on his doorstep every two days. His belly had swollen up like a drum, and because his eyes had turned lifeless and were popping out on sticks, and also because he was such a wild and coarse-looking creature, people called him The Toad. Before he died he kept saying, 'Don't worry, the master will take care of my children!' And on the last evening, he fixed those ghostlike uncomprehending eyes of his on the faces of the people standing round his bed, as they held the candle one after another under his nose.

The goatherd, Zio Menico, who was no fool, said his liver must have been hard as a rock and weighing a good kilo and a half.

And someone else said, 'He doesn't give a damn any more, after growing so fat and rich at the master's expense and seeing that his children no longer have need of anyone! Do you reckon it was on account of the master's good looks that he swallowed all that sulphur and all that eucalyptus for thirty years?'

The landlord of the lakeside tavern, Compare Carmine, had lost all five of his children in the same way, one after the other, three boys and two girls. It was not so much the girls that bothered him, but the boys died just at the very age they were old enough to earn a living. By the time it came to the last one, he had learnt a thing or two, and when the fever took a real hold on the boy after tormenting him for two or three years, he spent not a penny more on sulphur cures or any other medicines, but poured out quantities of good wine and prepared every fish stew he could think of, so as to stimulate the invalid's appetite. He would go out fishing on purpose every morning in his boat, return with a load of mullet and with eels as long as your arm, and stand there in front of his son's bed, with tears in his eyes, saying, 'Go on! Eat!' The rest of the catch was taken away by Nanni, the carter, to be sold in town.

'The lake giveth and the lake taketh away!' Nanni told him, whenever he saw Carmine crying his eyes out in secret. 'There's not much we can do about it, brother.' And in fact, the lake had been generous to him. Around Christmas, when eels fetch high prices, in the house by the lake they would settle down to a hearty supper in front of the fire, with macaroni, salami, and all the good food you can think of, while the wind howled away outside like a cold and hungry wolf. That was how the survivors consoled themselves for the ones who had died. But as their numbers dwindled one by one, the mother broke her heart so often that her body was bent over like a hook, and the father would set his big, burly frame in the doorway so as to turn his eyes away from the large, empty rooms where his children used to sing as they went about their work. His last child was utterly determined not to die. When the fever struck him he wept out of sheer despair, and he even went and threw himself in the lake because the thought of dying frightened him so much. But his father, who knew how to swim, fished him out again and talked to him severely, telling him that his cold bath would bring on his fever worse than before. 'Ah,' the young man sobbed, running his fingers through his hair, 'there's no hope left for me! I'm finished!'

'Just like his sister Agata, who didn't want to die because she was going to be married!' remarked Compare Carmine to his wife, who was seated on the opposite side of the bed. And she, who was able to cry no longer, just nodded her head, her body curved over like a hook.

For all that she was reduced to such a sorry state, she and her big, burly husband were tough-skinned, and they continued to look after the house by themselves. Not everyone goes down with malaria. There are people who survive for years and years, like Cirino the local idiot, for whom neither king and country, nor trade and spade, nor mother and father, had any meaning whatever. He had nowhere to sleep, nor bread to eat, yet everyone knew him for forty miles around, because he would forever be going from one farm to the next and taking on menial jobs, helping to look after the oxen, or to shift manure, or to skin carcases, in return for which he would be given a few kicks and a hunk of bread. He would sleep in ditches, on the edge of fields, behind hedges, or under stable roofs. He lived on charity, wandering about like a dog without a master, in shirt sleeves, barefoot, with the legs of his shorts secured to his thin black legs with pieces of string. He would go around singing at the top of his voice, with the bright yellow sun beating down on his hatless head. He took neither sulphur nor medicine, and caught no fevers. They had picked him up countless times as he lay stretched out on the road like a corpse, and in the end the malaria had left him alone, not knowing what to do with him. After eating away at his brain and the flesh of his legs, and puffing out his belly like a water bottle, it had left the local idiot happy as a sandboy to sing away like a cricket in the rays of the sun. His favourite place to stand was in front of the stables at Valsavoia, because there were people passing up and down, and he would run after them for miles, crying out, 'Hey! Hey!' until they threw him a few coppers. The innkeeper relieved him of the coppers and took him in to sleep in the stable on the straw put down for the horses. Whenever they started kicking, Cirino ran to wake the master, shouting, 'Hey!' and next morning he currycombed and groomed them.

Later on he took an interest in the railway they were building nearby. The coach-drivers and wayfarers were becoming a rare sight on the roads, and the idiot was unable to understand the reason. For hours on end, he would gaze up at the swallows flying through the air, blinking his eyelids in the sun to try and work it out. The penny seemed to drop for the first time when he saw all the people packed inside the railway carriages as they passed through the local station. Every day from then on he waited for the train at the exact time it was due, as though he had a clock in his head, and when it steamed past, engulfing him in its smoke and its noise, he flung his arms in the air and ran after it, bawling, 'Hey! Hey!' in the most angry and menacing tone he could manage.

The innkeeper too, every time he saw the train passing in the distance, puffing its way through the malaria, shook his head and silently cursed it for ruining his business, as he stood there in front of the deserted stables and the empty wine-jugs. In the past, he had done such a brisk business that he had married four separate women one after the other, earning himself the nickname of 'Wifekiller'. People said he was hardened to it, and he would have taken on a fifth except that Massaro Turi Oricchiazza's daughter put a stop to the rumours by saying, 'God forbid! Not even if the fellow was made of gold! He eats up wives like a crocodile!'

It was not true that he was hardened to it, because from breakfast-time on the day his third wife, Santa, had died on him, not a crust of bread or a drop of water passed his lips, and he stood there shedding real tears behind the bar of the inn. After that happened, he said, 'Next time I'll be taking a wife who's immune to the malaria. I won't go through all this again.'

The malaria killed off his wives one after the other, but left him the same as ever. Old and wrinkled as he was, you could never have imagined this man too could go the same way as his three wives, as he went about taking on a fourth. But he always wanted a wife who was young and attractive-looking, because nobody can run an inn without a wife, which was why, in the end, his clientele dwindled away. The only customer now left was Mommu, the permanent way inspector, who never uttered a word, and who came in to drink his glass of wine between trains, settling himself down on the bench by the door, and taking off his shoes to rest his feet. Wifekiller said very little either, but thought to himself that this fellow would never catch malaria, because if the people on the railway went down with it like flies there would be nobody left to run the trains. One of his customers had always made his life a misery, and once Wifekiller had seen the last of him, the poor wretch had only two enemies left to worry about: the railway that had stolen his business, and the malaria that had taken away his wives. At least all the other people in the plain, for as far as the eye could see, had something to look forward to, even if they had someone either breathing his last on his straw bed, or floored by the fever on the doorstep, wrapped up in his cloak, with his head covered in a handkerchief. They at least had the consolation of watching the sown fields coming up lush and green like velvet, or the corn ears undulating like the sea, and they could listen to the never-ending chanting of the reapers, strung out across the fields like lines of soldiers. And all along the country lanes you could hear the sound of bagpipes, followed by swarms of peasants arriving from Calabria for the harvest, covered in dust from head to foot, bent low beneath their heavy backpacks, the men in front and the women behind, their eyes fixed on the road winding endlessly ahead, their tired-looking faces burnt by the sun. And along the banks of all the ditches, beyond every thicket of aloe bushes, at the time when evening descended like a grey veil across the countryside, you could hear the watchman's whistle amid the silent ears of corn, now motionless in the still air, they too enveloped in the silence of the night. 'There!' thought Wifekiller to himself. 'If those people manage to survive and return home, they go back with money in their pockets.'

With him it was different. He had neither the harvest nor anything else to look forward to, and nothing to sing about. The evening brought an air of great sadness to the empty stables and the darkened inn. Mommu stood by his box, waving his flag as the train came whistling through from the distance, and after it had vanished into the night, even from where he was standing, in the doorway of the dark and deserted inn, Wifekiller could hear the idiot Cirino shouting, 'Hey!' as he ran along in its wake. And he muttered to himself that for some people there was no such thing as malaria.

In the end, no longer able to pay the rent for the inn and the stables, the landlord sent him packing after he had been there for fifty-seven years, and Wifekiller too was forced to take a job on the railway, and wave his flag when the train came by.

When he grew tired of running up and down the railway tracks all day, exhausted by his age and his misfortunes, he watched twice a day as the long line of carriages stuffed full of people came to a halt: bands of hearty huntsmen who would spread out over the plain, the occasional peasant playing a mouth-organ huddled up in the corner seat of a third-class carriage, fine ladies with veiled heads leaning out of carriage windows, the silver and burnished steel of their travel-bags and suitcases glittering in the light of the frosted lamps, the high, lace-topped backs of the padded seats. What a marvellous way to travel, taking forty winks when you felt like it! It was like seeing a part of the city going by, with its street lighting and its shops all aglitter. Then, as the train disappeared into the thick evening mist, the poor devil would take off his shoes for a moment and sit there on the bench, muttering, 'Ah! For these people there's no such thing as malaria!'

Property

If the traveller passing along the banks of Lake Lentini, as it lay there like a stretch of dead sea, and across the parched stubble-fields of the Plain of Catania, and through the evergreen orange groves of Francofonte, and the grey cork oaks of Resecone, and the lonely pasturelands of Passaneto and Passanitello, were to ask, so as to break the monotony of the long and dusty journey beneath a hazy, heat-laden sky, with the carriage bells jingling across the vast countryside, and the mules drooping their heads and their tails, and the driver singing his melancholy air to save himself from nodding off to sleep, 'Who does this belong to?' he would be told, 'Mazzarò'. And if he were to ask, as he came across a farm as big as a village, with barns like churches and great flocks of chickens squatting in the shade of the well, and women holding a hand over their eyes to make out who was going by, 'What about this place?' the answer would be, 'Mazzarò'. And going on still further, the malaria weighing down on his eyelids, suddenly startled by the barking of a dog as he passed through an enormous, dust-laden vineyard stretching motionless for miles over hill and dale, with its watchman lying flat out over his shotgun at the side of the valley, raising his sleepy head and opening one eye to see who was coming, the answer would still be the same, 'Mazzarò'. Then he would come to an olive grove thick as a forest, with not a blade of grass, where the harvest would last until March, and all those olives belonged to Mazzarò. And towards evening, as the sun was setting in a sky that was red as fire, and a veil of sadness descended over the countryside, he would come across the long procession of Mazzarò's ploughs as they returned at a snail's pace from the fields, and the oxen lazily fording the stream, dipping their muzzles into its murky water. In the distance he would see the pasture on the barren slopes of Canziria, with Mazzarò's flocks standing out in enormous pale-coloured shapes, and he would hear the shepherd's whistle echoing round the dales, and from time to time the sound of cowbells, and a solitary song petering out in the valley. The whole of it belonged to Mazzarò. Even the setting sun seemed to belong to Mazzarò, and the birds flitting down to their nests in the fields, and the scops owl hooting in the wood. Mazzarò seemed an enormous hulk that lay across the whole of the countryside, giving the impression one was driving over his stomach. 'Not at all,' the driver would say. 'To look at him, you'd think he hadn't a penny to his name. All the fat he has on him is his belly, and how he keeps it filled is a mystery, because he never eats anything except a hunk or two of bread, even though he's rich as a pig. But the fellow's as sharp as a tack.'

And in fact, being as sharp as a tack, he had piled up all that property, where once he had slaved his guts out from morning till night, digging, pruning and harvesting in the sun and the rain and the wind, with no shoes on his feet and not a rag on his back. Everyone could remember kicking him in the pants, the same people who now called him milord and spoke to him cap in hand. Nor did this cause him to put on airs, now that all the milords in the area owed him money, because, according to him, a milord was simply a poor devil who never paid his debts. He went on wearing a cap, except that it was made of black silk, this being his only luxury, and just lately he had taken to wearing a trilby because it cost less than a silk cap. The property he owned extended as far as the eye could see, and he had long eyesight. Everything belonged to him, to the right, the left and the centre, up hill and down dale. There were more than five thousand mouths feeding off his land, not to mention the birds of the air and the beasts of the field. He himself ate less than any of them, being content with a hunk of bread and a piece of cheese that he bolted down in a great hurry as he stood, faintly visible through the clouds of dust from the sacks of corn being laid in by the farmworkers, in a corner of the barn as big as a church. Or else he would eat as he leant against a haystack, with an icy wind roaring across the fields in the sowing season, or poking his head inside a skep in the sweltering days of the harvest. He never touched a drop of wine, nor did he smoke or take snuff, even though his gardens along the river bank produced tobacco leaves, tall and broad as a strapping youth, of the sort that fetched the highest prices. Gambling and chasing after women were no vices of his, the only woman he ever spent money on being his mother, who set him back twelve *tarì* when he had to have her carted off to the churchyard.

What it meant to own property was the one thing that had occupied his mind during all the years when he went around barefoot working on the land that was now his. He had known what it meant to earn three *tarì* a day, bending his back for fourteen hours in the heat of midsummer, with the foreman behind him on horseback, ready to give him a hiding if he stood upright for a single moment. That was why he had never ceased for a minute in his whole life from the business of expanding what he owned. And now his ploughs were as numerous as the long lines of crows that turn up in November, and there were mule trains winding endlessly across the land, and as many women trudging through the mud from October to March gathering his olives, as the magpies that came to steal them from him. At the grape harvest whole villages came swarming into his vineyards, and wherever you heard people singing on the land, they were singing as they picked Mazzarò's grapes. As for the corn harvest, Mazzarò's reapers spread out across the fields like a whole army, and to provide for all those people, with their early-morning biscuit, their bread and Seville orange for breakfast, their picnic lunch, and their lasagne in the evening, you needed fistfuls of money. The lasagne had to be served up in bowls as big as wash-basins. All of which meant that when he rode up and down on horseback behind the lines of his reapers, flourishing his whip, he kept a close watch on every one of them, and never stopped calling out, 'Put your backs into it, lads!' He was having to fork out good money the whole year round; in land tax alone the king was taking so much that Mazzarò broke out into a sweat every time he paid it.

But year after year all those barns as big as churches were so full of corn that their roofs would have had to come off to squeeze any more in, and every time Mazzarò sold off his wine he needed a whole day to count the takings, all made up of 12-*tarì* silver coins because he would have nothing to do with dirty paper. Dirty paper was something he only bought when he had to pay the king, or anyone else, and at the country fairs Mazzarò's herds filled whole fields, having cluttered up the roads so heavily en route that they took half a day to pass by, and sometimes the saint's procession, with the brass band, had to get out of the way and take a different route.

All those possessions he had got through his own efforts, with his own hands and his own brains, going without his night's sleep, breaking into many a sweat from palpitations and malaria, labouring away from dawn till dusk, and driving himself on in all weathers. He may have worn out his boots and tired out his mules, but he never tired himself of thinking about the property he owned, which was all he had in the world, for he had no children or grandchildren or relatives to occupy his thoughts. All he had was his property, and if that's the way a man is made, it means he's made for property.

Property came to him as though it were drawn towards him with a magnet, because property likes to be with people who know how to hold on to it, not people who waste it like that baron who first took Mazzarò on out of charity as a penniless drudge on his lands. The baron was the owner of all those fields, all those woods, all those vineyards, and all those flocks of sheep and herds of cattle, and whenever he turned up on horseback with his farm watchmen bringing up the rear, you would have thought he was the king. They had his lodging and his dinner waiting for the stupid ass, because they all knew the exact time he was due to arrive, and made sure they were not taken by surprise with their hands in the till. 'That fellow's just asking to be robbed!' Mazzarò laughed to himself, as he rubbed his hands over his backside where the baron had given him a good kick, and murmured, 'If you're as brainless as that you should stay at home. Property goes to the ones who know how to look after it, not to the ones who have it.' With him it was different. Once he had property of his own, he certainly never told anyone how and when to expect him to come and cast an eye over the harvesting of the corn or the gathering of the grapes. He would turn up unannounced, on foot or astride a mule, with a hunk of bread in his pocket and not a single watchman to accompany him. And he would lie down to sleep beside his hayricks, keeping his eyes open, with a shotgun between his knees.

That was how Mazzarò steadily took over all the property owned by the baron, who first of all gave up his olive groves, then his vineyards, then his grazing lands, then his farmhouses and finally the very palace where he lived. Not a day went by without his having to sign some legal document or other on which Mazzarò inscribed his splendid cross. The baron was left with nothing except the stone coat of arms that once stood over his front door, which was the only thing he was determined not to sell, saying to Mazzarò, 'Of all the property I owned, this is the one thing you are not the person to have.' He was right. Mazzarò had no use for it, and would not have given twopence for it anyway. The baron still looked down on him, but he no longer kicked him in the seat of his pants.

'What a fine thing it is to have the fortune of Mazzarò!' people said, unaware of what it had cost him to build such a fortune: all the thought, the labour, the lies, the risks of going to jail, and how, being as sharp as a tack, he had put his nose to the grindstone and worked day and night to amass all that property. Whenever a neighbouring smallholder refused to surrender his land, and vowed to wring his neck, Mazzarò would always find a way to disarm his peasant pride, bring him down a peg, and force him to sell. He would go along to him and boast, for instance, about the richness of a farm of his that would not even support a row of beans, get him to think it was the promised land, and persuade him to rent it by way of a good investment. And when the fellow could no longer pay the rent, Mazzarò would lay hands on his cottage and his smallholding for no more than it cost to buy a loaf of bread. But then, what about all those tiresome complaints that Mazzarò had to put up with? What about the tenant farmers who came and moaned about the poor harvests, the debtors who sent their womenfolk one after another to tear their hair out and beat their breasts, begging him not to turn them out on the street and take away their mule or their donkey, saying they had nothing to eat?

'Do you see what I eat?' he would answer. 'A crust of bread and an onion! And my storehouses are filled to overflowing, and I own all this property.' And if they were to ask him for a handful of beans from his enormous stockpile, he would say, 'Why? Do you think I stole them? Do you have no idea how much it costs to sow them, to dig out the weeds, and to harvest them?' If they asked him for a *soldo*, he told them he didn't have one to give.

It was true, because he never kept more than 12 *tarì* in his pocket. He needed the rest to make all that property pay, and money flowed in and out of his house like a river. Besides, he was not interested in money, because he said it wasn't property. As soon as he put together a certain amount of it, he spent it on a piece of land, because he was determined to own as much land as the king, and be better off than the king, since the king can neither sell his land nor call it his own.

The only thing that troubled him was that he was growing old, and would have to leave the land where it was. That goes to show that God is unjust, because you spend your whole life collecting property, and when you manage to get hold of it, and want more, you have to leave it all behind! He would sit for hours on a skep, cradling his chin in his hands, casting his eyes over all those flourishing green vineyards of his, and the fields of corn shimmering in the breeze like the sea, and the olive groves veiling the mountainside like mist. And if some half-clothed youngster were to pass that way, bent double like a tired mule beneath the burden he was carrying, he would hurl his stick between the boy's legs out of sheer envy, and mutter, 'Take a look at that fellow! He has nothing, and his whole life ahead of him!'

So when they told him it was time to forget about what he owned and think about his soul, he staggered out into the farmyard like a madman, and went round killing his ducks and his turkeys with blows from his stick, yelling, 'You're all mine and you're coming with me!'

Black Bread

No sooner had Nanni closed his eyes for the last time, with the priest standing over him in his stole, than his children were at one another's throats over who should foot the bill for the funeral. The priest was sent packing empty-handed, with the aspergillum[1] under his arm.

For Nanni had been sick a long time, with the sort of illness that costs you an arm and a leg, and the family furniture too. Every time the doctor spread out the sheet of paper on his knee to write the prescription, Nanni shot a pitiful look at his hands, and mumbled, 'For pity's sake, doctor, make it as short as you can!'

The doctor was only doing his job, like everyone else. It was when Massaro Nanni was doing his own job that he had picked up that fever, down at Lamia,[2] where God bestows his blessings so freely on the land that the crops grow as tall as a man. The neighbours told him over and over again, 'You're bound to snuff it, Nanni, on that Lamia farm.'

'Anyone would think I was a lord,' he replied, 'free to do whatever he liked!'

His children, who were like the fingers on the same hand as long as their father was alive, were now compelled to look to their own interests. Santo had a wife and small children, Lucia was left high and dry with no dowry, and Carmenio, if he wanted to eat, would have to go and find work for himself away from home. It was anybody's guess which of the three was going to maintain their old mother, sickly as she was, as they were all penniless. Mourning the dead is all very well when you have nothing else on your mind!

The oxen, the sheep, and the grain in the store had gone to glory with the master. All that remained was the gloom-filled house, with the empty bed and the orphaned mourners. Santo shifted in his movables along with The Redhead, saying he would take care of his mother, but the others claimed he was doing it to save paying his rent. Carmenio packed up his things and went away to become a shepherd for Vito the sheep farmer, who had a stretch of pasture land at Camemi. Lucia threatened to move out and go into domestic service, rather than live under the same roof as her sister-in-law.

'No!' said Santo. 'I won't have people saying my sister had to go and work as a maid for anybody.'

'He only wants me to work for The Redhead!' Lucia mumbled.

The big problem was this sister-in-law who had driven herself into the family as firmly as a nail. 'What am I to do about it, now that I've got her?' groaned Santo, shrugging his shoulders. 'I should have listened to my father, God rest his soul, when there was still time!'

His father, God rest his soul, had warned him, 'Steer clear of that Nena! She has no dowry, no roof over her head, and no land.'

But at Castelluccio Nena was forever at his back, whether he was digging or reaping. She would gather up the corn for him or clear the rocks with her own hands from under his feet. And whenever he was resting from his day's labours, leaning his back against the wall by the gate of the labourers' quarters in the hush of the evening, as the sun was setting over the fields, she would come up and say, 'God willing, Santo, this year you won't have laboured in vain!' or 'If the harvest turns out well for you, Santo, you should take that big piece of land down on the plain where the sheep have been grazing. It's lain fallow for two years' or 'This winter, Santo, if I can find the time, I'm going to knit you a pair of leggings to keep you warm.'

Santo had got to know Nena when he was working at the Castelluccio farm. She was the daughter of the farm watchman, a girl with red hair. Nobody wanted anything to do with her, which was why the girl made a fuss of any poor hound that came within her reach. She would go hungry to present Santo with a black silk stocking cap every year on St Agrippina's Day,[3] and to make sure a flask of wine or a hunk of cheese was waiting for him when he arrived at the farm, saying, 'Take this, Santo, for my sake. It's what the master drinks' or 'I was worried when you came without any lunch, the week before last.'

He was unable to say no, and accepted everything. The most he could do, out of politeness, was to reply, 'It's not right, Nena, for you to go hungry for my sake.'

'I feel happier if you have it.'

Every Saturday evening, when Santo returned home, his father, God rest his soul, would tell him all over again, 'Steer clear of that Nena. She doesn't have this, that, and the other.'

'I know I have nothing,' Nena would say, as she sat on the low wall gazing at the setting sun. 'No land, no property, and I've had to steal the bread from my mouth to put together my few bits of white linen. My father's a poor watchman living on his master's charity, and nobody's going to take a daughter without a dowry off his hands.'

But what she did have was a white neck, like most redheads, and when she lowered her head, with all those worries inside it, the sun lit up the golden hair behind her ears, and the downy complexion of her peach-like cheeks. And Santo stared into her deep blue eyes, and admired the fullness of her breasts as they heaved gently up and down like a field of corn. 'Don't upset yourself, Nena,' he told her. 'There'll be plenty of men wanting to marry you.'

She shook her head, and the red ear-rings that glistened like rubies brushed against her cheeks. 'No, Santo, no,' she said. 'Nobody'll ever want to marry a plain-looking girl like me.'

'Just think!' he said, struck by a sudden thought. 'Just think how wrong people are! They say red hair's ugly, and yet your red hair doesn't worry me in the least.'

His father, God rest his soul, on seeing that Santo was so wild about Nena that he wanted to marry her, said to him one Sunday, 'You've made up your mind to take The Redhead, haven't you? Go on, tell me.'

Not knowing where to put himself, Santo stood there with his hands behind his back, unable to raise his head and look his father in the face. But he agreed it was so, saying that without The Redhead he couldn't go on living, and it was God's will they should be man and wife.

'You need to work out whether you can support a wife, knowing I have nothing to give you. I and your mother here have just one thing to tell you: think twice before you marry, because bread is scarce and children come all too quickly.'

His mother, huddled up on the bench and pulling a long face, tugged the tail of his coat and whispered, 'Try and fall in love with the widow of Massaro Mariano. She's got plenty of money, and she won't be too choosy because she's paralysed.'

'That's a good one!' Santo mumbled. 'Massaro Mariano's widow'll be delighted to take a pauper like me for a husband!'

Nanni took the same view, saying that Massaro Mariano's widow was looking for a husband as rich as herself, even though she was paralysed. In any case the trouble was that his grandchildren might be born cripples.

'Think twice about it, that's all,' he repeated. 'Bear in mind that bread is scarce, and children come all too quickly.'

Then on St Bridget's Day,[4] towards evening, Santo had accidentally bumped into The Redhead, who was gathering asparagus shoots along the lane. She blushed on seeing him, as though unaware that he had to pass that way on returning to the village, and she lowered the hem of her skirt that was tucked into her waist as she went crawling through the cactus bushes. Blushing no less deeply, the young man stared at her and said nothing. Then finally he began to speak and told her he was returning home after finishing his week's work.

'Tell me, Nena, do you have any news for me to take back to the village?'

'If I wanted to sell the asparagus I could come with you, and we could walk along together,' said The Redhead. He nodded his head up and down like a fool, but then she added, tucking in her chin above those gently heaving breasts, 'But you don't want me to come, do you, because women are a nuisance.'

'I'd carry you there in my arms, Nena, honestly I would.'

Whereupon Nena began to nibble at a corner of the red headscarf she was wearing. Santo was equally at a loss for something to say, and simply stood and stared at her as he switched his knapsack from one shoulder to the other like an idiot. The air was heavy with the scent of calamint and rosemary, and up on the side of the mountain the cactus bushes were catching the last rays of the sun. 'You must go now,' Nena told him. 'You must go. It's getting late.' She then turned to listen to the great-tits singing merrily in the sky, but Santo stayed where he was. 'You must go,' she said, 'before people see us here alone together.'

Santo was at last on the point of proceeding on his way when he reverted to his earlier idea, and with a further shrug of the shoulders to adjust his knapsack, he told her he really would carry her in his arms if she would come with him. And he stared into those eyes of Nena's, that had turned away from him in search of asparagus shoots between the stones. And he stared into her face, that glowed red as if reflecting the setting sun.

'No, Santo, you must go alone. I'm just a poor girl without a dowry.'

'Let's leave all that to Providence, come on.'

She kept telling him that she was not for him, now with a dark and sulky expression on her face. Discouraged, Santo adjusted the knapsack once again on his shoulders and made to turn away, lowering his head. The Redhead insisted he should at least take the asparagus she had gathered specially for him. It would make a good meal if he agreed to eat it for her sake. And she held out the two corners of her apron to show him how much she had gathered. Santo put an arm round her waist and kissed her on the cheek, his heart melting in his breast.

At that very moment her father arrived on the scene, and the girl ran off in terror. The watchman had a gun slung over his shoulder, and vowed he would blast Santo to kingdom come for playing such a trick on him.

'No!' Santo replied, holding up his hands in an attitude of prayer. 'I don't get up to those sorts of tricks! I honestly want to marry your daughter, not because I'm afraid of your gun, but because I'm the son of a gentleman, and Providence will see us through because we've done nothing wrong.'

So the following Sunday the wedding banns were announced, with the bride-to-be decked out in her best clothes, and her father the watchman wearing new boots, which he waddled about in like a farmyard duck. What with the wine and the toasted beans, even old Nanni was in good spirits, though he was already going down with the malaria; and Santo's mother took from the seat-locker a roll of yarn she'd been saving for Lucia's trousseau. Lucia was now eighteen, and she would spend half an hour every Sunday before going to Mass prettying herself and admiring her reflection in the washbowl.

Santo, the tips of all ten fingers and thumbs stuck in his coat pockets, was in his seventh heaven as he surveyed his bride's red hair, the roll of yarn, and all the merrymaking that was going on that Sunday in his honour. The watchman, red-nosed, was skipping about in his oversize boots, determined to kiss one by one all the people who were present.

'Not me!' said Lucia, who was upset because of the yarn they were taking away from her. 'I don't want any of your kisses.' She stayed in a corner of the room, pulling a very long face, as if she already knew what was going to happen to her when her father breathed his last.

And, just as she had thought, she was now having to bake the bread and sweep out the rooms for her sister-in-law, who was off to the farm with her husband every day at crack of dawn, even though she was pregnant again. The woman was worse than a cat for filling up the house with offspring. Santo had more to think about now than those little presents they exchanged at Easter and on St Agrippina's Day, or the sweet nothings they had whispered into each other's ears when they met at the Castelluccio farm. That villain of a watchman certainly knew what he was doing when he married off his daughter without a dowry, leaving Santo to work out how to maintain her. From the moment he married Nena he was without the food to feed them both, and they just had to go and dig it out from the Licciardo fields by the sweat of their brows.

As they trudged along the stony lanes on their way to Licciardo, their knapsacks slung over their shoulders, wiping away the sweat on their shirtsleeves, all they could think about was the state of the crops on either side and ahead of them. To them, the crops were like an invalid with a weak heart, yellow at first, then turning limp and soggy in the pouring rain. And as they began to recover, there would be weeds everywhere, that Nena would pull out one by one on all fours, ruining her hands in the process, with her fat belly sticking out beneath her, and her skirt pulled up above the knees so as not to get it torn. She was quite unconcerned about the weight she was carrying from her pregnancy, or the pain in her back, and every time she freed a green stalk from the weeds it was like giving birth to a child. When finally she collapsed on the bank at the end of the row, panting for breath and brushing back the hair behind her ears with both hands, in her mind's eye she could see the cornstalks standing tall in June, touching one another as they swayed in the gentle breeze. Then she would reckon up with her husband as he stood on the bank untying his sodden leggings and cleaning his spade on the grass. 'So much was planted, so twelve, or ten, or even seven will see us through.[5] The stalks are none too strong, but it's a nice thick crop. As long as March is not too dry, and we only get rain when we need it, but Saint Agrippina, bless her, will see to all that.'

The golden sun lingered, shining down upon the green fields from a fiery and cloudless western sky, where larks were singing and descending like black specks to their nests. Spring, green as hope, was everywhere apparent, in the cactus hedgerows, in the thickets along the lane, between the stones, and on cottage roofs. As Santo trudged along behind his companion, heavy with child as she was and bent beneath the sack of animal-feed she was carrying, his heart swelled with tenderness for the poor woman, and he chattered away to her, panting for breath from the climb, about what he would do if the good Lord blessed the crops right to the end. There was no longer any talk of red hair, whether or not it was beautiful, and that sort of nonsense. But when May came along with its frosts to stab them in the back and destroy all their efforts and their hopes for the harvest, husband and wife sat on the bank surveying the field that was turning yellow before their very eyes, like an invalid on his way to the next world. Without uttering a word, they simply sat there, elbows on knees, white-faced, eyes staring from their sockets.

'It's God's judgement!' muttered Santo. 'My father, rest his soul, warned me what would happen!'

The ill humour of the gloomy, muddy paths penetrated the walls, also, of the poor fellow's cottage. Husband and wife sulked and turned their backs on one another, they quarrelled whenever The Redhead asked for money to go shopping, the husband came home late, there was no wood for the fire, or the wife's pregnancy made her seem slow and lazy. They pulled long faces, they swore, they even came to blows. Santo would grab Nena by her red hair, she would dig her nails into his face, and neighbours would come running to hear The Redhead screaming that her accursed husband was trying to make her miscarry, and that he didn't give a damn about sending an innocent soul to limbo. Afterwards, when Nena had given birth, they made peace, and Santo took the baby girl in his arms as though he had produced a princess, and ran around proudly showing it off to all his friends and relations. Whilst his wife was confined to bed, he prepared soup for her, he swept the house, he winnowed the rice, he stayed with her the whole time, so that she never lacked a thing. And when he appeared on the doorstep, looking like a wet-nurse, with the baby snuggled up in his arms, he would answer anyone who asked by saying, 'It's a girl, my friend. I was always unlucky, and now I have a baby girl. That's all my wife can manage.'

Whenever The Redhead had been beaten by her husband, she would take it out on her sister-in-law, telling her she never did anything to help around the house, whereupon Lucia would retort by saying that she had no husband but had to put up with other people's children.

The mother-in-law, poor woman, tried to stop their quarrelling, and kept saying, 'I'm the one to blame. All I'm good for now is to take the bread out of your mouths.'

All she was really good for now was to suffer all her troubles, and keep them hidden inside: Santo's hardships, his wife's wailing, the distance separating her from her other son, which was like a nail driven into her heart, the unhappiness of Lucia, who was without a rag to put on her back, and never saw so much as a dog passing beneath her window.

On Sundays, if the other girls invited Lucia to join them for a gossip in the shade, she simply shrugged her shoulders and replied, 'Why do you want me to come over? To show you the silk dress I haven't got?'

Sometimes the group of bystanders was joined by Tricky Joe, the frog-catcher, who never said a word but stood listening with his back to the wall, hands in pockets, spitting to the left and to the right. Nobody knew what he was doing there, but whenever Lucia appeared in the doorway he would pretend to turn his head to spit, and cast a furtive glance in her direction. In the evening, when all the doors were shut, he would even venture to serenade her on her doorstep, to his own basso accompaniment, 'Boom boom! boom!' Sometimes his voice was recognized by village youths going home late, who would taunt him by croaking away like frogs.

Lucia meanwhile pretended to busy herself about the house, keeping her head down and away from the light, so that no one could see her face. But if her sister-in-law were to come out with 'There goes that music again!' she would turn on her like a viper and answer back, 'The music bothers you, too, does it? Is nobody allowed to see or hear anything in this prison?'

The mother was listening also, and when she saw what was going on, she looked at her daughter and said that as far as she was concerned the music made her feel happy. Lucia pretended to know nothing about it. But every day, at the time when the frog-catcher was due to pass by, she appeared in the doorway with her spindle. As soon as he had got back from the river and done the rounds of the village, he would turn up in those parts with his string of frogs, yelling, 'Singing fish! Singing fish!' as if the poor devils in those back streets could ever afford to buy any from him.

'They're supposed to be very good for invalids!' said Lucia, who was dying to do a deal with Tricky Joe. But her mother refused to let them spend good money on her account.

Seeing that Lucia, chin resting on her chest, was looking towards him out of the corners of her eyes, Tricky Joe slowed down as he was passing, and next Sunday he plucked up enough courage to move nearer and seat himself on the veranda steps of the house next door, dangling his hands between his thighs. He told the women how he went about catching frogs, and how it required the cunning of the devil. He, Tricky Joe, was as cunning as a cartload of monkeys, and he waited for the women to go away before turning to Lucia, saying, 'The crops could do with some rain!' and 'There won't be many olives this year.'

'What does that matter to you? You live on frogs,' Lucia said.

'Listen, my love, we are all like the fingers of one hand, like the tiles on a roof, that let the water pass from one to the other. If no corn is harvested, and no oilseed, no money comes into the village, and nobody buys my frogs. D'you follow?'

That 'my love' was like sweet music to the girl's ears, and it kept coming back to her mind the whole evening, as she sat spinning beside the lantern. She turned it over in her head again and again, as often as she wove her spindle up and down.

Her mother seemed to read what the spindle was saying, and when a whole fortnight went by with no sign of the frog-seller and no sound of a serenade, she said to her daughter-in-law, 'What a sad winter it is! Not a soul to be heard in the neighbourhood.'

The front door had to be kept closed now because of the cold, and from the window all one could see was the window opposite, streaming dark with rain, or a neighbour returning home inside a sodden overcoat. But of Tricky Joe there was no sign whatever, and Lucia said that if any poor soul was taken ill and needed a drop of frog soup, it was just too bad.

'He must have found another way to earn his living,' her sister-in-law replied. 'That stupid job is for people who can do no better.'

One Saturday evening, Santo overheard what they were saying, and out of brotherly concern he gave her a scolding.

'I don't like the sound of this Tricky Joe business. No sister of mine will marry a fellow who makes a living out of frogs, and spends the whole day crawling about in mud! You must go and look for one of your own kind, a farm worker, even if he owns nothing.'

Lucia remained silent, with lowered head and knitted brow, and it was all she could do to stop herself blurting out, 'Where am I to find a farm worker?' As if it was up to her to find one! The only man she had found was no longer anywhere to be seen, perhaps because The Redhead had offended him with her jealousy and her gossip. That was the reason. Santo always said what his wife told him to say, and she went round telling everyone the frog-catcher was a good-for-nothing, and of course Tricky Joe had got wind of it.

So the sisters-in-law would be constantly bickering with one another.

'I can never be my own mistress in this house!' muttered Lucia. 'The mistress is the one who pulled the wool over my brother's eyes, and got him to marry her.'

'I wouldn't have pulled any wool over his eyes if I'd known what was coming to me. I only had one mouth to feed, and now I have five.'

'What does it matter to you whether the frog-catcher has a proper job? If he were my husband, it would be up to him to maintain me.'

The mother, poor thing, tried to pacify them, as gently as she could. But being a woman of few words, all she could do was to go from one to the other, running her hands through her hair, murmuring, 'For pity's sake! For pity's sake!'

The two women took not a blind bit of notice, scratching one another's faces after The Redhead let fly a term of abuse, yelling, 'You bitch!'

'Bitch yourself! You stole my brother!'

At that point Santo intervened, and gave them both a hiding to restore the peace.

The Redhead burst into tears, and mumbled, 'I only said it to help her! Troubles soon come to a woman who marries without a dowry.'

So as to pacify his sister, who was shrieking and tearing her hair out, Santo repeated, 'What do you expect me to do about it, now that she's my wife? But she cares about you, and what she says is for your own good. D'you see what good it did the two of us to marry?'

Lucia turned to her mother, complaining, 'I wouldn't say no to doing the same! I'd even be better off as a domestic servant! If a decent fellow shows his face around here, they drive him away.' And her thoughts turned to the frog-seller, who never showed his face there any more.

Later on they heard he had taken up with Massaro Mariano's widow, and the pair of them were thinking about getting married, because although it was true he had no proper job, he was a splendid specimen of youth, as good-looking as St Vitus[6] in the flesh, no doubt about it. And the paralytic was so stinking rich that she could make a husband out of any man who took her fancy.

'Look around you, Joe,' she told him. 'This is all pure white linen, these ear-rings and necklaces are all pure gold, this big jar has forty gallons of oil inside it, and that large wicker basket is filled with beans to overflowing. If you wanted to, you could live like a prince, without having to spend your time up to your knees in bog-water catching frogs.'

'I wouldn't say no,' said Tricky Joe. But then he thought about Lucia's dark eyes, looking out for him from behind her muslin-covered window, and the widow's paralytic hips, bobbing up and down like frogs as she took him round the house showing him all those belongings of hers. In the end, though, after three whole days without earning a penny, he was forced to call on the widow for a square meal and something to drink. And as he stood in her doorway, looking out at the rain, he decided to say yes, so as to keep body and soul together.

'Honestly, I had to do it to keep body and soul together!' he said, his hands joined as if in prayer, when he returned to Lucia's front door to look for her. 'If it wasn't for the poor harvest, I would never have married the cripple, Lucia!'

'Go and tell that to the cripple!' replied the girl, foaming at the mouth. 'All I want to tell you is to clear off, and never come back here again.'

The cripple told him the same thing, that he must never go back there again, otherwise she would throw him out of the house, as poor and hungry as when she took him in. 'Don't you realize it wasn't God but I who saved you from starving to death?'

Her husband had everything he wanted. Well dressed, well fed, and with shoes on his feet, he had nothing else to do but wander about the village-square all day on a full stomach, his hands clasped behind his back, chatting to the greengrocer, the butcher and the fishmonger as they served their customers. 'That's all he's good for, to do nothing!' said The Redhead.

To which Lucia replied that he did nothing because he had a rich wife to support him. 'If he'd married me he would have worked to support his wife.'

Santo, with his head in his hands, simply reflected that his mother had urged him to marry the cripple himself, and if anyone was to blame it was himself for letting go the food from their mouths.

'When we're young,' he sermonized to his sister, 'we fill our heads with foolish ideas like the ones you have now, and we only go for what we like, without thinking of what comes afterwards. Ask The Redhead here whether we would do what we did all over again!'

The Redhead, squatting on the doorstep, nodded her head in agreement as her offspring ran around her, shrieking their heads off and tugging at her clothes and her hair. 'The good Lord could at least spare us the pain of having children!' she whimpered.

She took with her to the fields, every morning, those of her children she could manage, like a she-mule with her foals, the baby girl tucked into her rucksack whilst she held the eldest one by the hand. The other three she was forced to leave at home, to persecute her sister-in-law. The baby in the rucksack and the little girl who trotted along limping behind her would cry out in unison along the path, in the cold air of the grey morning, and every so often the mother had to stop, scratch her head and sigh, 'Oh, my God!' Then she would breathe on the girl's tiny hands that had turned purple from the cold, or she would haul the infant out of her rucksack to suckle her, and carry on walking. Her husband meanwhile went on ahead, bent low beneath the burden he was carrying, scarcely turning round for a moment to allow her to catch up, all breathless, dragging the child behind her, her breast naked to the elements. No longer did he turn to admire The Redhead's flowing tresses, or her gently heaving breasts, as on the farm at Castelluccio. Nowadays The Redhead exposed her bosom to the sun and the icy cold, like something that was useful only for giving suck, exactly like a she-mule. She was truly a beast of the field (and her husband could have no complaints on that score), digging, reaping and sowing, better than a man, when she pulled up her skirts, with those half-white, half-brown legs of hers, in the open field. She was twenty-seven now, with more to think about than pretty shoes and bright blue stockings. 'We're growing old,' her husband would tell her, 'and we have to think of the children.' At least they worked as a team, like a pair of oxen harnessed to the same plough. That, nowadays, was what their marriage had turned into.

'Don't I know it!' mumbled Lucia. 'I have their children to cope with, and no husband at all. When this poor old woman passes on, they might still give me my daily bread, but then again they might turn me out on to the street.'

Her poor mother was at a loss for an answer, and simply sat by the bed with a scarf round her head and her face yellow with illness. During the day she would sit quietly without a word outside the front door until the light of the setting sun faded over the grey roofs opposite, and the neighbours called in their chickens. Except that, when the doctor came to see her, and her daughter held up the lighted candle to her face, she would ask him, with a timid smile, 'For pity's sake, doctor, is it going to take long?'

To which Santo, who had a heart of gold, responded, 'I'm not worried about spending money on medicines, as long as that poor old woman stays here, and I know she's waiting there in the corner of the room when I come back home. She too worked hard all her life, and when we're old, our children will do the same for us.'

Meanwhile, at Camemi, Carmenio too had gone down with the fever. If his master had been a rich man he would have bought him medicines, but Vito was just a poor devil who depended on that small flock of his, and he was employing the lad out of charity. He could easily have looked after those few sheep himself, but for the fear of catching malaria. Besides, he was anxious to do a good deed by providing Nanni's orphan child with something to eat, and thus winning the good graces of Providence, which would surely come to the boy's assistance if there was any justice in heaven. What could he do to help if all he owned was that scrap of pasture land at Camemi, where the foul air lay as thick as a blanket of snow, and Carmenio had picked up tertian fever? One day, when the boy felt the fever crushing every bone in his body, he dropped off to sleep behind a large boulder that threw its shadow across the dusty lane and, as the horseflies buzzed in the sultry air of the hot summer's day, the sheep burst through into the neighbouring field, a barren piece of ground no bigger than a pocket handkerchief, where the crop, such as it was, had been half-destroyed by the heat. But to Zio Cheli, the field was the apple of his eye. It had cost him gallons of sweat, it was his harvest dream, and he kept strict watch over it in the shade of the branches of an old tree. When he saw the sheep running about, he shouted, 'Ah! Why bother paying these people?' He laid into Carmenio with his fists and his feet, and Carmenio woke up to find

him running like a lunatic after the sheep, wailing and screaming. All
Carmenio needed was that barrage of blows to his body that was already
racked with malaria! But how could the neighbour feel compensated
for the damage with merely a stream of abuse and oh my Gods? 'The
crop's ruined,' he yelled. 'My children will go hungry next winter!
Look at the damage you've done, you murderer! If I were to finish
you off altogether, it wouldn't be enough!'

Zio Cheli sought out witnesses to cite them before the judge, along
with Vito and his sheep. When Vito was served with the writ, he and
his wife were in despair. 'Ah! That villain Carmenio has completely
ruined us!' 'This is the way they pay you back for doing them a favour!'
'How was I to look after the sheep with all that malaria around?' 'Now
Zio Cheli will end up by taking every penny we possess!'

It was mid-day, and the poor fellow ran to Camemi, out of his mind
with despair over all the misfortunes pouring down upon him, and
with every kick and every blow he dealt to Carmenio, he puffed for
breath and muttered, 'You've turned us into paupers! You've ruined
us, you villain!'

'Don't you see what a state I'm in?' Carmenio replied as he tried to
ward off the blows. 'How am I to blame if I collapsed from the fever?
It took me by surprise, by the boulder over there!' But it was no use,
he had to pick up his stick and bundle, say goodbye to the two *onze*
he was owed by Vito the farmer, and abandon the flock. After so many
misfortunes, Vito was prepared to catch the fever himself next time.

Carmenio said nothing to anybody when he returned home empty-
handed, with his bundle and stick slung over his shoulder. His mother
was the only one to worry on seeing how pale and emaciated he was
looking, but failed to discover the reason. She found out later from
Don Venerando, who lived nearby and also owned some land at
Camemi that bordered on Zio Cheli's field.

'Don't tell anyone why Zio Vito sent you away!' the mother advised
her son. 'Otherwise nobody will offer you a job.'

And Santo also put in a word of advice: 'Don't tell anyone about
your malaria. Nobody'll want you if they know you're unwell.'

However, Don Venerando took him on for his sheep flock at Santa

Margherita, where the shepherd was robbing him blind, and doing him more damage than any sheep straying into a sown field. 'I'll see you have medicine,' he said, 'so that you don't have to take a nap and allow my sheep to wander about where they like.' Don Venerando had taken a kindly interest in the whole family for the sake of Lucia, whom he admired from his balcony when he was taking a breath of fresh air after lunch. 'If you let me have the girl as well, I'll pay her six *tarì* a month.' Not only that, but he said that Carmenio would be able to take his mother with him to Santa Margherita, because the old woman was growing weaker by the day, and at least, living with the flock, she would not go short of eggs, milk, and meat broth when a sheep was slaughtered. The Redhead went to great lengths to put together a bundle of white linen for her. Harvest time was approaching, they would no longer be going to Licciardo every day, and everything became scarce in the winter. And this time Lucia said she would be really glad to go into domestic service at Don Venerando's.

They settled the old woman on to the donkey, Santo on one side and Carmenio on the other, with the goods and chattels behind her. And while this was going on, the mother turned to her daughter, pale and heavy-eyed, and said, 'Who knows, who can tell, if I'll ever see you again? They say I'll be back in April. You be a good girl now, and stay with your master. At least you'll have everything you need.'

Lucia sobbed into her apron, and The Redhead too, poor girl. At that moment they were at peace with one another, and wept in each other's arms. 'The Redhead's good-hearted really,' said her husband. 'The trouble is, we're not rich enough to love each other all of the time. When the hens have nothing to peck at in the coop, they peck at one another.'

Lucia was nicely settled now, in Don Venerando's house, and said she wanted to live and die there, as the saying goes, to show how grateful she was to her master. She had as much bread and minestra as she could eat, a glass of wine every day, and her meat dish on Sundays and holidays. Meanwhile her monthly pay remained untouched, and in the evening she even found time to weave white linen for her own trousseau. She already had her eye on her prospective husband. Brasi, who was living under the same roof, was the scullery-boy who prepared the meals, and who also lent a hand with jobs in the country when he was needed. Their master had made his fortune in the same way, starting out in the service of the baron, and now he had his Don's title and his farms and his cows and sheep in abundance. Because Lucia came from a decent family that had fallen on hard times, and was known to be a respectable girl, she was given the less demanding jobs, washing dishes, keeping the cellar in order, and looking after the chickens. Her sleeping quarters were a cubby-hole under the stairs that was like a small room, with a bed, a chest of drawers, and all the rest, and Lucia was so contented that she wanted to live and die there. Meanwhile she was giving Brasi the glad eye, and she confided in him that in two or three years she would have her little nest-egg, and would be able to 'take the plunge', if the Lord so willed it.

Brasi turned a deaf ear to all this, though he liked Lucia, what with those coal-black eyes of hers, and the grace of God she had about her. And she was just as fond of Brasi, who was stockily built and curly-haired, with fine features and eyes full of mischief. As they washed the dishes or stoked up the fire beneath the copper kettle, he got up to all kinds of tricks to make her laugh, as though she were being tickled. He would splash water down the back of her neck and stick endive leaves into her tresses. Lucia would stifle her yells to prevent her master and mistress from hearing, and take refuge in the corner of the fireplace, her features red as burning coals, and start throwing twigs and dusters at him, while the water ran deliciously down her back.

'It takes two to play,' said Brasi. 'I've done my bit, now it's your turn.'

'Oh no, it isn't,' Lucia responded, 'I don't like playing these games.'

Brasi pretended to be mortified. He picked up the endive leaf she had thrown in his face and thrust it down his shirt,[7] murmuring, 'This belongs to me. Touch who dares, it's mine, and it stays where it is! If you want to put something of mine in the same place, here you are!' At this he pretended to grab a handful of his hair and hand it to her, sticking out his tongue as he did so.

With her countrywoman's fists she thumped him so hard he pretended to double up, claiming she would give him nightmares. Then, grabbing him by the hair like a lapdog, she felt a thrill of pleasure as she buried her fingers into his soft woollen curls.

'That's it, let off steam! I'm not fussy like you. With those hands of yours you can beat me as hard as you like!'

Once, as they were playing these games, Don Venerando surprised them and created a rumpus. If there were any more goings-on of that sort in his house, he would boot out the pair of them. Yet when he found the girl alone in the kitchen, he tried to caress her, taking her by the chin between his finger and thumb.

'No! No!' she cried. 'I don't like playing these games. If you don't leave me alone, I'll pack my things and leave.'

'You play these games with him, don't you! But not with me, the master of the house! What's all this? Don't you realize I can give you rings and gold chains, and provide you with a dowry if I want to?'

According to Brasi he really could, because the master had all the money he wanted, and his wife wore a silk cloak like a real lady, now that she was all skin and bone and as ancient as a mummy, which was why her husband would go down to the kitchen to chat up girls. He went there to keep an eye, also, on how much wood was being burnt, and how much meat they were cooking. He was rich, yes, but he knew how to hold on to his fortune, and he was forever having to placate his wife, who was hard to please now that she was a fine lady, and regularly complained about the smoke from the fire and the smell of onions.

'I intend to make up my dowry with my own hands,' Lucia retorted. 'I'm my mother's daughter, and I'm going to keep my honour till a good man comes along in search of a wife.'

'Very well, keep it!' the master responded. 'Let's see what a fine dowry you put together, and how many men come looking for this precious honour of yours!'

If the macaroni were overcooked, or Lucia brought a couple of fried eggs to table that were burnt at the edges, Don Venerando abused her roundly in his wife's presence. He seemed another man entirely as he stuck out his chest, shouting, 'What's all this pig's swill? These two servants are eating me out of house and home! If it happens again I'll throw the food in her face!'

His wife, bless her, was afraid the neighbours might hear the uproar, and sent away the maidservant, shrieking in a high-pitched voice, 'Go back to the kitchen! Get out, you slovenly good-for-nothing!'

Lucia returned to sit weeping in the corner of the fireplace, but Brasi cheered her up with his prankish smile, saying, 'What's it matter? Let them squawk! A fine mess we'd be in if we paid attention to our employers! If the eggs were burnt at the edges, it's too bad! I couldn't be chopping wood in the backyard and turning over the eggs at the same time. They get me to do the cooking as well as the odd jobs, and expect to be served like royalty! Don't they remember the time he sat eating bread and onion under the olives, and she gathered corn for him in the fields?'

Cook and maidservant then told each other how they had been dogged by ill luck, and how they both came of respectable parents who had once been richer than their master. Brasi was the son of no less a man than a wheelwright. He himself was to blame for dropping out of the craft and taking it into his head to wander round the country fairs, chasing after the wagon of a trader, who had taught him how to cook and look after animals.

Lucia recited the litany of her own troubles: her father's death, the livestock, The Redhead, the poor harvests. She said they were so alike that she and Brasi, there in the kitchen, seemed to be made for one another.

'Like your brother and The Redhead?' Brasi replied. 'Thanks very much!' However, he was not going to fling that marriage in her teeth and leave it at that. It was not because she was a peasant girl that he refused to marry her. But they were both so poor it would be like throwing themselves down the well with a stone round their necks.

Lucia suffered all this in silence, and whenever she felt like crying she would retire to her cubby-hole under the stairs, or to the corner of the fireplace when Brasi was nowhere about. Spending all day with him by the kitchen fire, she had grown to love the fellow. When the master stormed and bellowed, it was she who took the blame, and she always saw that Brasi had the bigger helping and the fuller glass. She would go out to the yard and chop wood for him, and she learned how to turn over the eggs and serve up the macaroni at exactly the right moment.

When Brasi saw her crossing herself as she was preparing to eat, with the bowl on her lap, he said, 'Have you never seen food before?'

He was constantly complaining about everything, about living in a prison, or about having only three hours in the evening to drop in at the tavern to see his mates. Sometimes Lucia, blushing and lowering her gaze, would pluck up courage and say, 'Why go to the tavern? Stay away from it. It's no place for you.'

'Anyone can see you're a peasant!' he would reply. 'You people think every tavern has the devil inside it. My dear woman, I come from a long line of craftsmen. I'm no country bumpkin!'

'I say it for your own good. You spend good money there, and you could easily end up by picking a fight with someone.'

With a thrill of satisfaction, mollified by her words and by those eyes that were still turned shyly away from him, Brasi said, 'What does that matter to you?'

'Nothing. I'm saying it for your own sake.'

'Don't you get bored, spending all day inside the house?'

'No, I thank God for the way I am, and only wish my family could say the same. I have everything I need.'

She was drawing off some wine, crouching down with the earthenware jar between her legs, and Brasi had descended with her into the cellar to light the way. The cellar was big and dark, like a church, with not a sound to be heard, and the pair of them, Brasi and Lucia, alone together below ground, when he put an arm round her shoulders and planted a kiss on those coral-red lips of hers.

Poor Lucia, leaning forward and keeping her eyes on the jug, waited anxiously, with neither of them saying a word, and all she could hear was his heavy breathing and the gurgling of the wine. Then suddenly, trembling all over, she let out a strangled cry and started backward, spilling some froth from the red wine on to the floor.

'What's the matter?' exclaimed Brasi. 'Anyone would think I'd given you a slap! So you don't really love me at all!'

She dared not look at him, even though she was dying to do so. Red in the face, she stared at the spilt wine, murmuring, 'Poor me! What have I done? Poor me! The master's wine!'

'Oh, forget the wine, the master's got plenty more. Pay attention to me instead. Do you love me or don't you?'

This time, without replying, she let him take her hand, and when Brasi asked her to return his kiss, she turned and kissed him, flushed with something more than a feeling of shame.

'Has no one ever kissed you before?' Brasi asked, laughing. 'That's a good one! You're shaking all over as if I said I was going to kill you.'

'Yes, I do love you,' she replied. 'I've been dying to tell you. Don't worry about it if I'm still shaking. I was worried about the wine.'

'You too, then! When did it happen? Why didn't you tell me?'

'It was when we were saying we were made for one another.'

'Come on,' said Brasi, scratching his head. 'Let's go back up, in case the master comes.'

Lucia was enormously happy after being kissed like that. She felt that Brasi had sealed on her lips his promise to marry her.

But he never even talked about it, and if the girl were to mention the subject, he would answer, 'Why are you in such a hurry? Anyway, there's no point in tying a halter round our necks when we can be together here as though we were man and wife.'

'No, it's not the same. Now we each live for ourselves, but when we're married, we'll be one, and one alone.'

'A fine pair the two of us'll make! Besides, we're not made of the same stuff. Now if only you had some kind of dowry!'

'What a low creature you are! You're not in love with me at all!'

'Oh yes, I am. I'll do anything for you, but I don't want to hear that sort of talk.'

'In that case you'll get nothing out of me! Let me alone, keep your eyes off me!'

Now that she realized that all men were liars and deceivers, she wanted nothing more to do with them. She would rather throw herself head first down the well, she would become a Child of Mary, she would take her good name and hurl it out of the window! What was the use of it, without a dowry? Very well then, very well, she would go crawling to that dirty old man of a master, and trade her honour for a dowry. Don Venerando was forever at her heels with his compliments and complaints, looking after his interests, seeing whether they were putting too much wood on the fire or using too much oil in the cooking. He would send Brasi off to buy him an ounce of snuff, and try to give Lucia a pinch on the cheek, chasing her round the kitchen on tiptoe so that his wife would hear nothing, reproaching her for lack of respect by making him run after her in that fashion! 'No! No!' she shrieked, like a scalded cat. She would rather take her things and go away!

'And what'll you eat? And where will you find a husband without a dowry? Take a look at these earrings! And I'll present you with 20 *onze* for your dowry. Brasi would give his eye-teeth for 20 *onze*!'

Ah, yes! That low creature of a Brasi had left her to be mauled by the filthy, shaking paws of their master! He'd left her with the thought of her mother who could not survive for very much longer, and of the house now broken up and full of troubles, and of Tricky Joe who had ditched her to go and eat the widow's bread! He'd left her with her mind filled with the temptation of the earrings and the 20 *onze*!

So one day she came into the kitchen looking all perturbed, with the golden earrings dangling against her cheeks.

Brasi rubbed his eyes, and said, 'What a pretty picture you make, Comare Lucia!'

'Is that how you like to see me, then? Very well, that's good!'

Now that he saw her with the earrings and all the rest, Brasi did his utmost to make himself useful and solicitous as if she had become a second mistress of the house. He saw to it that she got the bigger helping and sat in the best place at the fireside. He opened his heart to her, pointing out how poor they both were, and how much good it did to a man's soul to share his troubles with the person he loved. If only he could manage to lay his hands on 20 *onze*, he would start up a little café and take a wife, with himself in the kitchen and his wife behind the counter. No longer would they have to take orders from others. If the master wished to do them a good turn, it was no trouble, because to him, giving away 20 *onze* was like taking a pinch of snuff. Brasi wouldn't be asking any awkward questions, not he! In this world, one hand washes the other. And no one could blame him for earning his corn in whatever way he could. Poverty was no crime.

But Lucia turned sometimes red and sometimes pale, and sometimes her eyes filled with tears, and she hid her face in her apron. After a while she no longer set foot outside the house, and never went to Mass or confession, not even at Easter or at Christmas.

In the kitchen she settled down, her head bowed, in the darkest corner, wrapped around in the new dress given her by the master, with its loose waist.

Brasi comforted her with a stream of fine words. He put an arm round her neck, he fingered the fine fabric of her dress and told her how much he admired it. Those golden earrings seemed to have been made for her. There was no need to feel ashamed and lower your eyes when you were well dressed and had money in your pocket, especially when your eyes were as beautiful as Lucia's.

The poor girl, though still upset, recovered her composure sufficiently to raise those eyes and look him in the face, murmuring, 'Is it true then, Brasi? Do you still love me?'

'Yes, yes of course, I want to love you,' Brasi replied, hand on heart. 'But how can I help it if I can't afford to marry you? If you had a dowry of 20 *onze* I'd marry you with my eyes shut.'

Don Venerando had by this time taken a liking also to Brasi, and gave him his cast-off clothes and old boots. Whenever he came down to the kitchen he would pour him a large glass of wine, saying, 'Take this and drink to my good health!'

And his fat belly shook with laughter on watching Brasi turn pale as death, pull a long face and turn to Lucia, muttering, 'The master's a real gentleman, Lucia! The neighbours can talk as much as they like, they're all jealous and starving to death. They'd like to be in your place.'

Santo, her brother, heard about it in the piazza a few months later, and ran back breathless to tell his wife. Poor they had always been, but at least they were respected. The Redhead, no less appalled at the news, rushed off to her sister-in-law in such a state of shock that she could hardly utter a syllable. But by the time she returned home to her husband, she'd calmed down entirely, and was all smiles.

'I wish you could see it! A chest, so high, full of white linen! Rings, pendants and necklaces, all in fine gold. Then she has 20 *onze* for her dowry. A real godsend!'

'It makes no difference!' said Santo, who was unable to come to terms with what had happened. 'She might at least have waited for our mother to close her eyes!'

All this happened in the year of the snow, when a whole lot of roofs collapsed, and – Lord deliver us! – the cattle in the region were dying like flies.

When people at Lamia, and on the hillside of Santa Margherita, saw the evening sky turning so dark with ominous thick clouds that the oxen turned round in distrust and began to low, they all came out of their cottages and peered silently into the distance towards the sea, shielding their eyes with their hands. The bell of the old monastery, at the top of the village, tolled to exorcize the Stygian gloom, and women, dark against the pale horizon, swarmed up the hill to the castle to view the Dragon's Tail[8] as it swept across the sky in a vortex black as pitch. They said it smelt of sulphur, and foretold an evil night. The women pointed their fingers at the dragon to ward him off, they spat in his face, they bared their breasts to display their scapulars[9] and dragged their crucifixes down to their navels, and they prayed to God, the souls in Purgatory, and St Lucy,[10] whose vigil it was, to protect their fields, their beasts, and those of their menfolk who were away from the village.

Carmenio had gone with his flock to Santa Margherita at the start of the winter. His mother was unwell that evening, and lay restless on the bed, her eyes wide open, no longer content to remain quiet, wanting one thing, then another, wanting to get up, wanting to be turned on to her other side. Carmenio ran around for a while, paying attention to her, trying to do what he could. Then finally he planted himself in front of the bed, not knowing what to do, with his head between his hands.

Their hut was on the far side of the stream, at the foot of the valley, between two enormous boulders that towered above its roof. The barren hillside, ascending steeply on the opposite bank, and strewn with black rocks among which the white trail of the footpath was lost, began to disappear from view as the darkness rose from the valley. Their neighbours from the flock by the cactus grove called at dusk to see if the invalid was in need of anything. She no longer moved on her pallet, but lay face upwards, her nostrils the colour of soot.

'Bad sign!' said Decu the shepherd. 'If I hadn't left my sheep up there, with the weather that's coming, I wouldn't leave you here by yourself this night. Call out, if you need me!'

Carmenio, resting his head on the doorpost, said he would do as Decu had suggested. But as he watched him walking gradually away and disappearing into the night, he longed to run after him, to start shouting, tear out his hair, or do something, anything.

'If anything happens,' Decu the shepherd shouted from the distance, 'run up to the flock by the cactus grove. There's always somebody there.'

By the little that was left of twilight as it penetrated the cactus groves and lit up the peaks of the mountains, the flock could still be seen high up on the rock. Suddenly, from the far distance, down at Lamia and towards the plain, the sound of howling dogs drifted up and made the blood run cold. The sheep, terrified, started running round in circles, as if they sensed that a wolf was coming for them, and at the jingling of their bells it seemed that a thousand eyes glittered forth all around from the darkness. Then the sheep stopped and huddled together motionless with lowered heads, and the sheepdog ceased its barking in a long, mournful howl, seated on its tail.

'If only I'd known!' thought Carmenio. 'It would have been better to tell Decu not to leave me here alone.'

Every so often, the sound of sheep-bells pierced the darkness outside as the flock took fright. Through the crack inside, all that could be seen was the pitch-black outline of the doorway. The hillside opposite, the lower part of the valley, the plain of Lamia, all were engulfed in a blackness so profound that the roar of the swollen stream below seemed to take shape within it and hover menacingly above the hut.

If only he had known about this also! Before dark he would have run back to the village to summon his brother, who would be there with him now for sure, along with Lucia and his sister-in-law.

At that moment his mother began to say something, but you couldn't tell what she was saying, as she groped around the bed with her hands, all skin and bone.

'Mamma! Mamma! What do you want?' Carmenio asked. 'Tell me, I'm here beside you!'

His mother made no reply, but simply waved her head from side to side as if to say she wanted nothing. Carmenio held the candle up to her face, and burst into tears with alarm.

'Mamma! Mamma mia!' wailed Carmenio. 'I'm here on my own and can't help you!'

He opened the door to call up to the shepherds at the cactus grove, but nobody heard him.

The hillside, the valley, the plain below, everywhere was silent, wrapped in a dense grey light like cotton wool, when suddenly the muffled sound of a church bell, tolling in the distance, came on the ears as though half-frozen in the snow.

'Holy Mary, Mother of God!' sobbed Carmenio. 'Who's the bell tolling for?' Then he shouted, 'You up there at the cactus grove, help! For God's sake, come and help me!'

Then at last the people at the cactus grove on the mountain-top, hearing a voice in the distance mingling with the sound of the bell at Francofonte,[11] called out, 'Halloa . . . What's up? What's the matter?'

'Help, for the love of God! Help, down here at Decu the shepherd's!'

'Halloa . . . Bring in the shee . . . eep . . . ! Bring 'em in . . . !'

'No, it's not the sheep! Not the sheep!' At that point an owl settled on the roof of the hut and began to hoot.

'There!' Carmenio murmured, crossing himself. 'Now the owl's caught the scent of the dead! Now my mother's going to die!'

Alone in the hut with his mother, who no longer uttered a word, he wanted to cry.

'What is it, Mamma? Say something, Mamma! Mamma, are you feeling cold?'

Her face now dark, she showed no sign of life. Carmenio lit a fire between the two hearth bricks, then watched as the sticks burned, forming a tongue of flame, that hissed as if to tell him something.

When he tended the sheep at Resecone, there was a fellow from Francofonte who, after dark, came out with tales of witches riding round on broomsticks and casting spells above the flames of the fireplace. Carmenio could still remember how the farmhands, their eyes popping, gathered round to listen below the lantern hanging from the pillar in the vast, dark winery, and how, that evening, none had the courage to return to his own sleeping place.

True, he was wearing the medallion of Our Lady round his neck and St Agrippina's ribbon, blackened by time, around his wrist. In his pocket he still carried the reed pipe that reminded him of summer evenings, 'Whoo! Whoo!' when the sheep are released to roam at will through the golden-yellow stubble, and noon is filled with the chirruping of crickets, and dusk with the warbling of larks as they descend to their nests in the earth, and the air is heavy with the scent of rosemary and calamint. 'Whoo! Whoo! Infant Gesú!'. When he went back to his village for Christmas, that was the tune they always used to play around the crib, all lit up and bedecked with orange branches, and outside every cottage the children would be playing pitch-and-toss, with the warm December sun on their backs. Then they would all set off in a big crowd with their neighbours to midnight Mass, joking and jostling as they made their way along the village streets in the dark. Ah! Why should his heart be aching so, with his mother no longer uttering a word? There was still some time to go before midnight. From every fissure between the stones of the unplastered walls, hundreds of eyes, ice-cold and black, seemed to be peeping out into the room towards the hearth.

In a corner of the room, a coat had been flung full length on his straw mattress, and now the arms seemed to fill out as the picture of the Archangel Michael that hung on the wall behind the bed came to life, and the devil tore his hair and bared his white fangs as he came bursting forth from the zig-zag flames of Hell.

Next morning, Santo arrived with The Redhead followed by the children, and Lucia, who in her distress did nothing to hide her condition. All looking pale as death, they gathered round the dead woman's bed, with no other thought but to tear their hair and beat their heads with their fists.

Then, catching sight of his sister's big belly, which was a disgrace to the family, Santo spluttered amid the weeping and the wailing, 'At least she might have waited until this poor old woman closed her eyes!'

For her own part, Lucia murmured, 'If only I'd known! If only I would've seen she had a doctor and medicine, now that I have 20 *onze*.'

'She's up there in Heaven praying to God for us sinners,' concluded The Redhead. 'She's quite content, poor soul, because she knows you've got your dowry. Brasi's bound to marry you now.'

Bigwigs

The trouble is, they know how to write. They're made of flesh and blood like the rest, so like any other poor devil they put up with the hoar-frost on a dark morning and the dog-days at harvest time, so as to keep watch on their workers and make sure they're not wasting their time and robbing them of a day's wages. But once they get their claws into you, they jot down your name, surname and parentage with those pens of theirs, and you never get out of their grubby little books, you're in debt up to your ears.

'You still owe two bushels of corn from last year.'

'But, sir, the harvest was poor!'

'Is it my fault if it didn't rain? Was I supposed to give the fields something to drink?'

'I sweated blood on that land of yours, sir!'

'That's what I pay you for, you rogue, to sweat blood! I sweat blood paying you to farm the crops, and when the harvest is bad, you quit the tenancy and sneak off with your sickle under your arm!'

They even pretend it's better to be poor than rich, because if you're poor you can't be skinned alive for what you owe. When you have no belongings you pay more for your land, because the owner is taking a bigger risk, and when the harvest is poor, the tenant is sure to be left with nothing, and go off with his sickle under his arm. All the same it's a nasty way to leave, after a year's hard work, and a long winter ahead of you without food.

The fact is that a poor harvest brings out the devil in everybody. Once, when the harvest seemed to be under a curse, the mendicant friar called around midday at Don Piddu's farm, spurring on his fine bay mule by digging his sandals into its belly, and calling out from the distance, 'Jesus and Mary be praised!'

Don Piddu was seated on a worn-out mule-pannier in the deserted farmyard, gloomily surveying the parched stubble that lay all around. He could not even feel the scorching sun as it beat down on his bare head, consumed as he was by despair.

'That's a fine mule you have, Fra Giuseppe! It's worth more than all four of these skinny jades of mine, with nothing to thresh or to eat!'

'It's the collection mule,' Fra Giuseppe replied. 'The charity of our neighbours be praised! I've come to gather alms.'

'It's lucky for you that you can gather without sowing, and amble down to the refectory when the bell tolls, to fill your stomach with your neighbours' charity! I have five children to think about feeding! You see what a fine harvest! Last year you collared a couple of acres of grain from me for St Francis to send me a good harvest, and what did I get in return? Three months of burning sun and not a drop of rain.'

Fra Giuseppe stood mopping his brow with a pocket handkerchief.

'Feeling hot, Fra Giuseppe? I'll give you something to cool you down!'

Whereupon he got some of his farmhands, seething with rage like himself, to pull the friar's sackcloth over his head and soak him with buckets of filthy green water from the horse pond.

'By all that's wicked!' shouted Don Piddu. 'If giving alms to Christ doesn't help, next time I'll give them to the devil!'

From then on he banned Capuchins from entering the farm, and only allowed the Minim Friars to come near the place.

Fra Giuseppe tied a knot in his handkerchief. 'So! Wanted to inspect my underpants, did you, Don Piddu? You'll have neither shirt on your back nor underpants by the time I've finished with you!'

He was a giant of a friar with a huge beard, and shoulders as broad as an ox, so that in the streets and the courtyards the peasants and their wives looked upon him as an oracle.

'Keep well away from Don Piddu,' he told them. 'Remember he's a heathen, and his land has a curse on it!'

When, towards the end of Carnival, the missioners came to conduct the Lenten spiritual exercises and preach on the doorsteps of sinners or street girls or people enjoying life too much, Fra Giuseppe joined them as they went along in procession, scourging themselves for the sins of others. He pointed towards the house of Don Piddu, who was suffering the torments of the damned: poor harvests, dead livestock, a sick wife, unmarried daughters, all dressed up and ready to leave the nest. The eldest, Donna Saridda, was nearly thirty, but she was still called Saridda so as to stop her growing up.[1] According to Pietro Macca, a servant at the town hall, she had finally grabbed a husband at the Mayor's ball on Maundy Thursday, because he'd seen her holding hands with Don Giovannino as they flung themselves about in the square dance. Don Piddu had starved himself for months so as to take his daughter to the ball in a silk dress with a plunging neckline. You never know! At that moment the missioners came to the Mayor's front door and started preaching against temptation and all the sinning that was going on inside, and the Mayor had to have all the shutters closed, otherwise the people in the road would have hurled stones and broken the windows.

Donna Saridda returned home in high spirits, as though she had the winning lottery ticket in her purse. She never slept a wink that night for thinking about Don Giovannino, unaware that Fra Giuseppe was about to tell him, 'Are you mad, young man, to be marrying into the household of Don Piddu, when the bailiffs are due there at any moment?'

Don Giovannino was not concerned about a dowry. But calling in the bailiffs was another kettle of fish! The shame of it! People crowded round Don Piddu's doorway to see them taking away his wardrobes and his chests of drawers, leaving white patches on the walls where they had been standing for years, while his daughters, pale as death, were doing everything they could to hide what was happening from their mother as she lay there on her sickbed. She, poor woman, pretended not to notice. She had gone with her husband to plead with the notary, with the judge, swearing they could pay the next day, or the day after that. But they returned home with bowed heads, she concealing her face in her shawl. After all, she did have barons' blood flowing through her veins! On the day the bailiffs came, Donna Saridda had gone round with tears in her eyes closing all the shutters, because people born with a Don to their name feel the disgrace of it all. When they took him on out of charity as a watchman at the Fiumegrande farmlands, at harvest time, when malaria was killing people off like flies, Don Piddu was not bothered about the malaria. What bothered him was that whenever the peasants got into an argument with him, they dropped the Don and addressed him as though he were one of themselves.

At least other poor devils, as long as they have strong arms and good health, can find ways of earning a crust, which is what Don Marcantonio Malerba said when he fell on hard times. He had loads of children, his wife was forever pregnant, and he had to make the bread, prepare the minestra, do the laundry and sweep out the rooms. Bigwigs are brought up differently, and need a whole lot of things that others can do without. The children of Don Marcantonio would go the whole day on empty stomachs without a word, and if the eldest was sent by his father to buy a loaf or some fresh salad on credit, he would go after dark, hiding his head beneath his patched-up cloak.

His father did all he could to make ends meet, either by renting a piece of land or taking up a tenancy. He would return from the fields on foot, later than everyone else, when nobody was passing down the lane, wrapped in what his wife called the plaid, her tattered shawl, having put in a hard day's digging like the rest.

Then on Sundays he would go and join the other bigwigs at the gentlemen's club, where they would stand around exchanging gossip among themselves, hands in pockets, noses tucked into the lapels of their overcoats, or else they would sit playing cards, wearing their hats, with their sticks between their knees. On the stroke of noon they would scatter like the wind in various directions, and he would go back home pretending that, like the others, he too had a meal waiting for him. 'What else can I do?' he would say. 'I can't very well take on daywork with the children.' And whenever the father sent the boys to Zio Masi, or Massaro Pinu, to ask for the loan of a quantity of spelt for sowing a couple of acres, or a bushel or two of beans for making soup, they turned red in the face, and mumbled as though they were already grown up.

When Mongibello[2] spat out fire, destroying vineyards and olive groves, at least the workers with a pair of strong arms were in no danger of dying of hunger. But the bigwigs who owned the land would have

been better off buried under the lava, with their farms, their children
and everything else. The people with nothing to lose went out from
the village to stand watching the fire, hands in pockets. Today it had
overrun so-and-so's vineyard, tomorrow it would get into so-and-so's
field, now it was approaching the road-bridge, tomorrow it would
surround that cottage on the right. The ones who were not gawping
were darting to and fro removing tiles, shutters and furniture, emptying
the rooms and saving whatever they could, driven out of their minds
by their haste and despair, like ants in an upturned nest.

They brought Don Marco the news while he was at table with his
family, tucking in to a plate of maccheroni. 'Don Marco, sir, the lava's
turned in your direction. The fire'll be in your vineyard very soon
now.' The wretched man was so alarmed that the fork dropped from
his fingers. At the vineyard the watchman was carrying away the
wine-making gear, barrel-staves, and everything else that could be
moved to safety, while his wife went round the edge of the vineyard,
planting canes with images on them of the saints who were supposed
to protect it, mumbling Hail Marys.

The great dark cloud was raining down ash on Don Marco as he
arrived, gasping for breath, driving his donkey ahead of him. From the
yard in front of the winery one could see the huge black wave,
smouldering as it piled up round the vineyard, crashing forward here
and there with a clatter like a pile of dishes being dropped, and splitting
open to reveal the red fire seething inside it. In the distance, before it
reached them, the tallest trees rustled and quivered in the still air and
then began to smoulder and to crackle. Then they suddenly burst
into flame, like torches lighting up one after another across the silent
countryside, in the path of the lava. As the canes with the holy images
caught fire one by one, the watchman's wife retreated and replaced
them with new ones, weeping in terror at the destruction all around
her, and thinking that the master would no longer need a watchman
and they would be out of a job. The guard dog, too, was howling as
it faced the burning vineyard. Even the winery, roofless and open to
the elements, with all its bits and pieces being piled in the courtyard,
seemed amid the cowering farmland to be shaking with fear as it was
emptied before being abandoned to its fate.

'What are you doing?' Don Marco asked the watchman as he tried to save the barrels and the contents of the winery. 'Save your breath. I've lost everything now, and there's nothing to put in the barrels in any case.'

He kissed the vineyard rake for the last time before casting it aside and going back by the way he had come, leading his donkey by the halter.

In God's name! The bigwigs have their troubles too, they're made of flesh and blood like the rest of us. Take Donna Marina, for instance, Don Piddu's other daughter, the one who threw herself at the stable-boy after giving up hope of ever getting married when they fell on hard times and had to live in the country, and her parents kept her with not even a shred of a new dress, and not so much as a dog would come near her. One afternoon, on a hot day in July, while the horseflies were buzzing round the deserted farmyard, and her parents were taking a siesta behind closed doors, she came across the lad as he lay behind a haystack. He turned bright red and mumbled to himself as she fixed her eyes on him, then she seized him by the hair to get him to kiss her.

Don Piddu would have died of shame. After the bailiffs and the poverty, he would not have believed he could sink any lower. The poor mother heard about it at communion on Easter Sunday. That woman was a saint! Don Piddu was in retreat at the monastery, doing his spiritual exercises along with all the other bigwigs. The bigwigs joined up with their farmhands to confess their sins and listen to the sermons. In fact, they paid to maintain them there in the hope that if they'd stolen anything they would repent, and hand back their ill-gotten gains. During those eight days of spiritual exercises, bigwigs and villagers returned to the Garden of Eden and treated one another as brothers. The masters served the farmhands at table with their own hands in such a spirit of humility that the peasants' food went down the wrong way in their embarrassment, and with all those jaws munching away the refectory sounded more like a pig trough while the missioners were preaching about hell and purgatory. That year Don Piddu would have preferred not to go as he was unable to pay his share, and besides, there was nothing left for his farmhands to steal. But the magistrate had him called, and forced him to go and purify himself, so as not to set a bad example. Those eight days were a godsend for anyone with business to attend to in some poor devil's house, without fear that the husband would return suddenly from the fields and ruin the party. The door of the monastery was locked for everyone, but as soon as night fell the young men with anything to spend sloped off and stayed out till dawn.

One night it was the turn of Don Piddu, after coming to hear a piece of gossip put about by Fra Giuseppe, to slip quietly away as if he were a lad of twenty with a girl-friend waiting for him, and goodness knows what he stumbled across when he let himself into his house. When he returned before dawn he was certainly as pale as death, and seemed to have put on a hundred years. This time the escape had been discovered, and the lady-killers returned to the monastery to find the mission father on his knees behind the door, praying to God to forgive them for the sins they had committed. Don Piddu, too, flung himself down on his knees to confess into the missioner's ear, shedding buckets of tears.

Ah! What a terrible thing to discover! In his own home! In his daughter's bedroom, where not even the sun ever entered! The stable-boy jumping out of the window! And Marina, pale as death, not daring to look him in the face, clinging desperately to the doorposts to defend her lover. At that moment he had a vision of himself standing with his other daughters, and his sick wife, and the magistrates and the police, in a river of blood.

'You! You!' he murmured. The sinner trembled all over, but offered no reply. Then she fell to her knees, hands clasped in an attitude of prayer, as though she could read murder in his eyes, whereupon he turned and fled, clutching his head between his hands.

The priest confessor advised him to offer up his suffering to God, but instead he should have told him, 'You see, sir, when ordinary folk face this kind of trouble, they say nothing because they're poor, they can't read or write, and the only way they can think of to put things right lands them up in jail!'

Freedom[1]

They unfurled a tricolour streamer above the campanile, rang the bells like merry hell, and began shouting 'Hooray for freedom!' in the square.

Like the sea in a storm, the crowd foamed and heaved in front of the bigwigs' club, outside the town hall, on the steps leading up to the church: a solid mass of white headscarves, axes and sickles flashing in the sun. Then they burst into a narrow street.

'You, baron, for a start! That's for getting your farm-watchmen to beat up the people!' At the head of the mob, a harridan with ancient hair sticking straight up, armed only with her fingernails.

'You next, priest of the devil, for sucking away our souls!'

'That's for you, rich pig, who grew so fat on the flesh of the poor that you can't even run away!'

'That's for you, constable, for prosecuting no one except the penniless!'

'And that's for you, woodkeepers, for selling the body and soul of yourselves and your neighbours for a couple of *tarì* a day!'

The smell of blood made them drunk. Sickles, hands, rags, stones were all dripping with it. 'Get the bigwigs! Get the felt hats![2] Kill 'em! Kill 'em. Get the felt hats!'

Don Antonio was slipping off home through the back streets. The first blow floored him, face bleeding, on to the pavement. 'Why? Why d'you want to kill me?'

'You as well! The devil take you!' A crippled street urchin grabbed his filth-covered hat and spat into it. 'Down with the felt hats! Hooray for freedom!'

'Take that! You too!' This to The Reverend[3] who preached that anyone stealing bread would go to Hell.

He was on his way back from saying Mass, with the consecrated Host in his belly. 'Please don't kill me! I'm in mortal sin!' Gnà Lucia was the mortal sin he meant. Her father had sold her to The Reverend when she was fourteen, the winter of the famine, and she'd been filling the Cloister Wheel[4] and the streets with starving brats ever since. If all that dog's meat were worth anything to them that day, they could have stuffed themselves with it as they went about carving it up with their sickles in the doorways and the cobbled streets. The same thing happens when a starving wolf turns up in a flock of sheep: it doesn't think of filling its belly, but just slaughters everything in sight from pure rage. First, the Grand Lady's son, who had rushed out to see what was happening; then the chemist, as he was shutting up shop in a tearing hurry; and then Don Paolo, who was riding back from the vineyard on his donkey with a couple of saddlebags that looked half-empty. And he was even wearing an old cap that his daughter had embroidered for him ages ago, before the disease struck the vineyard. She saw him fall at the front door, as she was waiting with her five children for the few vegetables he had in his saddlebags to make the minestra. 'Paolo! Paolo!'

One of them struck him in the back with a blow from an axe. Another fell upon him with a sickle, and ripped him open as his bloody arm was reaching for the door-knocker.

But the worst moment of all was when the notary's son, an eleven-year-old with a head of golden blond hair, managed somehow to fall in the midst of the crowd. His father had raised his head two or three times and called out, 'Neddu! Neddu!' before dragging himself to die in the gutter.

Neddu was running away in absolute terror, eyes and mouth wide open, unable to utter a sound. He took a tumble, and raised himself on one knee, like his father. The torrent poured over him. One of them put the boot in and smashed his cheek, and the boy still pleading for mercy with clasped hands. No, he didn't want to die in the way he'd seen his father killed! It was heartbreaking! The woodcutter, out of pity, landed him a massive blow with his axe using both hands as if he were felling a fifty-year-old oak, as he lay there shaking like a leaf

Another one cried out, 'What the hell! He would only have grown up a lawyer!'

What did it matter? Now they had their hands covered in so much blood, they had to spill all the rest. Get them all! All the felt hats! It was no longer the hunger, the bullying, the beatings, that were fuelling their anger. It was innocent blood. The women were even more ferocious, waving their skinny arms, shrieking with anger in high-pitched voices, their tender flesh showing beneath the rags they were wearing. 'So much for you, that came praying to the good Lord in your silk dress! And you, that loathed having to kneel alongside the poor! Take that! Take that!' Into the houses, up the stairs, into the bedrooms, tearing up the silk and the fine curtains. No end of ear-rings decorating those bleeding faces! And what a collection of gold rings on the hands trying to ward off the blows from the axes!

The baroness had ordered a barricade of wooden beams, country carts, and casks full of wine to be placed behind the main entrance. Her watchmen were firing away from the windows to sell their lives dearly. The crowd kept their heads down against the shotgun pellets, having no weapons of their own to fire back. Before all this, anyone carrying firearms faced the death penalty. 'Hooray for freedom!' Once they broke down the door, they charged into the courtyard and up the steps, trampling over the wounded. They left the watchmen alone. 'We'll get the watchmen later!' First of all they were after the flesh of the baroness, flesh fattened on partridges and precious wines. She was running from one room to the next with a suckling at her breast, hair dishevelled, and there were plenty of rooms for her to run through. You could hear the crowd yelling along the corridors, closing in on her like a river in spate.

Her eldest son, a boy of sixteen with a body still as pale as his mother's, propped up the door with his trembling hands, shouting, 'Mother! Mother!' At the first push, they crashed the door down on top of him. He clung on to legs stamping over it, but soon stopped shouting. His mother had taken refuge on the balcony, clinging frantically to the baby with a hand over its mouth to stop it bawling. Staring wildly around him, her other son was trying to shield her with his body, grabbing all those axes by the blades as though he had a hundred hands to do it with. They were separated in a flash. One of them took her by the hair, another by the waist, another by her dress, and they lifted her in the air above the balcony rail. The charcoal-burner seized the suckling baby from her arms. The other brother could see nothing of all this, only black and red everywhere. They were stamping on him and breaking every bone in his body with their hob-nailed boots; he had sunk his teeth into a hand that had him by the throat and refused to let it go. The throng was so tightly packed that they were unable to strike with their axes, that were glistening in the air.

And in that raging carnival of the month of July, amid the drunken shouting of the ravenous mob, the church bell went on tolling furiously away until evening, without either noon or Angelus, as if in the land of the Turks. Eventually they began to split up, weary of the slaughter, and crept slowly away, each avoiding his companion. By nightfall all the doors were closed out of fear, and in every house a lamp kept vigil. In the narrow streets all you could hear were the dogs, rummaging in the corners, gnawing hungrily away at the bones by the light of the moon, which washed over everything and cast its glow over the wide-open doorways and windows of the empty houses.

Daylight came. It was Sunday, with nobody in the square, and no bell ringing for Mass. The sexton had made himself scarce, there was not a priest to be found anywhere. The first group of people to form in front of the church looked suspiciously at one another, each wondering what his neighbour had on his conscience. Then, once a tidy number had turned up, they started to grumble, saying, 'People can't go without their Sunday Mass, like a pack of dogs!' The bigwigs' club was boarded up, and no one knew where to go to take the masters' orders for the week to follow. From the campanile the tricolour streamer still dangled flabbily in the stifling midsummer heat.

As the shaded area in front of the church grew gradually smaller, they all crowded together in a corner. Between a pair of shabby-looking houses, at the foot of a narrow lane that sloped down steeply from the square, you could see the parched fields of the plain, and the dark woods on the slopes of Mount Etna. Now it was time for them to share out those woods and those fields. Everyone was adding up on his fingers how big his own portion ought to be, and casting hostile glances at his neighbour.

'Freedom meant there was going to be enough for everyone!' they were saying. 'That swine of a Nino, and that Ramurazzo, would like to take over from the felt hats, and carry on the bullying where they left off! With no surveyor left to measure out the land, and no notary to put it down in writing, it's everyone for himself, and the devil take the hindmost!'

'And what if you guzzle up your own share in the tavern? Do we have to divide everything up all over again?'

'You call me a thief, and I'll call you a thief. Now there's freedom, anyone can go for a double helping and live it up like the bigwigs!' The woodcutter waved his arm in the air as if he were still wielding his axe.

Next day they heard the general was coming, the one who frightened the life out of people, to deal out justice. You could see the red shirts of his soldiers making their way slowly up the ravine towards the village. All that was needed was to roll boulders down on them and wipe out the lot. But nobody moved. The women were screaming and tearing out their hair. The men, black as coal and with long beards, waited on the hillside, dangling their hands between their thighs, and watched the young soldiers arriving, bending exhausted beneath their rusty old rifles, with that tiny general on his big black horse riding alone ahead of them.

The general had straw brought into the church, and put his boys to bed like a father. In the morning, before dawn, if they failed to get up at the sound of the trumpet, he would ride into the church on horseback, swearing like a Turk. That was the sort of man he was. The first thing he did was to order five or six to be shot: Pippo, the cripple, Pizzanello, whoever happened to come within reach. The woodcutter, while they were making him kneel against the wall of the cemetery, was crying like a child because of something his mother had said to him, and because of the scream she had let out when they tore him away from her arms. From a distance, in the remotest lanes of the village, behind closed doors, that series of rifle shots sounded like rockets going off at festival time.

Afterwards the real judges arrived, bespectacled gents perched on mules, travel weary, who were still complaining about being overworked as they were questioning the accused in the convent refectory. They were seated side by side on the bench, and letting out a groan every time they changed position. The trial went on and on for ages. The ones they found responsible were led away to the city on foot, chained together in pairs, between two lines of soldiers with muskets at the ready. Their womenfolk ran after them beside the country lanes, across plough-land, through cactus groves, vineyards and golden cornfields, staggering along out of breath, calling out to them by name every time the road turned a corner, and they could see the prisoners' faces. On reaching the city they were locked up in the great, tall prison, huge as a monastery, dotted all over with tiny barred windows. If the women wanted to see their menfolk, it was Mondays only, in the presence of warders, behind the iron gate. The poor wretches inside became more and more pallid-looking in that eternal half-light, never catching a glimpse of the sun. Monday after Monday they became more reticent, hardly giving an answer, complaining less and less. On the other days of the week, if the women were to buzz around the square by the prison, the sentries would threaten them with their rifles. They had no idea what to do for the best, where to find work in the city, or how to get themselves something to eat. The bed in the stable cost two *soldi*, the white bread was no more than a single mouthful and never filled their stomachs. If they huddled down to spend the night in the doorway of a church, the police arrested them. Gradually they returned to the village, first the wives, then the mothers. One fine-looking young woman disappeared in the city and was never heard of again. All the rest of the villagers had returned to what they were doing before. The bigwigs couldn't work their lands by themselves, and the poor couldn't live without the bigwigs. They declared peace.

The orphan of the chemist stole Neli Pirru's wife from him, and thought it a good way of avenging himself against the man who had killed his father. Now and again, when the woman had qualms because she feared her husband would slash her face when he came out of prison, he would say, 'Don't worry, he'll never come out.' Nobody gave them a second thought any more, except for a few mothers and a few older men whenever they cast their eyes towards the plain, where the city lay, or else on Sundays, when they saw the others calmly discussing their affairs with the bigwigs in front of the club, cap in hand, which only went to show that the poor always came off worse in the end.

The trial lasted three years! Imagine! Three whole years locked up without a glimpse of the sun. The accused looked like so many corpses dug up from the graveyard, every time they were led handcuffed into the courtroom. Everyone who could manage it dashed in from the village as though to a festival: witnesses, relatives, rubbernecks, so as to take a look at their fellow-villagers cooped up in the dock like so many fattening fowl, which was all they became after such a long time in jail. And there was Neli Pirru, standing face to face with the chemist's son, who had played him such a trick to become his in-law!

They were made to stand up one after the other. 'What is your name?' And each of them heard himself spouting it out, name, surname and what he had done. The lawyers fought it out in their broad-sleeved gowns amid the hubbub, getting over-excited and foaming at the mouth, then drying themselves off with their white handkerchiefs and taking a pinch of snuff. The judges were dropping off to sleep so often behind their spectacle lenses that your heart absolutely froze. In the jury-box opposite sat twelve good men and true, so tired and bored by the proceedings that they were yawning, scratching their beards, or twittering among themselves. Of course people said it was lucky for them that the good men and true were not from that village up in the hills, when they had struck a blow for freedom. The poor devils in the dock tried to read their faces. Then they went away to have a chat among themselves, and the prisoners waited, pale in the face, their eyes fixed on that closed door. When they came back, the foreman, looking almost as white-faced as the accused, speaking with his hand on his belly, said, 'On my honour and on my conscience . . . !'

As they were putting on his handcuffs again, the charcoal-burner muttered, 'Where are you taking me? To prison? What for? I never even got a square metre of land out of it! They told me it was all in the cause of freedom . . . !'

Other Stories

Springtime

When Paolo had arrived in Milan with his music under his arm – at that time of life when the sun shines every day, and all the women you meet are beautiful – he had met the Princess. The girls in the workshop called her that because she had an aristocratic little face and delicate hands, but above all because she was rather proud, and in the evenings, when her companions burst into the Galleria[1] like a flock of sparrows, she preferred to stride majestically through Milan to the Porta Garibaldi[2] alone, with her white scarf wrapped neatly round her head. That was how she met Paolo, as he wandered about engrossed in his musical thoughts, and his dreams of youth and fame. It was one of those wonderful evenings when he was feeling light as air, the better able to ascend to the clouds and the stars without being dragged to earth by the demands of his stomach and the emptiness of his purse. He took pleasure in linking his pleasant daydreams to the pretty little woman who was hurrying on ahead of him, raising her neat grey skirt whenever she was forced to descend from the pavements on the tips of her elegant, mud-flecked boots. He watched two or three times as she did this, and in the end he was at her side. When he first spoke to her she burst out laughing; in fact, she laughed every time he caught her up, then walked straight on. If she had taken notice of him the first time, he would no longer have bothered to pursue her. Then finally, one evening when it was raining and Paolo still possessed an umbrella, they found themselves walking arm in arm along the road, which by that time was almost deserted. She told him she was called the Princess, because, as often happens, she was still too shy to reveal her real name, and he walked her back to her house, a stone's throw from the Porta Garibaldi. She wanted no one, least of all Paolo, to see inside the sort of palace at thirty *lire* a month where the Princess's parents were living.

They carried on in this way for two or three weeks. Paolo would wait for her in the Galleria, near the Via Silvio Pellico end, shivering in his summer coat that stuck to his legs in the January wind. She would come quickly up to meet him, holding her muff to her face, red with the cold, and link her arm under his. Then they would amuse themselves counting the paving-stones as they sauntered along in two or three degrees of frost. Paolo would often chatter away about fugues and canons, and the girl would ask him in Milanese dialect to spell it out to her more clearly. The first time she went up to his tiny room on the fifth floor, and heard him play one of his romances on the piano, she began to understand all the things he had been telling her about. At once curious and bewildered, she gazed around the room in a sort of daze, felt the tears welling up in her eyes, and gave him a passionate kiss. But that happened some time later.

At the dressmaker's, behind the cardboard boxes and the heaps of flowers and the ribbons scattered across the big worktable, they whispered about the Princess's new 'sweetheart', and had a good laugh over 'this new fellow', who went about in an overcoat that looked as if it had come from the rag-and-bone merchant, and who never bought his girl-friend a shred of clothing. The Princess pretended to hear nothing, shrugged her shoulders, and got on with her sewing, quiet as a mouse and proud as a peacock.

The penniless budding genius had plied her with so much talk of future fame, and all the other splendid things that followed in its wake, that at least she couldn't accuse him of trying to pass himself off as a Russian prince or a Sicilian baron. On one occasion, just after the end of the month, he tried to present her with a slender gold ring with a chip of synthetic pearl mounted on it. She blushed and thanked him, overcome for the first time with emotion, and pressed his hands tightly into her own, but refused to accept it. Perhaps she had some inkling of the privations that the trivial bauble would cause her Verdi of the future to suffer. True, she had accepted a great deal more from the Other One without displaying so many scruples, or so much gratitude either. But anyway, to do her lover proud, she went on a spending spree, picked up a pretty little dress on credit in the Largo Cordusio,[3] and bought a shawl for 20 *lire* on the Corso di Porta Ticinese, along with some costume jewellery that was on offer in the Galleria Vecchia. The Other One had whetted her appetite for stylish things, and encouraged her to consider them a necessity. She enjoyed hearing Paolo telling her how beautiful she looked, as it pleased her to think that for the first time none of her attractive appearance was owed to her lover.

On Sundays, if the weather was fine, they would go for a stroll in the country, or along the city walls, to Isola Bella, or Isola Botta,[4] or one of those other dusty, so-called islands on terra firma. They spent freely on those days, so much so that when the time came to reckon it all up, the Princess worried about all the mad things they had got up to during the day. Feeling sorry for herself, she would go and rest her elbows on the ledge of the window looking out on the garden. He would come over and join her, and as they stood there, side by side and shoulder to shoulder, with their eyes fixed on the patch of green below them, while the sun slowly disappeared behind the Arco del Sempione,[5] they were overwhelmed with a sweet sensation of melancholy. When it was raining they had other diversions: they would take the bus from Porta Nuova to Porta Ticinese, and from Porta Ticinese to Porta Vittoria,[6] and for thirty *soldi* they would ride around like a pair of aristocrats. The Princess would spend six whole days with her brass needles, making lace and embroidering it with voile flowers, and thinking only of the delights in store on Sunday. On the day before and the day after, the young man would often go without a decent meal.

In this way they spent the whole of the winter and the following summer, playing at being in love as children play at being soldiers or at staging processions. She would not allow their relationship to go any further, and the enamoured youth felt himself too poor to ask any more of her. She was truly in love with him, but the Other One had been the cause of a great many tears, and she was now convinced she knew better. The poor girl never even suspected that by not throwing herself into his arms after what she had been through with the Other One, her delicate instincts were suggesting a way of proving she really loved him.

When October came along, he was seized with a bout of autumn melancholy, and proposed they should spend the day together in the country, at Lake Como. They took advantage of a day when her father was away to make good their escape, a costly escape that would leave them fifty *lire* the poorer, and spent the whole day in Como. On the way there, Paolo had asked the Princess what she would do if she were forced to stay away from home for the night, and she had laughed and said, 'I'd say I spent the night at the workshop to finish off some urgent work.' So when the hotel manager asked them if they would be going back by the evening train, she lowered her head and told him they would be leaving next morning. As soon as they were alone she was aflame with desire, and let herself go completely.

How different it now became from the carefree days when they wandered openly arm in arm beneath the blossoming horse-chestnuts, when she paid no heed to the fine silk dresses that passed her by in four-horse carriages, or to the splendid headgear of the young men who rode around puffing their cigars! How different from those Sundays they had spent together, painting the town red with five *lire*, or from those wonderful evenings when they would hold each other's hands as they stood for an hour on the doorstep before parting, exchanging a score of words at most, while people passed hurriedly on about their business! When they began they had no thought of one day becoming lovers in earnest, and now that they had the proof they were filled with new anxieties.

Paolo had never said a word to her about the Other One, whose existence he had assumed from the moment the Princess had first taken shelter beneath his umbrella. He had assumed it from a hundred trifling and insignificant details, from certain ways she reacted, from the way certain words were spoken. But now he was gripped by an insane curiosity to know more. She was fundamentally honest, and told him everything. Paolo said nothing, and gazed at the curtains surrounding that huge hotel bed on which unknown hands had left their indelible mark.

They knew that some day their happiness would come to an end. Both of them knew it, but they dismissed the thought from their minds, perhaps because the joys of youth still lay ahead of them. Paolo, in fact, experienced a kind of relief after hearing the girl confess to him, as though all at once her confession freed him from all scruples, and made the moment to bid her farewell less painful. At that stage in their relationship, they both kept thinking about it, but calmly, like something inevitable, a bad omen to which they resigned themselves in advance. But for the moment they were still in love, and held each other tightly in their arms. When the day came, it was another matter entirely.

The poor devil was badly in need of shoes and money. His shoes had got worn out in the pursuit of his youthful ambitions and his daydreams of artistic fame – those ill-fated daydreams that pour into Milan from every corner of Italy to turn pale and fade away beneath the shining glass canopy of the Galleria, in the cold hours of night or the rueful hours of the afternoon. The heedless follies of his love were costing him dear! When you are twenty-five years old, rich only in your mind and your feelings, you have no right to love any woman, even a princess; you have no right to avert your gaze for a single moment, under the penalty of plunging into the abyss, from the splendid illusion that has kept you under its spell and may turn into the glittering star of your future; you must constantly move forward, ever forward, your eyes fixed eager and intent on that distant beacon, with a heart that is sealed, ears that are deaf, and a step that is steadfast and relentless, even if it should trample upon your own better feelings.

Paolo fell ill, and no one heard anything of him for three whole days, not even the Princess. Then along came those days that seem dismal and unending, the days when people go for a stroll along the dusty roads beyond the city gates, or peer into the jewellers' shop windows, or read the newspapers pinned up on the doors of the kiosks, the days when the water flowing beneath the bridges of the Naviglio[7] makes you feel dizzy as you look up in fascination at the spires of the cathedral that are still reflected there. As he waited for her in the Via Pellico, he noticed the cold more than before, the time seemed to drag, and the Princess no longer had the same carefree spring in her step.

Around that time he came into an enormous fortune, something like 4,000 *lire* a year, to go pounding away at the piano in cafés and night clubs. He took the job on as happily as if he'd had any choice in the matter, and turned his thoughts to the Princess. That evening, like some dissolute man of means, he reserved a private alcove at the Biffi[8] and invited her to supper there. He had received an advance of 100 *lire* and spent a large portion of it. The poor girl was wide-eyed with amazement at seeing such a feast laid out before her, and after coffee, feeling rather weak at the knees, she leaned back against the wall behind the divan where she was sitting. She looked a little pale and a little sad, but more beautiful than ever. Paolo kept pressing his lips against the nape of her neck. She did not resist, but fixed her eyes on him in bewilderment, as though sensing that something unpleasant was going to happen. He felt his heart turn to stone, told her how much he loved her, and asked her what she would do when they no longer saw one another. The Princess said nothing, turned her head into the shadow, her eyes closed, and remained motionless in an effort to conceal the huge, glistening tears that rolled down her cheeks one after another. When he saw her in tears he was taken by surprise: it was the first time he had known her to cry.

'What's the matter?' he asked.

'It's nothing,' she kept repeating, choking back her tears. She was never very talkative, and was too proud to tell him what was upsetting her, like a small child.

'Are you thinking about the Other One?' It was the first time he had asked her such a question.

'Yes!' she said, nodding her head. 'Yes!' And it was true. Whereupon she began to sob.

The Other One! The very phrase signified the past; it signified days full of wonder and happiness, the springtime of her youth, her shallow affections destined to drag her in similar fashion from one Paolo to another, trying not to weep too much when she was sad, or rejoice too much when she was happy. It signified the present as it moved into the past, and this young man, bound to her body and soul, who like the Other would become a stranger to her within another month, within another one or two years. Paolo perhaps at that moment was vaguely turning over similar thoughts in his mind, but was not bold enough to tell her what he was thinking. He simply held her tightly in his arms and began to cry himself. How different from the laughter of their first meeting!

'Are you leaving me?' the Princess murmured.

'Who told you that?'

'No one, I just know, I can guess. Are you leaving me?'

He nodded. She stared at him for a moment with her eyes full of tears, then turned away, and wept quietly to herself.

After a while, perhaps because her mind was wandering or her feelings had got the better of her, she began to ramble on again, and told him what she had always concealed from him out of timidity or self-respect; she told him how the Other One had come into her life. Her family was not very well off, in fact; her father had an ill-paid job in railway management, and her mother took in embroidery, but her eyesight was getting weaker all the time, which was why the Princess had taken a job in the fashion shop to eke out the family's income. Once she had started work, the rest inevitably followed, in part because of the fine dresses she saw there, in part through the compliments they showered on her, in part through the example of others, in part through her own vanity, in part because it all seemed so natural, in part because her workmates encouraged her, and in part because that young man followed her wherever she went. She had never thought it was wrong, except when she felt the need to keep it a secret from her parents. Her father was a gentleman, her mother a saint; they would have died of grief if they had suspected she was having an affair, and would never have thought it possible that they had exposed their daughter to such a temptation. She alone was to blame, but not really, so whose fault was it, then? Certainly she would never have taken up with the Other One now that she had met her Paolo, and if Paolo left her she would never take up with anyone else.

She whispered all this as if she were half asleep, resting her head on his shoulder.

After leaving the Biffi, they were inclined to linger as they walked the length of the *via crucis* of their bitter-sweet memories: the street corner where they had met, the pavement where they had stopped to exchange their first words with one another.

'This was where it happened!'

'No, it was further on!'

They dawdled on in a kind of stupor. 'See you tomorrow,' they said, as they parted company.

Next day Paolo was packing his cases, and the Princess, kneeling in front of his shabby old trunk, was helping him arrange his few belongings including his books, sheets of music on which he had scribbled her name in those early days, and the clothes she had seen him wearing so many times in the past. She felt as if her heart would break as she watched each of his possessions disappear inside the trunk, one on top of the other. Paolo was handing her his clothes as he went over to take them out of the wardrobe and the chest of drawers. She paused for a moment to look at each of them in turn, folded them once, then twice, and packed them neatly away, ensuring they would remain uncreased, between the socks and the handkerchiefs. They said little to one another, and seemed to be in something of a hurry. The girl had put aside an old calendar on which Paolo was in the habit of jotting down occasional notes. 'May I keep this?' she asked. He nodded, without turning round.

When the trunk was full there were still a few bits of old clothes draped over chairs and suitcases, along with his old overcoat. 'I'll see to them tomorrow,' Paolo said, and the girl knelt on the lid of the trunk while he snapped the buckles into place. She then went over to the bed where she had left her veil and her umbrella, laid them aside, and sat down sadly on the edge of it. The walls were bare and sad-looking, all that remained in the room was the huge trunk, and Paolo rushing this way and that, rummaging in the drawers and wrapping up the rest of his things in a large bundle.

That evening they took their last stroll together. She leant on his arm with a timid sort of air, as if her lover was beginning to turn into a stranger. They went to the Fossati,[9] as they had often done on holidays, but they found the entertainment dull and left before the end. The young man was thinking about all the people who would go back there and see the Princess in the audience, whilst she thought about not seeing Paolo among all those people. They had grown accustomed to stopping for a beer at a small café in the Foro Bonaparte.[10] Paolo loved the great piazza there, through which he had walked so often on summer evenings, arm in arm with his Princess.

In the distance they could hear the sound of music coming from the Caffè Gnocchi, and could see the light coming from the rounded windows of the Teatro Dal Verme.[11] Along the darkened road there were countless splashes of light, where people sat outside the bars and the cafés. The stars seemed to tremble in the deep-blue sky, and at various points between the trees along the dark avenues, a pair of black, silent shadows would move across the light of the gaslamps. Paolo was thinking to himself, This is our last evening together!

They had chosen to sit at a table away from the crowd, in the darkest corner, with their backs turned towards a row of stunted shrubs that had been planted in old oil drums. The Princess plucked a couple of the leaves and gave one to Paolo, a gesture that in the past would have started them laughing. A blind man came along and strummed a whole repertory of tunes on his guitar, and Paolo gave him all the small change he had in his pocket.

They met for the last time at the station, when the train was about to leave, at the painful hour of the hurried, prosaic, careless adieu, uttered with no sign of enthusiasm or regret, amid the crush, the indifference, the hubbub and the throng that attend a departure. The Princess followed Paolo like a shadow from the luggage office to the ticket window, copying his every step without saying a word, her umbrella rolled up under her arm. She was white as a sheet. He, on the other hand, was all confused and distracted-looking. When they came up to the waiting-room an inspector asked for their tickets. Paolo showed him his own, but the poor girl had no ticket to show, so it was there that they hurriedly shook hands in front of a great crowd of people pushing to get through, and the inspector punching the tickets.

She was left standing there beside the door, clutching her umbrella, as though waiting for someone else to turn up, and casting her eyes over the huge posters pasted here and there to the walls. She watched the travellers as they made their way from the ticket office to the waiting-rooms, accompanying them all the way inside with that same expression of total bewilderment before turning to watch the next ones arriving.

Finally, after ten agonizing minutes, the bell rang, and the whistle of the engine could be heard. The girl gripped her umbrella tightly and walked slowly away, tottering a little as she went. Outside the station she sat down on a stone bench.

'Farewell, you that are going now, you that have shared the secrets of my heart! Farewell, you that went before him! Farewell, you that will come next, and you that will go as he has gone!' The poor girl was almost demented.

And you, penniless great artist of the cafés, go and drag your chains somewhere else! Go and dress more smartly, and eat every day! Go and allow the dreams of your youth to drown themselves amid the pipe-smoke of the gin-palaces of distant lands where nobody knows you and nobody wishes you well! Go and forget your Princess among the princesses of faraway places, after the small change you collect at the doors of the cafés has driven away the melancholy image of the last farewell you exchanged with her in that dismal waiting-room. And later, when you return, no longer young, nor penniless, nor foolish, nor eager to fulfil the splendid visions of those early days, and you meet the Princess again, don't remind her of the wonderful times you spent in each other's company, of the laughter and the tears, for she too has filled out a little, she no longer dresses on credit at the Largo Cordusio, and would no longer understand what you are saying. And that, sometimes, can be the saddest thing of all.

Wolf-hunt

That evening, in howling wind and driving rain – real weather for wolves – Lollo turned up unexpectedly at his house, like a piece of bad news. At first he tapped gently, poked an anxious head round the door, then finally decided to enter, red as a beetroot and soaked to the skin.

What with the raging storm, and her husband returning, purple in the face, at so unusual an hour, the poor woman began to tremble like a leaf, and could hardly summon up the breath to mumble, 'What is it? What happened?'

Lollo said nothing, not even 'drop dead'. He was a man of few words, especially when the moon was on the wane. He alone knew what he was chuntering between his teeth, as he went on casting sullen looks at everything around him: the lantern on the table, the neatly made-up bed, the heavy cross-bar on the door leading to the kitchen, where the chickens, terrified on account of the storm, were making a great uproar. The woman turned paler and paler, and hadn't the courage to look her husband in the face.

'Right ho!' he said. 'This won't take me long.'

He hung his shoulder-belt on a nail, placed on the table the lamb that was hanging below it with its four legs bound together, and without another word he sat down, legs wide apart, hands dangling between his thighs. His wife, meanwhile, not knowing what else to do in that tense situation, set bread and wine in front of him, as well as his pipe filled with tobacco.

'What are you thinking of? What's on your mind?' Lollo muttered. 'One thing at a time, dammit!'

He chewed slowly, taking in large mouthfuls, keeping his back to the wall and his nose over his plate. Every so often he turned his head to glance at the lamb, which was bleating as it tried to free itself, striking its head on the table.

'Calm down, calm down!' Lollo muttered, finally. 'Calm down, there's still some time to go.'

'What are you going to do? Say something at least.'

He looked at her as if he hadn't heard, through a pair of mean little eyes that revealed no hint of his intentions, at the same time calmly lighting his pipe, so that the poor woman grew more and more bewildered. Suddenly she threw herself on to her knees to untie his sodden leggings.

'No,' he said, pushing her aside with his foot. 'I'm going out again.'

'In this weather?' she said, heaving a great sigh.

'The weather's not important. As a matter of fact . . . !'

Speaking in that tone of voice, grim-faced, trying not to look her squarely in the eye, her shrunken little husband put the fear of God into her. Solitude lay all around, and in the raging storm there was no chance of her cries for help being heard.

She cleared the table in silence while he sat puffing away at his pipe and spitting here and there. All of a sudden the black hen began to cluck. An ill omen.

'Did you see anything of Angelo today?' Lollo asked.

'No . . . no . . .,' his wife stammered, very nearly dropping the plates from her hands.

'I told him to dig a pit . . . A nice big pit . . . I expect he will have done it.'

'Jesus, Mary and Joseph! Why? Why a pit?'

'There's a wolf around here somewhere. I'm going to catch him.'

She instinctively shot a brief glance towards the kitchen door, then fixed her eyes anxiously on her husband, who never even looked in her direction as he leant over his pipe with relish, as though he was already savouring the pleasure of catching the beast. Her face grew even paler, as with trembling lips she murmured, 'Jesus! Jesus!'

'Don't be afraid. I'm going to trap him, without putting my life at any risk. A fine thing it would be if someone came along to steal from you, and you risked losing your life into the bargain! I've already spoken to Zango and Buonocore. They're in this as well.'

Whether it was the wine that was loosening his tongue, or he was simply taking pleasure in chewing over the cause of his ill temper, he never stopped, scratching away at his wrinkled chin, sometimes almost nodding off over his pipe, then chattering away like a magpie.

'D'you want to know how it's done? You prepare a nice little trap for him . . . a lovely soft bed with leaves and branches . . . the lamb lying tied up on it, fresh meat to draw the crafty devil towards it. When he hears the bleating and catches the smell of fresh meat, along he comes like a groom to a wedding, his nose sniffing the wind and his eyes lit up with longing. But as soon as he falls into the trap he's a helpless booby, at the mercy of whoever wants to throw sticks or stones, or boiling water!'

As if it could understand what he was saying, the lamb started bleating again like a baby, in a heartrending tremor of a voice. Once more it leapt and shook itself, thrusting up its head, and beating it against the table like a hammer.

'Stop! For God's sake, stop!' the woman cried, clasping her hands together, almost out of her mind.

'Don't worry, he doesn't even touch the lamb when he finds himself in the trap alongside her. He prowls round and round the pit all night, trying to find a way to escape, even from temptation. It's as though he's realized it's all up and he has to ask God and men to forgive him. You should see him there, at daybreak, with his head turned upward, waiting for the hunters and the dogs, eyes glowing like a pair of hot cinders.'

Finally he dragged himself to his feet and began to wander about the room like some phantom, dragging his sodden leggings behind him, holding up the lantern to rummage here and there.

'What is it you're looking for? What do you want?' his poor wife asked, breathless as she crawled along behind him.

He answered with a sort of grunt, and thrust the lamp under the bed.

'There we are, that's it, I've found what I'm looking for.'

At that moment there came a fierce gust of wind that almost blew the house down. A clatter was heard in the kitchen, the woman let out a yell and stood against the door. Then, in the wind, the lamp went out, and suddenly it was pitch dark.

'Holy Mary, Mother of God! Wait! I'll look for the matches. Where are you? Where are you going? Answer me at least!'

'Shut up!' cried Lollo, who had rushed to bolt the outer door. 'Shut up! Don't you move!' He then began to strike the flint so hard against the tinder, green as the sulphur match he had lit, that the lamp flickered in his poor wife's shaking hands. Once again he wandered round the room without a word. He took up a stick of oakwood, cut out a notch at one end, and tied a length of rope to it fashioned out of goat's hair. Seeing that the storm had died down, his wife began to recover her spirits. Cupping her chin between her hands, elbows on the table, she seemed absorbed by what he was doing, and asked him, 'What's that you're making?'

'What's this? This, you say?' he mumbled, wheezing and puffing. 'This is the biscuit for shutting up the mouth of the wolf. We could do with another one for you, couldn't we! Aha! You're laughing now, are you? Getting a bit of colour back in your cheeks? You women are like cats, you have nine lives.'

Looking him straight in the eye, as if to guess what the grin on his face was concealing, she crawled on top of him, just like a cat, in fact, her breast heaving, with the hint of a smile on her lips.

'Keep still, keep still, or you'll spill the oil. It'll bring bad luck.'

'It'll bring bad luck all right,' she cried. 'But what is it you're up to? Tell me!'

'I see! Now you're turning on the bad temper! You know all the tricks, don't you! Want to know more, do you? Want to know how to finish him off. Well, all you do is lower this little toy into the pit. The wolf, being stupid, grabs it between his teeth, and in a flash you switch the rope from the other end of the stick and tie it behind his neck. After that the job's done. You can take the wolf and drag him up because now he can't harm anyone! And you do whatever you like with him. But you have to wait till broad daylight. I'm off now to get the trap ready.'

'Shall I wait for you, then? Are you coming back?'

Lollo went and unhooked his shoulder-belt, grunting as he did so. Then he turned to pick up the lamb. 'We shall see,' he said. 'The best part is seeing him caught there in the trap. And after that you can do what you like with him, without asking permission from anyone. You can even claim a reward from the town hall! All you have to do now is stay where you are and keep still.' Tucking the lamb under his arm, 'Keep still,' he repeated, 'the wolf won't touch you. He's too busy trying to save his own skin.'

Paying no attention to his wife, he then went out, locking the door behind him.

'Why are you locking me in?' his wife screamed, beating her fists against the door. 'Answer me! What are you up to?'

Lollo made no reply as he walked away through the rain and the wind.

'Ah! Holy Virgin!' exclaimed the poor woman, as she wandered about the room, clasping her head between her hands. Then the kitchen door opened and Angelo came in, looking pale as death, and moving unsteadily on his feet.

'Trapped! We're trapped!' she murmured, in a trembling voice. 'He's bolted us in!'

Without replying, the man rushed this way and that on tip-toe, exactly like a wolf caught in a trap. Pale-faced and out of his mind, he wrenched at the door and the iron grille over the window. Then he picked up the table like a feather and set it on the bed, placed a stool on top of it, and climbed up trying to reach the ceiling, clawing away desperately with his arms outstretched. Finally he gave up, exhausted, looked sideways at his companion, and swore at her.

'Ah!' she burst out, hands on hips. 'Is this the reward I get from you?'

'Be quiet!' he exclaimed, terrified, clapping his hand over her mouth. 'Be quiet! Can't you see we're staring death in the face?'

'I curse the day I ever set eyes on you!' the woman continued to mutter. 'I wish I'd dropped dead on the very spot!'

'Hush!' he whispered, fingers to his lips, in a croaking tone of voice. 'Hush!'

All one could hear was the wind, and the rain pouring down on the roof. She held her head between her hands, while he stared at her, utterly bemused.

'What did he say? What did he do?' he finally got round to stuttering. 'Perhaps we're just imagining he suspected us.'

'No!' Lollo's wife replied. 'He knew for certain! For certain!'

The lamp was running short of oil, and began to go out. In a fit of rage, he attacked the door and window once again, then split his nails tearing away at the plaster and moaning like a wild beast caught in a noose.

'Hail Mary, help me, help me now!' the woman begged.

The lamp finally went out. Turning round, he picked his way towards the woman, and in a low whisper he asked, 'What'll your husband do now? Will he come back here?'

On hearing the prayers she was mumbling, without waiting for the poor wretch to answer, he said, 'You should have recited your Hail Marys before! It's too late now!'

And so he began to unleash his bad temper upon her, calling her every filthy name under the sun.

Maps

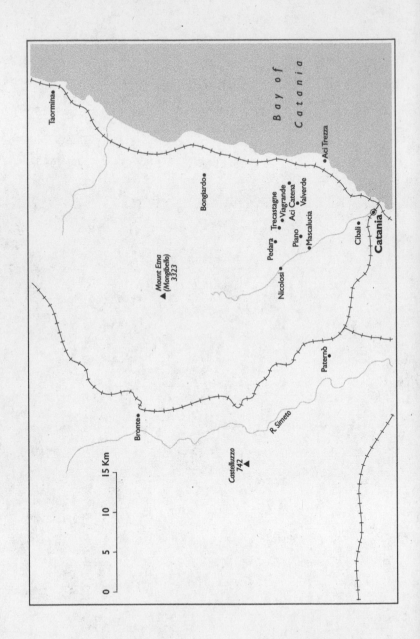

Bay of Catania

Taormina

Aci Trezza

Bongiardo

Trecastagne
Viagrande
Aci Catena
Pedara
Piano
Valverde
Mascalucia

Cibali

Catania

Nicolosi

Mount Etna
(Mongibello) 3323

Paternò

Bronte

R. Simeto

Castelluzzo
742

15 Km

0   5   10

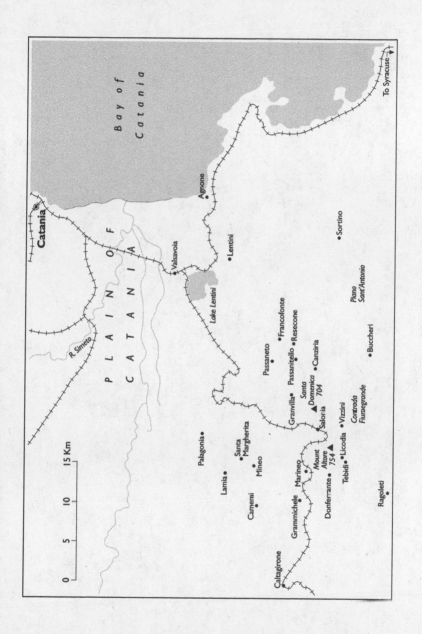

Notes

Nedda

1. Nedda's Sicilian nickname, meaning a woman born in Viagrande, a village in the Plain of Catania.
2. La Piana di Catania is the name given to the lowland area lying to the south of Mount Etna.
3. A knee-length, narrow-sleeved vestment of linen and lace worn by priests on occasions that require a high degree of solemnity.
4. 'It won't be long before I go and see her, the mistress of my soul.'

Cavalleria rusticana

1. A small town halfway between Licodia and Syracuse.

The She-Wolf

1. The scapular (*abitino della Madonna*), found in some peasant communities, consists of two small pieces of cloth, joined by string and worn back and front next to the skin.

Jeli the Shepherd

1. Sicilian for eucalyptus.
2. The Italian text reads *monte Arturo*, almost certainly a misprint for Mont'Altore, situated halfway between Licodia and Vizzini. There is no Monte Arturo in Sicily.
3. Sicilian for Phosphorus, the morning star.

Rosso Malpelo

1. Literally 'evil-haired', because of the popular belief that anyone with red hair was of a villainous disposition.
2. The slaughter-house, named after the district where it was situated, along the shore (*La Plaja*) south of Catania.
3. Etna.
4. The term given to the hardened lava scree on the slopes of Mount Etna.

Gramigna's Mistress

1. Salvatore Farina (1846–1918), a Sardinian, was the author of some fifty novels and editor of a Milanese literary review. Verga first met him in Milan in 1872.
2. *Gramigna* is dog-grass or couch-grass, which interferes with the growth of a farmer's crops, and must be dug out and burnt.

War of the Saints

1. San Rocco (St Roch), who lived in the fourteenth century, is the protector against plagues. He is supposed to have recovered from the plague himself after being befriended by a dog, and dogs invariably appear in the paintings and frescoes in which he is depicted. Rivalries between the devotees of various saints are a common feature of Italian as well as Sicilian life. The annual Festa dei Ceri at Gubbio, in Umbria, is a colourful pageant in which teams of strong young men race through the streets carrying enormously heavy statues of different saints under decorative canopies, or *baldacchini*, cheered on by their sometimes fanatical supporters.
2. A special cape worn by high dignitaries of the Roman Catholic church.
3. The feast day of San Pasquale is 17 May.

How, When and Why

1. Region bordering on the southern shores of Lake Como, favoured by affluent Milanese for their country villas.
2. Famous luxury hotel at Cernobbio, on Lake Como.
3. Literally Elysian Fields, in the hotel gardens.

The Reverend

1. Ferdinand II, Bourbon ruler of the Two Sicilies from 1830 to 1859. He earned the nickname by ordering the bombardment of Sicilian cities to crush the popular uprising of 1848.
2. Mortmain is the conveyancing of property to a corporate body, such as the Church, which then claims perpetual ownership of it. The law of mortmain was not abolished in Britain until 1960.
3. Garibaldi landed in Sicily with his thousand-strong army on 11 May 1860, proclaimed himself dictator and drove out the Bourbons with the help of a popular uprising.

Getting to Know the King

1. A litter was a sort of large sedan chair carried by mules, one in front and one behind. It was used on nearly all the inland roads of Sicily until almost the end of the nineteenth century.
2. The attempted assassination took place in the royal chapel at Capodimonte, Naples, on 7 December 1855.
3. *See* note 1 in 'The She-Wolf', p. 235.

Don Licciu Papa

1. The Grilli fields are a farming district 3 kilometres south-east of Mineo.
2. *See* the story about 'The Reverend', pp. 137–45.
3. Probably the tract of pasture land north-east of Mineo where there are grottoes in the hillsides.

Malaria

1. i.e. Etna.
2. The morning star.
3. A vine bush placed on the door served as an inn sign, like the garland of ivy that was hung outside taverns in England. Hence the proverb; A good wine needs no bush.
4. *'Il pane che si mangia bisogna sudarlo'*, (Genesis iii, 19).

Black Bread

1. Holy-water sprinkler.
2. The Plain of Lamia is a farming district lying a little over thirty miles north-west of Syracuse.
3. St Agrippina was a third-century martyr, the patron saint of Mineo, where she was buried. Her feast is 23 June.
4. 8 October.
5. The figures refer to the number of spikelets on each ear of wheat.
6. A saint much revered in Sicily, where in popular speech the attractive paintings and images of saints often serve as terms of comparison for a person's physical appearance.
7. According to popular superstition, an endive leaf carried about the person was supposed to inspire true love in the object of one's affection.
8. *Cuda di dragu* ('dragon's tail') is the Sicilian name for a twister or water-spout.
9. *See* note 1 in 'The She-Wolf', p. 237.
10. Lucy, a popular saint in eastern Sicily, was born in Syracuse. Her feast day is 13 December.
11. A town lying about nine miles south-east of Santa Margherita.

Bigwigs

1. Saridda, a diminutive of Sara, would normally be used only as a name for a child.
2. The popular name for Mount Etna.

Freedom

1. The story is based on an incident that took place in the hillside town of Bronte shortly after Garibaldi's redshirts entered Catania in 1860. The red, white and green tricolour was the Piedmontese, and later the Italian, national flag. The general who comes into the story later on was Nino Bixio, Garibaldi's lieutenant.
2. Felt hats were worn by the well-to-do. Peasants wore caps.
3. *See* the story about another 'Reverend' (pp. 137–45).
4. A revolving device in the wall separating the parlour of a convent from the

inner cloister, sometimes used by unmarried mothers to transmit their babies into the care of the nuns.

Springtime

1. The Galleria, or Galleria Vecchia, is the glass-covered arcade linking the Piazza del Duomo with the Piazza della Scala. Built in 1865, it is one of the main architectural features of Milan's city centre.

2. One of the several gates in the old city walls, the so-called Spanish walls (*mura spagnuole*) or *bastioni*.

3. A square lined with fashionable shops along the Via Verdi.

4. The two 'islands' referred to were tenement blocks outside the old city walls.

5. Monumental arch, built in honour of Napoleon III, at the western end of the Parco Sempione, the gardens of the Castello Sforzesco.

6. Like the Porta Garibaldi, these are gates in the *bastioni*, the old city walls.

7. The Naviglio Grande is a famous canal dating from the Middle Ages which connects the River Ticino with the centre of Milan. It was used in the sixteenth century for transporting marble from the quarries near Novara for the building of Milan's cathedral, hence the reference to the latter.

8. Fashionable restaurant in the Piazza della Scala.

9. A theatre in the Corso Garibaldi.

10. A broad, crescent-shaped thoroughfare in front of the Castello Sforzesco, with a large piazza at its centre.

11. A theatre in the Largo Cairoli, near the castle. The Gnocchi is a well-known café in the same area.